PRAISE FOR *DARK MOON*

"*Dark Moon, Shallow Sea* is as he........
A fantasy adventure rooted in compassion, the world building
and lore are exquisite, and the characters are so real it hurts
in the best way . . . I have waited my whole life for
an epic fantasy like this."
—SHAUN DAVID HUTCHINSON,
author of *Before We Disappear*

"Immersive world-building, compelling characters,
and a twisty plot. An excellent story!"
—GAIL Z. MARTIN,
author of the Chronicles of the Necromancer

"Breathtaking action, yearning so powerful that it hurts,
and that David R. Slayton signature wit combine like a
symphony to lift *Dark Moon, Shallow Sea* from
the extraordinary to the divine."
—BARBARA ANN WRIGHT,
Lambda Award–nominated
and Rainbow Award–winning author

"A thrilling, atmospheric fantasy . . . A twisty read,
with surprises aplenty, and a lead who will pick your pockets
and your heart. I look forward to more adventures
with Raef and his friends."
—K. A. DOORE,
author of the Chronicles of Ghadid trilogy

DARK MOON
SHALLOW SEA

BOOKS BY DAVID R. SLAYTON

THE GODS OF NIGHT AND DAY SERIES
Dark Moon, Shallow Sea

THE ADAM BINDER NOVELS
White Trash Warlock
Trailer Park Trickster
Deadbeat Druid

DARK MOON
SHALLOW SEA

DAVID R. SLAYTON

BLACK STONE
PUBLISHING

Printed in the United States of America
Originally published in hardcover by Blackstone Publishing in 2023

First paperback edition: 2023
ISBN 979-8-200-97730-7
Fiction / Fantasy / General

Version 1

Blackstone Publishing
31 Mistletoe Rd.
Ashland, OR 97520

www.BlackstonePublishing.com

To Alfred Utton,
who kept the faith even when I lost the light.

PART ONE

THE CITY IN THE GRIEF

❧

Only mortals die forever.
—GRAFFITI CARVED
ON THE GARDEN WALL

1
MOON

The smell of wilting flowers and spent candles almost masked the odor of decay. Raef pressed against a statue and fought to keep from trembling as the knight with the flaming sword paced nearer.

He didn't have much time. The sun would soon set, and the temple doors would close. If they did not find him, he'd be trapped. If they found him, they'd burn him alive.

Golden-haired and handsome, the knight approached Raef's hiding place, waving his sword like a torch. It should be easy. One jab to the neck would do it.

Raef drew his knife.

The Knights of Hyperion, god of the sun, had murdered Phoebe, goddess of the moon. With her had gone the tides and the path to the Underworld.

They'd razed her temples and burned her priests, the only family he'd ever known.

A decade later, the screams of the orphans still echoed in his dreams, and he shook at the sight of fire. No matter how tonight went, he'd need a long pull from the rum bottle if he wanted any sleep.

Raef gripped the blade and inhaled the crypt's moldy air.

It wouldn't be murder, not really.

He tensed, ready to spring, and . . . lowered his hand.

The knight deserved it. They all did, but Raef wasn't like them. They were his enemies, and yet . . . he couldn't do it.

Sinking back into the shadows, he waited for the chance to slip away.

New flames lit the direction of his escape. Another sword, another knight, approached the tomb where the handsome one stood guard.

"It's almost sunset," the second knight said. Older, he wore a beard of steely wool. "Get to your penance, Seth."

"I can guard with you," Seth protested.

He looked about Raef's age but sounded eager and youthful. Probably because he hadn't spent the last decade on the streets.

The veteran sneered.

"I don't need the likes of you. See that the dark doesn't seduce you."

"Yes, Zale."

Seth marched away, shoulders shrunk with disappointment.

Despite himself, Raef felt a pang of sympathy for the young knight.

Seth had been gone a few moments when Zale called out, "I know you're there, rat. I can smell you."

Raef froze.

"Get out here," the knight commanded.

Raef's breath caught. He could run, but Zale could call for help. Lowering his hood, Raef dropped his unsheathed knife inside it and placed his hands atop his head.

His stomach tightened to a stone as he stepped into the sword's light.

"I'm unarmed."

"You reek like a sewer. What are you doing down here?"

"Nothing," he tried to sound confused.

"Here to steal, I'd bet." Zale twisted the sword, aiming its flaming point at Raef's eye. "I should blind you, or take your hand. That's what they do to thieves in a civilized city."

The tremor spread through Raef as the flames danced closer.

The priests of Hyperion preached their god's mercy, but Raef had never seen it. Where Seth had seemed earnest, this man wore a cruel sneer.

Raef slid his hands to the back of his skull. The knife was the slightest weight there.

"I only came to pray. Really."

"Nobody prays in the dark," Zale said.

"Except heretics."

Zale flinched at the admission, giving Raef time enough to bat the sword aside with his right arm. He drew the knife from his hood with his left hand and punched it into the knight's shoulder, between the leather joint in the armor's plates.

The sword rang against the floor. Raef expected its flames to die, but they flared instead, growing brighter as Zale back-handed him with a growl.

The mailed glove felt like a hammer. Stars lit Raef's vision. He tried to turn, to run, but Zale lashed out with his boot. Raef felt something inside him crack as he flipped. Groaning, he landed hard against the stone of the floor.

Zale bent to seize him by the throat.

"Who do you serve?" he demanded, lifting Raef until they were face-to-face. The stars began to dance.

"No one," Raef sputtered.

"Don't lie to me, boy."

Zale tightened his grip.

"Phoebe."

"A moon worshipper?" The knight's eyebrows lifted as he grinned. "I thought we'd killed you all."

He began to squeeze.

The stars winked out as blackness grew at the edge of Raef's sight.

Raef, a woman whispered.

She sounded far away. Faint. She couldn't be a shade. Shades never spoke.

Raef.

"Lady?" he sputtered.

"Don't worry," Zale snarled. "I'll send you to her."

Something in Raef's left arm shifted, sliding like ice between his bones, burning with cold.

A glossy shard slipped into his palm. Raef blinked once, twice, but the double-edged blade remained solid in his hand. It didn't cut him when he gripped it and thrust it into Zale's wrist.

The black blade ignored the knight's bracer, passing easily through flesh and bone. It dissolved like ink in water as Zale released Raef and staggered back. Eyes rolling up into his head, the knight slumped to the floor.

Raef sat on the cold marble, gulping air. A bruise marked the inside of his wrist where the thing had emerged.

Darkness bloomed as the sword's fire died, but Raef could see.

The bronze doors of the tombs glinted in his shadowsight. The mournful statues stared with empty eyes.

"Lady?" he rasped again.

No one answered, not that he was surprised.

His prayers had gone unanswered since the knights had

trapped her in the Underworld, on the Ebon Sea, but Raef hadn't imagined that voice.

He certainly hadn't imagined the knife.

It had felt familiar, like an old dream finally remembered after nights of trying.

It hadn't killed Zale. His chest rose and fell like a steady bellows.

Raef wanted to spit on him but couldn't spare the breath. Finding his feet, he kicked the unconscious man, just to make certain he was truly out.

"I should kill you." Raef bent to jerk his metal knife from Zale's shoulder. "It's what you did to her."

He squeezed his eyes shut and let out a long breath.

"But I'm not you."

Raef cleaned his metal blade on Zale's sleeve, cut the strings to his purse, and pocketed it.

Zale slept almost peacefully, the trickle of red from the stab wound the only sign of the fight.

Raef scanned the crypt but saw no shades, no hungry ghosts crowding to drink the blood.

The temple of Hyperion and its crypt sat atop a warren of ancient tunnels. Rumor said they predated the gods, were left from the time of the demons, that Hyperion's priests had built their golden dome here and buried their saints and heroes beneath it to seal away the things that might rise out of the darkness.

Raef wasn't certain how much truth there was to it. Even he wasn't curious enough to explore those depths, but perhaps it explained why the shades, ever present since the moon had left the sky, did not intrude here.

Zale should be safe. Raef hadn't cut him deeply. Someone would come, probably soon, and he did not want to be there when they did.

Rising, he stepped toward the tomb, blinking when its door swung open at a touch. The darkness deepened, and a blue glow, Raef's shadowsight, settled over the room He saw no traps, no trip wire that might sound an alarm.

This seemed too easy. Perhaps the knights were just that confident in their flaming swords.

Raef rubbed his beard and immediately regretted it. His jaw was sore, not broken, but the pain made him want to go back and kick Zale again.

The tomb's walls were covered with restful frescoes, a temple on a rocky island surrounded by sheep and olive trees. They clashed with the long box of rough, pitted iron resting on the floor.

Raef had come on a tip from a friend. Maurin had said the Knights of Hyperion had brought a box by ship, that they'd carried it to the crypt and placed it in a tomb.

Grave robbing wasn't his usual style, but everything in Hyperion's temple was golden, or at least gilded. He could expect jewels if the coffin held the bones of a saint or bishop, and a little desecration of Hyperion's holy place would serve as some payback for what Raef owed the sun god.

Inching closer, he froze at the device spanning the lid, a series of interlocking crescents forged from tarnished silver.

Raef reached for the box and jerked back from the blistering cold.

That symbol, Phoebe's symbol, should not be here.

The knights had torn down her towers, her temples. They'd scoured her symbol from the world.

Seeing it, Raef could not turn back. A thousand flaming swords could come for him, but what, or whoever, was inside the box belonged to her.

Rubbing his hands together to get the feeling back, he ran

the tip of his knife along the seam of the lid, but found no key-hole, no catch or hidden button.

Choosing the hard way, he cast about for something he could use to smash the lock, seized on one of the brass urns in the corner, and reached for it. His wrist flared not with pain, but with a pulse, like a second, waking heartbeat.

The shadowknife slipped free of his skin. Solid before, it felt softer this time, malleable, like wax or clay.

Raef turned it back and forth, unable to shake the feeling of familiarity. It gleamed blue-black in his shadowsight, spar-kling like it held distant stars, a bit of glossy night made solid in his hand.

He tested the edge with a fingertip, but it didn't cut him, didn't knock him unconscious like it had Zale. Whatever it was, he was immune.

It had to be from Phoebe, a sure sign that she wanted him here, that she wanted him to open the box.

Instinct, or a forgotten memory, whispered instructions to him. Raef pressed the knife to the emblem on the lid. The blade slid in and hardened. He turned it like a key.

The box came alive as tumblers rattled and gears whirred beneath its iron skin.

Raef retreated to watch the tomb's door, certain the noise would bring more knights.

He could walk but breathing hurt where Zale had kicked him. He had no doubt how another fight would go. Whatever was inside had better not be too heavy.

It could be books. Phoebe's priests had treasured books and scrolls above all else.

It could be the bones of a Hierophant, one of her most cherished disciples.

The box fell silent.

The streets had toughened Raef's stomach. Bones he could handle. A fresher body, well—maybe. Raef took a deep breath and tugged the collar of his shirt over his nose. He pulled his hands inside his sleeve and reached for the lid.

He'd expected an old corpse, withered, not a fresh-faced youth close to his own age. Hair blacker than his framed a pretty face tinged in blue. The man's arms lay stiff, folded across a narrow chest.

He's dead. Raef thought. *Of course he's dead.*

The corpse wore a homespun shirt and sandals. He might have been a farmer, a laborer—anyone poor. He certainly didn't look worth a temple burial or an honor guard of Hyperion's devoted knights. They hadn't buried him with anything useful, anything Maurin could fence.

He had to be Phoebe's, but if so, why hadn't they burned him?

The inner lid of the box was marked with a design, a pattern of circles and lines Raef knew he recognized but could not place.

He leaned closer, squinting, and brushed the corpse's hand.

The man sucked in air as if surfacing from a long dive.

"Holy Moon!" Raef exclaimed, stumbling back.

He kept his distance and tried to force his heart to slow its pounding. The man sat up, his green eyes searching the darkness.

Raef recognized the look on the sleeper's face. He'd worn it himself when he'd fled the tower's smoldering ruins, seen it anytime he'd spied his reflection in a window or puddle. A lost boy had stared back, his pale features numbed by the loss of the only family he'd ever known.

Seeing it now, on the other man's face, twisted something inside Raef's chest.

Gently, trying to sound calm, he spoke.

"It's all right. You're safe now."

"Where?" the man asked, his voice still thawing. "Where am I?"

"Versinae," Raef said. "What's your name?"

"Keen—Kinos."

"I'm Raef."

"Raef," Kinos said with a smile that warmed him despite the cold still coming from the box.

Kinos struggled, stiff and puppet-like, to climb free. He was over the side when his strings broke. Raef caught him.

He lay cold, but alive, in Raef's arms. His heartbeat raced beneath Raef's fingertips. Raef's own heart sped to match it.

If Kinos had anything to do with Phoebe then Raef wasn't alone, not anymore. He wasn't the last of her children, the last to remember her. That hope was like a moonrise in his chest.

"Well, Kinos," Raef whispered. "It's nice to meet you. I don't know who you are, but I'm stealing you."

2
MOON

"Where did you come from?" Raef whispered as he half-carried, half-walked a groggy Kinos out of the tomb.

His other questions were more direct but he feared the answers, that they'd extinguish the light in his chest, this strange feeling that felt suspiciously like hope.

Why were you in that box? he thought. *What do you have to do with the moon?*

Raef choked them down.

Kinos couldn't be from Versinae. No one from the port city smelled that clean, so free of coal and brine, not even if they'd just bathed.

Zale remained sprawled on the crypt's floor. Raef considered pausing to drag the unconscious knight inside the tomb to hide him but wasn't certain he could, not with the weight of Zale's armor.

"Come on," he told Kinos, hurrying them along.

They had to make it out by sunset before the temple doors closed and the other knights discovered the unconscious man.

Wincing with each jarring step, certain they'd be caught, Raef steered them up the stairs.

Maurin would tell him to cut his losses, to leave Kinos behind, but the questions swam in Raef's guts as the haunted look lingered on Kinos's face.

Incense pricked Raef's nose as they surfaced behind Hyperion's altar, a grand circle of crimson marble capped in gold. Rich offerings of precious candles covered its surface. The oculus above glowed with the last of the day's light.

They still had time.

"Thank you, Lady," Raef whispered.

Chapels, each a scene writ in gilt and marble, ringed the dome. Many were dedicated to saints and heroes of Hyperion, golden knights and kindly priests cast in bronze. Raef smiled to see the rich scene marred by the city's derelicts.

Dressed in tattered clothes, sprawled in the chapels, they prayed to the sun, begged him for food and shelter. Raef could not hate them for it.

Like him, their former lives had died with the moon, leaving them without purpose or livelihood. His heart ached from a similar hurt, one the world shared.

The number of old sailors and fisherfolk thinned every year. They'd soon be gone, but for now they reeked of rum and emitted a sweaty warmth that eased Kinos's shivering as Raef helped him toward the temple doors.

Kinos collapsed, putting his full weight onto Raef. He swallowed a groan as his ribs pulled.

"What's wrong?" Raef asked.

"Still frozen. Need to rest."

Eyes watering, Raef settled them against a column of purple marble. They slumped to the floor together. Raef palmed his side and winced. His ribs had to be cracked.

"They'll catch us if we stay here."

"I'm so cold," Kinos said with a puff of icy breath.

Raef rubbed Kinos's hands between his, trying to impart some warmth. Kinos gave a happy exhale. His smile lit a very different warmth in Raef's gut, but now certainly wasn't the time for that.

"We have to go," Raef said. "It's not safe here."

The light from the oculus had faded. The priests would soon shoo out the derelicts. His plan was to leave with them, blend in with the crowd. He had to get Kinos moving. He was too much of a mystery to leave unsolved.

Even then, Raef knew he could not abandon Kinos to the knights.

"Your brother?" a young priest asked, pulling Raef from his thoughts. "Did he drink too much?"

Some of Phoebe's priests had been kinder than others, always good for an extra cookie or a little slack when Raef bent the rules, which had happened almost nightly.

If the tower hadn't burned, Raef might be like Seth, or this man, fresh to the order and eager to serve his god.

It would be a shame to stab him, but if he recognized Kinos or tried to sound the alarm, Raef would risk drawing blood and hope the temple's main floor was as safe from the Grief as the crypt below.

He slid his free hand into the pocket where he hid his knife.

"He's sick, Father," Raef said, pitching his voice just a little higher. "I brought him for a blessing."

The priest's lips pursed with sympathy.

"He's been this way since we lost our dad," Raef said. "He went too far out."

The priest nodded in understanding. Without the tides, many fishermen sailed beyond the point of safety. Their beaten craft returned, pushed back to port by the shallow waves, the salted corpses of their crew sprawled within. The prince had the boats burned lest the shades of their sailors came ashore and added to the city's ghosts.

"Since then, well, Mother—" Raef nodded to a tottering wretch. She chose that moment to hike her filthy skirts and scratch her backside. "She drinks. I care for them the best I can, but there's no work these days."

The priest gaped at the woman and pressed a pair of coppers into Raef's palm.

"Use this for bread. Do not give it to your mother."

"I won't," Raef said, nodding eagerly.

"If you need work, come around to the kitchens," the priest said. "It's hard, but honest."

"I will," Raef said, fighting off a grin as the priest went to berate the drunk woman.

"Your mother?" Kinos asked, voice still raspy.

"No," Raef said. "No parents."

"Orphan?" Kinos asked.

He had a little drool at the corner of his mouth.

"Not exactly," Raef said.

This wasn't the time to explain that he'd been an oblate, the extra child of a noble family given to a temple, and he couldn't imagine a more dangerous place to explain which temple his family had given him to.

Raef wanted more than anything to know if Kinos was the same, but instead he asked, "Can you walk yet?"

Kinos smiled and offered Raef his hands.

Raef helped Kinos to his feet with another wince and steered them out the temple doors.

They reached the bottom of the steps as the priests sang their sunset prayers.

The golden dome reflected the last of the sunlight as the Grief began to rise. A mix of ghosts and briny sea fog, it already coated the lower city in gloom.

The fires in Boat Town sparked to life, little islands in the mist. Always safer by dark, Raef exhaled and let the salt air scrub the incense from the back of his throat.

They reached the nearest alley. His questions wouldn't wait any longer.

"Who are you? Why were you in that box?"

The temple bells pealed an alarm.

Kinos stiffened.

"Knights," he hissed.

"Don't run," Raef said, trying to sound calm. He couldn't have anyway. His ribs burned as they staggered deeper into the alley.

He did not know what would happen if the knights caught them. Would Kinos go back into the box?

They may not burn Raef right away, but if Zale woke and told them what he was, what he'd done—Raef couldn't imagine he'd survive for long.

He pressed Kinos against a wall, counting on his darker clothes and the whorls of Grief to hide them. Kinos gripped the front of Raef's shirt, pulling him close. His breath was hot on Raef's neck as he turned to glance behind them.

The younger knight, Seth, burst from the temple, accompanied by a female knight Raef had neither seen nor stabbed.

Standing chest to chest, Raef couldn't help but notice how Kinos, a little shorter than him, fit against him. Kinos's heartbeat kept time with his as the flickering swords bobbed nearer, their light bouncing off the alley's entrance.

3

SUN

This couldn't be happening. The Hierarch himself had called them to this task.

He could not fail.

The Grief rose as Seth and Sophia raced outside. It pooled across the cobbles, drawn like skeins of shadow.

Seth spied two men standing face-to-face in an alley. Were they kissing? Flushing, Seth turned away. This city had no modesty.

"Help!" a woman cried.

She stumbled into view, skirts fluttering around her.

"What's wrong?"

"A carriage—" she gasped. "It nearly ran me down. They were loading something—" She pressed a hand to her heart. "I think it was a body."

Sophia charged in the direction the woman had pointed.

"Do you need help?" Seth asked.

"No, no." She waved him off. "I'm fine."

With a nod, Seth followed Sophia.

The fire coiled inside him, feeding on his excitement, his

anxiety and worry. Seth poured it all into the sword, felt the heat through the leather of his gauntlet as his blade flared, chasing back the gloom.

A body, the woman had said. The box was coffin-sized. It had weighed enough to contain a corpse. They'd carried it through the city, up from the docks, and interred it in a crypt. He'd felt the cold through the thick leather of his gauntlets.

A body. Seth was a fool. What else could it hold?

He wasn't supposed to question. He wasn't supposed to imagine. It wasn't his place, and he'd been happy to ignore a frozen box marked with the sign of the moon, but now he felt blind.

If the contents were stolen, then surely he must ask questions? Surely they must know more to fulfill their task?

Or was that the darkness calling to him, tempting him by way of curiosity?

He wished Father Geldar were there to guide him. He almost wished he was back in Teshur.

Seth stopped that line of thinking.

His dependency on his old mentor and the rigor of the monastery was another of his failings, one more reason he was not the knight he was supposed to be. The box was not the Inquisitor's mission, and if it had been, Geldar would not have lost its contents.

Seth's mind spun. This had been his chance, his one chance. He felt like he'd been thrown from one of the city's towers.

Sophia turned a corner, her boots rapping on the dark, mist-slicked cobbles as she charged ahead. None of the streets ran a straight course. Walled by brick and soot-stained granite, they all looked the same. Versinae's towers were high, casting deep shadows. There were few signs, and the windows were shuttered, giving everything a too-similar appearance.

Cocking an ear, Seth chased after the clap of Sophia's boots, but the city twisted the noise back on him. He called her name, but the rising Grief drank the sound. Seth did not fear its unsettling touch, only his own failings. He could call the god's fire but still shuddered at the grasping hands and vague eyes of the incorporeal dead.

"Sophia!" he shouted again. He thought he heard a response and turned a corner to find himself in a dead end.

The fire inside him tensed, feeding on his fear of it, ready to test his will.

Seth forced one long breath. Then another.

Versinae's air lacked grit, the sand of Teshur's desert. Damp and slick, it slid fingers beneath his armor and caressed the back of his neck, bidding him to relax his guard.

They'd brought the box up from the docks. Seth had taken in as many details as he could, but all of these buildings looked the same.

He'd return to the temple, look for the carriage. Maybe Sophia had returned.

Seth retraced his steps, but found himself somewhere new, a small plaza. Its wide ring of a fountain sported a trio of bronze statues. Green with age and verdigris, it gurgled softly. There were no people, no one to ask for directions.

The Grief curled around his feet, greasy and black, tendrils twisting around his boots like cat tails. It veiled the stars. Seth's sword provided the only light.

I should not be here alone, he thought unbidden.

Perhaps Versinae held the death of its patron goddess against him, against all the Knights of Hyperion, and the city meant to punish them. Zale had already paid the price.

"I am the light."

His words kindled the god's fire. It leaped, too quick, too

near the surface, and singed the leather of his gauntlet. It could consume him, and would if he unleashed it.

It could burn the city to the ground.

"Father guide me," Seth prayed.

He forced the fire back, begged it to sleep even as it crackled, snarling at him as it fought for its freedom.

One of the shallowed canals lay ahead, a bricked canyon with a gulley running down its center. Seth could follow it to the bay, find his way down and back up from the old docks.

Steadying his breath, he descended the nearest ladder. His boots sank into the garbage piled at the edge. He avoided the open sewer at the center, lifted his sword, and tried to shutter his nose.

He'd gone a while before he spied them. Three gray figures, like charcoal sketches against the darker bricks, they hunched over a fallen shape.

He could see through them, see the dog they lingered over. Dipping hands into its blood, they smeared it across their lips. Each sip of its life, each dart of their tongues, made them more solid.

Shades, new or greedy enough that they were not so starved of blood that they'd lost their forms and joined the Grief.

Seth took a step backward. He could leave them to their grisly meal, find another path, but he had his duty.

"No," he said. Forcing his cowardice aside, he lifted his sword. "No shadow shall stand against his light."

The blade flared. The god's fire wouldn't have burned Sophia or Zale. They were true knights, not marred by his flaw. Inside his gauntlet, Seth's skin blistered and bled, just a little.

Sensing it, the shades swam toward him.

Made stronger by the dog's blood, they flickered less, looked more real, more solid, but they hungered still.

A ghost in a nightgown led their charge. Her open throat spoke of a grisly death. Seth slashed out. She dissolved into mist.

The taste of rot, damp, and sizzling blood sent a ripple through his guts, breaking his focus.

The fire overran the hilt of his sword and crept toward his hand. It hungered for him like he was a shadow, just as the ghosts hungered for blood.

"I am the light," Seth spat through gritted teeth.

The fire halted at his gauntlet, but the time it took him to regain control gave the other dead the chance to flank him. Seth spun and nicked the one to his left, a boy in rough clothes. The third shade, a workman, retreated into the alley wall.

Seth's chest heaved as the fire fought its leash. It wanted out, to light the trash and seaweed, the dog's corpse. Above all, it wanted him. The flames surged.

The faintest touch of cold on his ear gave him warning. Seth stabbed over his shoulder to pierce the approaching workman. The spirit burned as the boy dove for Seth's face, his fingers extended like claws. Seth had no time to duck. He loosed the fire and let it have its way. It burst from him in a ring, rabid and directionless.

The flames incinerated the ghost and lit the garbage. It sizzled against the canal's fetid walls. He'd thought the dog dead, but it let out a high whine and fell silent as it burned.

"No," Seth said, dropping to his knees.

Ignoring his singed cheek and the ashes drifting like snow around him, he scooped the dog into his arms. It did not stir.

He'd done this. His failing, his inability to tame the fire, had killed it.

"I'm so sorry," he said.

The taste of stiff burned hair and flesh made his stomach heave again. He did not know how long he sat cradling the dog.

4
MOON

Maurin grinned as she approached the alley, pleased that the knights had fallen for her lie.

Raef let out the longest breath of his life.

"He was in the box?" Maurin asked, jabbing a finger at Kinos. "He doesn't look dead."

"This is Kinos," Raef said, forcing the huskiness from his voice as he shifted away from the half-frozen man. "He can't walk. Help me get him out of here."

Maurin's black face bent with consideration as she weighed the risk.

"Please, Maurin."

She sighed, draped Kinos's arm across her shoulders, and winced at the contact.

"He's freezing."

"That box was some kind of prison," Raef said. "He wasn't even breathing."

"What about the guard?"

"I knocked him out," Raef said.

"You took on the Knights of Hyperion?" Maurin asked.

"Just one."

"That explains your face," she quipped.

"Am I bleeding?" Raef ignored the pain and used his free hand to pat himself, checking for cuts.

Only a few strands of Grief had drawn together, but he could see the hungry faces in it. It would only take a drop of blood to make them manifest.

"No, no." Maurin lifted her hands. "Just bruised."

He exhaled, gave a little nod, and guided them into the maze of towers and emptied canals.

"You should have been an actress," he said.

"Thieves keep better hours."

"And it's more fun," Raef told Kinos.

Kinos's nose wrinkled at the joke, but he gained more strength as they led him over the Prince's Bridge.

Maurin cocked her head, listening for trouble as Raef watched for threats. The knights were far from the only danger.

"What will you do with him?" Maurin asked as they passed the statues of former princes and ship captains who'd died in service to the city.

Raef hadn't thought beyond the moment, but the questions he'd swallowed threatened to rise. Why had the box been marked with the moon? Why had Kinos been in it?

"I'll take him back to Eleni's," Raef decided. They'd be alone there, mostly, and he could ask his questions.

"That old con artist?" Maurin asked.

She'd never liked that Raef had gone to stay with Eleni when he'd left her gang, but it was safer for everyone.

"Can you trust her?"

"She does what she has to," Raef said. "Just like the rest of us."

Kinos scowled.

"You could come with me, back to the Lost," Maurin suggested.

Her gang of orphans and urchins were why she'd brought him the tip. She needed the money to see them through the winter. Even with Raef's help, she'd lost three last year. More would follow without food and heat.

The overland roads were too dangerous for peddlers or wagons now. Too few ships came since the tides had stilled. All over Aegea, trade and life ground to a halt as the Grief grew worse.

"I won't risk your kids," Raef said quietly.

Maurin's face pinched. She gave a little nod. She knew, after all, where he'd come from, who he'd been. The knights would be after Kinos, and he would not bring that sort of trouble to her door.

The Grief thickened as they sank into the lower city.

A shout, followed by a dog's barking, punctured the night. It could have been a simple mugging, or someone might have spilled blood and drawn the shades. Light glimmered ahead, one of the rare braziers the Watch set against the gloom.

Maurin shifted Kinos's weight to Raef and drew her knives. She'd fight for Raef, to a point, but her kids were her priority. She'd vanish if it came to knights and fire.

Luckily, Kinos carried more of his own weight as they walked on. He'd gotten his color back.

The priest had been wrong to mistake them for brothers. Kinos's sandy features had a gentler cast than Raef's sharp and ruddy angles.

Kinos was handsome, almost pretty, with long eyelashes, no beard, and olive skin. The V of his tunic hinted at a chest sprinkled with dark hair.

"You're staring," Kinos said.

"Sorry."

"Don't be," Kinos said with a smile. He nodded toward Maurin. "Are you two . . ."

"Nah," Raef said. "I like men."

"Like he can't tell by the way you're ogling him," Maurin grumbled.

Raef felt his cheeks heat, but it was Kinos who blushed. He smiled as he ducked his head and looked at Raef through the dark wave of his hair.

They walked to the edge of Boat Town.

"Fifty percent, remember?" Maurin asked. "That was supposed to be my cut."

"What do you want, his legs?"

"You can keep those. He doesn't walk so well. I'll take an arm maybe."

"I'm a person, not a prize," Kinos snapped.

"Don't be so certain," Maurin quipped before turning back to Raef. "We could sell him to the ships."

"She's kidding," Raef said. "She wouldn't do that."

He hoped she was kidding. Since the tides had stopped, some crews had gotten desperate. They'd coerce people aboard, force them to sail. They'd even buy people, prisoners from the Watch or indebted servants.

Maurin lifted an eyebrow.

"Here," Raef handed Maurin the purse he'd taken off the knight. "There's a bit of gold."

She sorted through it quickly.

"No silver?" she asked.

"He was Sun House," Raef said.

She didn't need to know about the coins Raef had tucked into his shoes.

Maurin threw up her hands and walked away, heading back toward the canals.

"Where are we going?" Kinos asked.

"Can you see?" Raef asked, trying to keep hope from his voice.

Kinos squinted at the empty bay.

"Only a little," he said.

The derelict ships had settled into the mud at every angle. Fetid water pooled around dead coral. The scattered fires provided the only light.

So Kinos couldn't see. That didn't mean he wasn't a child of Phoebe's. Among her faithful, only Raef had been able to pierce the dark. His gift had been unique and used far too often for mischief.

"I live with a woman named Blind Eleni," Raef said. "I have since—well, for a while."

He didn't want to just come out and say it. He wanted Kinos to guess, to understand.

"So that's home?" Kinos asked.

"No," Raef said. "It's a place I sleep. But there's nowhere safer these nights."

Because home was ashes. Home was a pile of ruins locked behind a wall with no gate.

"This way," Raef said, leading Kinos out onto one of the old docks.

Starting down the ladder, Raef tried to take two rungs at once. His ribs groaned with wrenching pain. He didn't quite choke down a gasp.

"What's wrong?" Kinos asked from above.

"Nothing," Raef said, going slower, sinking into the miasma of Grief and briny sea fog.

"What is this place?" Kinos asked, landing beside him.

"We call it Boat Town now, but it used to be the bay. It went shallow when the tides stopped."

They'd built new docks out beyond the wall. The old ones served as streets or bridges to nowhere. The place reeked of burning wood, salt, and long-dead fish.

"It's a good place to hide," Raef explained. "Too dangerous for the Watch and the priests of Hyperion have given up on it."

"But how can you live here?"

Raef shrugged.

"Because I have to." He palmed his knife. "Stay close. We need to keep out of the firelight when we can. Are you bleeding anywhere?"

"No," Kinos said.

"You're certain?"

"Yeah."

"All right, then," Raef said. He offered Kinos his right hand.

Kinos took it. His palm felt a little sweaty, but Raef did not blame him. Kinos had every right to be worried.

The fires guarded against the shades but the living were just as desperate these nights.

"I can't see," Kinos whispered.

His eyes darted side to side, chasing shapes in the whorls of Grief and acrid smoke.

"I can," Raef said.

"What do you mean?" Kinos asked. "How can you see?"

"I'll explain later," Raef whispered. "Just keep quiet and don't let go of my hand."

A pair of cats, one orange, one paler, picked their way together among the bones and refuse. They shot Raef and Kinos a surly, challenging glare before stalking off in search of something more interesting.

Some boats were husks, charred victims of a cook fire gone

wrong. Their hulls were slowly disappearing, broken up to feed the warding fires. Others were piled together into ramshackle buildings, their upper stories reached by rope ladders salvaged from old rigging.

Raef watched the shadows, the eaves, and hiding places. Rough shapes huddled everywhere, hungering for coin or blood. Even he couldn't always tell the living from the dead.

They skirted a fire. A moth flew too close to the flames. It ignited with a sizzling pop.

The group huddled in the light eyed their passing. Raef flicked his knife at them, threatening to call down the shades if they made trouble. His stomach clenched at the idea. He hoped it never came to that.

"Almost there," Raef whispered, leading Kinos through the last of the darkling maze.

"I don't know how you survive here," Kinos whispered back, his voice a mix of pity and awe.

"It's not like we have a choice. There's no work without the sea, without the fish or the whales."

Raef nodded to the salt-stained tidal wall. Beyond it the Shallow Sea, once named the Eastern Sea, glittered in the starlight.

"Surely they're still out there?"

"If they are, we can't find them," Raef said. "Ships that go too far out don't come back."

"Why?" Kinos asked.

"Pirates, storms. Versinae has enemies, other cities, like Tethis."

He added a few extra twists and turns to their path, working to lose any interested eyes. They squeezed between two keels leaned together like an arch ready to topple. Eleni's ship appeared on the other side.

The shade of a man drifted nearby. Burned beyond

recognition, he worked his mouth, rasping like a fish seeking water. Raef didn't know who he'd been, but he always lingered near Eleni's. Fresher ghosts, or those who ate well, remained solid. The rest dissolved, becoming part of the Grief.

"What is this?" Kinos asked, squinting to discern the boat's shape and garish, mismatched colors.

The bright paints, purples and magentas, were chipped and aged. Much of the railing was gone. The sails, tattered, were more like streamers than anything that had ever been seaworthy.

"Welcome to Blind Eleni's," Raef said with a wave. "She'll be up. Probably."

The gangplank creaked beneath them as they climbed it.

"Eleni?" Raef asked.

"You're late," she said from below.

"The Sight told you we were coming?" Raef asked, a smile tugging at his lips as they descended into the hold.

"Of course," she said.

"Then why do you need that?" he asked, nodding to the crossbow resting across her lap.

"Can't see everything," she said. Her face pinched. "Who's with you?"

"Can you light a lamp?" Raef asked. "Not all of us are blind you know."

"Smart-ass," she said, setting aside her crossbow to reach for a jar of matches. "You've never complained before."

Raef chuckled.

"We have a guest tonight."

Eleni lit a match with the tinderbox and set it to a lamp, burning a bit of their precious oil.

He watched Kinos take in the skulls and the cheap tapestries depicting fake star charts.

Eleni herself was reed thin, with a river of white hair mixed with streams of gray and yellow like dirty snowmelt. The lines in her skin were fine, like cracks in ivory.

Kinos leaned toward Raef and whispered, "Is she a witch?"

"No," Raef said. "Not really."

Eleni's expression soured. "I was up, wasn't I?"

"You're old," Raef said. "Everyone knows old people don't sleep."

"I'm not too old to shoot you," she said, chin jutting toward the crossbow. "Who is this?"

"Kinos," Raef said. "He's a friend. He needs shelter."

"You don't pay enough for two, rat."

Raef shook his head, but he fished a pair of coins from his shoes.

Eleni sniffed but took the money.

"Two nights," she said.

"Come on, Eleni, I feed myself. Give him half a fortnight."

"Three nights, and he stays with you."

"Fine," Raef said, taking up the lamp.

"I'll make it one if you use up all the oil," she snapped.

"Yeah, yeah, you old sea crow," Raef cawed back.

He worked hard to make certain Eleni ate and to keep them stocked with oil, but supplies were getting scarce. Only reeds and weeds grew in the briny land surrounding Versinae. The prince and the other nobles hoarded what remained of the city's light stores.

Three nights should be enough to figure out what to do with Kinos. Raef could always dole out a bit more of his stash, buy more time from Eleni if he didn't think of something.

He led Kinos to a ladder and brought him up to the crow's nest. Raef had covered it with oiled sailcloth to keep the rain and mist out.

The bedding was worn, stained, and thin, but it was the best he could steal. He shuffled and folded the pallet of blankets, trying to make it wide enough for two before eventually giving up.

"You sleep up here?" Kinos asked. A little blue from the chill of the box still clung to his features. "It's like a treehouse."

"Most nights," Raef said. "I'll go below and find a spot in the hold when it gets too cold."

He didn't add that the height and slight swaying with the wind reminded him of the tower, and that, more than the motion, allowed him to sleep without the rum on his better nights.

Kinos slumped atop the pallet. He looked ready to fall asleep. Staring at the bed's narrow width, he nibbled his lip.

Raef swung the trapdoor to the nest closed and winced as his ribs pulled. His limbs felt leaden, but he couldn't sleep yet. Too many mysteries buzzed around him.

"Who are you? Why were you in that box?"

"I don't know," Kinos said, shaking his head. "We were at the Columns. At the summer festival . . ."

"Where?" Raef asked.

"You wouldn't have heard of it." Kinos waved a hand. "It's just a little rock between here and Delia."

"An island?" Raef asked.

"It's called Eastlight. We weren't doing anything wrong. Then the knights came. They said they wouldn't hurt my family if I went with them, if I went into the box, so I did."

"That box had a moon on it," Raef said, broaching the subject he most wanted to.

Kinos blinked.

"So?"

"Are you . . ." Raef trailed off.

He wanted to ask how Kinos was connected to Phoebe, but the answer of "I'm not" wasn't one he could bear, not in this moment, not after their escape and the knowledge that the knight he'd left alive knew what he was, knew his face.

"Raef," Kinos said quietly. "I don't know why I was in that box."

A childhood of mischief had made Raef a good liar even before he'd reached the streets. Father Hanel, one of the priests, had nicknamed him the Fiend, calling him that often during his thirteen years in the tower. Raef's instinct said Kinos was sincere, that his confusion was genuine, that he was telling the truth, but it still hurt, sinking the hope he'd known better than to let sail.

Frozen, he watched the lamplight flicker on the sailcloth roof and felt the crow's nest tremble in the wind.

"I don't know why they took me," Kinos said. "But the Hierarch was there."

"What?" Raef straightened.

"The Hierarch. He was on the ship when they brought me to the box."

"Tell me everything you can," Raef said. "Everything you remember."

"He said Hyperion had a purpose for me," Kinos said. He looked so lost.

"And these columns, what are they?"

"An old temple. They're everywhere on the island, mostly collapsed. But we keep the Columns, clean them and don't let anything grow on them."

"Are there any statues?"

"There's a goddess. We call her the Lady, but she doesn't have a face."

It could be her. It could be Phoebe. Maybe there was a little hope after all.

"Anything else?" Raef asked.

"Oh and there's a carving. Like a door. It's made of glass."

"Glass?"

"Black glass. We're very careful with it."

The knife, the thing that had opened the box and knocked out Zale, had looked like that.

Something Raef couldn't remember wanted to rise, but it lay beneath the dust of his memory, in the ashes of what had been before the fire.

He needed to think, to sleep.

Sitting on the edge of the pallet, Kinos bent to unlace his sandals.

"Sleep in them," Raef said. "We might need to run."

Kinos gave a little nod.

Raef reached to douse the lamp.

"Wait," Kinos said, looking up at him. "Show me."

"Show you what?" Raef asked.

"Your ribs. They've been hurting you all night."

"I'm fine."

"Show me," Kinos said. Leaning forward, he lifted the hem of Raef's shirt.

They shared a grimace over the bruise covering his right side.

Kinos pressed a careful palm to the mottled purple and red.

Raef tensed, not breathing, not moving. The cold of Kinos's palm soothed the ache.

"What happened?" Kinos asked.

He let the shirt drop but didn't shift away.

Raef couldn't mention the shadowknife or how he'd won the fight in the crypt without Kinos knowing him for a heretic, a moon worshipper.

The knights had hunted Phoebe's priests and followers, burning them to death. Maybe a few had been thrown into Drowned Gate, the Inquisitor's prison, but only they knew where it was.

"The knight, the one guarding the box. He kicked me," Raef said. "When I went to get you out."

Kinos reached to snuff the lamp.

"I can't believe you did that for me," he said.

Raef couldn't either. Now that he had, he wasn't certain what came next.

Raef settled into sleep next to Kinos. Only as he drifted off did he realize that he wasn't trembling and didn't need the rum.

5
SUN

"Seth?" a voice called. Sophia. The light from her sword fell over him. "What are you doing down here?"

Gently, he set the dog aside and rose, wiping his eyes before he faced her.

"There were shades," he explained.

Her mouth crinkled with a sneer that reminded him of Zale. They were two of a kind, a matched pair with no room for him.

"You lost control again," she said, eyeing the charred body and singed garbage.

"I—I did."

Seth almost lied, but that would've been worse in Hyperion's eyes. Night obscured. Hyperion's light revealed the truth.

"Good," Sophia said, nudging the dead dog with her toe. "This cesspool of a city should be burned to the ground."

Seth stiffened at her tone.

"I didn't find anything," he said. "Did you?"

"No. We should return to the temple."

"Yes," he agreed, adding a silent *please*.

Seth needed to pray. For guidance. For forgiveness. For a return of his fleeting control.

It hadn't been like this in Teshur. There were no ghosts there. The days were too long, the sea of sand too flat and sparse. Perhaps there were too few dead, or perhaps something about Hyperion's sacred spaces burned them away.

From Teshur he'd been called to Ilium, to Hyperion's great temple. Seth had not spent enough time in the Hierarch's city to know the state of her shades, but the roads there were broad, easy to navigate, and lined in rose bushes of every color. The plazas were marked by obelisks with gilded caps and all streets led to the great, golden dome at its peak. He couldn't have lost his way there.

He kept close to Sophia as they made their way back through the alleys. Dawn lit the sea, chasing back the Grief and the city's malice. They turned a corner and stepped into the temple plaza. Seth could not shake the idea that Versinae had allowed them to find it, or that the sun had forced it to give them back.

Seth fell to his knees before the altar. The priests encircled it, their faces and arms uplifted, their cupped palms open to catch the light falling from the oculus.

"Thank you, Father, for your light," Seth whispered. "Thank you for our safe return."

He considered the dog, the spirits of the dead he'd burned away, and the people who had to live in this haunted place. His armor felt heavier than usual.

"Help them all, Father," he prayed. "Help me."

Hyperion seemed to answer as the brightening day eased the night's terrors and light filled the temple. Seth remained on his knees. Sleep tempted him, but he focused on his prayers.

He'd failed his mission. He'd failed the Hierarch.

He must perform penance. He must beg forgiveness.

Seth inhaled the familiar incense, sharp laurel and black poplar, trees sacred to the god.

"Father, make me whole," he prayed.

He never should have come here, but he'd been ordered to. The Hierarch himself had chosen him for this mission.

From the ship, approaching at dusk, Versinae had appealed to Seth's curiosity. Spires of dark granite made a forest crisscrossed by bridges that he'd itched to explore. They sloped up from the Shallow Sea. At the top sat Hyperion's temple, its golden dome a lesser sun on the horizon.

Then they'd docked and the reek of rotting fish from the bay had tilted Seth's stomach, costing him his dinner and another measure of his fellow knights' respect.

Versinae's people had seemed nearly as gray as the spirits gathering in the shadows. Gaunt and hollow-eyed, they looked hungry. Guarding the cart with the box, Seth had wished for some way to bring the light to them, to ease their desperation.

Lamplight had been rare in the streets, but music from a lonely violin had leaked from a window, surprising him as the Grief whorled about their feet.

He never should have come here.

A shadow blocked the sunlight, pulling Seth from his memories and silent prayers. Expecting Sophia, he opened his eyes.

"Father Geldar!"

Like all of his order, he dressed in simple robes of brown linen and dusty sandals. The old priest clapped a hand to Seth's back as he stood.

Seth beamed.

"I didn't know you'd be here," he said.

Geldar hadn't sailed with them, not that Seth would have noticed with his head hung over the ship's rail. He was relieved that Geldar had not seen his weakness.

"I have duties in the city," Geldar said. "Still, I am glad to see you."

"It has been too long."

"Walk with me, Seth. I wish to hear of your progress along the knight's path."

"I would like that."

Seth spoke truly, though his feelings warred within him.

Geldar had been the first to believe that Seth could serve Hyperion. In Teshur, he'd too often felt like Geldar was the only one who had, himself included. The memory of the old man's kind face had been the thing to get Seth through the worst of his penance. Now the box lay plundered. Seth had failed in his duty, and he could only think, again, that he never should have come here.

Geldar led Seth out into the long plaza stretching between Hyperion's dome and the blackened wall that sealed away whatever remained of Versinae's tower.

Curiosity snaked through him, but Seth would not look, would not be tempted by the ruins of Night.

He focused on Geldar instead. The pale hair crowning his bald pate nearly matched the white rope he wore as a belt but his steps were deliberate and unfaltering.

It couldn't be a coincidence that Geldar was also in Versinae, but it wasn't Seth's place to ask questions. Curiosity was discouraged in a Knight of Hyperion, and Inquisitors answered only to the Hierarch.

He tried again to ignore the black wall.

"They call it the Garden," Geldar said, following the reluctant direction of Seth's eyes. "A joke. They say Versinae's prince wanted a new garden, so he tore her tower down. I suppose it's easier than calling it the Tomb."

"But it was the knights who brought the towers down," Seth said quietly.

"It was," Geldar agreed.

Phoebe's priests had consorted with demons, the gods' enemies, who they'd nearly eradicated in their ancient war.

It was the worst of heresies. The knights had been left with no choice. Of course, they'd destroyed her temples, burned her priests, and trapped her in the Underworld.

Some bit of the tower might remain behind the wall. Some bit of the dead goddess might linger, but even if Seth had dared it, he couldn't go and see. They'd built the wall without a gate, without a means of entrance.

Seth forced aside his curiosity with a shudder.

"I do not like this city," he admitted.

"It will test you," Geldar said. "But your mission is important."

"But Father," Seth said, choking to hold in a sob as he confessed. "I have failed in my mission."

"It may seem so," Geldar said. "But Hyperion has a plan for all of us, as does his Hierarch."

Seth hung his head but gave a little nod. It did not surprise him that Geldar already knew what had happened. His order had the task of bringing hidden truths to light.

"What are you doing?" a voice broke in.

Sophia. She'd come to meet them on the temple steps.

"We must see to Zale," she barked.

If Geldar were offended by her tone, he did not show it.

"No shadow shall stand," he said.

"Against his light," Seth finished.

Geldar smiled, and gave a nod.

It warmed Seth as he followed Sophia through the temple. Golden braziers caught the light falling from wells in the ceiling. Even the sandstone walls held a glint of mica, spreading Hyperion's gift through the halls.

It eased the tightness in Seth's chest. Hyperion would not abandon him, and Seth would never abandon the god who'd saved him from a life of darkness.

Zale lay unconscious in the temple's infirmary. A priestess stood beside his bed, examining a small bowl of his blood. The light from the window caught on the heavy glass and copper wire of her spectacles.

"Why won't he wake?" Sophia demanded without greeting.

Seth inched into the room.

Zale lay stripped to the waist. Pale and still, he looked like a corpse, though his muscled chest rose and fell. He had a lot of scars.

The sunlit infirmary had a sharp, astringent smell, nothing like the city's reek of garbage and coal smoke, but the taste of burned fur clung to the back of Seth's throat.

"I've drained the wound," the priestess said, ignoring Sophia's tone. She shook the bowl and peered into it again. "It's not poison, at least none I've seen."

"And how many is that?" Sophia asked.

"This is Versinae," the priestess said as though that should answer the question.

Sophia glared at her.

"Then it's magic," she said.

"That would be my guess."

The priestess peeled back Zale's eyelid. The pupil was covered in black, in darkness.

"No shadow can stand against the light," Seth whispered.

"True," the priestess said, lifting her eyes in his direction. "But I've never seen this, not even before the tower fell."

"So, it is new?" Seth asked.

"Or very, very old."

A chill ran up his spine. There were demons left in the world, in the wild places. The knights were sworn to destroy them lest they corrupt the people, lest the high demons, once mistaken for gods, returned.

Zale muttered something and shifted in his sleep.

"He dreams," the priestess said, running a hand across his brow. "Nightmares mostly. He cannot kindle the fire, not in this state, so he cannot drive out the darkness that smothers his light and clouds his mind."

"I could try to light it within him," Seth said.

Zale was not flawed as Seth was. The god's fire wouldn't burn him.

"I'll do it," Sophia snapped. "Your faith is too weak."

She jerked the glove from her hand. The priestess gently wrapped a hand around her wrist.

"You should wait," she said. "We've called for the Bishop."

"I will not."

The room warmed as Sophia jerked free.

Looking resigned and a little angry, the priestess took a step backward.

Sophia spread her fingers and pressed her hand to Zale's face.

Seth began a whispered prayer, "Father, guide her—"

"Shut up," Sophia hissed through clenched teeth.

She conjured the god's fire. Seth's flames were like burning wood in an iron forge. Sophia's were different, still intense, but more like sunlight concentrated through a lens.

The priestess looked to Seth, silently pleading with him, though he did not know how to alleviate her worry.

Steam rose from Zale's body. He convulsed. His eyes opened. The blackness swirling over them ran like ink. Cold leaked from him, driven out by the fire.

Sophia grimaced as she struggled against something unseen. Her eyes narrowed with their usual determination, then widened as she paled too.

"Help me," she said.

Seth pulled off his glove and pressed his hand to Zale's bare chest. The dimpled flesh felt clammy beneath the woolly hair. Seth took a breath and closed his eyes. He willed the fire to rise, to fill Zale and burn away whatever shadow plagued him. Seth's palm blistered as the fire poured out of him. The ink coating Zale's eyes burned away.

He jerked upright, wisps of smoke wafting off him.

"Demons!" Zale shouted. "Heretics! The Day of the Black Sun—"

Tears lit Zale's wide eyes. Crazed, he seized Seth by the arms, knocking Sophia aside and spilling the bowls of ichor. The priestess made the sign of Hyperion and muttered a stream of prayers.

"Shadow. Heresy. Lies," Zale hissed, spraying spittle. He fixed his gaze on Seth. "Not a relic. Not a corpse. It's a man."

"What?" Seth gasped.

"The box," Zale spat. Foam flecked his lips. A puff of smoke spilled from his mouth as tears ran down his cheeks. "I heard them in Ilium. The Oracle. The Hierarch. It's a man. A living man. I confess. Father Hyperion save me. I confess."

"What are you confessing to?" Sophia said. She put her hands on Zale's shoulders. "You're fine. You're going to be fine, Zale."

Zale never took his eyes from Seth's. "The Oracle. She told the Hierarch it had to be him. Black hair. Green eyes. You have to find him."

"A living man?" Seth said. "You mean he was in the box?"

"Black hair. Green eyes," Zale repeated. "It had to be him."

Seth remembered the weight of the box, the cold of it, like the Ebon Sea, like death itself.

"Forgive me," Zale said, his wide eyes fixed hard on Seth's.

He collapsed back onto the bed and lay limp, his fever spent.

Seth struggled to find his voice. His arms ached where Zale's fingers had dug into them.

"What do we do?" he managed to ask.

"We get back what they stole," Sophia said. "We find this man, and we put him back."

"But the Bishop—" the priestess began.

"Is not here," Sophia snapped.

She glared at Seth, challenging him to argue, but he said nothing as Zale twitched and shook from the fire and darkness warring inside him.

"Come," Sophia ordered, jerking her head for Seth to follow her out of the infirmary.

"What are you going to do?" Seth asked, straining to match her pace.

"I am going to fulfill our mission," Sophia said, her face as hard as marble as they passed through the temple doors and out into the plaza. "At any price. This is what Hyperion wills, what the Hierarch set us to. I will find this man and return him to the box if we have to burn this city to the ground."

6

SUN

Sophia pressed her fists to the heavy desk and leaned forward. The Watch captain didn't smile, but the corner of her mouth twisted. Seth got the feeling she was enjoying herself.

The room was stone, like the rest of the Watchhouse, with smoke-stained mortar and shelves that could use a dusting. The acrid-sweet taste of the captain's cigar filled the air as she settled back into her heavy chair.

"It's a man," Sophia said. "With black hair and green eyes. What don't you understand about that?"

The captain blew out a long stream of white smoke. The bitter flavor stuck to the back of Seth's throat. He knew he'd be smelling it all day.

"Because it's not a lot to work with." A pale patch at the front of the captain's temple clashed with her darker hair. She reminded Seth of Zale, another person roughened by life in a way he hoped to never be.

"Do you have any other details?" the captain asked. "I'm happy to take notes."

Her tone was even, but Seth suspected she was mocking Sophia. He hoped Sophia did not think so too.

"We have a score of gangs, some with dozens of members. Half of them are men," the captain explained. "We have old men in droves, fishermen past their prime."

"He's not from this city," Sophia said, her tone close to seething.

"Well, that narrows it down," the captain said. "You can't even tell me how old he is or how tall?"

"No," Sophia spat.

"So then how do you expect us to help you?"

The room began to warm.

Seth did not want to intervene. Sophia was his elder, but she could not bring Hyperion's fire against innocents. Surely, she wouldn't, but he'd seen her with the priestess and had his doubts.

The captain's near smirk did not falter. Broad of body, she wasn't tall like Sophia, but she gave no impression of weakness. There were muscles beneath her gray shirt.

"You could help us search," Seth suggested.

"I don't have the people for that," the captain said. "I can't help you."

"We are Knights of Hyperion," Sophia said.

"The prince pays my wages, not the temple. I don't work for you."

Seth narrowed his eyes. Father Geldar had tried to warn him about Versinae, that they did things without Hyperion's guidance.

Sophia leaned forward. "Then perhaps we should take this to him."

"You do that. Be sure to tell him you spoke to Captain Regan and that she laughed you out the door."

Seth trailed Sophia as she stormed out of the Watchhouse. It occupied its own small square, a patch of dead soil in the shadow of the greater towers. He shuddered at the gallows tree. A murder of crows perched in its black, leafless branches. At least no one hung from its nooses. Any bodies would be burned to avoid adding to the Grief.

"This city will not aid the light," Sophia said. "It should burn."

Seth felt his heart divide as Sophia repeated her now familiar threat. The people in this city eyed the knights with a mix of resentment and curious greed, but that did not mean they deserved death.

The captain had been right. Sophia had given her nothing to go on, no useful information.

Sophia had stormed out of the temple and gone straight to the Watchhouse, but they knew nothing.

She could have tried another approach, used some tact to try to learn more. That's what Father Geldar would have done. Seth would have sought his guidance, or waited for the Bishop as the priestess had suggested, but he did not think Sophia would hear such a suggestion, especially from him.

A crow fixed its black eye on him and cawed, perhaps to beg for a meal.

Sophia paused at a column plastered with wanted posters, sketches of cutthroats and murderers. If their quarry were an innocent, he could not be in a more dangerous city, but if he was the source of the darkness infecting Zale, someone demon-touched, he could not have found a better place to hide.

The woman from that night had mentioned a carriage. That implied horses and money. Sophia had yet to question the nobility, but the time would come. She was brazen enough to approach the prince himself. Seth did not expect it to go any better than it had with the Watch.

"We don't know enough," he said, following her.

"Hyperion will guide us," she repeated. She'd said it so many times, but each avenue they'd followed had reached a dead end. Perhaps Hyperion did not hear Sophia's prayers, or perhaps she did not hear his answer. Seth chided himself.

Forgive me, Father.

He was tired, and it was not Seth's place to question Sophia's faith, not when he himself was so flawed. Who was he to judge her? The god showed him mercy, showed them all mercy. It should be simple enough for Seth to do the same.

"Perhaps Zale has woken up."

"Perhaps," Sophia agreed with a little gentleness.

Returning to the temple was something Seth could agree to.

Weariness had slowed his steps, but he found some renewal when the golden dome came into sight.

Perhaps Sophia would clear her mind and consider better solutions. He would pray. Hyperion would guide them to their quarry. They would redeem themselves. They had to. Seth had to. This was his chance to prove himself to the Hierarch, to become a full knight, perhaps to join a cadre and not be so alone.

"We will see to Zale," Sophia said, sounding determined once more. "Then we shall search again. The city will bring us our prey."

"Then what?" Seth asked. "We were ordered to guard the box."

"You do not eat an eggshell." They entered the temple. "The contents are what matters. We'll guard the man and burn the thief, after we've learned what they did to Zale and if it can be reversed."

"It cannot be reversed," a woman said.

She waited near the altar, the candlelight gleaming on her black skin. Another knight stood beside her. Both wore freshly polished armor, but it was marked with the dings and dents of battle.

"Shadow is a corruption," the woman said. "Once it touches you, it festers and grows. It infects."

Seth drew up straight. Sophia crossed her arms.

"Kneel," the woman ordered with such force that Seth did not doubt she'd draw the mace hanging from her back if she felt it necessary.

"Who are you?" Sophia asked.

Seth dropped to his knees while Sophia remained standing.

"All knights in this city are under my command," the Bishop said. "You will kneel, Knight, or I will have you stripped as I have your fellow."

"Zale? Stripped?" Sophia sputtered.

Seth had not thought anything could cow her. She looked both stricken and furious.

"He has been touched by darkness, by shadow," the Bishop said. "He no longer wields the god's fire."

"It is not his fault." Sophia seethed. "This city is corrupt. It needs cleansing."

"Who are you to pass such judgment?"

"I am a Knight of Hyperion."

The Bishop's expression promised fire and penance.

"You are for now. Now pray."

The daylight falling from the oculus was not strong, as though Hyperion hid his face from them. Seth looked from the Bishop to Sophia and back. Sophia did not have his problems. Her judgment should not be flawed like his.

Sophia followed the Bishop to her knees.

Seth closed his eyes. He let the temple with its marble and statues fade away. He ignored the others, until he felt only the falling light, its warmth and the fire inside him that answered it like a song.

Father, forgive this city. Help them. Show them your light.

He repeated it, over and over until some of his weariness lifted.

It felt selfish to ask for more. Turning to the light, letting it brighten his closed lids, he added, *Make me yours. Make me whole.*

Father Geldar had taught Seth that a sacrifice must be willing. The gods would take no life that had any reservations. You had to grow your sacrifice inside you before you could gift it to them. It had to be real. It had to hurt.

Seth had offered himself, what he was and where he'd started, but Hyperion had not changed him.

The monks in Teshur had said he must not truly want it, that some part of him clung to the flaw in his blood, the reason the fire burned him. Seth's birth wasn't his fault, but he remained imperfect. The monks had doubled his penance, tripled it, and still the god's fire burned him. Seth did not think Hyperion failed to hear his prayers, only that the answer was always no.

The Bishop exhaled. Her armor gleamed.

The knight beside her watched the altar, like he had some prayer left on his mind. He had a trimmed red beard and a lean face. He was handsome, and Seth felt a little pang to notice it now.

"What have you learned?" the Bishop asked, her voice a little warmer, like prayer had softened her edges.

"Nothing," Seth said. "We do not know where he's gone, who he is, or even where we should look."

"We know that the box contained a man," Sophia snapped, breaking the calm that sunset had brought. "And we know that he was stolen. This city hides him. We must find him and punish the thieves."

"You would bring the god's fire against those responsible?" the Bishop asked.

She narrowed her bronze eyes at Sophia. Seth thought it a warning, but Sophia answered without flinching.

"Of course."

The other knight stiffened at her answer.

"And the innocents caught between you?" he asked. He was tall, taller than Seth and leaner of shoulder.

"They are not innocent," Sophia hissed. "This city corrupts."

The Bishop cocked her head.

Sophia seemed so certain and so devoid of mercy. What chance did anyone have, did Seth have, if the gods were not merciful?

The tall knight opened his mouth to speak, but the Bishop held up a hand.

"Hold, Lathan." She turned to Seth. "Do you share her belief?"

"It is not my place to question Hyperion," Seth said, eyes dropping to the floor.

"I'm not asking you to question Hyperion. I am asking you to question the stance of your fellow knight. Is she your bishop?"

"No," Seth said, voice faltering.

He did not like the turn, to have all eyes focused on him. He felt measured by their stares, but they needn't have bothered. Seth knew he was unworthy.

"Does she outrank you?" the Bishop asked.

"No."

"Look at me, Seth."

He did. How could he not? There was no question of the Bishop's rank, no falter in her voice. Her eyes were piercing, like they saw every bit of him. Seth felt exposed, like she'd stripped away his armor and skin to read his failures in his entrails.

"You were both chosen by the Hierarch for this mission, were you not?" she asked.

Seth nodded.

"Speak up."

"Yes, Bishop," he said. "We were both chosen."

Seth could not miss Sophia's sour expression.

"Then who is Sophia to command you?"

"She is my elder."

"So she is. But age does not always grant wisdom. Who are you, Seth?"

"I don't understand," he said.

"You are a Knight of Hyperion, trained at Teshur. The monks there are among the hardest of the faithful, their discipline almost as strict as the Inquisitors'."

"What does it have to do with the box? With the man?" Sophia demanded.

"I seek to understand," the Bishop said. "In understanding there is truth."

Seth said nothing. He could feel the others watching him, examining him. He flushed a little when he noticed Lathan's eyes on him.

"Have you kept up your training, Seth?"

"Yes, Bishop," he said. "Each day along with my penance."

"Yet the order has not recalled you, has not assigned you to a cadre. In fact, you've had no missions, though you are more than old enough."

"No, Bishop," he said. She didn't sound judgmental, merely curious. She was a bishop, the commander and spiritual leader of her cadre, of the knights under her command. It was not Seth's place to question, but it was hers.

Sophia snorted.

"You have something to add?" the Bishop asked.

"His faith is not pure," Sophia said. "The god's fire burns him. He would not be safe in a cadre."

Seth flushed. He did not look up. He did not want to see the Bishop's or Lathan's expressions. He knew he was flawed. Did Sophia need to voice it to everyone, to shame him publicly?

He felt the fire stir inside him. It wanted to be loosed in retribution, to vent his shame on one of Hyperion's own. Seth had never wanted to hurt another knight before.

"That is for the cadre's bishop to decide," the Bishop said. "The Hierarch called the three of you to this mission. Sophia from Tethis and Zale from Ilium, where he has been reprimanded more than once for gambling and drinking to excess."

Seth blinked. He'd thought Zale a better knight, a better man.

"The Hierarch chose three knights, none of them part of a cadre, each a problem to the order in a different way. Now one of you has fallen to shadow."

The Bishop turned from Sophia to Seth and back.

He tried not to wilt beneath her gaze. He failed and fixed his eyes on a statue, a golden hero crushing a basalt demon beneath his boot. If only Seth could crush the darkness inside himself so easily.

He'd known he wasn't perfect, that he'd come to Hyperion from a past without the light. He'd always suspected that was why he'd been left at Teshur so long after his training was complete, but to have it dredged out into the open, spoken of so bluntly—

Seth ducked his head to his chest.

"I thought this mission was my chance to prove myself worthy."

"And so it may be," the Bishop said. "It is not my place to question the Hierarch's decisions. You are far from perfect, Seth, but that is true of all of us."

He did look then. The other knight, Lathan, nodded, agreeing with her. Something stirred inside him. Perhaps there was a chance for him after all.

"We were sent to guard the box and its contents," Sophia said, her anger obvious. "A man. We must find him."

"But we have failed."

"We have not failed!" Sophia barked. "We will find the man and return him to the box."

"Perhaps," the Bishop said. "Versinae does not like parting with her secrets."

"What can we do?" Seth asked.

"Come with me," the Bishop said.

She led them away from the temple dome, into the halls of the complex. The priests averted their eyes or narrowed them at Sophia. Most looked at the Bishop with respect or gave her the god's sign, cupping their hands above their head as if to catch the falling light.

The Bishop led the knights outside, into a courtyard where several golden shapes sat or lay curled into a ball. Their fur gleamed in the torchlight. The scent of dog, not unpleasant, filled the space.

"Hounds," Seth said, eyes wide.

He'd never expected to see one. Hounds of Hyperion were rare. Bred for the demon wars, they were sacred. They'd fulfilled their purpose when the gods defeated their ancient enemies, so their numbers had faded.

Only the noblest of knights were chosen by a hound. Seth saw the Bishop's wisdom. The Hounds of Hyperion were superb trackers. If the box held any trace of its occupant, a hound could find him.

"We should have thought of this."

"Yes, you should have," the Bishop said.

Even Sophia seemed awed by the beasts.

"I did not realize there were hounds here," she said.

"Because you have treated the priests with disdain," the

Bishop said. "They are Hyperion's faithful. They are not beneath you. The people of this city are not beneath you."

We all have something to offer Hyperion, Father Geldar was fond of saying. He'd told Seth that many times on the journey to Teshur, trying to assure him, but Seth saw now that it could have another meaning, that a knight might mistake themselves, consider themself to be above other people. Sophia seemed to.

"With a hound we can find the man quickly," Sophia said, too excited to have heard the Bishop's scolding. "Which is yours?"

"I have not been blessed that way," the Bishop said. She nodded to her companion. "Lathan has."

The slender knight smiled, just a little, a spark of pride. Seth doubted he would have been able to contain it either.

The biggest hound, all muscle and legs, stalked forward.

Sophia extended a hand.

"Here," she commanded. "Come here."

The hound growled a warning.

"Easy, Targ," Lathan said. He cut his eyes at Sophia. "I don't like her either."

"Enough," the Bishop said. "Bring her, Lathan. We'll take her to the box."

Sophia clenched her jaw to hold back some comment.

The growl she'd received from Lathan's hound had been enough to make Seth keep his distance. Targ's jaws could have fit around his neck.

Tufts of golden fur lay everywhere. He was tempted to pocket one, just to remember this moment.

The Bishop turned to go. Lathan led Targ forward. Seth lingered a breath, getting one more look at the sight.

A hound far smaller than Targ unwound from the pile of sleeping dogs. A pair of eyes, yellow like Seth's, peeked out.

Seth smiled.

"That's Argos," Lathan said, calling back from the courtyard entrance. "He's still growing."

"Argos," Seth repeated, smiling.

He waved goodbye, knowing he'd likely lose a hand if he approached.

7
MOON

Kinos smiled as Raef reached out to tug the hood of the tunic Eleni had lent him over his face. A mossy green, it went well with his eyes.

"Should we be going out in the day?" he asked.

"We have to eat," Raef said. "And I want news, to find out what people are saying. We can get both at the market."

Kinos still wore the light pants and sandals he'd worn in the box. Those wouldn't do when winter came. He'd need something warmer. He'd need heavier shoes immediately. A stray nail or broken bottle could be a death sentence. Perhaps the market would provide those too.

It filled one of the city's biggest plazas. Vendors kept stalls under awnings of oiled sailcloth to ward back the rain. They'd been colorful once but most were drab and faded now.

Kinos took in the scant offerings of fresh cloth and slightly withered fruit. The flowers were thin and straggly, even for autumn. He fixed on a row of fish speared on sticks lining a fire pit.

"It's rude to stare you know," Raef said.

"They're staring back." Kinos gestured at the glassy eyes.

"Are you cold?" Raef asked.

"A little bit," Kinos confessed. "It's warmer back home."

"What is it like there, on your island?"

"Small," Kinos said. "You could walk across it in a day."

The same could be said of Versinae, at the ground level. If you started climbing the towers it would take months. Square, dark-stoned, and often capped in spires, they were like a forest of stone.

"What do you do there?" Raef asked.

"Fish. Garden," Kinos said. He looked east, toward the docks with its grove of ship masts. "My mother makes wine. She wants me married."

"Any prospects?" Raef asked. He felt the corner of his mouth curling.

"Are you asking?"

"Oh, I'm sure you could do better than me," Raef said.

"Probably," Kinos said with a laugh. "I mean, if I wanted to."

Raef scoffed to cool the warmth the flirting brought and turned back to the market.

"It used to be very different," he said, eyeing a stall full of scrap wood, bits of broken furniture, and a once beautiful parasol. Anything that could be burned for light would fetch a decent price. "There were fresh flowers, books. You could get almost anything here."

Now the café tables stood empty, their tops cracked and unoiled. There were only a few paper lanterns. Everything had seemed bright and colorful when Raef had been a boy, shopping with the other novices. Now it looked dull, the signs faded. Everything could use a coat of paint and the stalls sold mostly junk.

"I wish I could have seen it," Kinos said.

"Me too."

Father Hanel had liked to bring the orphans and oblates here to seek any books the goddess's library might be missing. They'd rarely found anything, and Raef had always suspected it was just an excuse to give the Hierophant and Scribes a break from the restless children.

He missed the smells the most. The market had been a riot of bitter, boiled coffee and horse-drawn carts, the yeasty tang of fresh bread, beer, and herbs. Now it just smelled like Versinae, like grit and brine, though the bread and coffee lingered in the corners.

Eyeing a weathered gondola, now useless without water in the canals, Raef almost wished he hadn't brought Kinos here. His stomach gurgled, reminding him that they had business.

"Come on," he said, leading Kinos past a wagon of empty birdcages.

The bread stalls showed the most life. They ringed the prince's fountain in the plaza. A statue of him kneeling, just slightly, so the Hierarch could crown him, was the centerpiece.

"Pirate?" Kinos asked, reading the word scratched into the prince's bronze back.

"It's how he got enough money to buy his crown from the Hierarch," Raef said. "I thought everyone should know."

Kinos waved a finger at the graffiti.

"You did that?" he asked.

"Nearly froze to death standing in the water, but yes," Raef said. "Dulled my knife too."

He'd worked at it until the word had been gouged too deep to buff away and had laughed to see the watchmen try.

Kinos followed Raef's example and washed his hands and face in the fountain.

The clouds threatened rain. Raef did not want them to thicken. Too dark of a day meant the Grief would rise early.

"Over there," Raef said, leading Kinos to one of the make-shift stalls.

He passed a few coppers to the mostly toothless woman on the other side, trading for a pair of fish pies and tin mugs. The pie had chilled. They'd probably been hot for the morning workers on their way uptown or to the docks. At least the coffee was still steaming. Just holding it chased away a bit of the cold.

"You surprise me," Kinos said, unwrapping his pie from the waxed paper.

"How so?" Raef asked.

"I thought you'd steal something to eat."

"It's daytime," Raef said, shrugging as he took another bite. "And she needs the money as much as I do."

The coffee, strong enough to not be greasy, sat good and warm in Raef's belly.

Raef felt the pressure of Kinos's stare, as fixed as the smoked cod.

"What?"

"You're—you're just not what I expected," Kinos said.

"Well, you haven't known me very long," Raef said. "And I'm still a thief. I noticed you didn't much care for that."

"There are other ways to get money," Kinos said.

"There are," Raef agreed. "But I like my fingers. I'm not keen on the idea of losing them in the mills or getting branded as a guild apprentice."

"Don't they cut your hand off for stealing?" Kinos asked.

"Not in Versinae. Not even before the Grief." Raef lifted a shoulder toward the fountain. "They'd have to start with him."

Raef didn't mention the nights he'd spent in the Watch's cells with the worst the city had to offer. The first time, right after the tower fell, he'd tried to steal a loaf of bread.

Not that it had stopped him from stealing or joining the Lost after they'd hazed him. He hadn't had another choice.

In many ways he still didn't.

Survival came first for everyone. People picked lemon rinds from the gutter to squeeze the last of their oil for candy-making. The lowest used to sell matches, splinters dipped in jars of phosphorous, but with light so precious, even that work was guilded now, and any competitor soon found their legs broken.

Raef listened to the people around them but heard only the usual chatter, grumblings about the prince throwing a ball while the city suffered, and complaints about the lack of trade. One woman mentioned losing a dog to the Grief.

No one mentioned Kinos. No one mentioned the Knights of Hyperion or a looted box.

It didn't rain, but the clouds thickened, and the Grief rose. The browsers trickled away.

Raef set his empty cup atop the planks the stall keeper used as a bar. He threw the wax paper into her fire, hoping the extra light would keep her a little safer while she packed up.

"Come on," he said. "We should get back."

Kinos followed him into the streets. They were alone. Something inky lay against the gray of the cobbles. Blinking, Raef knelt to get a closer look.

"What is it?" Kinos asked.

Raef held it between two fingers.

"A rose petal," he said.

He knew it. Specifically. A petal from a Night Rose. They bloomed perfectly black and only in the dark. It was said they'd first blossomed on the Day of the Black Sun, when Phoebe rose by day. Raef hadn't seen one since the tower, since its fall had crushed the gardens there.

Now he remembered—the pattern inside the box. It was a calendar, a countdown to a certain day.

The Day of the Black Sun.

It hadn't happened in Raef's lifetime.

He still counted the nights, kept the cycles, even though he no longer had the moon to go by. The priests had drilled the patterns into their charges, teaching by rote, by chant, until they'd made a drumbeat like a second heart inside Raef's chest.

The day wasn't that far away. A matter of months.

The timing could not be a coincidence.

It had to have something to do with Kinos, with the box.

Movement caught Raef's eye. A cloaked figure, a woman, stood at the entrance to an alley. She moved silently, but quickly as she turned to dart away.

He couldn't see much of her shape, but the petal and her dark cloak . . .

"Wait!" Raef called, chasing after her.

She turned a corner ahead.

He followed through the shadows and the Grief swirling around him. She might be no one, but if she'd dropped the petal she might be—he couldn't finish the thought.

He turned another corner and found a dead end, heard nothing but his own ragged breath.

He'd lost her, but he'd taken the right turns, hadn't he?

Raef realized his mistake. He'd run into the Narrows.

This was a hard part of the city, even by his standards. The towers stood so near each other that you sometimes had to turn sideways to pass through the alleys. With only a few cracks of gray light, even on the brightest day, it was the perfect place for a mugging or for the Grief to catch you.

Someone had learned that the hard way. A withered body

lay slumped against the wall. A crack of dusty light lit their face. It hadn't been enough to save them.

A hand touched Raef's shoulder. He drew his knife, spun, and froze when he met Kinos's frightened eyes.

"Sorry," Raef said.

Kinos lifted his hands and stepped back. "What was that? What happened?"

"Did you see someone?" Raef asked. "A woman?"

"No," Kinos said. "Can you put that away?"

"Sorry," Raef repeated, sheathing the blade.

Kinos crouched over the body.

"Poor soul," he said. "The shades drank him dry."

Raef knelt.

"Look, though," he said. "Boots."

"Are you kidding?" Kinos asked. "You want me to take a dead man's shoes?"

"It's not safe to have you walking around in sandals," Raef said. "And it's not like he needs them anymore."

"Raef, I . . . I just can't."

"Fine," Raef said, unlacing his shoes. "I'll take his and you take mine."

The exchange took a moment. Kinos tested Raef's shoes then knelt to scoop up a handful of dust.

"Rhea, our mother in which we lay," Kinos whispered as he sprinkled the corpse with dirt. "Hyperion, the flame to light your way."

It was the blessing for the dead, simple enough that every child knew it.

Raef held his breath, waiting to hear if Kinos would say the part no one dared to anymore.

"Two coins for Phoebe, to carry you away," Kinos whispered.

Turning, Kinos looked up at Raef.

Something, understanding, passed between them, and the glint of hope that Raef had felt in the crypt rose again.

Kinos held out his palm. Raef passed him the two coppers the priest had given him.

"Why did you run in here?" Kinos asked as they made their way out of the alleys.

"I thought I saw someone," Raef said.

He'd dropped the rose petal along the way, but retracing their steps was no use. He'd never know if he'd imagined it, but he could remember the silky texture between his fingertips.

Yes, the moment had felt like a waking dream, but dreams, especially prophetic ones, had been Phoebe's domain.

"You're acting very strange," Kinos said.

"I'm sorry. I shouldn't have left you behind like that."

It couldn't have been her. She was dead, trapped in the Underworld. But that cloak, so black, like the night sky . . .

"You!" a voice yelled, jarring Raef out of his thoughts.

A pair of watchmen ran toward them.

"Stop in the name of the prince!" one called.

They drew their truncheons, steel rods wrapped in leather. They wouldn't draw blood, but they'd break bones.

"What do they want?" Kinos asked.

"You, obviously. Run!"

Raef heard the slap of Kinos's feet behind him as they raced away.

Usually, alone, he wouldn't have looked back. Now he paced himself, careful not to leave Kinos behind.

The watchmen gained. They blew their whistles, sending screeches echoing off the granite. That wasn't good. Raef could lose two graycloaks, but a mob would catch them.

He turned, heading back into the Narrows, into the tight alleys and little uneven streets.

It wasn't enough. The whistles drew nearer.

"There," Raef said, leading Kinos to the end of an alley.

It ended at a blue door, its paint chipped and weathered. Kinos tried the knob and was met with a rattling lock.

"Maybe they just want to talk," Kinos suggested.

"That's not how things work here," Raef said. "Let me try something."

He pressed his left wrist to the lock.

Please, Lady . . . Raef silently pled.

"What are you doing?" Kinos asked.

"Just keep a look out," Raef said.

The whistles shrieked as the watch spotted them, using the shafts of daylight as a guide.

Please. Please, Raef silently pled.

The mark on his wrist answered him, but the knife didn't come.

It needed darkness.

Raef bent to better shield his wrist from the sun.

He almost gasped as the shadowknife slipped free, as cold as before. He got a quick glance at it, a blue-tinged shadow. Almost shivering, concentrating so he didn't fumble, Raef slid it into the lock. It hardened.

He turned his wrist, heard the latch click, and yanked the door open. Raef pulled Kinos inside and turned the bolt.

"Thank you, Lady," he whispered. "Thank you."

They'd entered a tall stairwell illuminated by the open ceiling high above them. Raef jumped as the watchmen hammered at the door.

"That won't hold forever," Kinos said.

"It won't matter," Raef said. "Not where we're going."

Racing again, he led Kinos up the stairs. They reached the roof, a square patch of slate tiles. Versinae opened out beneath them. The next roof was close, then another, stretching like a causeway in the sky.

"Can you keep up?" Raef asked.

He ran, leaped, and landed on the next roof.

Kinos looked back once, dashed, jumped, and skidded to a halt beside Raef when he landed.

"I guess so," he said, lips bent into a smile that Raef could have kissed.

Grinning, he leaped again. Raef followed and together, they ran across the sky.

They went on like that until Raef's ribs would bear no more. He picked a spot where two towers met in a corner and settled them into its lee with huffing breaths.

"What did they want with us?" Kinos asked.

"I think the Watch is helping the knights look for you," Raef said. He shook his head. "I left that knight alive. I shouldn't have. He's probably told them everything."

"Don't feel bad that you're not a murderer," Kinos said, nudging Raef's shoulder with his. "I'm glad you didn't kill him."

"Me too," Raef said, meaning it.

The clouds were clearing, the Grief thinning. Beyond the towers, Boat Town, and the docks, silvery water stretched toward the horizon.

He didn't often think about leaving Versinae. For all its grime, this was his home. Versinae had been Phoebe's city, but if word was out, if the knights knew he lived, then his borrowed time was up at last.

"This isn't who I was supposed to be," Raef whispered.

"Who were you supposed to be?" Kinos asked, his expression earnest.

A scholar, Raef thought. *A scribe. Hers.*

Raef hadn't known why he'd been the one to live, the one to get away. It certainly wasn't fair.

He'd never had an aspiration or a thought beyond a life in her library, beyond reading and copying books. Now he almost couldn't imagine what he would have been like, who he might have become. It all seemed so distant, so vague and half forgotten.

The tower had fallen. The priests had burned.

Raef felt the tremble start. Had he been alone, at Eleni's, he'd have reached for the rum bottle and passed the rest of the day in fitful sleep. It didn't always stop the shaking, but it usually calmed the dreams.

Raef didn't have whatever it would take to trust Kinos with who he'd been before. At least, not yet. Kinos's prayer had planted a seed, but it needed time to grow.

Kinos laid his hand atop Raef's. He gave a gentle squeeze.

"Tell me when you're ready," he said.

A little crack in the tightness around Raef's heart opened, and the tremble stilled. Standing, he offered Kinos a hand and said, "We should get back to Eleni's."

8

SUN

Sophia led the knights as they followed Targ into the lower city. She swept her sword out before her, chasing back the night. The Grief and briny reek worsened as they neared the shallowed bay.

Seth felt stronger, safer in the company of the other knights, but he could not stop thinking about the Bishop's revelation. The three of them chosen for this mission were broken, flawed.

He hadn't been alone, all that time—yet they were not anything like him or what he aspired to be.

Seth knew he wasn't to question—but why them, why had the Hierarch set them to such an important task?

He marched beside the Bishop. Lathan flanked her other side. This must be what it felt like to be part of a cadre, a team.

Thank you, Father. For this. For the Bishop. For them.

It had to be a sign. Hyperion could not think Seth too broken, not if the Bishop had included him. Geldar believed in him. Geldar had saved him. Perhaps he could still become the knight they believed he might be.

Targ had a scent, but she led them in circles across the old docks and between the broken ships.

"Why does she dither?" Sophia asked over her shoulder.

"The scent in the box was too weak," Lathan said.

Seth was thoroughly lost, but he did not sink into the despair of the night before. He wasn't alone now. The Bishop marched with such confidence that he suspected the Grief might retreat from her.

Lathan strode, tall and confident. He had narrow shoulders, less broad than Seth's. Perhaps the topic of the hounds would give them the chance to speak more.

"Focus, Seth," the Bishop said.

He felt his face warm. She'd caught him staring.

Sophia scoffed.

She straightened when Targ let out a long, rumbling growl. Sparks lit along her fur.

"She's got something," Lathan said. "No, Targ—wait!"

The hound bolted ahead. Bursting into flame, she took off, darting between the stacked and broken ships.

Seth blinked. Targ hadn't obeyed. Was Lathan imperfect, like Seth and Sophia? Or was that the nature of the bond, that if the hound chose the knight, the knight did not command?

"After her!" Sophia said.

"No," the Bishop said.

"Why not?" Sophia demanded, the light from her sword flaring with her conviction.

"Because we are not alone here," the Bishop said.

A dozen shadows separated from the hulls. They moved toward the knights, so quiet that Seth thought they might be shades. As they neared, he saw them by the light of the swords. They were dirty and roughly dressed, but alive.

The fire stirred in Seth's belly. It always lay there, coiled, waiting for something, usually his fear, to stoke it. The mob encircled the knights.

"Knights of Hyperion," one said. "Last time you came around, we lost everything, the whales, the fish."

"We're looking for a man. He's lost here," the Bishop called. "We want no fight."

"Well maybe you've found one anyway," the man spat. "Maybe a fight is all we have left to give you."

He stepped into the light of Sophia's burning sword. He was younger than Seth had expected, probably no more than twenty-five, but hard years had weathered him to roped muscle and rough skin. He wore beaten leathers and a frayed red scarf about his neck. He wielded a long, jagged bit of iron like a club. Many of the gang carried similar weapons, bits of broken ships and blunt, rusted metal.

They were a mix of ages, men and women. Some were weathered, some fresh-faced, but all wore the scarves and looked ready for a fight.

The knights were outnumbered. Seth could not see Targ. She'd run too far ahead and he'd lost sight of her in the Grief.

"I will pray for you," the Bishop warned without a trace of meekness. She kept her glare leveled at the leader.

Lathan and Sophia stepped toward the Bishop, forming a circle around her. Seth copied them, joining their formation.

"We don't wish you harm," the Bishop said. "But we will defend ourselves if you force us to."

The ragged man sneered. He opened his mouth to say something, probably a curse, but Sophia pointed her sword at him. Fire engulfed him. A brief scream was all he managed.

Seth hadn't thought anything could shock the Bishop, but she gaped at Sophia's gleeful expression. Seth's stomach churned as much from her grin as the reek of burning flesh.

The man fell, charred and dead to the mired dock.

Howling with rage, the gang came at them, emerging from the Grief with real numbers, their weapons raised.

"To me," the Bishop commanded. The knights lifted their shields.

Seth copied Lathan's stance.

The monks had trained him. They had drilled him day and night. He could use a sword and shield, but he'd never fought in a cadre, never trained to the exact tactics of standing beside other knights.

The first club, a metal pipe, hammered against Seth's shield, harder than he'd expected. Staggered, Seth cursed himself for worrying about his experience, for not keeping his focus on the enemy, on the Grief and what it hid.

The fire rose inside him. It wanted out, to burn them all. It would be so easy to unchain it. Hyperion would leave only the knights standing, but the Bishop did not command them to attack.

Seth forced the flames down and felt it singe him from the inside. The gang hammered at the knights. Sweating, the bones of his arm ringing with the blows, Seth held firm.

"Defend only!" the Bishop yelled. "Stay with me."

Seth struggled to batter back the strikes with his shield and sweep aside the clubs with the flat of his blade.

"Murderers!" someone shouted. "Butchers!"

The words landed almost as hard as their blows.

The crowd pushed the knights back, away from Targ and their quarry.

"Retreat!" the Bishop shouted, her voice breaking over the din. "Now!"

A wall of crimson fire fell, dividing the knights from the crowd. It silenced their attackers and pushed them back. Unburned by the flames, Sophia turned, her face twisted with wrath.

Her hair had come loose from its tie. A cut on her scalp had marked her face with a trickle of blood, adding to her wrathful expression.

Seth shouted, trying to warn her as eyes opened in the Grief. "Sophia, you're bleed—"

"Enough!" she shouted over the hammering. "We must press forward."

"We retreat," the Bishop commanded. "We are not here to spill blood."

"They spilled it first," Sophia spat. Seth did not know how she could not see the truth. She'd been the first to strike. "And I will do what Hyperion wills, even if you cowards will not."

Seth looked to the Bishop, expecting her to command Sophia again, to order someone to stop her, but she only narrowed her eyes as Sophia lifted her shield and leaped through the flames.

"So be it," the Bishop lifted her mace. The flames contracted, encircling her, Seth, and Lathan. Through them, Seth watched Sophia charge.

The gang descended. Sophia sliced out, again and again, hacking into them and ignoring the blows she took. She bashed them with her shield, throwing them off balance.

It looked as though her faith and sheer force of will would keep her afloat in the tide of violence. Then Seth saw the eyes of the dead, pale and green, like the eyes of wild animals, shining in the smoke.

The Grief surged, swirling out of the shadows.

The shades grew more solid as they ripped the blood from the wounded. Sophia called forth a jet of fire, sending it from her sword, but it went wide, lighting one of the upturned ships. The old wood burned quickly, brightly red. The hungry dead were not deterred.

They rose around her, shrouding her in fog. She went down with a scream that Seth knew he'd always remember. The burning ship provided light enough for him to see the blood ripped from her in a cloud. Several of the gang died the same way. The injuries Sophia had inflicted dragged them down with her.

"Are you cut?" the Bishop asked, her voice steely.

"No," Lathan said.

Seth could not answer. The smell of burning flesh and blood overwhelmed him. The Bishop's fire lit the dark in flashes, illuminating the charred boats and bodies around them. Somewhere nearby a child wailed.

"Seth!" the Bishop's shout was like a slap. "Are you bleeding?"

"No," he said, gulping air and almost choking on the char. "What—what do we do?"

"We wait. Then we take her back to the temple. She was a Knight of Hyperion. She will be burned in his fire. May he forgive her sins."

It was clear from her tone that the Bishop would not.

9
MOON

Raef raised his hand and asked the question that had squirmed through his head all evening. "Where does she go, Father, during the new moon?"

Always smiling, often laughing, Father Hanel wasn't like the stricter priests, especially the Hierophant, Father Polus. He always hid an extra cookie for Raef, the little lemon crescents the cooks baked for the snow moon, the one closest to the solstice. He took one from his pocket now.

Raef liked this game. If he proved himself clever, he'd get the cookie. If he didn't, Father Hanel would eat it, and Raef would just pinch another from the kitchens later.

The novices sat in a circle, a clutch of smaller, black-robed versions of the priest standing in the center. Father Hanel turned back and forth, including all of them in the lesson.

"She dies," he said. "Because you must be dead to enter into the Underworld. Then she sails the Ebon Sea, in her boat, the crescent moon." He bobbed the cookie through the air. "But she doesn't go alone. She takes with her all the souls she's gathered, the dead."

"Everyone who paid the way?" Raef asked, then cringed at Hanel's smile.

Hanel always laughed when Raef won. A smile meant he hadn't been clever enough. At least Hanel was gentle. Father Polus scowled when he corrected the oblates.

"The coins are but a courtesy, Raef," Hanel said. "What needs our goddess with money?"

"For books!" most of the children said together.

Hanel laughed.

"But why does she go?" a girl asked.

Raef didn't remember her name. She was younger, one of the orphans. She had a sweet face and had recently lost her two front teeth. Catching Raef's glance, she stuck her tongue out. He returned the favor.

"For three nights she rows the souls across the sea, to the gates of the Underworld and returns," Hanel said. "Then she rises, emerging from the Door to fill the sky until she descends again."

"Where's the Door?" the girl asked.

It hadn't been Raef's question, but Father Hanel looked to him when he answered.

"It is a mystery. One of her greatest," Hanel said.

He snapped his teeth shut on the cookie.

Raef woke from the dream.

It hadn't ended in fire, in screams, but he still shuddered. Some truth lay beneath it, some memory, something he needed to know, but it refused to surface.

Usually, he'd reach for the rum, put himself back under, but Kinos lay facing him, snoring faintly.

He was a drooler, this one, but Kinos slept deeply. He must feel safe here. Raef lightened to see it, and the shudders subsided.

He shifted to try and settle back to sleep, but movement at the edge of his sight caught his attention.

A ghost hovered in the darkness at the edge of the crow's nest. It was the burned man, the spirit always lingering near Eleni's boat. He mouthed a single word, over and over, his hands held in a pleading gesture.

Fire. Fire. Fire, he mouthed.

Raef took a long breath and tasted smoke.

"Fire!" he said, bolting out of the bed. "Kinos, wake up."

"Wha—?"

"Fire!" Raef shouted. The shaking threatened to overtake him, but he forced it away. There wasn't time.

Kinos sprang from the bed.

"Thank you," Raef said to the burned man.

He chased Kinos down the ladder.

"Eleni!" Raef called.

"No need to shout, boy," she said. She sat in a chair in the wheelhouse, watching the gangplank. "I can smell it."

The odor of burning wood and singed mud grew stronger. The flames were coming.

"Then get a move on!" Raef called, looking out the door.

Out across the wooden streets, flames wreathed a four-legged form. As big as a horse, with ears raised to the hunt, it raced toward them. Boat Town resisted, beating at it with boards and whatever they could throw. They slowed it, but still it came on, shrugging off the blows and missiles to charge toward Eleni's.

"That's a Hound of Hyperion," Kinos whispered, his voice raspy with awe.

"We have to go," Raef said. "Now."

Eleni shook her head.

"I can't outrun that thing," she said.

"Eleni . . ."

"If it is my time, it's my time," she said with a shrug.

"We'll lead it away."

Eleni settled back into her chair, her crossbow balanced on her lap.

Kinos bolted down the gangplank.

Catching up, Raef grabbed Kinos by the arm and jerked him back toward the city. "Not that way. We're done if they trap us at the docks."

"I can barely see," Kinos said.

"Trust me?" Raef asked, offering his hand.

"Yes," Kinos said, taking it.

"Then come on," Raef said. "Run."

He pulled Kinos onward, warning him of gaps or the chance to trip over broken boards.

"That's a Hound of Hyperion," Kinos said.

"So you said, and so I noticed."

The nimbus of fire had paused behind them. The hound had slowed, no doubt catching on Kinos's scent inside the ship— Eleni's very flammable ship full of old cloth and too-dry wood.

Raef knew of the hounds. Left over from the demon wars, they could track anything once they'd tasted its blood. There'd been nothing in the box for it to eat, so Raef and Kinos should be able to get away.

"Stay here," he said. Letting Kinos go, he turned back.

"Where are you going?"

"I'm not letting her die, especially not like that."

Raef ran back toward the broken ship. The hound hadn't crossed the gangplank.

Skidding to a halt, Raef cast about for a weapon, anything, and found half a brick.

"Hey!" he called.

The hound's ears straightened. It tensed, perhaps sensing a threat.

Damn, it was big.

Raef threw the brick with everything he had. It slammed into the hound's side, not hard enough to hurt it, but he got its attention.

It leaped, leaving the ship behind.

Raef didn't pause to watch. He ran back to Kinos, grabbed his hand again, and yanked him into Boat Town's depths.

"That. Was. Very. Brave," Kinos panted out.

"Or very stupid. Maybe we can lose it in the canals."

He could try to stop it with the shadowknife, but the hound burned with sun fire. That would probably douse the knife before Raef could strike.

It would also mean revealing it, and himself, to Kinos. It was likely too late anyway. He already knew Raef could see in the dark. That was more than enough to connect him to Phoebe.

The planks shook beneath their feet as they splashed and clomped their way through the wooden streets. Raef ignored what remained of the stitch in his side and caught his breath when they squeezed between ships or ducked under keels, forcing the hound to find another way.

Every instinct said to rush ahead, but Kinos couldn't see.

The hound's fire, and the screams of panic, told them how close it was.

Flames leaped from boat to boat. Dry wood crackled beneath its hunger, the smoke mixing with the Grief, obscuring the stars and the few lamplights in the upper city.

Raef and Kinos reached the broad canals where the biggest ships used to moor. Maurin's gang, the Lost, lived nearby, in a crack in one of the canal walls. They couldn't run that way, but heading farther into the docks meant nearing the warehouses where Versinae stored its dwindling coal and oil. If those were lit, the entire city could burn.

"Into the canal," Raef said. Its mouth loomed ahead.

It was a risk. He didn't know if the ladders were missing or too broken to climb. The hound could trap them, though the open sewer at the center might help mask Kinos's scent.

Many bodies lay piled by the brick walls. Shades lurked by the score.

Raef felt their fingers, damp and slimy, on his cheek and neck.

Just a scratch, he thought. *Just a drop.*

Kinos's grip tightened on his hand. They were nearing the canal's last bend. There had to be a ladder there. There had to be.

"Did we lose it?" Kinos asked.

"I doubt it," Raef said. He'd never be that lucky.

A splashing followed a howl that echoed off the moldy walls. Firelight chased them.

"Hyperion's balls," Raef cursed.

They rounded the bend.

A steel rung ladder was bolted to the bricks.

"Thank you, Lady," Raef whispered.

"You first," Raef gasped out.

Kinos climbed quickly. Raef followed.

The hound charged around the bend and leaped, his jaw closing on Raef's ankle. The creature's flames licked at his pant leg, singeing the cloth.

His boot kept the hound from drawing blood, but its jaw had clamped on tight. It began to shake and twist, trying to pull Raef from the ladder.

Gods, the thing was strong.

Raef's grip on the rungs took everything he had. The ladder rattled, starting to come loose from the wall.

"Hold on!" Kinos shouted. "Just hold on!"

He disappeared over the top of the wall as Raef swung his other foot to kick at the hound. They didn't have long. The knights would catch up. The dead man's boot was laced too tight for Raef to work it free of his foot.

His grip on the rung began to slip as the hound shook him back and forth.

A broken oar fell, narrowly missing Raef's head, but slamming into the hound, delivering enough of a shock that the beast let go.

Raef scrambled up, and took a moment to get his breath.

The hound wouldn't be able to climb out of the canal but it could circle around.

They didn't have long.

"We have to go," Raef panted.

"Where?" Kinos asked, casting about, still trying to see through the gloom and Grief. "It'll just find my scent again."

"I have an idea."

10

MOON

Nothing would catch their scent over the greasy, meaty reek of tallow.

Raef had snuck them into the Guild District and used the shadowknife to open the gate to the courtyard where the chandlers' cauldrons simmered, rendering fat for candles.

He'd barely slept, stirring at any sound. They'd been careful to rise and leave before sunrise, before the apprentices caught them.

Now he led Kinos back toward Boat Town, afraid of what they'd find.

There would be fresh ghosts tonight.

A black scar ran the length of the bay. Many of the wrecks still smoldered. Raef couldn't see Eleni's boat through the smoke.

He wanted to believe that she'd made it, but the sight of the dazed, wandering people stilled his heart.

He'd done this. He'd stolen Kinos and brought him to the part of the city most likely to burn when the knights pursued them.

"This isn't your fault," Kinos said, settling a hand on Raef's shoulder. "They did this, not you."

Raef reached up to squeeze Kinos's hand.

"How did you know what I was thinking?" he asked.

"It was all over your face," Kinos said. "Let's go check on Eleni."

They followed the scar.

Some of the citizens tried to salvage possessions from the burned ships they'd been forced to scuttle the last time the knights had upended their lives. Now many of them would have nothing, and nowhere to live.

There were more than a few bodies, all burned and bloodless.

Raef exhaled, squeezed between the two keels, and froze. His heart stopped. He barely noticed Kinos squeezing past him, nudging him aside.

The scar of the hound's fire marked the streets, but the garish ship remained untouched.

Raef climbed the planks, hopeful, but didn't risk calling out for Eleni. It might not be safe.

He stepped into the wheelhouse and wished for the first time that he had no shadowsight, that he was as blind in the dark as anyone else.

Eleni sat slumped in her chair, her old crossbow on her lap, its bolt driven into her neck. The shades had come, drank her blood, and left her dry as a husk.

"Raef?" Kinos called from behind him. "What is it?"

Raef stumbled back into the light.

"Why?" he asked, voice rough and choking.

Kinos did not answer. He went to look, squinting at the interior.

"They killed her."

He clenched his fists hard enough to feel his nails almost

draw blood. Maybe he should. Maybe he should cut himself and see if she could talk to him.

"She was just an old woman," he said. "Why kill her?"

"Raef . . ." Kinos tugged at his sleeve, forcing him to look away. "You don't know it was them."

"Who else?" he asked, jerking free. He waved a hand at the smoldering slum.

So she'd told fortunes, so she hadn't really been blind. They hadn't had to kill her.

Eleni had claimed to have magic, sure, but palm and card reading weren't from the demons. She'd faked all of it, not that the knights would see a difference.

Black and red and blue mixed in Raef's blood with such force that he swayed on his feet as the tremor came over him.

"There's no fire," Kinos said quietly. "The knights would have burned her."

"Who then?" Raef asked, but even as he said it, he knew. Realization doused his rage. "No. No."

"What?"

"We have to go," Raef said. "Right now."

"Why? What is it?"

"There's no fire. You're right. The knights didn't do this."

But Hyperion had other servants. They could not call the flames because it required a purity they did not possess.

"An Inquisitor," Raef whispered.

Knights were dogmatic, but naive. They could be deceived, avoided, but an Inquisitor was like Raef—sneaky. They were Hyperion's spies, and more than a match for him.

"How do you know?" Kinos said.

"You said the Hierarch was there," Raef said. "Whoever you are to them, to her, you're that important."

"Where do we go?" Kinos asked, eyes wide with fear. "To Maurin's?"

"No." Raef shook his head. "I can't bring that down on her. I won't."

"Where then?" Kinos asked.

"The only place we can," Raef said, leading Kinos back toward the top of the city.

They hadn't gone far before Kinos reached out and took Raef's hand.

"It's not that dark," Raef said. "You can see."

"I just wanted to."

Kinos dipped his face to look at Raef through his hair. His smile faltered with an unasked question.

Raef looked at their entwined fingers and squeezed. Kinos smiled again.

The bit of dream from the night before, the lesson with Father Hanel, echoed in Raef's memory as they walked.

They rose through the city, back through the market. Raef kept his senses tuned for anyone following them or taking note of their passing.

"Keep your hood up," he said, tugging his own forward with his free hand.

"What did you mean?" Kinos asked, mirroring the gesture. "About the only place we can go?"

"We need shelter," Raef said. "I need time to think, to figure out what to do."

"Where is that?" Kinos asked. "Back to the chandlers?"

"No," Raef said. "It's too visible. They'd spot us and tell the Watch. They're way too rich to tolerate the likes of us."

The chandlers were the prince's new favorites, freshly moneyed and anxious to buy his respect. The graycloaks were already after Kinos, and Raef wouldn't trust the city's ruler on any point, not after he'd opened the city gates to the knights.

Eleni was gone. Maurin was out.

The only place left was the one he'd avoided until now.

"Home," Raef said. "I have to take you home."

"Where is that?" Kinos asked.

"It's best if I just show you," Raef said.

He led Kinos upward, over bridges, toward the prince's palace and Hyperion's golden dome. In another life it would have been a chance for him to show Kinos the upper city.

Versinae was as awake as she got these days. The clouds were thin. People ate on the go, picking up bread or a meal from bakery windows and eating as they walked. Some cafés had patrons. They sipped tea or coffee, ignoring the shuttered businesses around them and trying to pretend that all was normal.

A cobbler eyed their shoes, hopeful for some work, but Raef waved him off. The barbers were long closed. Long hair and beards had become the fashion since the Grief had risen. Few wanted to risk a nicked ear or scalp. Raef's own hair curled over his ears.

"Raef . . ." Kinos muttered, nodding to the looming temple, the golden dome.

"It's all right," Raef said, stepping sideways to nudge Kinos's shoulder with his. "Trust me."

"I do," Kinos said, giving Raef's hand a reassuring squeeze.

"We're going to walk past like it's no big deal," Raef said. He sniffed, making certain the tallow still cloaked their scent.

The priests had come into the plaza for noon blessings. Now they lingered to pray over injuries and ill fortunes, most of which their god had caused. It made Raef's face hurt to return their smiles.

They crossed the plaza. The city gates were near. They could just keep going, but the marsh beyond the walls was as alien to Raef as the other side of the horizon.

He steered Kinos away from the imposing, granite arch and its portcullis of heavy iron.

They were behind the Garden's wall now, in the little alley of shrines to lesser gods. They lined the city wall, tucked among a row of withered cypress trees. Some were crushed, taken down by the tower's fall. Most were just abandoned.

The Grief was thin despite the shadow cast by the city and the walls. That was a small blessing. Raef turned to the wall of charred, uneven stone. Three stories tall, it loomed.

He'd avoided it, told himself he'd never come back, but he didn't see a choice now. The hounds could not scale these walls, and there might be answers to the mysteries, to the shadowknife, to the vision of the woman in the alley, to Kinos.

Raef found a spot.

"No one will see us if we climb here."

"This is it?" Kinos stepped forward to run his fingers over the stone, feeling for holds and gaps in the mortar. "This is where you grew up?"

"Yeah," Raef said. "In the tower. In her tower. I was an oblate."

"Your family gave you away?" Kinos asked.

Raef nodded.

"It was common then. Families donated an extra or un-wanted kid, usually to earn favor from the goddess. Phoebe took anyone. That's why most of the kids were orphans."

"You have no idea who your parents are?" Kinos asked.

"No." Raef trailed out his fingers, felt the cold stone. "I don't think about it that much, to be honest. Her tower was my home. I know what they say, that her priests summoned demons, that she betrayed the other gods, but it wasn't like that. They weren't like that. They—we—just collected books and watched the stars. We prayed a lot."

Kinos stared upward, to the sky beyond.

"Do you think it's safe?" he asked.

"It's the only place I can think of," Raef said. "No one will look for us here."

It wasn't like the tremble, what came over him. It was more like those times when the city was too loud, or too quiet. The rum didn't help those moments. It was like his skin didn't fit. It tingled and he spun inside it. The only thing that helped was to sit or lie in the dark, to try and force all the noise from his ears and all feeling from his body.

"Do you want me to go first?" Kinos asked.

"Can you climb it?" Raef asked.

"It's a very rocky island," Kinos said, eyes lighting with the challenge. "Just watch."

He moved up the uneven stone with a speed Raef envied, finding divots for his hands and toes, leaving tracks in the char.

Raef had only come back once, when the ground still smoldered, before they'd built the wall. He took a long breath and let it out slowly. It was time to put away his fear. It was time to see.

He scrambled upward, following Kinos's path and paused at the top to catch his breath, pressing himself flat between two crenels in case anyone looked up.

From here, all of Versinae stretched beneath them, from the dome to the bay. Raef could look down but did not. He put it off as long as he could, descending slowly, pausing here and there to catch his breath.

Raef let go and dropped the final distance. He landed with a thud among the ruins of his past.

11
SUN

Seth and Lathan carried Sophia's body back to the temple. Seth expected it to be easier, that without blood she'd be nearly weightless, but her armor made her heavy, and her limbs, not yet stiff, flopped awkwardly. They'd lift and carry her, then rest when one of them called for it. They paused constantly to catch their breath and fold her arms over her chest.

By dawn, Seth's muscles were stretched to the point of aching, almost worse than any training he'd had. He tried to hold in his grunts, to not feel the slick of sweat inside his armor, to steer his thoughts toward kindness. There was penance in this work, and duty to the gods or others was not often easy.

They reached the temple and placed Sophia in the courtyard.

Targ had returned, carrying the charred remains of an oar. Lathan just shook his head and laid a hand on the hound's forehead.

"Why did you run off like that, girl?" Lathan asked.

"Why didn't she come when you called?" Seth asked.

"We don't command the hounds," Lathan said. "They choose us. We're not their masters."

"Go sleep," the Bishop said, breaking into the conversation. "I will watch over Sophia and build her pyre."

"We could help," Seth offered, despite the fog of weariness wrapping his thoughts.

The Bishop shook her head.

"This is my penance. I led us. I should have brought us all home. Go."

Her back remained straight, but Seth could see regret and weariness in the lines around her eyes.

"Yes, Bishop," he said.

He started to follow Lathan inside. Turning back, he saw the Bishop make the sign of Hyperion as she knelt to pray over Sophia's body.

Seth's stomach grumbled, and he quickened his steps to catch up to Lathan.

"We could, uh, get some food," Seth offered. "Take some to the hounds. You could show me—"

"She was terrible," Lathan said, cutting him off. Anger flushed his skin. "But you are almost no better. You are corrupt. The fire burns you. I will do as the Bishop commands. I will fight beside you and tolerate you as I have been ordered to, but that doesn't make us friends."

Seth took a step back.

"I could never be friends with the likes of you."

Lathan spun on his heel and marched away.

Seth remained in the corridor, frozen in place, breathing hard. He'd known it was there, that the knights would never accept him, but he'd never expected to be slapped with it, to be so openly condemned.

The temple complex was all broad hallways, bright stone,

and light wells. He felt exposed, with nowhere to hide his shame.

Grateful to find the barracks empty, he stripped off his armor and wiped the soot from it. The steel needed polishing and the leather joints needed oiling, but it would keep.

The Bishop had commanded him to sleep, but the loneliness, more than the pain of Lathan's words, had worked its way too deep beneath his skin. It would prove fatal if he did not somehow rip it out.

Seth found his way back outside, to the courtyard where they kept the hounds.

Targ had returned to the pack. The hounds lay in a pile, curled together, most of them snoring.

Seth wondered what it would be like to live so simply, to just be happy, a family.

Careful not to provoke them, he kept his distance and sank to his knees, making himself smaller. He'd watch for a while then sleep as the Bishop had ordered.

A pair of golden eyes opened. The pup, Argos, uncurled from the others and stood. Though not fully grown, he already outsized most of the dogs Seth had seen.

Seth did not move. It would be a quick end, by tooth or fire, if the hounds chose to attack.

Argos padded forward. Seth remained on his knees as the pup tried to squeeze atop his lap. He curled into a ball and pressed himself down, flattening Seth to the ground.

He laughed and stroked the hound's coat, expecting something coarse, but the golden fur was soft. Content, the pup slept, his body rising and falling with his breath.

The weight of the prior night, the labor of carrying Sophia's body, settled onto Seth.

He woke there, on the ground, wearing his doublet, and

found the light above him waning. Argos remained, but he had shifted to Seth's side.

"I have to go," Seth said, measuring how much of Hyperion's light remained. If he hurried to the barracks, he'd have time to wash, to rearm, and make himself presentable.

Argos let out a yip and wagged his tail. Despite the weight in his chest, Seth smiled.

He washed his face and changed his tunic, ran damp hands through his hair, doing his best to comb its short length into some ordered shape.

The priests had arranged Sophia on a bier in the main courtyard. They waved censers, the incense filling the air with laurel and rosewood to mask what would soon come.

If the long night and full day of keeping watch had worn on the Bishop, it did not show in her stance, but Seth spied dark rings around her eyes.

She stood at Sophia's feet, the dents and marks on her armor lending it an earned beauty. Her hair, arranged in fine twists, fell about her head and brow. The priests gathered at a distance. If any held resentment for Sophia, it did not show in their somber expressions.

Sophia had not been kind to them, no kinder than she'd been to Seth. Nor was Zale there to see her pyre. He'd been her friend. He should have been there, and Seth should have gone to check on him. He hung his head. Flawed or not, stripped of his rank or not, Zale was a Knight of Hyperion.

Lathan stood with several knights Seth did not know. Something black and red stirred in Seth's gut at the fool he'd made of himself. Of course he was alone. He'd always be alone, even in a cadre. He was the only one like him, the only one the god's fire burned—but Seth remembered the pup's weight against him, the comfort of someone touching him without fear of the taint that clung to him. It struck him hard, from nowhere, an ache he hadn't named, and Seth forced down his sudden tears. He fed them to the fire within him and let them burn away.

"Rhea, our mother in which we lay," the Bishop intoned. She crouched, lifted a handful of dust, and walked the length of Sophia's body, sprinkling it around her.

Sophia's bloodless skin looked waxen. It shone slightly, ready to join the flames.

The assembled crowd repeated the Bishop's words.

"Hyperion, the fire to light your way."

The crowd echoed back the phrase.

They said it again, three times, and each time, the stricken part threatened to rise.

How could it not?

Every child had learned the blessing for the dead. Three gods—three lines—three invocations older than the world.

It wanted to be said.

Seth fed the echo, the memory, to the fire.

The Bishop called the flames. They fell in a column, consuming flesh and wood.

The knights burned their dead, mixed their ashes with the god's fire, which set their spirits free. It was a necessity when they marched to war, even before the moon had died.

It took only a moment before Sophia and her pyre were consumed. Ashes drifted over the courtyard like early snowflakes. The god's fire burned even her bones, leaving behind only her scorched armor. They'd inter that in the crypt, among the other faithful, to warn anything that rose out of the dark of what they'd face should they dare creep into the light.

Seth could only watch.

He could not help. The heat would burn him. Lathan and

another knight stepped forward, doing the grim work of piling Sophia's remaining gear upon her shield.

))) ꝺ ● ꝺ (((

Seth took a seat at the long table. The other knights and priests gathered at the other end. It was so much worse this way, to be alone within a crowd. He ate quickly, chewing without really tasting. He would finish, then sleep again. He hoped the dawn and his morning penance would bring solace.

The fire rose like a bubble of heat, up his throat, in his head. Looking into his spoon, Seth could see a gleaming flicker in his eyes.

He needed to pray.

He pushed his chair back and stood.

No one asked where he was going.

Sophia had been so angry. It hadn't been knightly behavior, but she'd also seemed so unhappy. Maybe given time and the chance she'd have found a way to let it go, to find happiness. Now she never could.

Seth did not want to be like that but wasn't certain how to purge these feelings.

By dark the space beneath the dome remained beautiful. The brazen statues and gold cap of the altar reflected the wealth of candlelight. Seth approached the altar, ready to kneel, and found a robed figure leaning there, hands pressed flat to the ring of red marble.

Seth turned to go. He did not want Father Geldar to see him riddled with doubt.

"It is all right, Seth." Geldar straightened. He turned, his smile slipping into place. "You must be distressed to pray by night."

"It is nothing, Father," Seth said, chin dipping toward the floor.

"Knights are not to lie, my boy." He looked to the altar. "Especially not here."

"You're right, Father," Seth admitted. "And you were right before. This city tests me, more than I expected. I have failed Hyperion. I have failed the Hierarch."

Geldar put his arms on Seth's shoulders.

"Hyperion is forgiving. You must remember that. Our lord is light. Mercy is his."

"And the Hierarch?" Seth asked.

Geldar's smile faltered.

"I do not know," he said. "I have known him a long time, since he was simply Father Logrum of my order, but I do not often understand his will."

"I don't know how I can face him," Seth said.

"You must. And very soon."

Seth lifted his face to meet the Inquisitor's eyes.

"The Hierarch is coming. I've word that he will arrive to-morrow."

Seth's heart fell.

The people here, the ones who'd attacked them, were rough. But they were also desperate. How could they not be? They lived in darkness.

Hyperion was the light. Geldar said he was merciful, but was the Hierarch?

Would he be merciful in a search for the man from the box, or would he be like Sophia?

"Seth," Geldar said, putting a hand on his shoulder. "I think I may need your forgiveness."

"Father?" Seth asked, blinking.

"Living among monks all these years, among the old, you've

had no company your own age. And the isolation of Teshur . . . I fear that it, that I, did not prepare you for this world."

"I am not the knight I am supposed to be," Seth said.

His eyes dropped to the floor, to the pattern of tiles and squares, white broken by spirals of bronze.

"I'm not talking about the knight's path," Geldar said. "You did not have the chance to grow as you should have."

Seth's face pinched with questions.

"You lack some experiences," Geldar explained. "Ones that should be had by one your age."

Seth remembered Lathan and flushed.

It was true. He'd never been kissed, never played games or run through the streets the way the children did here. He'd been the youngest person in the monastery by decades, and the solitude had suited him for a while, but now he could see the gap inside him, the things he'd never done or learned. It was another kind of flaw, something he lacked, but perhaps one more easily corrected.

Geldar watched him come to this conclusion. He smiled what Seth called his Inquisitor's smile, which he wore when he'd unfurled the path of Seth's thoughts like a scroll.

"I often think that one should not come to belief too quickly," Geldar said, turning to regard the altar. "Phoebe's priests kept orphans and oblates, and I think that was a mistake, to bring them up in a temple."

Seth glanced around them, eyes darting side to side. That Father Geldar should mention her, here of all places.

"I think one should come to belief when they are older, have had the chance to live," Geldar explained. "Then they would not pine for things they did not experience. I feel it's that way with you, Seth. I should not have left you to be raised by the old."

"I am sorry, Father," Seth said. "I shall do better. I promise."

"You misunderstand me. I am not saying that you must be a better knight, my boy. I am saying you must be a better person."

"Are they not the same thing?"

"Somewhat," Geldar said. "But to grow, you must first live. The knight's path, your path, it is part of who you are, but not all of it. I think you must find out what else you can be, Seth. You may never be whole otherwise."

"But I want to be a knight."

"I know that's your dream, your goal," Geldar said. "And it is a worthy one. But I'd like you to dream bigger, to want more, to become more."

"I don't understand."

"I know, my boy." Geldar looked to the ring of sky visible through the oculus. "And perhaps I think of you too fondly, too much like a son, because I want happiness for you, and that requires more than mere duty and discipline."

Geldar's words lit a mix of things in Seth's heart and stomach. He did not cringe from them, to do so would be dishonest.

The fire would always be inside him. It would always contend with the darkness that dwelled there too. Seth wasn't certain he had room for another struggle. The question, the constant question, had always been which of the two would win.

12
MOON

It really had been a garden once.

The priests had cultivated anything that grew in the colors of night, pale moonflowers, black apples, and the night roses. A few vines with the bluest flowers still peeked out of the mist that carpeted the ground.

Kinos stood apart, watching Raef by what light the wall let in.

He shuddered at the chill and checked his palms for scrapes and nicks. He would not have been able to bear meeting the faces of the dead that lingered here.

He almost scoffed. They'd killed her and torn down her temple, only to seal it in artificial, everlasting night.

A bit of the base remained, part of the curving wall. A few of the flying buttresses hadn't broken in the collapse.

A pillar of white marble and black basalt, the tower had once crowned Versinae. Now nothing rose higher than Hyperion's dome.

Raef had known better than to expect scraps of paper or

bits of books, but still, he looked for them among the ruins and blackened ground.

Much of the tower's rubble had gone into the wall, but a vast pile remained.

A marble eye stared up at Raef from the dirt.

He crouched to brush the dirt from a bit of broken statue.

"Who is it?" Kinos asked as Raef lifted the piece.

"I can't tell. Probably some Hierophant."

"He was the head of the order?"

"Yeah," Raef said. He laid the half-face back among the rubble. "Father Polus was the Hierophant in my time. He was stern, but he wasn't mean."

"You got in a lot of trouble, didn't you?" Kinos asked.

"How did you know?"

Kinos smiled.

"Just a guess."

Raef shook off the attempt at lightening his mood.

"He was always punishing me, usually for running or pinching extra food."

"How did he punish you?" Kinos asked.

It was hard to answer, not because the details were dire, but because the memories hurt now. Maurin knew where he came from, but she'd never asked, had never wanted or pressed to know.

"By making me sit in his office and read while he wrote letters," Raef said.

His voice creaked on the well of emotion, the long-swallowed feelings finally surfacing from the depths of his gut.

"That doesn't sound so bad."

"It wasn't," Raef said. "But I was a kid. It bored me to tears. It took me a long time to realize that he wanted me to learn, that he was trying to teach me . . ."

Raef trailed off, remaining silent for a while.

"I miss him," he said, looking over the ruins. "I'd give anything to have them back."

"I can't understand," Kinos said, hanging his head. "Not completely, but I do, a little."

"Your family?" Raef asked.

He sank. He hadn't even asked. Of course Kinos was worried about them. How could he not be?

"I don't even know if the Hierarch kept his promise, how long I was in there, or if they're even alive," Kinos said.

Raef reached out. He wanted to put his hand on Kinos's shoulder, maybe embrace him, but dropped his arm to his side.

"We should see if there's anything we can use for bedding," he said.

"Yeah."

They circled the rubble, their soft steps the only noise. They could sleep in the lee of the wall. There wouldn't be any wind, but it was already cold.

"What's that?" Kinos asked, nodding to a slab of bronze peeking out from the rubble.

"The doors to the undercroft," Raef said. "If it's intact there will be stores, maybe even food."

"I'd settle for a cloak," Kinos said, rubbing his arms with his hands.

"Let's go see," Raef said.

He didn't mention that there might be other reasons, a slim chance for answers to the mysteries of the shadowknife and the box.

They shifted stones to clear a door, rolling them more than lifting, cautious of their edges. Dirt and ash gloved their hands. Finally, they could swing one door open.

The stairs were intact. The roof remained standing, its arched vaults held aloft by thick, fluted columns.

"I won't be able to see," Kinos said.

"Do you want to stay up here?" Raef offered.

"Maybe—Yes." Kinos let out a little breath. "Just be careful."

"Always."

Flashing a smile he didn't feel, Raef took a long breath, and descended.

The tower's fall had cracked the ceiling of the main chamber, but not broken it. Roots had wormed their way inside, marring the beauty of the blue plaster and the inlaid silver stars. They peeked out from the ash that covered most of the space. Many of the smaller vaults had collapsed.

Raef's steps unveiled bits of the polished marble floor. No Grief gathered here, which was a mercy he sorely needed.

The memories of the last time he'd seen this place were rising, whispering at the edges of his mind.

For a decade he'd bottled them up, swallowed them down, and dulled his senses. He had no rum with him tonight, and he knew it was time. He had to let them rise and surface.

Passages ran between the pillars, doorways leading farther into the dark. Raef explored one, and found it full of ledgers. It had flooded. He lifted one book, but it was too stained to read, so he set it back in its watery grave.

Other tunnels led to statues, hooded figures, her priests and children, the other gods of the Night House. Her cult statue had stood on the tower's main floor. It would have been crushed in the fall.

Raef's wrist pulsed faintly. He wasn't even certain he'd felt it until he took another step and it came again. The shadowknife stirred like a waking heartbeat. It sped up as Raef progressed deeper into the vaults.

A narrow door stood open, and on the other side, a rectangle of black glass, polished obsidian, hung on the far and final wall.

It gleamed in the shadowsight, reflecting Raef's fractured image back at him.

The glass was broken.

This had been what Kinos had described, the carving on Eastlight, on his island.

Raef reached out, brushed a hand over its surface, felt the faintest touch of cold.

He knew it would not open again, though it had once before. This was the thing, the memory he'd avoided. How he'd escaped, and how they'd died.

)))) ● ● (((

"Lady Moon," Raef chanted. "Sail the Ebon Sea. Mother Moon, daughter of the deep. Midnight Moon . . ."

He trailed off. He'd forgotten the hymn's third line again.

Shaking his head, he reached for the blindfold but left it alone with a sigh. The priests required him to wear one in the prayer rooms, to keep the shadowsight from breaking his punishment, a meditation on sacred darkness.

He was the only one who could see in the dark, so he was the only one who had to wear a blindfold. It was stupid. He shouldn't be punished for a gift she'd obviously given him, just like he shouldn't be punished for running up the stairs. Walking was a waste of time.

He wasn't old. His bones didn't crack or creak like the priests'. Nor was he one of them. That was years away. He didn't need to appear dignified no matter what they told him.

Raef pinched himself to stay awake. It had to be close to noon. He should be asleep, tucked in among the other novices, sharing snores with them in the barracks, but the old man had given Raef this punishment, probably because the prayer room smelled like feet.

He sighed again. A hand jerked his blindfold away.

Raef twisted to see Father Polus, Phoebe's Hierophant, the old man himself, looming in the doorway. Raef hadn't heard it open.

Polus's stern face met Raef's stare.

How did Father Polus always sneak up on him?

All of the priests were taller than Raef, but the old man loomed.

"Father?" Raef asked. What had he done now? Worse, what had the Hierophant found out about?

Polus tossed him a robe, the sort they wore for winter prayers.

"Get dressed, Raef."

Raef pulled on the heavy garment. He didn't intend to argue, not when Father Polus was wearing that expression, but he opened his mouth to ask a question.

"Don't speak," the priest said, cutting him off. "Just follow."

Father Polus had definitely found out about something. Probably that fight in the yard, or maybe that Raef had skipped midnight prayers last full moon to spy on the Initiates.

Father Polus took him by the wrist and dragged him from the prayer room as soon as he'd finished lacing his sandals.

All the tower should have been fast asleep in the middle of the day. The priests kept all-night vigils, watching the eastern sky. That was their duty during the new moon, to await her return from the Underworld. It bored Raef. Most priestly duties bored Raef, but he accepted their importance and usually went along with minimal grumbling.

The curtains in the halls should have been drawn against the daylight, but they stood open, letting the noon sun touch the darkness of her temple. Raef wanted to protest, to ask the

Hierophant about it, but experience with the old man's moods said he'd allow no questions. Cowed, Raef let himself be carried along in the old man's wake.

Something cold ran up Raef's spine to see the priests and Initiates running for the roof, where all the order prayed at moonrise, where they sang to the temple of the sun when Hyperion set. His priests would sing back, making a chorus that ran through the city's highest plaza. Father Polus pulled Raef against the tide, toward the cellars.

It wasn't fair. Running was what had gotten him punished. Something had to be terribly wrong for the priests to do it and for the Hierophant to not punish them too.

They reached her statue on the main floor. The chant of many voices, strange and brassy, rose from outside. Raef gasped at the sacrilege. This was new moon.

The Initiates were forbidden to speak. They fasted. They waited for her to complete her descent to the Ebon Sea and to return through the secret door.

Novices like Raef were granted a child's leniency, but they were still taught to keep quiet and silence was encouraged.

They had to pray her back from the Underworld, not offend her with noise and light. Even Raef respected those rules.

He didn't know the consequences. No one had ever told him, but he had this terrible notion that she'd be trapped there, unable to return to the sky.

Sweat stuck the robe to his skin. It should not be so warm.

They passed a casement. Outside, a horde in brazen armor wove flaming swords. Their chant, almost guttural, reverberated through the tower's stones.

The sight of them made Raef forget the Hierophant's command for silence.

"Father, what's happening?"

"We are out of time, Raef." Polus grabbed Raef's wrist, harder than before. His touch burned like ice. "I'm so sorry. I thought we would have longer."

"But what's happening?" Raef demanded.

"The Knights of Hyperion have come for us."

It made no sense. The knights were their cousins, the children of their goddess's brother.

Hyperion's light was Phoebe's light. They reflected each other. She glowed because of him.

His knights and priests guarded the day as Phoebe's own watched the night. Why would they come to her temple armed for war?

Raef looked to her statue, her cloak of black basalt and her boat of silver-veined granite. Her marble face, half hidden, gave no answers.

Heat surged through the air. The fine hairs on Raef's arms stood straight. Something struck the tower in a whoosh, a blow of unseen force. He smelled fire.

Another blow struck and Raef's world shook.

The acrid reek of burning vellum burst over him, falling in a noxious wave.

"The library!"

Raef tried to pull away, to start back up the stairs and reach the books so precious to the goddess.

Father Polus's grip on him tightened until it hurt.

"Down," the Hierophant commanded.

The tower shook.

High above, an acolyte screamed as she toppled from the stairway's railing. She fell, still screaming. Father Polus shielded Raef's eyes with his hand, but it did nothing to silence the wet snap of her landing.

Raef felt something in his chest break at the sound.

His sobs turned to choking coughs as the knights' chant grew louder, deeper, more menacing. Father Polus dragged him into the cellars and closed the doors behind them. It muffled the chanting, but the ceiling above them smoldered. The mortar between the stones lit with an orange glow. The bronze doors steamed.

The cooler darkness of the cellars relieved the oppressive heat, but the smoke soon found them. The screams of those trapped above drowned out the chanting.

Raef wiped his tears and breathed through the sleeve of his robe.

Their journey ended at a black door. Pure obsidian, it shone like a mirror.

"You have to open it, Raef."

Raef blanched at the tears on the Hierophant's face and whimpered, unable to make words. He could not have imagined anything making the old man cry. Raef's own tears froze inside him at the sight.

"You have the key," Father Polus said. "Use it."

Lessons rushed back. A room full of doors. Father Polus ordered him to call the shadowknife and open every lock, one by one, in secret practice.

Raef blinked, remembering it all.

The attack on the tower, the fire the knights lobbed against it, stopped. They'd done their work. A great rumble began above them. Father Polus pushed Raef toward the door.

"You have to leave us now, Raef. You have to survive. For her."

"Please, Father. I don't want to."

"You have to," the Hierophant growled even as he threw his arms around Raef.

Raef didn't want to die, but he didn't want to leave his brothers and sisters, his fathers and mothers, behind.

The screams above grew louder. A great crack, like a hot mug dropped into icy water, silenced them. The flames found them. Fire swirled in the darkness.

"It's time," Father Polus said, letting Raef go. "The tower is breaking apart."

Raef called the shadowknife and plunged it into the black door. The obsidian grew darker. Its gloss flattened to matte. The starless night on the other side sucked the heat from the air around them. He shivered despite the fire, the smoke, and his heavy robe. The sweat turned clammy all across his body.

"Come with me," he said, hearing the plea in his voice and not caring how young he sounded.

"I cannot," Father Polus said. "That door will only open for those of your blood."

The flames were all around them. They seeped into the undercroft like hunting serpents.

Raef's tears froze to his face as he went through the waiting doorway.

The memory let him go. He gasped like a diver surfacing from the bottom of a frozen lake and woke in the undercroft. He slumped to the ground, pressed his back to the cracked obsidian, and sobbed.

"I ran," he said. "I ran through this door and left them to die."

13
MOON

Raef left the cellars to find the circle of sky above the wall filled with stars beyond counting. He felt like he'd been skinned, and yet that was a relief. He felt strangely free of a weight he hadn't known he'd been carrying.

He did not know why he alone could see in the dark. None of the other priests or Initiates could. And the shadow-knife—he'd forgotten about it. Stepping through the black door had made him forget. Sifting through his memory now, he knew he'd been somewhere else. Somewhere freezing. He'd awoken in the smoldering ruins later, dazed but alive.

Prodding the memory, all he'd forgotten, he found the edges jagged. The tower's fall and his escape had left him unable to remember the knife. He had the shape of it now, of the hole inside him. Pieces were still missing.

Stumbling into the night, Raef pressed a hand to his belly to quell its rumbling.

Cricket song filled the air. He heard nothing else. The

wall muted the city's clamor. He hadn't even heard the temple bells ring the sunset.

Kinos waited outside, perched on the base of a broken column, his night-blind eyes wide as they sought the light. He looked a little afraid, a little lost, but not as much as he had when Raef had found him. There was almost something bird-like, something delicate, to his lean frame.

Raef approached cautiously, filled with the notion that Kinos would fly away if startled.

"Was there anything down there?" Kinos asked.

"I don't think so," Raef said. "I mean, I didn't find anything."

"What do we do?" Kinos asked.

"We won't freeze," Raef said, letting out a breath that Kinos had changed the subject. "And the shades won't bother us if we're not bleeding."

"Then we should check." Kinos inched in Raef's direction.

He lifted his shirt over his head, showing Raef what he'd wanted to see since he'd first opened the box.

Kinos smiled. He knew that Raef, and only Raef, could see him.

"Check my back?" he asked, turning.

"You're, uh, fine," Raef said, unsurprised that his voice had dropped low.

"Your turn then," Kinos said, stepping closer and nodding to the hem of Raef's shirt.

Raef's breath caught. He'd done this before, but this time felt different, new, like showing any part of himself to Kinos went deeper than any water he'd ever dove into. Turning, Raef tugged off his shirt before he could think himself out of it.

He knew he wasn't beautiful. He had pale skin that reddened at a touch. His wiry shape was formed more from hunger than labor. His heart thrummed, surely Kinos could hear it.

Then Kinos touched him. His palms were cold, but Raef did not pull away. Raef closed his eyes. Kinos's hands were warmer by the time he'd worked his way to the small of Raef's back. Raef held his breath as Kinos trailed the tip of his thumb along the waist of Raef's pants.

"Turn around," Kinos said, voice husky. "Show me your arm."

"I'm fine," Raef said. "I can see, remember?"

"You've been sneaking looks at it since we met," Kinos said. "Let me see it."

Raef had clutched his wrist to his chest.

He'd come this far, brought Kinos here, and told him how he'd been raised, but this was another step, another dive into deep, deep waters.

"You asked me to trust you," Kinos said. "Trust me back."

Raef nibbled his lip.

He didn't fight as Kinos took his arm.

The black crescents had darkened and spread. A second ring of moons now encircled the first. The mark had grown.

"What is this?" Kinos asked. Squinting in the darkness, he brushed two fingertips along Raef's arm, sending a jolt through his body. His fingers traced around the mark but did not touch it.

They were a contrast. Raef, pale; Kinos, golden-skinned.

Kinos stood just a little shorter. Raef would have to stoop if they were to kiss, and how he wanted to kiss Kinos in that moment.

Raef tried to keep his voice calm and not betray the leaping beat in his chest.

"I don't know," he said. "Really."

He wished he couldn't hear the want in his voice.

Someone like him. That's all he'd ever wanted, but there was no one like him.

He'd gone through the door. Father Polus had sent no one else.

Only Raef had survived and he had no idea why. Kinos was the first person he'd met who didn't feel like a stranger. Raef couldn't explain it better than that.

"It showed up when I fought the knight," he said. "The one guarding the box, when I went to save you."

"You mean when you went to steal me."

Kinos moved, trailed his fingertips up Raef's arm to lay his hand flat over Raef's heart, his palm warm on Raef's smooth skin.

Raef didn't move. He didn't want to break whatever spell had this beautiful man touching him.

Kinos's secret smile deepened.

His thumb shifted to Raef's jaw. He tilted Raef's head downward and leaned in.

The kiss filled Raef's chest, his skin, with pressure. It knocked on his heart's closed door, and for the first time in a long while, he considered opening up.

It was far from his first kiss, but it felt like so much more.

When Kinos pulled away, Raef had to remember to exhale, to inhale, to start the bellows of his lungs again.

"Thank you," Kinos said.

"For what?" Raef asked, still feeling like all the air had left his world, like he'd swam to the bottom of the bay. "You kissed me."

"For stealing me."

14

SUN

Seth hid in an alley. Back pressed against the rough brick, he shivered, trying to keep his breathing silent, to keep still, but knew it wouldn't matter. The fire always found him.

He knew he was dreaming. He'd been here many times, had hidden so many times in so many places, but it always found him, embraced him, and granted him a screaming, golden death.

His clothes were strange, a rough tunic that bared his arms, leather bracers, and sandals. He looked like one of the ancient heroes, like the temple statues.

The night sky above was clear, but no stars shone. The darkness shielded him, hid him. Seth shivered, but not with discomfort. The air felt silky on his skin.

He hunched his shoulders.

A Knight of Hyperion should not crave the shadows, but perhaps this once, the darkness could save him. He straightened. He would run. He'd escape.

Versinae's towers stood lightless and thin, like skeletal trees in a burned forest.

Seth turned a corner and the fire lunged like a hulking brute. Seth threw himself aside. Landing hard, he scraped his skin along the dirty cobbles. The dream should not feel so real. And yet there was no Grief, no hungry shades. This place felt both real and not at the same time.

The fire caught up to him in a burst of light.

Squinting, Seth could see a broad-shouldered form wreathed by the flames. It lifted its arms, ready to embrace him.

Seth ran. The figure floated after him, not with haste, but with the inevitable pace of a hunter certain his prey would not escape.

The darkness gathered ahead, so thick that even the pursuing flames did not breach it. Seth dove into it. Cool and concealing, the shadows swirled around him, soothing his hurts, guiding him toward a shape—a door. Feeling his way with outstretched hands, Seth stepped through it.

He fell to his knees in relief.

He'd escaped.

The grip on his heart relaxed. He could breathe here.

In this perfect darkness he'd finally found a place the fire could not reach.

Standing, blind, he pawed at the air, but he did not start or shriek when fingertips walked across his bare back.

The touch should have surprised him, but Seth realized that he'd been waiting for it, expected it, all of his life.

Arms embraced him. He turned inside them, seeking the face of whoever held him. The touch lit a different heat inside him. Then the arms withdrew. Seth shook his head, stepped forward, and felt only the darkness.

"Where did you go?" he asked, hating the broken sound of his voice.

A spark, the barest glimmer, lit the blackness like a green

ember dropped into water. It rippled, and gave Seth the slightest view of a black mirror. He saw himself reflected in the darkness, smiling back from the glossy stone.

There were other shapes there, statues. Some were broken, missing their features or upper bodies, but there had been twelve once.

He squinted, straining to see more. The fire brightened in the glass, turning red and orange, lighting around him. He felt something vital burn to cinders.

Seth awoke, bolting upright in his bed, sweat-soaked, chest heaving.

He cast about the barracks, but no one else was awake. At least he hadn't shouted, hadn't woken the others.

The odor of burned fabric drifted up from the bed.

He'd conjured the flames in his sleep. The sheets were singed, the fabric stiff and browned. He'd nearly lit them aflame.

Seth fought to get his breathing under control, to cool the fire inside. Sweat rose off him in a steam.

He'd nearly calmed, nearly settled the race of his heart to a normal pace when the temple bells rang, jarring him again. Seth leaped from the bed, hurried to splash water on his face, and dressed. The other knights were faster, their reflexes not slowed by dreams. He glanced once at the bunk where Sophia had slept.

The bells continued, a long song that should be joyous to a knight.

They signaled the arrival of the Hierarch, the living voice of Hyperion in the world, but Seth's shoulders, and with them the scars from his scourging, tightened.

The Hierarch had come, but the box lay empty. Sophia and Zale were gone, dead and stripped of rank, leaving Seth alone to answer for their failure. His first instinct was to run, but where would he go? Who would have him?

No, these were cowardly thoughts. He'd face his punishment. He joined the rush of the other knights and priests, dressing, donning armor, and hurrying outside to fall in line in the plaza.

Behind them, the temple priests made a line, their yellow cassocks cheerful in the gray daylight. Father Geldar came last. Wearing a placid expression inside his hood, he stood next to Seth.

They waited as the bells continued. Seth's eyes watered from the incense as the priests waved censers. He followed Geldar's gaze to the Garden wall and repressed a shudder, remembering his dream of the fire and how the dark had soothed him. That cool comfort had been terrible.

"It calls you," Geldar whispered. "Doesn't it?"

"A little," Seth confessed. "Maybe more than a little."

"It is natural to seek one's opposite. Are the gods not related, siblings and spouses? Are they not linked to one another?"

"Father?" Seth asked.

The Bishop was listening. Her eyes weren't on them, but she stared at the plaza's entrance, the one facing the city gate, her face frozen in an expression Seth could not read.

"I am merely saying that you must be strong, Seth," Geldar said. "No shadow can stand."

"Against the light," Seth finished.

"Now look elsewhere. He's nearly here."

Seth imitated the Bishop. He forced his gaze to the plaza's entrance and tried to adopt her stiff demeanor.

A crowd of citizens gathered on the cobbles, rising like a tide from the lower city.

Most were commoners, dressed simply, their dull clothes worn. All were pale from living beneath Versinae's gray skies. Many were thin. So much of the city looked hungry.

The nobles were fewer in number and easily spotted. Better

dressed, better fed, they held to the plaza's edges, close to their carriages, with guards to protect them.

The nobles had a right to be afraid.

The derelicts in Boat Town had risked their lives against the knights. They'd made it clear that they had nothing left to lose.

All of them had come to see the Hierarch's arrival, and the air buzzed with a feeling almost as palpable as the Grief at night. Seth recognized it easily. He'd worn the same expression when Geldar had delivered him to Teshur. He'd felt that same taste of hope.

Seth was trained to fight, trained to defend, but he had no skill to calm or comfort. Was that what Geldar had meant, that he should dream for more, to feel and be more?

He'd enjoyed singing, once, had thought he would learn the lyre—where had that desire gone?

The priests looked more at ease with the throng. Perhaps they were used to Versinae's desperation.

Seth closed his eyes and lifted his face to the sun.

Father Sun, give us light. Give us bright peace.

The buzz of the crowd was joined by another sound, the march of boots, but Seth did not stop the flow of his prayer. The gray burned away and he felt the light brighten.

Show us the road out of darkness. Heal us.

He always heard the words in Geldar's soft, firm voice. The priest had taught him these phrases on the long trek into the desert. Seth remembered answering in a much younger tone.

The memories, as much as the prayers, eased the weight in his limbs. His breath steadied. He could face this, and perhaps he might still be of use to Hyperion. Perhaps he still might help Versinae.

Seth opened his eyes as two columns of knights, each numbering a dozen, marched into the square. Their armor was a sight better than his or the Bishop's. It gleamed with inlaid gold. Red capes hung from their shoulders. These were the Knights Elite, those who guarded the Hierarch and served him alone as his personal guard.

The crowd of onlookers murmured, humbled by the spectacle.

Seth shared their awe.

The Knights Elite stopped marching, the final slam of their boots on the plaza cobbles a clap of thunder. Perhaps he could dream of more, but he could not dream of that. Such a lofty height, such perfect faith, was beyond his nature.

Several figures entered the plaza, carrying a large palanquin, a great box on poles that was like a whole room, a traveling house. A number of pages, young neophytes of the priestly order, preceded it. They rushed to unfurl a crimson carpet.

The box settled slowly to the ground.

The plaza fell silent, and the bustling crowd froze in place.

The Hierarch emerged.

His golden robe and crown gleamed as brightly as the temple dome. The white cape that trailed behind him was as pure as a cloud.

Most fell to their knees as he passed. Many called out prayers to Hyperion, though some sounded as if they were to the man and not the god.

In a wave, the priests and knights fell to their knees. If Geldar was a breath slower than the rest, surely it was out of awe or due to his age.

The Hierarch turned. He was not an old man, at least not as old as Geldar, forty or fifty perhaps. He had tanned skin and more gold in his hair than gray. Facing the crowd, he gave the god's sign, bending his head and making a crown of his hands.

Still smiling, he looked to the priests and knights of Versinae.

"Inside," he said, the terse command at odds with his expression.

A commotion in the square interrupted the faithful's motion to obey.

"Already here," the Hierarch said with a sniff. "You think he'd at least give me time to bathe."

As one body, the Knights Elite tensed, but the Hierarch lifted a hand to stay them.

"He's no threat," the Hierarch grumbled, low enough that only the faithful would hear. "Merely an annoyance. Let him approach."

A much smaller palanquin, this one painted a deep green with silver details, was lowered into the square. A dozen guards, dressed in teal and black livery, held a much shorter line against the red-caped knights.

A man, flanked by a pair of stiff-coated attendants, emerged from behind the curtains. He had a prodigious nose. The dark hair of his scalp was thin, yet he wore fine clothes, a coat of black velvet, and a white shirt. He carried himself with confidence and strode past the gauntlet as if the knights were statues.

"Your Holiness," he said, bowing just the right amount. "You did not tell us you were coming."

His words sounded pleasant, but his eyes were creased with anger.

The Hierarch squinted in kind.

"I am not beholden to you, Deslis," he said. Lifting his voice for the people, he added, "The will of our god dictates where I go. I obey only that, only Hyperion."

So this then was the city's prince. Adrian, Geldar had called him. It was hard not to compare him to the Hierarch, the way they faced off, one golden and white, the other dark-clad and scowling.

"As you should," the prince said. "But your visits would sow less chaos were you to inform us in advance."

"I believe you said the same last time," the Hierarch said. "Did he not, Geldar?"

"I believe so, Your Holiness."

The Inquisitor's face had gone blank. None of the warmth or laughter Seth got to see in private leaked through his mask.

Seth had asked Geldar, when he'd been brought to Hyperion, why he could not follow in the Father's steps. He admired the man, wanted to be like him.

You have no guile, Geldar had said. Inquisitors must be able to lie in order to do the god's quieter work.

But Hyperion is the god of truth, of light, Seth had said.

He is, Geldar had agreed.

And he hadn't explained any further, never reconciled the contradiction, but Seth was glad that he'd become a knight and not followed in Geldar's footsteps.

"As you can see, your knights have caused quite a stir in the city," the prince said.

The Hierarch's eyes followed the prince's gaze over the square, the press of the masses, and the assembled faithful.

He landed on Seth, just for a moment, and something Seth could not read, pleasure perhaps, danced in his eyes.

"I am here on the god's business," the Hierarch said. "When that is done, I will tend to the soul of this viper's nest you call a city."

"I must insist—" the prince started.

"You will insist on nothing," the Hierarch snapped, his voice deepening to a growl. "As I have always made clear, as I have already said today, I do not answer to you."

The temperature rose. Seth blinked. As far as he knew, Inquisitors like Geldar could not conjure the fire as the Knights of Hyperion could. The Hierarch had been an Inquisitor before he obtained his title, but perhaps his elevation to the head of the temple had brought that power.

The prince's expression went stony. The man might be everything Geldar had said, but he clearly was no coward. He straightened, rising to the challenge.

"What will you do, Deslis?" the Hierarch asked, voice low. "You have nothing to threaten me with. The only ones who might have offered me a challenge died when last we came here. Do you not remember opening the gates to us?"

The prince smiled. It was a sly, cunning expression. Seth did not like it.

"You misunderstand, Your Holiness," the prince countered, his voice lifted for all to hear. "I did not come to insist you or your knights leave Versinae. I came to welcome you."

The Hierarch lifted an eyebrow.

Deslis lifted a hand. Behind him, a thin man stepped forward. He wore a tidy suit coat of gray and green. Kneeling before the Hierarch, he offered an envelope in his raised hands.

"An invitation," the prince said. "I am hosting a ball, you see. Hyperion must have guided your arrival to coincide with tonight's event. You and your entourage are most welcome."

The Hierarch seemed confused.

"Do bless us with your presence," the prince said, looking around the square. "Not all of you, of course. My house is not as grand as the god's. My masquerade could not accommodate all of his knights."

The Hierarch's face pinched. Several nobles had filtered into the crowd. They watched the scene from the sides like spectators at a sparring match.

"This is most gracious of you," the Hierarch said, smiling. Lower, so that only those standing near might hear, he added, "Scurry away, you rat. You've won this round."

The prince withdrew, beaming, his head held high.

Seth blinked, uncertain how what had transpired was a victory, but no good could come from angering the Hierarch.

"Inside," the Hierarch repeated his earlier command. "Now."

Seth was swept up in the tide of robed and armored bodies hurrying to obey. The thick walls muted the buzzing of the throng as the Knights Elite held them back.

Seth had never seen so much armor. Whatever the Hierarch wanted in Versinae, whatever Geldar's purpose, it was of prime importance to Hyperion, but Seth could not help but wonder what such a force would mean to the city's common people.

They were already afraid. They were afraid of Hyperion.

The Hierarch turned to Father Geldar when they'd reached the altar.

"Well?" he asked, his voice deep, thick, and commanding.

"Your Holiness," Geldar said with a slight incline of his head.

"Report."

"The box was opened. We do not know how."

"Someone had a key," the Hierarch said.

His eyes flashed again, not with anger, but something else.

"The contents were stolen," Geldar confirmed. "A young man, by Zale's report."

The Hierarch's eyes narrowed.

"Zale is dealt with, as ordered."

Seth blinked. What did that mean? Was Zale dead? The Bishop had said he'd been stripped of his rank. Had Geldar killed him at the Hierarch's command?

"And Sophia is dead, lost to the Grief," Geldar continued.

"Which leaves you, Seth," the Hierarch said, turning in his direction.

"Yes, Your Holiness," Seth answered. He tried to sound strong, but his voice faltered.

"Approach us," the Hierarch ordered.

Seth obeyed. He knelt and kissed the offered ring. The cold of the stone floor seeped through his armor and breeches. The fire within him writhed. He pushed it down, but knowing that Hyperion's light was still inside him was a kind of comfort.

Seth had played this game often at Teshur during penance. The monks would command him to sit for long stretches. He would try to push the fire into the floor, to see how much of it he could warm before they released him.

It had been one of his small comforts. The other had been to sing, usually in the cistern, the underground cavern where they stored their water. His praises would echo off the stone, his voice low and pleasant in his ears.

"What did you see of the thief, the one with the key?" the Hierarch asked.

"Nothing, Your Holiness. Zale was unconscious when I found him. The box was open and the thief was gone."

Seth would never forget the moment, Zale lying in darkness, the light of his sword extinguished.

"We must be vigilant," the Hierarch said, looking over the assembled faithful, lifting his voice so all would hear. "This city lies. It hides from the light. Go to your duties. Prepare the temple. We shall let the people in and grant them blessings. As they come, listen to them. Question them, learn what they may know. Perhaps that will cast some light into the shadows."

Dismissed, shaking slightly, Seth rose to his feet. The Hierarch had not even chastised him. He hadn't been berated or expelled from the order. He did not understand.

The other knights went to their duties or drills. The priests drifted into the chapels. Geldar vanished, slipping away in that mysterious manner of his.

"Attend me, Seth," the Bishop called his name.

"I don't understand what's happening," he said, following her through the temple.

"Sophia caused a panic. The city feared us before. Then the Hierarch arrived with an army. Fear, especially from the common people, does not serve Hyperion."

That hadn't been what Seth had meant, but he did not mention it. He would pray as soon as he could.

"What must the Hierarch now do?" the Bishop asked.

Seth knew this tone well. The monks had also liked to test his wits.

"The Hierarch must show Hyperion's mercy," Seth said. "Show them that the god is good."

"Yes," the Bishop said. "And the prince forced him to show that he is a man, to lower himself, lest the nobility withdraw their support of the temple."

"So he won? The prince, I mean. He won."

"I do not know that," the Bishop said. "But this invitation, forced so publicly, will delay the Hierarch's purpose here. The prince is surely aware of that."

"Is he our enemy?" Seth asked.

"He is a politician, as to a degree, is the Hierarch. That is their work. We have our own."

They reached the courtyard where Seth performed his penance, where the knights practiced with their arms. He wished they'd gone to the one where the hounds were kept. Seth expected the Bishop would demand something of him, likely more penance, more punishment for his questions.

She might lash him. The monks had done that, whipping

him when he lost control. They'd bid him to whip himself when he was old enough.

The monks had always called for witnesses, but the courtyard was empty. Seth's shoulders lifted a little so that others, Lathan especially, would not see his shame.

The Bishop pulled a short blade from the weapon rack.

She nodded for him to take a blade as well.

"Show me what you can do."

"I do not understand."

"You know to stay ahead of me, to shield me, I saw that in the slums, but your training has been with monks. You know your weapons, but did they teach you to be part of a cadre? I must know how you would fare as part of a larger group. Arm yourself, and show me."

He obeyed, taking a stance. She moved beside him, holding her own sword and shield.

"Copy me," she said. "Advance!"

She took a step. Seth followed.

"In one breath, each time. Again!"

He matched her better the second time.

They repeated this, again and again, crossing the courtyard. The round shield was mostly metal, but Seth had no trouble lifting it. The lack was not in his body.

"Now backward," she commanded. "Go!"

They took several steps, her calling out and him reacting, matching her movements as best he could.

"Good, Seth. The key to fighting as a cadre, to your survival, is formation. Never break it. There is no more important command I can give you. If you break formation, the entire unit is at risk. Do you understand?"

"Yes, Bishop."

"You will practice this. With Lathan. Every day."

"Bishop?"

"Every day, Seth," she said, setting her shield back on the rack with enough force that it clanked. "With sword and shield."

"Yes, Bishop."

She left him there, alone.

Shoulders slumped, Seth returned his arms to their rack.

It was what he'd wanted, to be a Knight of Hyperion. He'd wanted it since Geldar had taken him to Teshur, speaking the entire way of the faith and the roles within it.

Yet Lathan had made his feelings clear. To be in the cadre, the Bishop's cadre, meant Seth would have to work with Lathan, fight beside him. Disdain or no, they would have to trust each other.

His spirits lifted. He could see the Bishop's intent, and he could accept this price. His need to be part of something was stronger than his embarrassment or the hurt he'd felt.

This too was a kind of sacrifice.

Geldar had seen his loneliness, how it plagued him.

Seth would practice with Lathan. He would find his place within the cadre, if the Bishop wanted him. That would have to be enough. He would not find friendship there.

If he wanted that, or more, what he'd felt in the dream, then he'd have to look beyond the order.

15
MOON

The temple bells rang long enough that the wall could not muffle them. They dragged Raef back to consciousness. Stiff and cold, he found himself alone on the ground.

It had only been one night, that one stretch of kissing, then sleeping in each other's arms. His body had pressed for more, but he hadn't been ready, even though Kinos had given him every sign. Raef had not trusted the depth of his desire, so they'd slept. And now . . .

"Kinos?" Raef asked, sitting up.

He was alone in the rubble.

Raef found his feet.

"Kinos!" he called quietly.

It might echo up the wall. Someone might hear.

The cellar door remained shut, as he'd left it the night before, and Raef could not imagine Kinos being foolish enough to descend into the dark alone.

Kinos had climbed the wall. Something inside Raef sank. He hadn't asked for anything.

He'd held back his trust and as soon as he'd started to open, to give up his secrets, Kinos had run away.

Something flickered beside the wall, in the deepest shadows where it met what remained of the tower's base.

Raef hurried toward it, his body tensed, worried about what he'd find.

It was the burned man, the shade from Eleni's who'd warned him of the fire.

His shade was so pale, so thin. He must have used all of his strength to come here.

Bits of him flaked away like ash as he mouthed new words.

Dome. Hurry. Dome.

Raef blanched.

Hurry.

"Who are you?" Raef asked.

He could cut himself, feed the ghost a drop of blood—but no, that was madness. The spirit would consume him. The Grief could rise. This shade might retain some of his mind, but those who had fallen fully into mist would not.

Raef bit his lip and reached for his knife. He had to know, but the shade faded, its strength expended.

"Damn it."

Raef took a long breath and scrambled up the wall.

His heart pounded as he crested it and descended again, landing behind it, away from the plaza where some commotion had started. It sounded like the entire city had assembled.

He did not understand why Kinos would have left shelter, what would have driven him into danger. The knights couldn't have come for him. There was no way Raef could have slept through that.

He dropped to the ground and thought of Eleni, slumped dead in her chair.

There was an Inquisitor in the city.

If Kinos was under Hyperion's dome, then he had been captured.

Shaking, Raef worked his way around to the plaza and stepped back into the shadows.

Now he understood the bells.

People filled the square. They crowded the temple steps, vying to squeeze through the open doors.

Knights stood guard everywhere. Many wore red capes.

It couldn't be a coincidence that Kinos had gone. He might have run from the sight of the Knights Elite, worried that they'd search the Garden, but it still stung that he'd left Raef behind.

Raef could walk away now. To find Kinos meant facing the man who'd ordered the towers razed and Phoebe killed.

He put his back to the wall, let the cold seep into him, and fought to stop his shaking.

Whatever had caused Kinos to run, the mysteries remained. Slighted or not, Raef had to know.

He slipped into the crowd, used it to hide as he crossed the plaza and squeezed inside the temple. Raef cleared the crowd and froze.

The Hierarch was impossible to miss.

The voice of Hyperion in the world stood inside the ring of red marble, dressed in a robe of golden fabric. The value of the thread alone could have fed Boat Town for a year.

Hands cupped toward the oculus, the Hierarch prayed in a deep, confident voice.

His eyes were closed as he faced the falling light.

Raef saw exactly how he could do it.

He'd dash forward, past the priests and knights. If he was quick, and he would be quick—if he was strong, and he would be strong, he could leap the altar and drive his knife into the Hierarch's throat.

Now he trembled for an entirely new reason.

It wouldn't bring Phoebe back, but it would be revenge.

He gripped his hidden knife.

But no . . . everything he'd felt in the crypt remained true. He was no murderer, and even if he was, he'd never escape. He wouldn't be there to save Kinos from the box or whatever they'd done with him.

Raef clasped his hands together and squeezed, the closest he could safely come to making Phoebe's sign, to holding his cupped palms together over his heart to make a sphere.

Raef joined the milling crowd to walk from chapel to chapel. He couldn't stare at the Hierarch. Someone might spot him, recognize the temptation behind his focus.

Bowing his head, Raef tried to look reverent, knew he probably failed, and circled the altar. He descended to the crypt and bought a prayer candle, the thin ones sold to leave as offerings or remembrances at the tombs. Raef walked on as if he intended to place it at the little altar to Helios, Hyperion's son, who'd died in the demon wars. No one was down here. All were above, watching the spectacle of the Hierarch, and yet he still felt like eyes were upon him.

The tomb where he'd found the box was unguarded, the door shut.

Checking that no one was near, Raef slipped inside. The box remained, open and empty. They did not have Kinos, or at least they hadn't returned him to his former prison.

Raef shook his head. He should have fed the shade, tried to get more information.

Head bowed, hands pressed together, he left the crypt.

They wouldn't keep Kinos in the temple. Too many pilgrims

crowded there to see the Hierarch. If the knights had him, they'd keep him in the courtyards and buildings that lay behind the dome.

Raef didn't know much about that space. It was private, locked away from the rest of the city. The shadowknife pulsed inside his wrist as if to remind him that locked doors were not a problem. Raef pulled at his sleeve, making certain the mark was hidden. Perhaps it wanted to warn him that it would be smarter to come back at night, when the priests and knights were sleeping, but Raef had no guarantee that Kinos would live that long.

There were Inquisitors in the city, at least one.

If they questioned Kinos, they'd learn about Raef, and he'd burn, all because his loneliness was eating him alive. Yet he didn't regret telling Kinos the truth, didn't regret the kiss, even if it had led to this.

Clenching his jaw, Raef left the temple and worked his way around to where the limestone walls met the complex. There were servant gates, all guarded by knights. Raef aimed for the kitchen and knocked.

A scullion in a stained tunic swung the door open.

"What?" he demanded. His dark hair was matted to his head with sweat and effort.

"I'm looking for work," Raef said. "One of the priests told me you might need help."

"What?" the lad repeated. He was young and possibly a charity case himself. "I've no time for more chaos today."

"The Hierarch is here," Raef said, speaking slowly. "And he brought all of these knights. I figured you might need help with dishes. Or chopping things. I'll work for a meal."

He rubbed his belly for emphasis.

"Fine," the scullion said, rolling his eyes so hard Raef wasn't sure they'd descend. "You can scrape the bowls and plates. I hate that part. You can eat any leavings."

Raef smiled and tried to look appreciative. He wouldn't need that long. He was already planning a convenient lie when the boy eyed Raef's hands and said, "You need to go wash."

"Sure," Raef said. "Where?"

"Through there." The scullion waved a knife with a bit of a potato peel stuck to it toward a door.

Raef considered palming an orange on his way, but thought better of it. In another life he might have been grateful for this work. He'd eat scraps. He'd eaten worse.

Not that he had ever had that problem in the tower.

He shouldn't have thought of that, not here. His hand started to shake.

He forced it away, forced himself to steady.

Kinos needed him.

Raef walked past the barrel and basin set for washing and darted around a corner. The temple was a maze, a series of narrow buildings and courtyards designed to maximize the sunlight.

At some point the scullion would realize Raef had snuck off.

The first courtyard opened into another, smaller space which led to another, then another.

He'd never find Kinos in this maze. Raef's concern had gripped him so hard that he almost didn't notice the old man. He sat on a stone bench, tossing out bread crumbs for a flock of doves. They cooed, their wings ruffling as they jostled one another.

"Some would say it's a waste of bread," the man said, looking up from inside the hood of his brown robes. He had a low voice.

Raef held back a wince as he met the man's eyes. The man's gaze was piercing, and Raef felt seen, exposed in a way he hadn't been since the last time Father Polus had caught him at something.

"Why?" Raef asked, trying to keep from shaking.

"To feed birds in a city on the verge of starvation."

"Then we'll just eat the birds," Raef said with a shrug.

The man chuckled before focusing his full attention on Raef.

"Why are you here?" he asked.

His eyes were a deep blue. He had a white beard and not much hair.

"I came looking for work and got lost." Raef jerked a thumb back toward the kitchens.

The man seemed to ignore the answer.

"I would pray with you, if you'd like," he said.

"I'm not that lost," Raef said.

"Are you so certain?" the priest asked. "We often cannot see the shape of the maze we're trapped in."

More than his words, his piercing stare sent a tingle of warning, like a spider's creeping steps, up Raef's spine. Trying to keep his expression neutral, Raef looked more closely.

The man wasn't like the other priests. Most strolled through the temple, well fed, often drunk, and slow-witted. This one seemed contemplative, but he had a sharpness that reminded Raef of Father Polus. The shadowknife pulsed in warning.

"That's all right," Raef said. He looked over his shoulder, trying to appear relaxed, as he kept the man in the corner of his eye. "I should get back to the kitchens."

"Many have come here today. Mostly to see the Hierarch," the man said, eyes narrowed. "All of them are seeking something. Have you found what you came for?"

"Not yet," Raef said.

"Even the prince came," the man said casually.

"Deslis?" Raef asked, pausing.

"He wanted to invite the Hierarch to a ball, a masquerade," the old man said, scattering more crumbs. "Can you imagine?"

"No," Raef said. Unless he had something to show the Hierarch, something he wanted to trade or sell. Something like

Kinos. The knights hadn't caught him. They would have returned him to the box. The Watch had found him first.

"Can you point me back toward the kitchens?" Raef asked.

"It's to the left, but go carefully, my son."

Lips pressed tight, Raef gave a little nod of thanks and retreated.

He went right, continuing his search, creeping through hallways to peek into barrack rooms and glance into courtyards. One was full of hounds and he went no closer.

More and more he felt he was right. The prince had Kinos, not the Hierarch.

Raef could go to the palace. He could get Kinos back.

He could do it alone, but it would be easier, much easier, with help.

Raef left the temple by another door.

He'd always wanted to go to a ball.

16

MOON

"You're insane," Maurin said.

"Think about it," Raef countered. "It's a masquerade. We'll blend right in. I'll find Kinos and get out. You watch my back and pocket whatever you can. We both win."

He took a seat on a pipe.

"You can't just walk right in, Raef. You'd have to look the part, have the right clothes, not to mention a bath."

The Crack was a gap in one of the canal walls. The interior, a network of bricked-off tunnels and pipes, was warm, but he'd never slept comfortably here.

She wasn't wrong. He remembered the knight in the crypt calling him out. How many days had it been since he'd paid a few coppers to scrub himself clean? If Kinos cared, he hadn't mentioned it. Raef almost flushed at the thought.

They paused to let one of the rumbles that sometimes moved through the underground pass. He didn't know what caused them, but guessed it was something ancient, something in the deep tunnels Raef wouldn't dare to enter.

"I know how to get us clothes, or at least enough money for them."

"It's an awful risk, Raef."

The bricks reflected the red light of the Lost's few fires. It danced over Maurin's features as she stepped closer.

"Why does the prince have him?" she asked. "How do you know he's not dead?"

"I think the prince wants to show up the Hierarch. He's playing some game. I still don't know why, but Kinos has value. The prince wouldn't kill him, not if he's worth any leverage. He's important to them. I just need to know why."

"I've always said that your curiosity would be the death of you."

Maurin reached over and straightened his hair. She used to cut it for him, in those years when he'd been among the Lost, when the Grief was new and a simple nick hadn't been such a risk.

"You should let this go, let him go," she said gently.

"I can't," he said.

"Why not? You can't care about him. You barely know him."

Memories of waking alone, of that sinking feeling in his guts, came back.

But there was also the box, the moon, and the obvious importance Kinos had to the Hierarch. He'd brought the Knights Elite to make certain Kinos went back inside.

More than that, there was Kinos's importance to Phoebe. She'd sent Raef the shadowknife. Dead or not, she'd spoken to him. He had to believe it.

Raef couldn't tell Maurin any of that, so he said, "You didn't see him when I opened the box, or his face when he talks about his family. I have to get him out of there, Maurin. I have to get him home."

"He's nothing like you," she said.

She took his hands in hers. It was a motherly gesture, one she might use with one of the kids under her protection.

Raef would normally bristle at it. They were the same age after all, but in the moment he took the comfort.

"Nothing like us," she stressed.

"I know," Raef said, squeezing her hands. "I think that's why I like him. I can't give him back to the Hierarch and I can't let the prince keep him. He is dangerous. All of Versinae could burn if they fight over him. I have to take him away from here."

"So you're leaving?" Maurin asked. "With him?"

Raef inhaled and gave a little nod. "I have to, I think. They won't stop hunting him, not if he's so important that the Hierarch himself came here."

She let out a breath and nodded.

"You're right," she said.

"So?" he asked.

"So what?"

"One last job?"

"One last job," she said, dark eyes sparkling. "But how? Where will you get the money for the clothes?"

"Don't worry, I know just where to go."

))) 🌒 ● 🌘 (((

He'd never try this on any other day, but with the Hierarch in the city, most of the Watch would be in the temple plaza.

The houses here shone with fresh paint. The chandlers could afford windows of cut glass and servants to keep the panes free of soot and tallow grease.

Raef didn't spy any rats. The Grief was ridding the city of vermin. Blood was blood to the shades, so there were fewer rodents and birds as the months passed by and the ghost mist thickened.

He picked a newer building with an open window on the second story and circled it for a while, watching from the shadows. He saw no one. The Hierarch's visit had pulled everyone to the plaza to get a blessing or maybe buy his mercy.

Lady, he prayed. *If you can hear me, bless me just a little more.*

Raef shimmied up a drainpipe. The cast iron held his weight, and for once he was glad he hadn't eaten better the past few months.

A little more climbing, a careful swing from the pipe, and Raef crouched on a broad window ledge. Pausing to get his breath back, he peeked inside.

Endless rows of dipped candles were hung to dry. There were devices, cranked molds, enough to keep a score of apprentices busy, but they'd gone to the plaza too. Even commerce and new wealth could not deny the Hierarch.

Raef probably could have walked in the front door and gone unnoticed.

He dropped to land in a pile of dried rushes and stayed there several moments, listening.

No one came but he still eased his way out of the pile, making as little noise as possible as he moved past the cauldrons of wax, the bottled dyes, and the clay jars of scented oil.

The iron door at the end of the hall looked promising. Its casters squealed when Raef opened it. Wincing, he moved it only as much as he had to and slipped inside.

He'd caused no alarm, but it didn't mean he shouldn't hurry. The Hierarch's blessings wouldn't take forever. Still, he grinned to be getting away with a daylight burglary.

The office on the other side doubled as a supply room. Metal racks stocked with unrendered fat rose to the ceiling. The pale stuff resembled lumpy, bundled cotton. Raef debated closing the door behind him but did not want to risk another squeal or chance getting trapped inside.

The thick walls must shield the suet from heat and any ghosts that might be drawn to the purple veins running through it.

An iron strongbox rested on a beaten desk. Raef licked his lips and drew the shadowknife. It came easily now, perhaps from practice, perhaps from his accepting what he hadn't before.

It opened the padlock as easily as it did a door.

Raef bit his lip.

There were more than enough coins to afford what they needed.

Perhaps, just perhaps, Raef's luck was changing. They could pull this off, save Kinos, and buy passage on a ship.

He tucked the money into his shirt and made his way to the door. He'd walk out like he belonged. Then a bath and Maurin could dress him. She'd known what to buy and how to get it on short notice.

Smiling, Raef had barely stepped outside when a shout rang out. Turning, he saw a watchman running toward him. It was one of the men who'd chased him and Kinos into the Narrows.

"Damn it," Raef said.

He bolted for an alley. It should cut through to Iron Street. He'd lose the graycloak among the forges. He found a wall instead, its mortar still new and bricks unstained by soot. He'd run so fast that he almost slammed into it. The chandlers' wealth had them expanding their shops and homes.

The watchman stalked into the alley. Too many patrols on rainy nights had given him a fleshy, undercooked pallor. Too bad it didn't slow his gait.

"Give it up," he said. "Whatever you took."

"So you can take your cut?"

The watchman sneered. "So I can take all of it."

"I thought you were looking for someone else," Raef said.

"Already found him."

That was confirmation at least.

Raef backed up until his foot touched the wall. He risked an upward glance. They both knew he didn't have time to climb. The watchman slid his iron baton free of his belt.

Raef drew his knife. The watchman stopped his advance.

"It's a tenday in the cells for carrying a cutting weapon. You so much as nick me and it's the noose."

"I wasn't going to cut you." Raef lifted the edge to his right wrist. "Back off."

"You wouldn't." The watchman's eyes flicked to the edges of the alley, checking for Grief. It may not work. The day was overcast, but it wasn't that dark. "Whatever you got can't be worth dying for."

"I'm not bluffing," Raef said.

He pulled his sleeve up with the tip of the knife, exposing a strip of pale flesh. The watchman's eyes bulged. Raef didn't break eye contact.

If the man spotted the tremble rippling through Raef's limbs the bluff would be up. He'd be forced to try spilling blood, and if that failed, he'd have to fight. The other man wasn't a knight, but he was armed and had a lot of bulk on him.

They stood there, Raef's knife upheld, the watchman's expression unreadable.

"One of us is going to have to take a piss eventually," Raef said. "And it's only going to get darker. So what will it be?"

The watchman slid his baton back into the loop on his belt. "You'd better hope I don't catch you again."

If Raef had any luck, he and Kinos would be long gone before he had the chance.

He scoffed at the thought. Counting on luck had gotten him caught.

Raef left the alley carefully, making sure the watchman wasn't lying in wait.

It had been too close. He'd never done anything stupider. Yet, he hadn't had a choice. It was this or leave Kinos to the prince and the Hierarch.

Raef couldn't do that, which was good, because what they were about to attempt was even riskier.

17

SUN

"Why is he doing this?" Seth asked, polishing his breastplate.

"The prince or the Hierarch?" Lathan asked, rubbing his bracer with a cloth to buff it.

Seth blinked. He hadn't expected the other knight to answer. "The prince."

"He knows Hyperion despises deception," Lathan said. "Throwing a masked ball is just one more insult. And inviting us, even more so. The Hierarch can't refuse without seeming ungrateful, without looking like he's set himself too far apart from the people, and the nobles' gifts to the temple pay for many of its works."

Seth nodded. He did not want to speak and risk Lathan being angry with him again, but he did not think Lathan was completely right. The Bishop had encouraged Seth to think, to challenge his elders. He hoped this was what she'd meant.

If Hyperion despised deception, then why had they brought the box into the city by night? Why had they worn cloaks over their armor? Why were the Inquisitors trained to lie?

"Basically, it's a pissing match," Lathan continued. "The prince is flaunting his power. What he has of it. Now the Hierarch will do the same. Expect him to condemn the ball, the excess, the waste of food and light."

Seth turned the breastplate side to side, looking for spots. It hadn't been made for him. Like his sword and shield, the monks had dredged it up from the depths of the monastery's vaults. It would never be perfect, just like he'd never be perfect, but it was his and he cherished it.

He'd been surprised that the Bishop had chosen him to join them at the palace. The Hierarch had left the choice of escort to her, and she'd ordered them to bathe and make themselves gleam. Seth felt there had to be more to this outing. He did not know why she'd included him, but he forced himself to not question her motivations.

In Teshur the monks had conserved every drop of water. He'd scrubbed himself with sand and oil, scraping it off with a strigil before using what little rainfall he'd been allowed.

He'd marveled at the baths in Ilium, how the knights used them regularly, wasting what the monks would have considered an endless bounty. When Seth had first arrived there, he'd been told he'd have an audience with the Hierarch, to make himself presentable. He'd marveled at the soap and steam.

They'd met before, once, when he'd been a boy. He'd hoped to be better prepared the second time. He'd been too worried to feel embarrassed as he washed himself, naked and exposed among the other knights.

In the end Seth hadn't even approached the Hierarch's throne, only seen his Holiness at a distance, conferring with cardinals and bishops.

Intermediaries had given Seth his mission, taken him to the docks, and brought him to the box. They'd spent the entire time warning him of the mission's importance, speaking of the honor he'd been given, that he'd been chosen by the Hierarch himself, and most of all, to not fail.

Yet he hadn't been punished for losing the man in the box. Seth lived when Sophia and Zale did not.

Worse, ever since he'd approached Lathan, he wanted something, to feel something beyond fire, devotion, and pain.

He felt tempted to pack it away, to cram it down into his gut and feed it to the fire. That might have been what Father Geldar had meant by trying to do more, to be more, but Seth did not think so. He felt lost in a wholly new way that had nothing to do with his impurity or Hyperion, and he had no one to ask, no one to seek advice from.

Did everyone go through this, or did their parents guide them? Seth could not say, and for once, being an orphan felt like a true disadvantage.

He'd bathed quickly when the Bishop ordered him to, made certain to avoid noticing anyone around him. He especially did not look in Lathan's direction and kept his eyes forward.

Now they worked to make their armor shine, to oil any exposed leather.

The Hierarch wanted them to impress, to intimidate, and to embody Hyperion's light.

They'd wear their helms, which would hide most of their faces. In a manner, they'd be joining the masquerade, and Seth smiled at the thought.

It was nearly sunset. They would pray, assemble in the temple, and depart for the palace.

The Hierarch had spent the entire day among the people. Surely he had blessed them all, but a number of parishioners remained. Some prayed in the chapels, kneeling quietly. They turned when Seth and Lathan entered, hoping for a sign of his Holiness.

But the Hierarch wasn't there.

Seth shuffled closer to the Bishop.

She'd cared for her armor too, but the dents and scratches caught the light, as if the blows she'd taken in Hyperion's service were jewels she wore with pride.

"Straighten your posture," she told him.

Seth squared his shoulders.

"Please," a voice said from his left. "Please bless me."

Seth looked to the woman. She knelt before the Bishop, a straggler as the priests shooed others from the temple.

"I cannot bless you, sister," the Bishop said.

"Not you." The woman lifted a crooked finger toward Seth. "Him."

"Me?" Seth held up his hands. "I'm . . . I am no priest, sister."

"But his fire burns within you." The woman staggered to her feet, swayed there, fixing Seth with sharp, slightly glazed eyes. "Burn away my darkness, my lord. Please. You must."

"I am no lord, and I am not worthy of such a request," Seth said.

The Bishop looked from Seth to the derelict and took her gently by the arm, escorting her to the temple doors, praying with her in a calm, soothing tone. She looked back at Seth with a question. He shrugged. He did not understand the woman's intensity, and he squirmed that she would focus her faith upon him.

He was no god, no priest, and unworthy of forgiving anyone for anything. He felt like he'd trespassed just to hear it suggested.

"Father, forgive her," he prayed aloud. "Forgive me. I know such is not my place."

Seth did not look to see if Lathan had overheard. He did not want to see the other knight's reaction, did not want more shame.

The Bishop returned to him.

"I didn't . . . I don't understand," he said, trying not to stammer.

"It is all right, Seth," the Bishop said. "The woman must offer her darkness to Hyperion, as must you, and I. The night comes for us all."

But it didn't, not anymore. They would die, but go nowhere. Eventually their shades would join the Grief. Phoebe no longer rowed her boat to the Ebon Sea. The Moon's Door no longer opened to admit the dead.

He didn't feel like it could be all right. Pride. Hubris. These were not for him. He prayed for forgiveness, repeating it like a mantra as the light from the oculus faded away.

Seth prayed until the Hierarch entered the candlelit temple, his body shielded by armor, a suit of golden rings. Geldar would have looked absurd in armor, but the Hierarch wore it well.

Even the Bishop straightened at his approach. The man's presence commanded attention. Here was Hyperion's voice in the world. This was who the woman should have approached.

Seeing the Hierarch now, Seth remembered that the first of them had been generals. They'd led the faithful in battle against the demons when the gods had warred to make this world theirs.

While the knights had their helms, the Hierarch had chosen to wear a mask. It covered his brow and eyes. Rays fanned from it, crowning him in gold.

The costume represented Hyperion, girded for war and armed for battle. Seth needed no guile to read the message.

It had been a long while since the knights had truly gone to war. Even the crusade against Phoebe's priests had not been much of a conflict. The Hierarch had orchestrated careful attacks against the goddess, destroying all her towers and temples at the same time, on the same day.

Almost none had been spared.

"Knights," the Hierarch said. There were eight of them, including Seth, Lathan, and the Bishop. "We will show our strength, his strength, to this city and its prince. He will tempt you. We will retrieve what was stolen. Remember whom you serve."

With that, he led them from the temple.

He was Hyperion's voice in the world, and they were his escort.

They crossed the plaza and descended into the city, but not very far.

These weren't the alleys where Seth had lost his way. They weren't the sodden, trash-littered canals. The houses of the Palace Quarter were as ornate as temples. Polished braziers stood at their gates, chasing back the Grief. They looked like cakes, with marble flourishes and statues. Everything and everyone, even the servants and personal guards, was polished and clean.

It was another Versinae, a secret district of light and wealth laid atop the true city.

Sitting behind a tall fence of iron, the palace was the largest house of all. A heavy, florid structure of the same dark granite as the towers, its domes were verdigris. Its spires rose almost high enough to challenge the temple, but wisely stopped short.

Light was everywhere. Lanterns hung in rows from chains strung across the street, highlighting statues, pillars, stone scrollwork, and a fountain larger than any Seth had seen.

Phoebe's towers had been black and white spires. Hyperion's houses leaned toward gold and gilt, but this was ostentation for its own sake. Everything in the god's house spoke to who Hyperion was. This was man's ego inflated and nakedly displayed.

Seth liked none of it, even as the lively music drifted from the many open windows.

People lined up outside, departing from carriages, surrounded by waiting, anxious servants.

The nobility. The wealthy. Their clothes were layered and rich, the men in silk and velvet coats, the women in full gowns. Most wore large hats, and all wore masks of every shape, beaded or decorated with gems or pearls. The colors were a riot of blues and greens, wine reds, and the brightest of yellows. Seth thought them akin to birds, and they preened as such.

The crowd parted. Even here, bloodlines and money still bowed to Hyperion and his knights.

"So many windows," Seth gasped. "So much light."

The sheets of glass let the lamps inside shine like beacons into the dark.

"It is a waste," the Bishop said. "All of that oil could protect so many. Its value could feed so many."

"Still," Lathan said, his tone begrudging. "The shades will not intrude here tonight."

Both statements were true. Glancing back toward Hyperion's golden dome, Seth had to admit that the same could be said of it, that the statues and gilt could feed the hungry, could change or save many lives.

He pushed the thought down. He had to. He'd feed his doubts to the fire, pray harder during his next penance, but he could not deny that he was floundering. He'd always been told it was not his place to question. Now the Bishop had encouraged it, and it had opened a box of doubts Seth did not know how to address.

The more questions he asked, the wider and deeper the gulf between him and his peace of mind.

They marched inside, flanking the Hierarch in a narrow V. It reminded Seth of a sword's point. The crowd of nobles, for their part, whispered behind their fans or dipped their heads to hide their expressions with their extravagant hats.

Here was Versinae's corruption, the greed at its core, those who wore pearls while those who dove for them starved. The fire stirred in Seth's belly and he let out a breath to soothe it.

Marble and glass were everywhere, but the sweeping space was set for comfort, not piety or contemplation. Seth found it a relief. He did not know if he could have tamped the fire down if it had felt like the prince had set himself at the same height as the gods.

The floor was dark wood, not stone. Laid in a swirling pattern of waves and islands, it shone with a glossy polish that reflected the forms of the people mingling atop it.

There were dancers. Seth knew he gaped but could not stop himself.

They turned and pranced in coordinated steps that reminded Seth of his lessons with the Bishop and Lathan, but they had such grace, something he did not think he could ever possess.

Seth swallowed and forced his gaze away. This place, this world—it wasn't for him. Maybe if he were another person, had grown up in a house like this—then he could be more.

Seth averted his eyes lest he crave a life he could never have and spied a figure moving through the crowd.

He wore a long open coat over a velvet vest. Both were black and worked with silver braiding.

Like Lathan, he was slender, though not as tall as either Lathan or Seth. He had a round, brimmed hat with a flat top and a white mask that covered most of his face. Seth warmed with curiosity. He wanted to see more of what the mask concealed.

He turned to see what Lathan was doing, if the others had noticed his distraction, but they'd gathered away from him, talking among themselves, leaving him to drift into the party as if he wasn't one of them. Because he was not. He did not belong.

Cadre or no cadre, he'd always be alone.

Seth let out a breath. For the moment, he had no orders, no immediate directive, so he would do what Geldar had suggested. He would try to dream a little bigger. With a nod to screw up his courage, Seth set off in pursuit of the masked man.

18
MOON

Raef tried to bathe a few times a month. It was worth a few coppers to scrub away the grime of the streets. Getting clean enough
to pass as a rich merchant at the prince's party had taken a lot
more time, a lot more soap, and had cost him way more skin.

He risked shaving and cut his hair, applying pomade so it
fell in spikes where the hat did not cover it. He did not hate its
scent, ginger and black pepper. Maurin had come through with
a costume. The long coat and the second mask he'd concealed
in his hat should be enough to disguise Kinos.

Raef still had some of the gold he'd taken from the chandlers. It should be enough to buy them passage away from
Versinae. He wanted to be excited, to imagine sailing off and
seeing new lands, like Kinos's home—but first he had to find
Kinos. He had to get him out.

Maurin sat beside him in wide, ruffled skirts. Ready for a
pirate queen's take, she'd sewn pockets throughout to conceal
any number of candlesticks, silverware, or purses.

Like him, she wore a black velvet hat, but hers was

wide-brimmed with a single, giant feather like a plume of white sea spray. Her mask was white like his, though she'd opted for something edged in pearls. Raef's was plain plaster and crafted to look aged, the glaze crazed with fine cracks. It left a little of his face exposed.

He'd never owned boots or clothes this fine. In the tower he'd worn a wool robe and sandals. Since then, he'd mostly worn stolen clothes, favoring black, but none had ever been wholly new or unstained.

They'd hired a carriage, a first for him, to carry them the short distance.

"I'm enjoying the ride," Raef said, leaning close as they bounced along. "But this seems unnecessary."

"We have to look the part," Maurin said. "Keep the pitch of your voice higher, and remember to walk like you've got a cane up your ass."

"Language," Raef teased. "I thought you were playing the part of a proper noblewoman."

"I am," she said. "And proper noblewomen don't want muck on their kidskin boots before they hock them. Hence the carriage."

Raef turned to the window as they arrived. A gleam of brass caught his eye.

"No . . ."

"What?" Maurin said, though she did not crane her neck.

"Knights," he said, nodding to the group marching toward the palace. "And the Hierarch is with them."

Maurin frowned. "It's not too late to turn back."

"I can't," Raef said. "Kinos is in there. Are you going to run?"

He watched Maurin calculate the odds. Raef was staying. He had to find Kinos, and he really didn't want to do this without her, but he would understand.

"The score is worth it," she decided. "I left Simon in charge, just in case. But if we pull this off, I can keep the kids safe through the winter. Maybe even keep them off the streets through the worst of it."

The carriage came to a halt. Maurin bounced out and shot Raef an impatient look.

He made sure the ribbons that tied his mask on were tight and followed her.

"My lord," she said, offering her hand.

"My lady," he said, dredging up a smile though it felt tight.

When had running jobs with Maurin stopped being fun? Raef had changed. Maybe he'd grown. He could not decide if it was a good thing or not, but tension thrummed along his limbs as they waited their turn in the line of bustling nobility. Maurin slid close to him, her hand on his arm.

The stiff-backed porter looked them over. Did they need an invitation?

Focused on the party, Raef swaggered forward, certain to walk as though he belonged. If challenged, he'd either have to risk making a scene or trying to find another way in.

The man stepped aside with a nod. Raef choked back an exhale but he shouldn't be surprised. Money bought access. These people had never faced a hungry day, never had to risk the Grief creeping into their homes. They deserved for Maurin to loot them into Boat Town.

Opulence swallowed them as they stepped inside. Raef felt filthy despite his bath. All was finery and marble. Even the ceilings and pillars were polished to a perfect gleam. No, he could never belong here.

He did not glance back at the porter as he leaned toward Maurin.

"I can't believe that worked," he whispered.

"Why not? This is so ballsy they'd never expect anyone to try it."

She tugged him to the edge of the dance floor. The crowd thickened around them and he relaxed a little.

Maurin really did look amazing. Feathers, so black they were tinged in blue, lined her skirts. Her bodice sparkled.

"Are those gems real?" Raef asked.

"Glass and paste," she said. "But I'll try to pass them off as real when I sell them."

"Always a plan," he said as a new song started.

"Always," she agreed with a sharp smile.

The music was lilting, with strings and a pace set for the graceful, slow dancing that occupied the main room.

Raef tensed.

"I don't know—"

"Just let me lead," she said, guiding him with a hand on his back. "You count the knights and guards."

They went round in circles. He knew he was nowhere as graceful as the nobility, but Maurin had tucked them among the crowd.

"How many?" she asked.

"Six."

"I count eight. That's not bad, but you need to hurry. I'll create a distraction if I think you're in trouble."

She laughed delicately, as if he'd told a little joke. Her eyes sparked with genuine mirth. Danger aside, she was having fun.

This was it. They'd be parted. He may never see her again, and realizing it, his heart sank.

"Maurin. I . . ." He closed the distance between them, dancing face-to-face with her and asked, "You'll be all right?"

"Without you?" She scoffed. Her smiled deepened, part of the ruse, but with a little of her usual edge. "Of course. I'll be better. With a little luck I'll be rich."

"I don't know what to say," Raef said. "All you've done. Coming here, taking me in . . ."

She smiled, pausing her steps as the beat required. Raef's heart sank a little further. This was it.

"Just say thank you, Raef."

The dance ended and she walked him back toward the edge of the crowd.

"Thank you, Maurin. For everything."

"I spied guards on the main doors, but not the servant passages," she said. "Go get him and get out of here."

He nodded and they parted.

Raef was alone.

He hadn't thought he'd feel so crestfallen, but he could not escape the sense of everything changing. Again. Hopefully, it would not hurt so much this time.

He took a step back, let the dancing crowd spin Maurin away from him. Turning, he collided with a broad, brazen chest.

Raef looked up to see Seth, the eager knight from the crypt. Raef's stomach tightened. He rocked back on his heel, ready to run. The main door probably wouldn't work, but he could find another exit. He tensed, ready for Seth to strike him or call the other knights.

"Hi," Seth said with a smile.

Raef blinked and remembered to breathe.

"Hi," he echoed.

"I, uh—like your mask," Seth said nervously.

It disarmed Raef a little, despite his mounting panic. How could it not?

Seth wasn't trying to burn him. He was trying to what, flirt?

"Thank you," Raef said. "I like your, uh, helmet."

Seth wasn't threatening him. He didn't seem capable of it, but Raef still tensed. A Knight of Hyperion, no matter how earnest or good-looking, wielded the same fire that had brought the tower down.

Raef had to find Kinos. He had to escape this awkward, confusing conversation.

"I'm Seth."

His eyes were golden, like summer wine. They matched his fair hair.

"I didn't realize Knights of Hyperion went to parties," Raef said. "Or is that a costume?"

"It's real." Seth's smile dropped a bit, though his eyes remained fixed on Raef's. "We were invited."

Raef returned Seth's smile. How could he not? The knight was cheerful, and a little intense in the way he stared into Raef's eyes.

He'd smiled at a Knight of Hyperion. He must be losing his mind.

"Do you want to dance?" Seth asked.

"I don't really know how."

Seth ducked his head.

"Me neither," he admitted shyly.

Behind him, the crowd parted for the Hierarch. His mask glinted in the candlelight.

Raef's breath caught as the shadowknife pulsed. It wanted out. It wanted something, vengeance, or maybe just to warn him. The cold it sent through Raef's arm broke the spell of Seth's awkward charm.

"I have to go."

"Did I? I mean . . ." Seth trailed off, his expression confused and sad.

"It truly was nice to meet you, and I'd like to stay, but I really must find my friend."

"You too." Seth failed to hide his disappointment as he clasped Raef's extended hand.

In another place or time, had they not been knight and heretic, if not for Kinos, he would have dragged Seth back to the floor and they could have fumbled their way through a dance.

A lifetime ago, the Knights of Hyperion had been his cousins, worshippers of his goddess's brother. No one would have batted an eye to see them friends or even more.

But now Phoebe was gone and there was Kinos. At least Raef hoped there was Kinos. He'd disappeared after a kiss and Raef didn't know why.

Raef had to focus, to remember that the mystery was the thing, the box with the moons, Kinos's importance to Hyperion and his connection to the carving on Eastlight, his little island.

Raef was used to seeing nobles on the streets. There, they'd had guards, but here they assumed they were among their own. They crowded together, chatting and gossiping, leaving most of the palace for him to explore.

He searched the quieter halls, avoiding the guarded doors until he'd found a way around, the servants' routes. He hurried while trying to look like he wasn't in a hurry, hoping that if caught, he could claim he'd been admiring the elaborate landscapes and dour portraits worked into the scrolling woodwork of the ceiling.

Raef found more than one locked door and opened them with the shadowknife. Most sported comfortable beds and private hearths, but no sign of Kinos. He pocketed nothing, though he left the doors unlocked in case Maurin made it this far.

The library gave him pause. It was a decent collection, or what passed for one in these moonless times. He ached to consider all that had been lost. The towers had traded books, shipping them from one to another for copying and distribution, but now all were burned.

How could he have smiled at Seth, found him charming for even a moment? The knights brought only fire and death.

Room by room, he searched. Sometimes he encountered revelers too engaged in each other to notice him and servants who pointedly ignored his presence, but he found no sign of Kinos.

Raef reached for a knob when a voice behind him asked, "Did you expect him to just be locked in a bed chamber?"

Raef narrowed his eyes. He didn't like that someone had snuck up on him. From the question, the man knew what Raef was searching for.

He was dressed like most of the revelers, with a broad hat and a black mask that covered half his face.

"I'm Cormac." The man offered a hand. "Captain of the *Ino*."

Raef couldn't easily draw his metal blade, but the shadow-knife would serve if it came to a fight.

"I don't know you." He did not take the man's hand. "What do you want?"

"To help," Cormac said. "The prince isn't that stupid. You won't find him up here. But I can tell you where he is."

"Why?" Raef demanded.

"I can't just be a good person?" A smile tugged at the corner of Cormac's mouth.

"This is Versinae," Raef said. "No one does anything out of the kindness of their heart."

"True, but we don't have time for this."

"Why not?"

"Because the prince is stupid enough to flaunt what he's stolen. As soon as he does, the Hierarch and the knights will tear this place apart."

Cormac put a hand to his collar. Raef reached for his knife and paused when Cormac withdrew a leather cord. A little silver crescent dangled on it. A moon.

"That's an Initiate's cord," Raef said, gaping. "Where did you get that?"

"Where do you think?" Cormac asked.

Raef almost reached to touch it. A bit of the tower, a bit of the past, a bit of her. He'd almost been old enough to join the Spring Rites. He would have been initiated the next year.

"Why aren't you dead?" Raef asked.

"I wasn't a priest," Cormac said with a shrug. "And I was at sea when the towers fell."

"I thought everyone forgot." Raef hated the sorrow and vulnerability in his voice. "I thought everyone forgot her."

"I suspect there are more of us than you think, but no one is going to talk about it, especially not with the knights in the city."

"How did you—" Raef stammered. He had to focus. "Why are you here?"

"I still have the dreams sometimes," Cormac said. "They told me to come here, to find you and help you."

Phoebe was the goddess of knowledge, both learned and secret, conscious and not. She'd whispered to her Initiates, sent them prophetic dreams. Perhaps she whispered still. Raef had heard her voice in the crypt, when he'd been close to unconsciousness. That had felt something like a dream. Perhaps sleep was the key.

For now, he had to decide whether or not to trust this man. Raef examined Cormac quickly. Slim, he had a rich voice and black hair tied back in a neat rope behind his head. He had enough lines on his face that Raef would have placed him near forty. Nothing in his eyes said he was lying, but it could be a trap. Raef put his trust in the cord.

"Do you know where Kinos is?" he asked.

"This way," Cormac said.

Raef kept his hands free, ready to draw his knife from where he'd hidden it in his coat.

"The prince was a pirate once," Cormac said, leading Raef deeper into the palace.

"I knew that. He bought his title from the Hierarch."

"Strange isn't it?" Cormac asked. "That the Hierarch should decide who rules and who doesn't?"

They took the backstairs, slipped passed a pair of kissing servant girls, going lower and lower.

"There are tunnels leading out to the bay," Cormac said. "Kinos is there, hidden behind the entrance where the knights won't find him."

"How do you know all this?" Raef asked.

Cormac turned and tipped his hat to Raef.

"Pirates tend to run together," he said.

"You said your ship is the *Ino*?" Raef asked. He didn't know it.

"She's at the docks. If you can reach her, I can get you out of the city."

They stopped at a wall.

"Here's the entrance," Cormac said. "Get him, get out. Don't go any lower. The shades are thick down there."

Reaching past Raef, Cormac pressed a point on the stone. A section of the wall swung open.

Raef had to admit that he was impressed.

"Are there guards?" he asked.

"Not at the moment. I'll try to buy you time."

"Thank you," Raef said.

"Don't you need a light?" Cormac asked, looking to a lantern that hung nearby.

"No," Raef said.

The wall clicked in place behind him.

No dust or cobwebs marked the floor or walls.

Raef doubted the prince did his own sweeping, so some of the palace servants must know about the tunnels. That meant more chances for someone to tell the Hierarch where Kinos was, for the secret to slip when the knights started throwing their weight around.

He passed supplies, crates of food and barrels of oil. Of course the prince would keep a private stash.

The walls here were rougher stone, far from the painted plaster and tapestries of the halls outside. The floor was cold granite. This was the real palace, the face beneath its mask. This felt more like the rest of Versinae—his Versinae, grayer, dingier—more honest.

He turned a corner, and there was Kinos, sitting in a barred cell. He had a narrow but comfortable-looking bed and a lantern for light. Raef's guts tensed even as his heart sped up.

"This doesn't look so bad," Raef said. "I mean, except for the bars."

Kinos leaped to his feet. He leaned close, taking Raef in.

"What are you wearing?"

Raef took off his mask, mostly to give himself a chance to break eye contact.

"A disguise." He nodded to the passage. "There's a party out there. Are you hurt?"

"No," Kinos said. "They grabbed me but they didn't hurt me."

"Why?" Raef asked. "Why'd you go?"

There wasn't time to ask, but the question refused to stay bottled.

"I had to see if it was really him, the Hierarch." Kinos wrapped his hands around the bars. "Then the Watch grabbed me. I'm sorry."

Raef wasn't certain he believed it, but he tried the cage door and found it locked.

"We have to hurry," he said. "The knights are here."

"What?" Kinos asked, straightening. "Where are we?"

"The prince's palace. He's playing games with the Hierarch." Raef gestured to his clothes. "And throwing a masquerade."

"That's really stupid," Kinos said.

"No kidding. He's going to get burned alive if he's not careful."

Raef could use the shadowknife, but Kinos would see it.

"Close your eyes."

"Why?"

"Just trust me, please?"

And there it was. Had Kinos run away because of where Raef had come from, because he'd shown him the Garden? Raef wasn't ready to show Kinos more, not if he'd just disappear again.

Kinos closed his eyes and turned to face the wall.

Raef brought out the shadowknife and unlocked the bolt.

"All done," he said, swinging the door open.

"How do you keep doing that?"

"Practice," Raef said. He slipped out of his coat, transferring his metal knife to his vest pocket.

He took off his hat and pulled a second, black silk mask from inside it.

"I don't understand," Kinos said.

The night before, he'd been ready to share everything, but for now he'd keep the rest of his secrets.

"I'll tell you later," Raef said. "But right now, we're going to walk out the front door, past the Hierarch."

He tugged the mask over Kinos's eyes. When Raef reached to place the hat atop his head, Kinos leaned forward and kissed him quickly. Its warmth curled through Raef despite the tendrils of suspicion roiling in his guts.

"You came for me," Kinos said, shrugging into the coat.

"Always," Raef said, mostly meaning it.

The kiss didn't stop the swirl of questions, but it stilled them enough for them to do what they had to do.

They followed the tunnel until it met a wall.

"I think this is an exit," Raef whispered. He laid his ear to the stone wall and heard loud voices.

"I know you're hiding him," a voice on the other side said. "These old walls. What do they conceal?"

Kinos blanched.

"That's the Hierarch," he whispered, stepping backward.

Raef wanted to call after Kinos as he retreated down the tunnel.

"Wait!"

"We can't go out there," Kinos said, green eyes wide behind the mask. "He'll find me. He'll put me back, Raef."

"We don't have a lot of options."

Kinos lifted the lamp in the other direction.

"Where do these lead?"

Raef shuddered. He could practically feel the dead retreat from the light.

"Down. Out to the bay, I think. They're smuggling tunnels from the prince's pirate days, but I don't know what's down there, or how many shades we'll find."

Something hard hammered on the wall behind them. The knights. They'd be through soon.

Raef did not think Cormac or Maurin would be coming this time.

"Come on."

He took Kinos by the hand and led him into the dark.

19
MOON

The dead were silent, but whispers rustled along the deeper paths. Most of those ways were boarded up or blocked by piles of rubble.

Down and down they went. Raef didn't know if they'd moved out of the city proper, but rumblings came, the same noises that sometimes reached the Crack. The air cooled, grew damp. He could taste salt. Everything smelled old, of dust, dirt, and a little rot.

"What is all this?" Kinos asked, holding up the lantern.

"Versinae is ancient," Raef said, trying not to notice how the light flickered. "She was here before the gods."

"It can't be easy to smuggle this way," Kinos said. "Can't be worth it."

"Depends on the cargo," Raef said.

The prince and his crew would have had to haul their loot uphill over a long distance to reach the palace. In the days before the shades, when there'd been a moon, it wouldn't have been so risky.

Kinos hefted the lantern toward another boarded-up passage. "What do you think is down there?" he asked.

"I don't want to find out. Our gods didn't make this world. They found it, but it was ruled by demons when they got here. They freed it, defeated the demons."

"Hyperion lost his son," Kinos said.

"Yeah, Helios," Raef said. "But if most of the gods survived . . ."

"Then some demons might have too," Kinos said.

Their eyes met over the lamp's flame.

"We should hurry," Raef said.

A backward glance revealed that the shades had crowded behind them. They hovered, lost and unfocused.

"We have to be careful," Raef said.

These shades were the worst of the Grief, too far gone to have a form. They were smoke and hungry eyes.

Just a scratch, a drop, and they would tear Raef and Kinos apart. No light would hold them back when they were this far gone.

The taste of salt intensified as they walked on, trying to hurry but not rush and risk a slip or scrape.

They'd gone lower than Raef could have imagined when the lantern died.

The shades whispered over his skin, cold and slick like winter fog. He almost regretted giving Kinos the coat.

"What do we do?" Kinos asked, voice shaking.

Raef took his hand. "Just stay with me. We can make it."

Kinos started to tremble. Raef felt it through his palm.

"Raef . . ." Kinos gasped. "I can feel them."

"Just walk carefully," Raef said, as though the press of the Grief didn't pull his heart into his throat. At least he could see. "They won't hurt us if we're careful."

The dead stared in no direction, their hollow eyes unfocused. They swam through the air like sniffing sharks, seeking any hint of a meal.

"You're shaking," Kinos said, squeezing Raef's hand.

"You're one to talk," Raef said, trying to sound confident, but his voice had grown hoarse. "Just keep walking."

He carried them forward on cautious steps, spying hints of ancient stonework through the swirling Grief. They passed columns, archways carved with geometric patterns, nothing like the temples and shrines he knew.

The air tasted of dust and sodden wood until the path began to rise. Then something rotten, like old meat, rode the breeze.

"What is that?" Kinos asked, covering his nose and mouth with his arm.

"The whaling beach. We're almost out."

The Grief parted and a bit of starlight shone ahead. They exited into the night, and Raef could hear the sea.

Normally, he'd have exhaled, gulped down fresh air, but the reek of the black sands remained potent after all these years.

A bramble thicket hid the tunnel entrance. The touch of the shades had receded, but Raef and Kinos picked their way clear, careful to avoid the thorns.

Kinos squinted, trying to discern their location. They'd come up outside the walls, putting the city and the docks ahead of them.

Between them and Versinae lay piles of discarded bone, the great cauldrons they'd used to render the blubber, and the whaling boats, moored forever in the sticky sand. Streamers of thin, flapping skin wrapped around the bones and skeletal ships.

Kinos made out the shape of a great rib cage and paled.

"They used to haul them in to make oil," Raef explained. "It was terrible. So much blood, so much life, just gone. They were getting harder to find even before the shallowing. Maybe it saved the rest of them from us."

"It's terrible," Kinos said.

"It is."

Kinos's hand slipped out of Raef's. He stared east, no doubt questioning if his family was still out there, still alive. Raef would get him home. He would, but couldn't hold the question back any longer.

"Why did you leave?" he asked. "It wasn't safe outside the Garden, and . . ."

He drifted off. The doubt was like a hunger pain. It had to be fed.

"I told you," Kinos said. "I'm sorry. I didn't think. I heard the bells and I just had to know if it was really him. I thought maybe I could find out why he'd put me in that box."

"What aren't you telling me?" Raef asked.

"Nothing." Kinos took a step away from Raef. "If you don't trust me, why did you come for me?"

Raef inhaled, uncertain how to answer.

"I'm sorry. I am," Kinos said. "I shouldn't have left like that. I wasn't thinking and I wasn't trying to run away from you."

If Kinos was lying, he was very good at it. Raef wanted to believe him.

"What now?" Kinos asked.

"We get to the docks. There's a ship there. We can get away."

Kinos chewed his lip.

"We?"

The box and the mystery were still waiting.

"Yes," Raef said. "We. Us."

"All right."

Fire flashed behind them, glinting across the oil-blackened beach.

"No . . ." Kinos said.

"Run."

The knights had followed them. The dead were less of a problem when you could conjure the sun's fire to drive them back.

The docks were far ahead. Hopefully Cormac was where he'd said he'd be. Raef didn't worry about Maurin. She'd use the commotion to make her escape.

The beach sucked at their feet as they panted and stumbled forward. They were halfway across, the sea to one side, the hills to the other, when a cry like a birdcall came from the cauldrons. It started with one. The number increased until the sounds filled the air like a flock of loons.

"Not now," Raef said. He skidded to a halt.

"What are they?" Kinos asked, peering into the night, trying to see by the distant flashes of the knight's fire.

"The Sharks. A gang."

"Like Maurin's Lost?" Kinos asked.

"Not like the Lost." Raef lifted an arm to block Kinos from moving forward.

The Sharks rose from the muck or climbed out of the cauldrons. They dressed in cloaks of old whale skin and clothes pierced with bits of bone. Their flesh was a sallow, sickly color.

There must have been a dozen of them. Caught between the Sharks and the approaching knights, Raef turned back and forth, trying to find a way out.

"Toll. Toll," the Sharks chanted. "Blood or gold."

"How about fire?" Raef asked, jerking a thumb behind them.

He knew the Sharks only by reputation, but that was enough. Some of the kids who'd aged out of the Lost had gone to join them. Maurin had never heard from them again.

The Sharks widened their eyes and stopped their stupid chant.

"Thought so."

Grabbing Kinos by the hand, Raef ran toward the cauldrons, but the Sharks encircled them. More than a dozen now. Maybe a score.

"Toll," they said as one. "Blood or gold."

"You really want to do this, right now?" Raef asked, drawing his knife.

"You can't take all of us," one of the Sharks said.

"I don't intend to," Raef said. "Then again, I don't have to."

"Raef . . ." Kinos gasped, understanding what he was about to do.

He'd been bluffing in the alley, but the time for empty threats was over.

Raef had never intentionally hurt himself before. It was harder than he'd expected. His hand quivered.

"Screw this," he said.

The knife bit into his wrist.

"Are you crazy?" one of the Sharks asked. "You'll kill us all!"

The Grief rose like a curtain. The Sharks shrunk away from the rising dead.

"You said you wanted blood," Raef spat. "Come and get it."

He leaped forward and slapped the nearest Shark with his bloody palm.

The Shark screamed as the tide of shades broke over them. The other gang members fell back so quickly that Raef almost laughed.

"Run!" he screamed, hoping the knights' fire gave Kinos enough light to see by.

The ghosts swirled after them. The Sharks screamed, but they shouldn't be harmed, not if they weren't bleeding. Raef didn't look back to check.

"Into the water!" he shouted. "The shades can't follow us there."

The first cold fingers brushed his cheek, ran down his arm, racing for the cut in his flesh. He couldn't outrun them.

Something yanked the shade away.

Raef jerked to a stop.

The Grief poured on, but a number of shades had made a wall. They pressed together, protecting him, forcing back the others.

Raef blanched. He'd never seen ghosts do anything like this, but there they were, shielding them from death.

At the center of the shade wall stood a figure taller than the rest.

The ash man, the burned man. He waved for Raef to go as the Grief broke against him.

"Come on," Raef said, pulling Kinos with him.

They splashed into the water. Raef dove, kicked out, sinking to his neck.

He looked back once more.

He knew them then, the shades who'd saved him. He could make out their black robes between the flickers of mist and the knights' fire.

His family.

They'd been trapped here, on this side of the door when she'd died.

"Father," Raef gasped.

Go, the ghost of Father Polus mouthed. *Go, Raef.*

Raef kicked after Kinos, swimming out to sea.

They surfaced together, shivering, their hands on each other's arms.

"Who was that?" Kinos asked. "You knew him."

Raef shook his head, unable to find the words.

All this time—Father Polus had been right there, watching over him. Raef should have seen it. He should have known.

His heart ached with a deep pain he'd buried for so long.

"Are you all right?" Kinos asked, swimming close. "Raef?"

"Yeah," Raef said. "Yeah."

The Grief had overtaken Father Polus and the others, but it could not cross the water. It swirled angrily, a storm of mist and fury, seeking its escaped quarry.

"Is there somewhere we can swim?" Kinos asked.

"Toward the docks," Raef said, though he doubted they'd make it. It was too far away.

The beach exploded in fire, a sudden inferno like a storm of pure flame.

Kinos gasped. Raef shook uncontrollably as the oil-soaked sand lit. The light blinded him. Screams came and died as the Sharks burned.

Raef could feel the heat despite the distance. Ashes sizzled on the water. The fire raged, massive, wild, enough to burn the world.

"Raef!" Kinos called.

He sounded so far away. Raef couldn't turn from the flames, couldn't still the shaking that had filled his body.

He was burning. He'd been burning since that day. The fire had found him. He wouldn't get away again. He—

Kinos slapped him.

"Ow!" Raef said, though it pulled him back to the moment, to the dark water and the creeping cold.

"We have to get out of the water," Kinos said. "We'll freeze if we stay here all night."

"All right," Raef said.

His teeth were already chattering. They could swim toward the docks and try to make it. They couldn't go back to the beach. The flames had reached the city walls.

Raef wondered if Seth had been among the knights. He

had the odd wish that Seth would be all right, but of course the flames wouldn't harm him.

Raef scanned the dark and let out a sigh at the sight of something black and hulking sliding across the water.

"There," he said. "A ship."

"I don't see it," Kinos said.

"Follow me."

They splashed out into the bay. Kinos could swim, and his strokes kept pace with Raef's.

The black ship had her sails furled. No lamps were lit. Her oars were graceful, almost silent.

Behind them, the last of the screams had died.

PART TWO

DARK MOON, SHALLOW SEA

*There is no death more
hated than drowning.
The gods wish us buried
in Rhea's arms.*

—RHEITE TENET

20

SUN

They'd fought their way through the tunnels, driving back the shades with the light of their swords, pursuing their quarry at the Hierarch's command.

Then the gang had barred their way. One of them had sprung out of nowhere, stabbing toward Seth with a jagged bit of broken ship.

The fire lashed out before he could call it back. The man died in a column of golden light. It happened so quickly that he didn't have time to scream.

Unleashed, the fire spread like wine from a split cask. It sloshed and raced across the oiled sand. The dried-out ships exploded. The Grief burned away.

The flames caught the gang, incinerating them.

Blinded by the smoke, Seth and the knights retreated.

Dawn revealed the devastation. The whaling beach lay scorched, with much of its sand turned to glass. The iron cauldrons remained, soot-coated and lonesome, but everything else, the boats, the bodies of the gang that had barred their way, the bones and skin of the whales—all was ash. It rained like flecks of snow.

"Bastard," one of the knights said.

Seth squeezed his eyes shut.

He didn't look, didn't want to know who'd said it.

"We will return to the temple," the Bishop announced, turning to lead them toward the city gates. "We must report to the Hierarch and seek his guidance."

They followed her into a Versinae hushed and cowed by fear.

Seth slunk into the Bishop's shadow as the common people turned from them. Parents put arms around their children to protect them from a monster—from him.

The cadre reached the temple. Seth flushed at the relief the dome brought, the shadows that would hide his shame. He deserved no shelter. He'd brought fear to the people. He'd murdered the gang.

Geldar stood beside the altar, deep in contemplation, looking as still as the statues. Seth had to force himself to not rush forward and throw himself at the old priest's feet.

The Inquisitor met Seth's gaze and gave the smallest shake of his head. Seth froze as the Hierarch entered the temple. His morning robes were crimson. They flowed around him as he walked. Over them, he wore a coat of golden scales. A number of Knights Elite trailed after him.

Seth forced himself to straighten his spine. He would face the god's wrath as a knight should.

"Clear the temple," the Hierarch commanded.

The common folk trickled away, hurried along by the red-caped knights if they loitered.

The doors were shut, sealing out the dawn. Only the wide beam of the oculus and the altar's candles lit the dome's interior.

Standing in the light, the Hierarch lifted his arms, held

them high, and prayed, "Eos, Dawn, open your gates. Give to us your insight. Show us your brilliance."

Seth knew the goddess of the dawn, but he did not know this invocation.

He echoed the Hierarch's prayer.

The Bishop prayed quietly beside Seth, though he could not make out her words.

"Show us the will of your father," the Hierarch continued, his voice booming through the temple. "Send us your Oracle to speak your truths."

The Hierarch pressed his hands to the altar.

The light from the oculus pooled like burning honey, molten and sparking. It splashed upward. Seth flinched, ready for it to rain down and burn only him, but the light gathered instead, flowing into a liquid, winged form. She hovered over them, robed in amber light.

The Hierarch turned to the faithful with an expression of pride.

Seth held in a breath and regarded the golden figure as the Hierarch faced her. It was a wonder, a mystery, and despite his failing, he felt his heart lighten at the sight.

"Lady," the Hierarch said. "Daughter of Eos."

Her voice was not a voice. More of a warm whisper, like a spring breeze, like a song inside Seth's mind.

What would you know? What would you know that I may tell? Not all is meant for mortals and those who walk beneath his light.

Seth gaped. He'd never seen or heard anything so beautiful. It made him want to be better, to be the knight he should be. It made him want to confess all of his failings, to purge them, to become more.

"All has come to pass," the Hierarch said. "The box has been opened."

So it was said, she sang. *The demons long to return. All you've done, in his name, to prevent this, shall be rewarded.*

The Oracle dipped her golden head. She fixed a molten eye on Seth and the sight burned through him.

"The thief has fled the city," the Hierarch said.

Dark draws dark as light draws light, but only one may cast the other out. The lesser demons will serve the elder as the noble will serve the gods.

The Oracle bowed her head in thought.

He must be found, and the demon captured. It holds the key to the Moon's Door, to the return of Phoebe and the one she will bring with her, the one who would end Hyperion's light.

Seth did not completely understand, but he shuddered to hear her mention demons. The gods' ancient enemies must not return. That might explain what had happened to Zale, how someone, a demon, could have opened the box.

"We need guidance," the Hierarch said. "Where will we find the thief?"

The Oracle raised her face to the sun. The light fell prettily, glittering over her wings and her shifting robe of molten amber.

To dead, sad Thiva, send one cadre. There, in the eastern heights, they will find the one you seek. Her wings stretched as she looked them over. She faced the assembled faithful, her golden, pupilless eyes lingering on the Bishop, on Seth, and Lathan.

Your quarry lies on the Isle of the Dead.

The light dissolved, and she was gone. Seth cooled as if a storm cloud had obscured the sun.

"Bishop," the Hierarch said, turning to her. "Your request is granted. Ready your cadre to sail for Thiva."

"Yes, Your Holiness," she responded with the slightest of bows.

"Geldar," the Hierarch said. "Bring your charge to my quarters."

Geldar's head dipped low.

The Hierarch left, the awed priests bowing as he passed.

Seth waited for Geldar to gesture to him.

"This way," the Inquisitor said.

Seth followed him into the temple complex, holding his questions until they were far from the dome and the other knights.

"Why, Father?" Seth asked. "What does he want with me?"

It had to be his overdue punishment, come at last.

"Not here," Geldar chided. "Not now."

His eyes darted to the walls. They seemed too thick for spying, but Geldar would know best.

They made their way into the finer apartments, to the quarters reserved for his Holiness alone.

Attendants were removing his golden coat. The weighty scales clinked like coins as they carefully set it aside. The change did not diminish the man's power or Seth's rising dread. He took a knee and fixed his eyes on the floor.

The Hierarch waved away the attendants with a muttered blessing and washed his hands in a basin, sending the scent of laurel and rosemary through the room.

"You can lower your hood, Geldar. Are we not both in his service?"

A rustle told Seth that his mentor had obeyed. Seth would not tremble. He was not the boy he had been the first time he'd met the Hierarch, when he'd announced that Seth could live, but that he would train in Teshur, in the desert, far from Geldar and Ilium.

"You came early to the city," the Hierarch said.

"I thought it best to show haste," Geldar said, his tone even.

Seth held his breath.

"And did you find anything interesting in your time here?"

"Only an empty box guarded by a corrupt knight, and another, too vocal in her pride."

"Now both are dead," the Hierarch said. "I assigned the boy a simple duty. One to bring him honor. Bring a box to Versinae's crypt and guard it."

Geldar's expression remained stony. "If I may ask, Your Holiness, did the Oracle request this duty for him?"

"You may ask, but I need not answer to the likes of you."

Seth froze. He had been here before. Perhaps if he did not move, if he made himself a statue—as small as possible—the Hierarch would spare his life.

"I will send the boy with the Bishop. She has asked for him to join her cadre."

Seth blinked, his fear forgotten. He could not have heard it correctly.

If it was true, would she regret it now? Would even the Bishop decide he could not be redeemed after the fire on the beach?

"This business began with him and the box," the Hierarch said. "It is fitting that he see its end."

"Yes, Your Holiness."

Seth kept his eyes fixed on the heavy purple rug carpeting the floor of golden wood.

He had another chance. By Hyperion's mercy, he had another chance.

The Hierarch turned to him.

"Tell me, Seth, do you continue your penance, that which the monks of Teshur set you to?"

"Yes, Your Holiness."

"Double it." His voice was like a lash on Seth's ears. "Your lack of control has forced another visit from Versinae's prince, and there is little I hate more than that odious man."

Seth nodded. "Gladly, Your Holiness. Thank you."

"You may go." The Hierarch waved them away. "Both of you."

Outside, Geldar left his hood down. He walked ahead, turning back once to gesture for Seth to follow. They came to the courtyard where the knights drilled. Above, the sun's disk hung high. Seth took comfort in it even as he cringed to remember the fire consuming the beach and the lives he'd taken. Geldar settled himself atop the steps to the colonnade and gestured for Seth to do the same.

"You are punishing yourself. I do not mean just the penance."

"The Hierarch gave me a great responsibility. I failed. I failed again outside the walls—I lost control of the flames."

"I know, my boy, but the Hierarch is another matter. Have you forgotten what I told you, that he was once an Inquisitor?"

Seth squinted, trying to discern what Father Geldar was trying to tell him. It was something that he could not state too directly. He'd questioned the Hierarch regarding the Oracle and Seth's role in the mission.

"Father, why did the Hierarch choose me for this?"

Geldar gave him a sad smile, telling Seth that he would not like the answer.

"I suspect he chose the three of you to be rid of you, to let this mission remove you from the order."

"He wouldn't do that, would he?" Seth asked.

Hyperion was supposed to be merciful. Where was the mercy or forgiveness in such an act?

If it were true, then the Hierarch would sacrifice the Bishop, Lathan, and the others just to be rid of Seth, just to see him dead.

Send one cadre, the Oracle had commanded.

She hadn't specified which cadre. The Hierarch had made that choice.

Seth had believed he'd had a chance, that he could grow beyond his failings. He saw now that he'd never had a chance at all.

"You are kind, my son," Geldar said. "And good. But the world often does not honor that. This is why we have Inquisitors, to do what good people cannot."

"You are good, Father."

Geldar smiled weakly.

"No, no I am not."

"I wish . . ." Seth stammered. "I wish you had not told me."

"I know, my boy, but you had to know."

"Why?"

"Because I won't be there to protect you."

21
MOON

Raef laid a hand to the mast and felt for the *Ino*'s pitch and yaw, her rhythm and response to the waves and wind.

"See anything?" he asked, peering out from the crow's nest with a grin.

"No." Kinos grumbled. "Same as the last twenty times you asked."

Raef had thought he'd miss Versinae, but he liked the sun. He liked the sea. From up here, in the crow's nest, he could see everything, and this view had none of Boat Town's squalor. The prince was generous with provisions, and Raef especially liked having something to eat every day.

Leaving the city had mostly unknotted the ball of worries in his gut. The knights and the Grief were behind them, but Kinos didn't seem happy.

"At least we're headed in the right direction," Raef reminded him.

"You've said that twenty times too," Kinos said.

He only grew more tense as they approached their

destination, like proximity to his island made it less possible, less real.

They'd passed islets and rocks, some home to birds, some dotted with ruins that might have meant something in another age.

"That's what matters, isn't it?" Raef asked, bristling. He wasn't used to being the one finding the positive side of things. "That we're sailing east?"

"And I can cook all the way," Kinos groused.

He did have a point.

Cormac had fished them from the bay and taken Raef's stash for payment, handing it off to the hulking quartermaster. It wasn't enough to pay for their passage, so they earned their keep by working off the difference.

"That doesn't sound too bad," Kinos had said.

"It wouldn't be if we were just hauling cargo," Cormac had answered. "But we're at war."

Raef and Kinos had exchanged glances while Cormac explained that the prince had given him a writ of privateering against Tethis. Versinae's southern rival had long contested their trading routes to Delia, the eastern continent, and the *Ino* was allowed to attack any ship flying Tethean colors.

The crew were in it for the money, their cut of the spoils. They were a rough, superstitious lot, and Raef was glad that he and Kinos had a little room in the hold where they could lock the door. That they had the space to themselves, privacy and proximity, was a boon.

Stripped and dried, they'd laid down that first night with a finger's distance between them. Despite the terror of the fire and his exhaustion, Raef had been restless, almost fevered, wanting to close the space.

Then Kinos had.

Somewhere in the middle of it all, he said Raef's name, and it unlocked him.

"What's that?" Kinos asked, leaning over the rail and snapping Raef back to the moment and out of the warm reverie.

Raef squinted.

Something bobbed on the horizon.

Sails came into view.

"A ship," Raef said.

The hull rose, wider than the *Ino*, built more for transport and cargo. "Definitely a merchant."

"You don't have to tell them," Kinos said.

Raef could see the merchant's flags. She wore the trident of Tethis, bronze on a bottle green field.

"This isn't our fight."

Kinos wasn't wrong, not exactly. Raef was from Versinae, not that he'd ever consider the prince his ruler or himself one of the man's subjects. Raef couldn't imagine killing people over trade routes and spoils.

They owed Cormac, but more than that, Raef did not trust the crew not to turn on them if they held back.

"It's too risky," he said. He wouldn't let anyone hurt Kinos.

He rang the bell. The crew scrambled into motion, climbing into the rigging to sight the ship.

Raef put his hands to the new knife on his belt, a gift from Cormac. Most of the crew wore blades. They really had left Versinae where only the knights were allowed to openly carry cutting weapons.

Raef and Kinos's clothes had been spoiled by their escape from the palace. Cormac had found them cast-offs from his quarters. Kinos's were a little loose, but Raef's fit him near perfectly. He wore a leather cuff, another gift from the captain, one wide enough to hide the shadowknife's growing mark on his wrist.

The *Ino* was long and narrow, bigger than many of the warships Raef had seen at the docks. Her four masts gave her black hull the speed to cut the waves like a knife.

"Sails!" Cormac called from the wheelhouse.

As dark as her hull, they went taut with the wind.

The *Ino* rushed forward, the ram at her prow aimed toward the merchant. Wood creaked. The waves splashed, and Raef's heart raced to match her stride.

Spotting the danger, the merchant turned, filling her sails, but they'd caught her unaware. She'd be no match for them.

Raef leaned out from the nest to watch the crew ready themselves.

"You're enjoying this," Kinos said.

"It is exciting," Raef admitted, feeling the wind rush through his hair.

"People are going to die, Raef."

"Maybe not," Raef said, though his guts tightened.

They did not ease as the chase went on.

No one laid claim to this piece of sea, especially since the Grief had silenced powerful islands like Thiva.

Raef's dread slackened and tightened as the merchant gained and lost distance. The merchants tossed items overboard, barrels and furniture, anything that might weigh them down.

"They'd drop their cargo if they were clever," Raef said. "The crew would stop for that."

Kinos didn't say anything. The wind whipped his hair about his face.

"It's not like we can stop it," Raef said.

"We didn't have to help make it happen," Kinos snapped.

Raef didn't answer that.

He didn't say it, but part of him wanted a fight. He itched for action, any kind of action. The sea and sun were beautiful, the constant taste of salt fresher than the city's air, but the days were long. They gave him too much time to remember the beach, the screams of the burning Sharks, and the sight of the priests, those he'd lost, who'd been there the entire time. If he'd known, he might have fed them blood, might have given them all of his own to keep them from joining the Grief. That was probably why they'd never revealed themselves to him. They'd known he'd sacrifice himself. There had been moments, far too many nights, when he might have done it just to see their faces one more time.

Raef welcomed the chance to act, to do something other than chores and wait for his nights with Kinos. He turned back and forth, scanning the horizon for other ships as the *Ino* closed with her prey.

Cormac shouted orders from the wheel, bringing them alongside the merchant. They'd have her soon.

"Come on," Raef said. Worried about the impact between the ships shaking them from the nest, he tugged Kinos's sleeve. "We don't want to be up here when they collide."

"Will we be safer down there?" Kinos asked.

"They're merchants. I don't think they'll try to board us."

Kinos squinted at the other crew as he reached for the rope ladder leading to the deck.

"They're blue."

"Yeah, they're Tetheans."

Spreading his feet when they reached the deck, Raef braced for the collision. Closer. Closer.

The ships slammed together, rattling Raef's teeth. Kinos kept his footing, but Raef stumbled to the deck. He straightened as the *Ino*'s crew leaped the rail, crossing to the merchant.

The battle spilled back onto the *Ino* and Raef drew his knives.

"Then again, they are Tetheans," he said.

"We should have stayed in the nest," Kinos said.

"Climb up," Raef said. "I'll cover you."

"Hardly," Kinos said. He drew a pole from the rigging and gripped it with both hands.

A Tethean charged them, sword held over his head, his eyes mad with panic. Raef gripped his knives. He'd never killed anyone. He still didn't want to, but he'd defend himself. He'd defend Kinos.

Raef's stomach roiled and he tried to pretend it was the rocking of the ship and not his rising gorge. He tensed as the man came on.

Kinos jabbed out, popping the Tethean between the eyes with the butt of his improvised staff. The sailor staggered back and Kinos swung, sweeping the man's legs out from under him. His sword clattered to the deck. Raef leaped forward to kick it away.

The man scrambled backward as Cormac stalked toward them.

"Not bad," the captain said.

A pair of merchants charged them.

Cormac whirled to engage one. Raef did not have time to watch for Kinos as a large man came at him.

The sailor swung out, his sword as long as Raef's arm.

Raef ducked inside his reach, jabbed his knife into the man's side. The Tethean screamed and shifted his swing. His blade bit into Raef's arm.

"Raef!" Kinos called from somewhere.

Raef dropped his knife to clasp the cut. Blood welled between his fingers.

The merchant took a heaving breath.

"Sorry, kid," he said, raising his sword for a final blow.

Frozen, Raef could only watch, tasting his own terror.

The merchant's eyes bulged. He choked and stilled as

Cormac shoved him off the tip of his lean sword. Raef hadn't seen the pirate captain dart in to stab the man from behind.

"Bad?" Cormac asked with a concerned look at Raef's arm.

"I don't think so," Raef said.

"Good," Cormac said. "I'll be right back."

He dove into the fray.

The merchant Kinos had disarmed kept his hands up. He shook, clearly wanting no more trouble.

"Are you hurt?" Raef asked.

"No," Kinos said, eyes fixed on Raef's bloody arm.

The sun stood high above them, and no Grief gathered on the open sea, but Raef still eyed the shadows.

The merchants surrendered and the *Ino*'s crew tied them to their mast.

Kinos stared, his eyes fixed on the bodies.

The Tetheans followed the goddess of storm and surge, but most Aegeans would loathe a burial in water. There wasn't a prayer to her in the blessing for the dead.

"They drink silver water to make their blood less palpable to the shades," Raef said, though he could see from the dead man that it ran red enough. "That's why they're blue."

"Does it work?" Kinos asked, his voice hoarse.

"I don't know, but they say Tethis is particularly haunted. That's why they've been moving farther north."

They inched forward as the *Ino*'s crew swarmed over the captured ship like ants across a mouse. One pirate lay swooning on the *Ino*'s deck. His leg hung crushed and limp.

"What happened?" Raef asked a passing crewman.

The man didn't answer.

"He got caught between the ships when they met," Cormac said. The captain swigged from an open bottle. "Try not to let that happen to you."

Raef's blood began to cool. The battle had chased away the burning beach and his memories of fire. He hoped they would stay gone, but knew the merchant with his bulging eyes would join the Sharks and the other things he saw when he closed his eyes. Even lying in Kinos's arms couldn't completely chase them away.

"Are you all right?" Cormac asked.

"Yeah, just . . ." Raef trailed off.

"Let me see that cut."

"It's just a scratch."

Cormac took Raef by the arm and dribbled wine into the wound. Raef winced.

"You don't need stitches," Cormac said. "But we should have the surgeon check to be certain."

Raef felt Kinos watching as Cormac pulled the black scarf from around his neck. He tied it around Raef's upper arm as a bandage.

"You should use a sword next time." He still hadn't let go of Raef's arm. "It has better reach."

"You'd have to teach me how to use it."

"I can do that." Cormac gave the scarf one last tug to tighten it. "But keep practicing with the knives. You're good with one in each hand. Not everyone can say that."

"Now what?" Raef asked.

"Now we see what they're carrying," Cormac said. "Go help."

Before Raef could start walking, Cormac put a hand on his arm.

"I'm glad you're all right."

"Thanks," Raef said.

Kinos kept his distance, clearly trying to look like he wasn't watching.

"What?" Raef asked.

"Nothing." Kinos shook his head. "I'll tell you later."

It took Raef a moment to match his balance to the heavier ship's softer rhythm. He breathed deeply, relieved that the smell of fresh blood remained above.

The merchant's hold was broader, with fewer bulkheads, to ease the storage of more cargo.

"I've always wanted a look inside one of these," he said, eyeing the nets the crew used for bunks. "They don't sail into Versinae anymore."

"Have you been on a lot of ships?"

"Only for jobs with Maurin," Raef said. "Come on, let's see what we can find."

He led Kinos into the lower hold.

"Stay here," Raef said.

Leaving Kinos in the beam of daylight falling from above, Raef squeezed into the smaller spaces where the larger pirates couldn't fit or wouldn't be able to see.

The merchant ship was cleaner than the *Ino*, with none of the refuse and unwashed clothing that gave the black ship's tighter spaces a sour odor.

Raef wriggled between the beams, letting instinct and the shadowsight carry him, exploring until his fingers brushed something pliant.

"Got you," he said.

"What is it?" Kinos asked.

"Let's find out," Raef said.

He hooked a finger into a drawstring and tugged a thick leather purse free of its hiding place.

Raef opened the bag and dropped a heavy gold piece into Kinos's palm. Kinos held it up to the light.

A golden Hierarch, the coin minted in Ilium with the man's visage.

Raef took another from the bag. Everything was supposed to go into the common pile, but he could take some, maybe one for each shoe. They were worth a lot.

Kinos put his hand over Raef's and shook his head.

"That's not a good idea."

"How did you know what I was thinking?"

"You had that hungry look on your face. It's not worth the risk."

Raef sighed and dropped the coin back into the bag.

They searched for a while longer.

Kinos found a sack of dusty wine bottles squirreled beneath a bunk, but nothing else.

"That can't be all of it," the quartermaster said, bouncing the purse in his palm when Raef and Kinos took their loot topside. A broad-shouldered black man, he had a book and quill to take account of the crew's finds.

"I didn't take any," Raef said.

"That's not what I meant," the quartermaster growled with a nod as Kinos put the wine with the rest of the tools and food.

"There's no cargo, so there must be payment," Cormac said, eyeing the captured survivors.

The youngest, a boy, stared at the deck like he wished to throw himself overboard. An open cut on his cheek bled freely, the line of red a stark contrast against his blue skin and yellow curls.

Cormac drew his sword a hand's length from its scabbard.

"Where's the rest?" he demanded. "Where's your trade?"

The curly-haired boy's eyes brimmed with tears. The captive beside him elbowed his ribs in warning.

"You gave us a good chase," Cormac continued. He let the sword slide back into the scabbard, pulled it out a hand's length and let it slide back. "I'd prefer to let you live, but my patience is slim."

The merchants did not answer.

Kinos moved closer to Raef.

Cormac stopped playing with his sword and called over his shoulder, "Burn her mast."

"No," Raef said, unable to hold it in.

The pirates lit torches and the smell brought back the blistering heat, the screams, the tears of the orphans.

"Tell them what they want to know," he begged. "Please."

"There's a compartment," the man who'd elbowed the boy said. "Under the helm."

The pirates raced to check, but Raef's eyes stayed fixed on the torchbearers.

"Lamp oil!" someone cried. "Barrels of it!"

"Douse those torches!" Cormac shouted. "Quickly!"

"You're shaking," Kinos whispered in Raef's ear.

"I need a drink."

Kinos put a hand on his shoulder. Raef reached to grip it and steadied himself with the touch.

The quartermaster added the oil to his ledger, listing the spoils by crew member, and setting aside an extra portion for the injured man. Raef's eyes widened at the amounts the crew would make. Versinae's crown paid well for strikes against its rival.

The crew started in on the wine before the quartermaster put away his quill. One pirate, a ruddy-faced woman with cauliflower ears, offered Raef her cup.

He reached for it, but waved her off when he noticed Kinos's frown.

The *Ino*'s crew were criminals and cutthroats, but they'd been kind, easygoing even. Raef admired Cormac's hold over them. It stretched and slackened, tethered by his smile and the pitch of his voice as he moved among them, patting backs and checking injuries, tossing out praise and compliments.

The captain climbed the merchant's mast, rising above the din with a bottle in his hand. A few strands of his glossy hair came free as the wind tossed it side to side. Beneath him, the bound merchants watched, wide-eyed and terrified.

"Do we keep her?" Cormac shouted.

"No!" the crew responded.

The woman with the swollen ears waved at the merchant ship as if shooing away a fly.

"Burn her!" she called.

Raef tried to keep his face neutral, to not let his feelings show, but he squeezed the hilts of his knives hard enough to leave marks pressed into his palms. He should have taken the drink.

A stain darkened the front of the curly-haired boy's breeches. Cormac caught Raef staring and followed his gaze.

"Cut her loose," he said.

The *Ino*'s crew booed and hissed their discontent.

Raef let out a long breath as the captain dropped to the deck. The sober ones among the crew worked at separating the entangled ships. Cormac tossed a knife at the prisoners. It skidded to a stop near their feet.

"With a little luck you'll soon be free and underway," he said. "Be grateful we left your sails."

Raef did not know how the merchants could serve such a cruel goddess. Tethis was no friend.

He thought, as the ships parted, that he saw the blond boy give him her salute, three fingers spread in a trident. He lifted his hands to hold them before his chest as if a sphere rested between them but stopped himself in time. He could not risk making Phoebe's sign, not even among pirates.

"You spared them," Raef said when Cormac came near again.

"Why wouldn't I?" Cormac asked. "The battle was over.

We got what we wanted from them."

"The crew didn't want to let them live," Kinos said.

"The crew aren't in charge."

"But they have a say," Kinos argued.

"They do," Cormac agreed.

Raef snaked out an arm to catch Cormac before he could dash off.

"We're still heading east, right?" Raef asked.

"They have a say," Cormac said with a smile. "But I set the course."

They stayed on deck until the merchant had slipped beneath the horizon and the *Ino* sat alone on the Shallow Sea. The calm came too quickly, as if there hadn't been blood and the threat of fire moments ago. True, few of either crew had died, but Raef could not shake the look of terror on the blue boy's face.

The crew scrubbed the blood from the deck with seawater and brushes as Raef and Kinos descended into the hold. Screams met them as the surgeon sawed off the ruined leg of the man who'd been crushed between the ships.

Raef exhaled as they left the noise behind. Their little cabin was near the aft, somewhere beneath Cormac's own.

Raef's stomach fluttered every time they approached it. It was barely large enough for the single bed they shared.

Cormac had given them the room without comment, another odd gift that Raef had accepted but did not know how to take.

After days at sea, he'd become accustomed to sleeping beside Kinos, breathing the same air, occupying the same narrow space. They slept tangled up in one another, skin to skin, and Raef knew every bit of Kinos's body by sight and touch.

His thin beard had almost grown back. He scratched at it now. The light from the little window was bright enough that

Raef did not need the shadowsight. Music, badly played on a pipe and violin, drifted in with the light.

"Hungry?" Raef asked as he closed the door. He hoped not. He did not want to be among the crew while they celebrated their victory, especially with the wine flowing so freely.

"No," Kinos said.

He frowned, and Raef hoped it was because he felt the same about the crew.

"We should check your arm," Kinos added.

Raef flexed it and barely felt the sting.

Kinos moved closer. He pulled up the scarf to check the red line of the cut.

"I thought it was worse." He tugged the scarf tight again. "I'm glad you didn't hurt anyone."

This near, Raef could smell Kinos. Spice from the kitchen and salt from their baths in the sea. Not bad, just human— alive. Raef shifted nearer and Kinos trailed fingertips from his shoulder to his palm. He took Raef's hand in his. They stood together, swaying with the ship. It almost felt like they were dancing.

"I cut that one man," Raef said.

"At least you didn't kill him."

"I couldn't let him hurt you."

"I appreciate that, but I'd rather we weren't in a situation where it could happen."

"We need to pull our weight," Raef said. "We're still a long way from Eastlight."

"We'll be there soon."

Kinos didn't sound excited.

"What is it?" Raef asked.

"I—I don't know what we'll find, Raef. I don't know if they're all right."

"We have to hope," Raef said. "The knights are a lot of things, but they're honest."

"And . . ." Kinos stammered. "I don't know what you'll make of it, of me, when we get there. It's not at all like Versinae."

"I'm sure I'll love it," Raef said.

These days and nights together had given him something he hadn't had before, and he could, maybe someday, love Kinos too. But he wasn't ready for that. He held those words back, just like he'd held back telling Kinos about the shadowknife. It felt too soon, like a leap off a cliff. It also felt inevitable, but he wasn't ready to take that step.

"How far is it now?" he asked instead.

Kinos looked to the bed. He made it each morning, though Raef didn't see the point.

"We're here," Kinos said, using his fingertip to draw an X on the blanket. He drew a large shape to the south. "And here's Thiva."

Kinos dragged his fingers toward the foot of the bed and made a smaller dip with his thumb.

"That's Eastlight."

Then he sat, looking over his shoulder at the rough map, then at Raef from the corner of his eye. He smiled, inviting Raef to join him.

Raef sat and Kinos moved his hand, brushed it down Raef's back, settling it just behind him.

Raef leaned closer, offering an invitation. He could feel Kinos's breath, warm and a little ragged on his lips.

"Raef," Kinos whispered, once, before leaning to kiss him.

22
MOON

Raef's first lesson was not very exciting. Cormac chose a clear space on the deck and offered him the hilt of a practice sword.

"I feel like a kid with a stick," Raef said, trying to ignore Kinos where he sat coiling ropes.

"Wood can do plenty of damage, and unsharpened steel a lot more, so we start here. Copy my stance."

Cormac spread his feet and gestured for Raef to mimic his pose.

It was harder than Raef had expected, to match someone's pose while the ship rolled beneath his feet.

"Good, but it's not a knife," Cormac said, stepping behind Raef and adjusting his grip. "You can stab, but most often you'll slash and hack. Don't extend your arm too far. Keep some flex in it, and don't use all of your strength at once."

From there it was more stances, more foot placement, and too long before they got to swinging at each other. Kinos finished sorting his ropes and started on Raef's neglected pile.

"Where did you learn all of this?" Raef asked Cormac.

"Nobles get training in arms and combat," Cormac said.

"You're a noble?"

"Yep." The pirate nodded and lifted his sword. "Now let's see if you can defend yourself."

They began at last, and Raef quickly realized he had no idea how to swordfight.

Cormac tagged him again and again, his wooden blade slapping against Raef's back, arms, and shoulders. The man was too fast for Raef to catch.

Panting and gleaming from effort, they finally stopped.

"I am really bad at this," Raef said.

"You're just new at it," Cormac said with a shake of his head. "It takes practice, dedication. I was a boy when I started training."

There were strands of gray in the captain's dark hair, and some laugh lines around his eyes. The open sea had browned him. Even Raef was tanning after their time aboard the *Ino*. A little longer and he'd be the same shade as Kinos.

"You should have started years ago," Cormac continued. "But you can still learn, and I'm the best teacher for you."

"Why?" Raef asked.

"You're left-handed, like me." Cormac nodded to Raef's sword. "That will give you an advantage in most fights. Again tomorrow?"

"I'd like that," Raef said with one more long breath. "Thank you."

Cormac took the practice swords and walked away. He looked back once, quickly. Raef could not read his expression.

Kinos's expression was thoughtful when Raef rejoined him.

"You've got that look again," Raef said.

"Ask me later," Kinos said.

Raef blinked at him, opened his mouth to press, but Kinos shook his head.

"Later. I'm not sure yet."

>))) ● ◖ ◖ ◖ ◖

Raef and Kinos helped with the cooking, which Kinos particularly hated, but the crew was large. Spreading the work among so many helped.

"I thought it would be worse," Raef said, chopping carrots.

"Worse?" Kinos asked.

"Life at sea. I didn't think I could bear it, but this isn't so bad."

"Unless you're one of the merchants," Kinos said.

"I didn't mean that part."

"I know." Kinos sighed. "I just worry that you'll want to stay, that you'll want this for your life."

"That's not me, Keen. I'm not going to hurt people, not unless I have to defend myself or you."

He meant it. Whatever was between them continued to grow. Raef guarded it carefully, a sliver of light in his chest.

"Keen?" Kinos asked, raising an eyebrow, though a smile tugged at the corner of his mouth. Raef quickly kissed it.

"It just slipped out," he said.

"I don't hate it," Kinos said, moving on to the mushrooms and onions.

"I just mean that you don't have to worry. I know I don't belong here."

"I don't think Cormac agrees with you."

Raef added the carrots to the pot.

"How so?"

"He wants something from you. He wants you to stay."

Raef scoffed.

"You don't see it, do you?" Kinos asked.

Raef narrowed his eyes, trying to guess his meaning.

"You," the quartermaster called, squeezing his way through the door. He practically filled the little space.

"What?" Raef asked.

"Captain wants you to dine with him tonight."

"Why?" Raef asked. "What does he want?"

"He's the captain. Ask him when you see him."

"Who else will be there?" Raef asked.

"Just you," the quartermaster said with a grin that sent a shiver up Raef's spine. "He wants to talk to you."

Raef looked to Kinos.

"See?" Kinos asked.

))) ● ● (((

Cormac's cabin dwarfed the one Raef and Kinos shared. Windows opened at the back, giving a broad view of the dark, glossy sea. The starlight glittered on the ship's wake, and Raef could not help but wonder how the moon would have looked hanging over it all.

Spirits dampened, he turned to examine the cabin.

Bits of random art, clothes, and half-full wine bottles shared space with bags of coin. Flags and swords adorned the walls without any kind of order.

A long fish on a wooden trencher waited on the cluttered table. The cushioned chairs, battered and mismatched, had probably been looted solely for their padding. The sack of gold Raef had found aboard the merchant ship lay among the loot.

His stomach clenched at the sight of it. Kinos judged the *Ino*'s crew for their greed, for turning to piracy, but he'd grown up with a family, with a garden. He hadn't gone without. He did not understand that gold meant food. It meant security and light. It meant survival and safety from the Grief.

"They're quite pretty," Cormac said, surprising Raef as he snuck up from behind him.

"How do you keep doing that?" Raef asked, whirling.

"Practice," Cormac said, his eyes laughing. "You'd think you'd be better at it after a life on the streets."

"You'd think," Raef groused. Maurin had always said he was too cocky, relied too much on the shadowsight, that he needed to tune his ears.

"I'll teach you that too, if you like."

Cormac lifted the little bag, withdrew a coin, and held it up to the lantern light.

"It's strange that the Hierarch mints his own money, don't you think?" Cormac asked. "He's a priest, the head of Hyperion's faith, and yet he rules his city and lands like a prince."

He tossed the little bag back onto the table and took his seat, adjusting his sword belt so he could sit. He wore a shirt of black silk, a contrast to Raef's white.

Cormac gestured to the chair across from his. "Eat. Fish is best warm."

"I thought we were having soup."

"The crew is."

Raef looked at the meal. It was more than enough for the two of them. Cormac had gone out of his way. Again. Kinos was right. He wanted something.

Raef took an oversized chair covered in beaten red velvet. The coarse stuffing crackled like old leather as he settled in.

Cormac stretched to fill Raef's cup from one of the wine bottles he and Kinos had dug out of the merchant ship.

Raef sipped. It tasted not quite sweet, like cherries rolled in oak ash. It did not burn like rum. He could learn to like it, maybe even prefer it.

"I wanted to talk to you," Cormac said.

Years of eating with his hands had almost cost Raef the memory of how to handle a fork, but he managed. He took a few quick bites, worried that whatever Cormac might say would end the meal. It floated in the captain's expression. He nibbled his lip, clearly nervous.

"I just want to get to Eastlight," Raef said.

The closer they got the more he felt the need to know what they'd find there. The Moon's Door, he hoped, another carving. The Day of the Black Sun was still months away, but Raef could count to it. Maybe then, he hoped. Maybe he'd find the door and open it. Maybe, just maybe, he could bring her back.

"We'll be there soon," Cormac assured him. "We'll round Thiva in a tenday and drop you off on our way to Delia. We'll only stop if we spot another ship."

"Do you only go after Tetheans?" Raef asked.

Cormac nodded.

"Anyone who flies their colors. They're getting bolder, and I want to drive them back."

"Why?" Raef asked. "For Versinae? You said you were a noble. Is that why you were at the prince's palace?"

"It was," Cormac said, a bit of a smile playing at the corner of his mouth. "But like I said, a dream told me to be there."

"What was it like?" Raef leaned forward. "Did you hear her? See her?"

"No. I'm sorry. I just saw myself there, at the party, talking to you. I woke up and brought the *Ino* home. It didn't take long to realize what the prince was up to and why you were there."

Raef stared at the table, at the meal.

"I don't understand why you're out here," he said, changing

the subject because he'd almost hoped that Cormac had seen and heard her too. "You can afford light. You could be safe in the city, not putting yourself at risk."

Cormac looked to the windows.

"I started sailing when there was still a moon. Maybe I'll tell you about it someday, but it was beautiful, watching her rise over the ocean."

Raef had to fight a smile. Hadn't he been thinking the same thing?

"The freedom suits me, but it's not for everyone," Cormac continued. "Not everyone is cut out for this life, Raef. Not like you and I."

"Me?"

Cormac faced him again.

"You've taken to this. You're sharp, and you can already read and write. You'd make a fine captain someday."

Raef bought time with a few more bites. Cormac wasn't wrong. He enjoyed life on the ship, the freedom, and a full stomach.

But then there was Kinos. The idea of giving him up now, of leaving him behind once he was home—Raef knew he couldn't do it.

There was also the other thing, the harder truth of what Cormac did to live this way.

"I'm not a killer," Raef said. "I can't do what you do."

"It's not murder if it's war."

"We aren't at war, not openly. Why do you care so much anyway? Sure, the prince gives you a great cut, but he's an asshole."

"Yes, he is, but he's still my brother."

"What?" Raef asked.

Cormac laughed.

"That's why he treats you so well?"

"Yes. We take what we can and use it to keep Versinae alight. That merchant's haul will help the city."

"So it's charity?" Raef thought of Boat Town. None of that largesse seemed to trickle down from the palace.

"We do what we can, but it's getting harder."

"I saw your brother's party. He's not hurting. Not like some people."

"He could do more for the city," Cormac admitted. "And I will push him on it, but he's playing a delicate game, keeping the nobles happy and the Hierarch at bay. He has to look powerful, impressive, or either side will turn against him."

"Is that why he sold out Phoebe? To make the Hierarch happy and keep the crown he bought?"

Cormac let out a long breath. He swirled his wine, took a heavy gulp, and sunk into his chair.

"He thinks he didn't have a choice. I disagreed with him, stopped speaking to him. I would have stopped him if I'd known what he was going to do. I wish every night that I'd known."

He took another long sip.

Raef's appetite had fled. He watched the sea through the windows. Ten days. They'd be there soon.

"You could stay," Cormac said quietly. "There's a lot I could teach you, that I want to teach you."

"Why?" Raef asked, voice quiet, though it had begun to settle on him, the truth he hadn't seen, that Kinos had. "You don't even know me."

"I know you better than you think, Raef. I left because I thought you were dead. I used to watch you in the tower yard, playing with the others. I never spoke to you, Father Polus wouldn't have allowed it. There were a lot of children your age, but when I saw you playing catch with your left hand, I knew you were mine, that you were my son."

Raef sputtered. "How?"

Cormac chuckled.

"The usual way. I was just a boy myself, only fourteen."

"And my mother?" Raef asked. "Who is she?"

"I don't know. We wore masks at the Spring Rites. Hers was polished silver. I could see myself reflected in it. You have her eyes, just as black. Phoebe must have liked that."

Raef squinted, and he could see it. The lines of their faces weren't so different. Cormac had no beard whereas Raef could almost grow one.

He'd always known his family was noble, that they'd given him to the tower. He just hadn't expected them to be so close. All this time, and the prince, the damn Prince of Versinae was his uncle. Raef took a long breath and let it out slowly.

"Tell me everything."

23

MOON

The *Ino* drifted in open, glassy water, her sails furled, her anchor dropped. The sea lay as still as it ever was, but Raef rocked as though he'd been hit by a storm.

He missed Maurin with a sudden fierceness. She would have known what to make of this, and probably would've made some crass joke. Her blunt manner always helped him sort his thoughts.

He had a father. He had a parent, alive, and he'd been nowhere nearby when Raef had needed him.

The crew had abandoned the deck. Raef circled it and found Kinos standing near the prow, staring out across the water, toward the east, toward his island.

Raef almost walked away. He could climb to the crow's nest, give himself the chance to untangle the ball of barbed feelings writhing in his guts.

A father would have meant everything during his years on the streets, and a noble father? He needn't have starved. He needn't have eaten garbage. He needn't have felt so utterly alone.

But he was grown now. He didn't know what sort of relationship they could have.

Kinos stared east as Raef approached, his green eyes so intent, like he might leap overboard and start swimming toward home.

"What are you doing out here?"

"Waiting for you," Kinos said without turning. "How did it go?"

Raef did not know what to say, how to explain, or if he even wanted to try.

He'd meant what he'd told Kinos on their way to the Garden. Phoebe's tower had been his home, her priests and children had been his family. Only during his worst punishments, the most boring of them, or the hardest nights after, had he fantasized about the life he could have led, the food he would have eaten, if he hadn't been gifted to the goddess.

It had happened how it had happened. Cormac had thought him dead and sailed away.

"You were right," Raef said. "He wants me to stay."

"And will you?" Kinos asked.

He still hadn't looked at Raef, and Raef was glad for it.

In time he could make peace with it, with what had been and what could have been. It would not be tonight, but some night, sometime, it would not hurt.

Raef moved to stand beside Kinos at the railing. Had there been a hymn for when the moonlight made a silver road atop the waves? He could not remember one, but perhaps, just maybe, he'd have the chance to write one someday.

"No," he said. "Not right now. I promised to get you home, and I will."

"You don't . . ." Kinos trailed off. His chin dipped toward his chest. "Thank you."

"Tell me about it," Raef said, trying to make a joke of it and knowing he failed. "Tell me about what I'm giving all this up for."

"Eastlight isn't a big place. We get people passing through, sailing between Delia and Aegea, but no one really stops there. There are olive trees. We shake them in the fall and press the oil. There are grapes, closer to town. There's almost nowhere that you can't see the ocean."

"It sounds pretty," Raef said.

"You mean boring." Kinos nudged him. "Don't you?"

"I'm never bored by food," Raef grinned. "But no, it sounds peaceful. Sometimes, we'd be up until dawn for moonset prayers. It surprised me, every time, that Versinae could be so quiet."

Raef rested his hands on the rail and slipped a little closer.

"You know, Raef—you're a bit of a poet."

The churning ball of revelations settled, and Raef smiled.

"Is that why you slept in the crow's nest at Eleni's?" Kinos asked. "It reminded you of the tower?"

"Yeah," Raef said.

There it was again, that way Kinos had of knowing him without having been told.

He was thoughtful, careful. He didn't do things without intention. The way he looked at Raef when they lay together was hopeful, wide-eyed, in between the gasps and the kisses.

"I'm glad you're coming with me," Kinos said.

"Are you certain?" Raef asked.

Kinos often sounded hesitant about it, like he might not want Raef there.

"Yes. I want you there," Kinos said.

"What happens then?" Raef asked. "When you're home?"

He did not add *with your family*. Raef did not know how he'd fit into that portrait, and he did not know how Kinos would respond to the fear that they might not be there.

"I don't know," Kinos said. He reached, put his hand atop Raef's on the rail. "But I am hoping we can make this work."

"This?"

"Us. I wasn't expecting you, Raef, and I'm glad that it's you I feel this way about."

))) ◗ ● ◖ (((

The sweat from his morning lesson chilled Raef as the *Ino* sailed into fog.

"Here," Cormac said, handing Raef a long coat in his usual black.

"Thanks . . ." Raef trailed off as he shrugged into it.

He still hadn't come to terms with the idea of calling Cormac *father*. He probably never would.

Cormac reached to tug the coat straight on Raef's shoulders.

"I'm glad she led me to you, Raef. I'm glad that you're alive."

"But she's dead."

It was one more sign, one more chance that he had heard her in the crypt, had seen her in the alley. He'd felt the rose petal between his fingertips and knew he hadn't imagined it.

She hadn't spoken to him before, not in the hardest times, the moments when his faith had nearly broken. Maybe she'd saved it for when she most needed it, when he could open the box. Then again, he had to wear the cuff to hide the mark. Perhaps she'd only given him the knife when she had to. Perhaps she'd protected him from exposure.

Raef wished he could ask her, but he hadn't seen or heard her again. His own dreams had been quiet. Even the flames had let him be, though he had to wonder how much of that was from having Kinos lying beside him.

He'd never been initiated, but it pained him to think that

she hadn't come to him. He had to hope, had to take it on faith, that some piece of her, some echo, had reached beyond the Ebon Sea. He decided that he could understand why Kinos was both excited and not to reach their destination.

"Perhaps she's not dead, just trapped," Cormac said.

"The priests said she had to die, to descend. Every month, she died and was reborn as her light returned to the sky."

"Whatever it means, I'm grateful she brought me to you, that she gave me the chance to know you."

Raef did not know how to take that. Were he still a boy, he'd have beamed. His heart would have swelled.

The bell rang.

"Ship!" Kinos called from the crow's nest. "There's a ship in trouble!"

The crew gathered at the prow.

Raef willed the shadowsight to part the mist, but it clung too thick atop the water.

"Spill wind!" Cormac called.

The crew rushed to obey, letting out the sails.

A corpse, floating facedown and unmoving, drifted by as the *Ino* slowed. A barrel knocked against the hull.

More refuse and bodies emerged from the fog.

Kinos reached the deck.

"I don't see her," Raef said.

"It's there," Kinos said. "I only caught a glimpse, but she's big."

"It's a Turtle Ship," Cormac said, squinting as the wreck emerged from the swirling gray. "She's Delian."

Raef had never seen a ship so large.

A wooden dome covered her upper deck. She listed to the side, broken. Something had ripped a hole into her. She bled cargo and corpses like a dying beast.

Kinos gripped the rail.

"Do you think there's anyone alive in there?" he asked.

"We should try to help them," Raef said.

Cormac squinted at the break in the hull.

"That's a big hole."

"A rammer?" the quartermaster suggested.

"Maybe," Cormac said. "But the height's off. Whatever hit her is a lot bigger than us. It would have to be to crack her open like that."

"Could have been a storm," the quartermaster said. "They left a lot of cargo."

Raef could see the calculations behind the big man's eyes.

The rest of the crew leered at the lilting turtle.

"We'll take a long boat, see what and who we can find," Cormac said.

Raef eyed the ship's dome.

"There's bound to be Grief in there."

"Then we'll need to be careful," Kinos said.

"You should stay," Cormac warned. "Both of you."

"I want to help," Kinos said. "We're supposed to earn our keep, right?"

"And I want to see," Raef said.

He didn't mention the shadowsight. He wondered if Cormac knew about it, and how close his father had really been to Phoebe's priests.

Father. He'd thought it. Maybe in time it wouldn't seem so strange. Maybe someday he'd even say it aloud.

"All right," Cormac said. He turned to the quartermaster. "Keep sharp. Be ready to sail."

Raef kept close to Kinos as the longboat descended, jarring them with every turn of the winch and grunt of the man at the crank. They settled into the water with a gentle splash. Raef couldn't see more than a few arm's lengths ahead as the sailors rowed.

Their excitement had dimmed and they kept quiet.

The fog rose goose bumps on his skin. Kinos hugged himself and Raef pulled him inside Cormac's coat. They shivered together until the warmth built.

The shadowknife woke. It began to pulse, perhaps responding to Raef's concern over what they would find.

"Why isn't she drifting?" Raef wondered, watching the waves brush the wreck.

"She's heavy," Cormac said, cocking his head to the side. "I don't see any longboats. They might have tried to escape."

"Not all of them made it," Raef said, watching another waterlogged corpse drift past. Waxy, green, and black, it had already half dissolved, leaving no way to tell who they'd been.

"Bring us alongside," Cormac told the rowers. "Let's hook her."

The pirates tossed ropes with iron hooks into the breech, snagging holds and dragging the longboat to tap against the turtle's tilted hull.

Cormac strapped a bundled ladder to his back and climbed. He held the rope tight, planted his feet flat against the wreck's hull, and ascended.

Raef held his breath as the captain disappeared inside.

He poked his head out a moment later.

"It's fine," he called, unspooling the ladder for them.

One by one the pirates climbed. Raef checked that his knives were on his belt and went ahead of Kinos.

The wreck's interior was vast, wider than some of Versinae's canals. Her tilt made it hard for Raef to find his footing, but at least she was heavy and didn't rock much.

"We're going to need more boats," one of the pirates said, eyeing the crates and barrels strewn about in piles. He brandished a crowbar.

"Let's not jump to conclusions," Cormac said. "See what she was carrying first."

"We'll look for survivors," Kinos said, nudging Raef to follow.

"Empty," one of the pirates called as he pried open a crate.

"No Grief," Raef said, eyeing the shadows. Glass prisms set in the decks cast greenish light here and there. "I thought there'd be shades. There's plenty of bodies in the water, but none in the ship."

"So far," Kinos said. "Maybe it's all the saltwater?"

"I don't know," Raef said as the shadowknife pulsed again. "Something feels wrong."

"You're turning into one of them," Kinos said, nodding back toward the crew. "Superstitious."

"Maybe," Raef hedged. "Let's keep looking."

They went farther inside. The cargo was piled in the main hold, tossed back and forth by the wreck's tilting. Most of the space was open, with bunks and hammocks enough for a crew of hundreds. There should have been something, someone.

A pile of toys, woven dolls and wooden swords, occupied a corner.

A flicker of black, like a dark-robed figure retreating up the tilted stairs, caught the corner of Raef's sight.

"This way," he said, leading Kinos by the light of the prisms.

The wreck pitched suddenly, rumbling with a death throe. Raef and Kinos held fast to the stair rail until she settled again.

He remained there a moment, hand clutched to the rail, hoping that he'd seen what he thought he had.

"She's not drifting," Raef said. "She's dragging her anchor."

"So?" Kinos asked.

"So who put her in place?" Raef asked. "Let's get to the wheel."

Open on all sides, the wheelhouse stood soaked in spray. The fog remained, but the waves had deepened to a heavy roll.

Raef wasn't surprised to see that the wheel was chained.

"She wasn't fully abandoned," he said. "Someone fixed her in place."

"There's blood," Kinos said, peering out at the deck. "A lot of it."

It stained the edges. The crew had died here, likely had their throats slit, and been pushed overboard.

"Who would do this?" Kinos asked.

"Someone desperate. Someone powerful," Raef said. "Tetheans, most likely. They took her cargo, but didn't sink her . . ."

"Why?" Kinos asked.

"Bait."

Raef looked to the sea, to the fog, and tried to force the shadowsight.

He'd never pushed it like this before, willing it to work despite the gray light filtering through the mist. He'd never been able to use it during the day.

Something snapped between his eyes. The fog didn't part, but it became translucent, thin like spiderwebs.

The *Ino* floated in the distance. Beyond her, he saw sails.

"There's another ship," he said. "We have to warn them."

He raced to the stairs, shouting.

"Cormac!"

"Here," the call came from below.

"We've got to get back!"

They reached the hold and found the crew in the middle of a pile of empty crates.

"There's nothing here," Cormac said.

"The Tetheans took it all," Raef said. "This is a trap. There's another ship."

"How do you know?" Cormac asked.

"I can see it," Raef said. "You have to believe me."

"Back to the longboat," Cormac ordered without hesitation. "Quickly."

The crew scrambled for the hole. The shadowsight flickered. Raef could see through the fog and the water. Dark hulks, sunken ships, surrounded them. He couldn't discern their make or markings, but each bore a gaping hole like the wreck. Raef felt certain they were victims of the trap the *Ino* had sailed into, the same bait she might become.

"Get us back," Cormac told the rowers. "Now."

A needle of pain pierced Raef's forehead. The shadowsight flickered and faded.

"You're bleeding," Kinos said, sounding worried.

Raef felt the drip on his upper lip. He wiped it on his sleeve. He swayed, almost tipping over. Kinos caught him.

"What is it?" he asked.

"Just light-headed," Raef said. "I've never done that before."

"Put your backs into it!" Cormac shouted before looking to Raef. "How many masts did you see?"

"Four. Tall ones."

"That's a carrack," Cormac said. "Not good."

"Can she catch the *Ino*?"

"Not at speed, but we're not at speed."

The *Ino*'s bell pealed through the fog.

"They've spotted her," Cormac said. "They're calling us back."

"Will they leave us behind?" Raef asked. He gripped the longboat's side as a wave of dizziness washed through him.

"They won't get the chance."

Raef lay still, trying to stop the spinning inside himself until the *Ino*'s hull loomed over them, a glossy wall of blackened wood. Their longboat knocked against it as Cormac caught the rope the quartermaster tossed him. The big man went back to shouting orders without waiting for Cormac to climb up. The crew dragged the anchor onto the deck.

"You first," Cormac said, handing Raef the rope. "They won't cut us loose."

"Why haven't they closed?" Kinos asked as Raef scrambled up after him. "They could have hit us by now."

"We're missing something."

They reached the deck. Raef stared, forcing his way through the pain, trying to see again.

The carrack remained at a distance. Raef looked back toward the wreck. The pain felt like a nail hammered between his eyes. Blood snaked out his nose, but he saw.

Another ship, flying the Tethean flag, sliced the roiling waves. She'd been hiding behind the turtle.

"There's another ship!" Raef shouted, his voice shaking. "She's coming at us from the other side."

"Turn!" Cormac bellowed. "Hard to port!"

Cormac reached the wheel and gave it a spin with all his strength.

"Toward the carrack?" the quartermaster asked.

"The carrack isn't the threat." Cormac shot Raef a proud glance before saying, "Go keep an eye on her."

Kinos at his side, Raef dashed to the opposing rail. The new ship raced toward the *Ino*. Propelled by dozens of oars, her strange, wide nose curved beneath the water's surface.

"What is she?" he asked.

"A rammer," the quartermaster said, speaking up from behind them. "She'll break our hull and sink us."

"Oh, Raef. That's a lot of blood," said Kinos with concern.

"I'm fine," he said, wiping it on the coat sleeve.

He could hear something over the crew's frantic work, a whine like a mosquito.

"Down!" Raef shouted, tackling Kinos.

The deck exploded. Bodies and wood flew. Raef lost his grip on Kinos. Raef threw his arms up to shield his face. He swallowed a yelp when pain erupted in his side. His vision cleared slowly. His ears rang.

A giant splinter had buried itself in his side. Raef yanked it out with a groan.

The quartermaster had vanished along with much of the upper deck. The *Ino* listed, weighed to her side by the giant bolt fired from the carrack. The rammer closed at a deadly speed from the other direction.

"Kinos?" Raef called, looking for him through the dust and fog.

A terrible crunch, louder than anything Raef had heard, cracked like thunder in his ears. He flew through the air and slapped against the water to sink limply into the cold.

He broke to the surface, tried to shake the stars from his vision. A bit of broken deck floated nearby.

Raef swam, clung to it, and cast about for Kinos, for Cormac—for anyone.

The *Ino* groaned as she sank. She tilted into the water, gulping as she went down. Raef screamed for Kinos. He screamed for Cormac. No one answered.

He tried to call the shadowsight and was rewarded with only pain and the taste of copper on his lips.

PART THREE

THE ISLE OF THE DEAD

❧

Rhea, our mother in which we lay.
Hyperion, the flame to light your way.
Two coins for Phoebe, to carry
you away.

—PRAYER FOR THE DEAD

24

SUN

"Will I be a knight, Father?" Seth asked as they marched into the sea of sand and rock.

"You will," Geldar answered from the depths of his hood. "The Hierarch has sent you here, and the knight's path is the best means to show you are worthy of his trust and Hyperion's mercy. Let your faith guide you and you will be rewarded with faith in return. Do you understand, my boy?"

"I think so."

Seth was thirteen. He'd met the Hierarch in Ilium, kneeling, and tried to still his shaking bones the entire time.

The man wore so much gold that he glowed like the sun himself. Surely he could see into Seth's heart, read his every thought.

The worry had eased when they'd left Ilium, heading north. With the ocean far behind, the air dried.

The fields of green wheat, apple trees, and grape arbors shifted to harder ground. Geldar led them around the great chasm that nearly split Aegea's south from the north. He told

Seth how it was a wound from the demon wars, the place where Helios had fallen in battle.

They trekked beyond its depths, passing into the red sands of Teshur.

The monasteries lay there, resting high atop five narrow mountains that rose like fingers from the desert.

The grit wore the skin inside Seth's shoes. He took it as penance and did not complain.

They slept at night in the lee of stones that had soaked up the sun's warmth, to fend off the sudden cold and hide from whatever dwelled here. The rocks were riddled with curving lines, carvings like the trails of worms through an apple.

Geldar kept his satchel unclasped and his hood raised. He must be sweating inside his robe, and Seth wondered if that was how he performed penance.

The sun lightened his hair to a golden yellow and reddened his skin. The linen tunic he wore did little to cover him, but he considered the sun's fire cleansing. It had to be. It must be.

At night, the moon shone, a waning crescent that lit the waves of sand stretching out before them. In a few days it would disappear when she reached the Underworld, then emerge again when she returned, reborn and ready for her next cycle, her next death.

Seth slept with a blanket, his crooked arm his only pillow. He did not rest well without the sounds of the city around him. The silence felt too different, but he also felt free, like the two of them were alone in all the world.

After a few days of nothing but sand, Geldar pointed ahead.

"We must pass through Open Skies on our way to Teshur. It's a trade village. I want you to stay close to me, Seth. Do not wander off. Do you understand?"

He understood. He wasn't a child.

"It's dangerous," he said.

"Yes," Geldar said. "In more ways than one. These lands are outside the bounds of a polis. No prince or priest rules here. Faith in Hyperion, in any of the gods, has not reached these people. Some still follow the demons and many a traveler has gone missing."

Seth trembled at the mention of the gods' enemies.

The ignorant, the lost, still worshipped the greater demons.

They'd bred with beasts, made abominations, the sort of monsters the Knights of Hyperion had hunted during the wars.

They should be extinct, but rumors always said they still existed in the wild places or on the continents beyond the horizon.

Seth curled against the rock and fell to sleep, but his dreams were strange. In them he fought beside the gods, battling a tide of monsters arrayed in fur and tooth, tentacles and so many eyes.

He saw Teshur, once a garden, burn to red, dyed with a god's blood, when Helios fell from the sky.

Open Skies emerged from the sand and heat haze the following morning, a half-buried sprawl of tents and corrals set in a dry oasis. Crumbling walls and sand-blasted ruins peeked from the sand. A six-legged ox lumbered past. Seth ogled the rough people clothed in worn reds and blues. Many wore masks of caked and crackled mud.

"Little towns like this dot the red desert," Geldar explained without prompting. "They give the wanderers and disaffected a place to gather, to trade and share news."

Seth held in a shudder. The place was so bright to the eye, but also felt so dour. It had none of Ilium's mica-capped obelisks or broad, clean streets.

Geldar led Seth onward, past vendors selling chunks of meat roasted on sticks. Seth's stomach grumbled despite the swarming flies. They'd eaten sparsely on the road, the fasting meant to help prepare him for life in the monastery.

A voice rang over the sand-battered tents and stands. Seth cocked his head to better hear.

"Come, Seth," Geldar said, gesturing that way. "Let's see what this is."

They came in sight of a man standing atop one of the riddled stones. His head, fully shaved, was marked with green and black lines, tattoos running in a rough pattern Seth could not follow. He was browned from sun and time, like a walnut shell left near a fire.

"The Twelve are a lie!" the man shouted. He jabbed his staff, a long-dead root, at the listeners. "They have destroyed us. We must return to the old ways, to blood, to sacrifice!"

"Observe, Seth," Geldar said wryly. "He's almost the last of them, a demon priest."

"That's heresy." Seth felt glad for his empty stomach.

The only sacrifice the gods asked for was something you grew inside you, a feeling, like pain, or love.

This man raged, begging for goats and babies.

"Yes," Geldar said, turning away from the man's ranting to regard the passing people. "Yes, it is."

Geldar paused at one of the sand-dusted trade tables. Several amulets, crude etchings carved on bits of desert stone, were laid atop a cloth so worn that it had no color. Geldar tapped a disk carved with an open hand. An angry eye was scratched into the palm.

"Should we do something?" Seth asked, looking over his shoulder at the ragged priest. The same symbol was tattooed on his chest.

"What would we do?" Geldar asked. "He is surrounded by ruffians, most of whom do not listen to him. I suspect they grew weary of his raving long ago, but they would defend him were we to act."

Turning, Geldar walked away. "Do you know what Inquisitors are for, Seth?"

"No, Father," he said, striding to keep up.

He could not read the man's expression inside his hood, which was probably its point. Giving up, Seth turned to the ox splashing in the trade post's shallow, filthy water. He envied them their bath. He felt so dry, so caked in sand and dirt.

"We are for what the knights do not do. You are to be a knight, to uphold our god's laws and set an example to the people. My order has other work."

"You'll kill him?" Seth asked. His stomach tightened.

"Yes, but not at this time," Geldar said calmly. "He's doing little harm, and I would not delay us. The Hierarch has commanded me to deliver you to Teshur. I must obey him, just as you would."

Seth could see the warning there, the thing left unsaid. Should it come to it, the Inquisitors would not hesitate to kill him either.

"Why does Hyperion not speak to us himself?"

"Hyperion is the light above. He is powerful, but removed from us, and so he anoints the Hierarch to speak his will. All of the gods like their mysteries. They are part of our world, and yet not so near that they speak to us directly, at least, not often. Perhaps in Teshur you will hear their voices."

The waning moon vanished that night. Seth knew she would return in three days. She'd carried the souls of the dead to the Underworld. Now new souls would come forth, brought into the world by Rhea, Phoebe's sister, the Harvest Mother.

They came to Teshur, to the five Sun Stones, great pillars rising from the desert floor like the fingers of a giant's hand. They rose higher than the temples of Ilium, higher than even Phoebe's Tower. Atop them, within them, were open squares, cut windows and doors, the monasteries where Hyperion's most devout withdrew from the world to contemplate his light.

There were statues everywhere, many several stories tall. They depicted hooded figures, monks of the order, he supposed. Many were wind-blasted past recognition. Some had toppled to lie partially buried so only a single eye or half an enigmatic smile peeked from the red tide.

Seth coughed, hinting.

"No water yet," Geldar said. "We must fast to reach the stones and make a sacrifice of our thirst to prove our resolve to the god."

With a nod, Seth bit his cheek. He bundled his thirst in his belly, squeezing it tight. He would build and offer it, more penance for who he'd been.

Sunbaked, the air held almost no taste. He did not know how long he'd be here, how long he'd train among the monks. The Inquisitor could not say, but he promised that Seth would emerge a knight. He'd squared his shoulders to hear the priest's confidence. He would make Geldar proud.

They finally came to the base of the largest pillar. Seth imagined falling from its height, from the structures he could just spy atop it. Father Geldar had warned him this place would call for silence, that the monks would require him to go days without speaking, so he did not ask how they would climb.

Geldar raised his arm. He held a knife, a small curve of polished bronze. Lifting it, he caught the sun, and flashed its gleam to a point high above. An answering flash responded.

A net, suspended from a crane, descended. Seth watched it approach, his stomach a stone in his belly. When it reached the ground, Geldar moved to open it, spreading its thick ropes into a circle. The gaps were wide. He'd need to hold tight or he might slip through.

"In you go, Seth. Cling tight. Be brave."

"You will not come with me?"

"I cannot." Geldar wrapped his arms around Seth and pulled him into a hard embrace. "I have my duty, as you now have yours. Be strong, and you will be a knight. Make me proud, and I will see you again."

Seth would not cry. Though everything had changed so suddenly, he would not cry. Though these months with Geldar had come to an end, he would be brave. He would be a knight.

The net closed around him. It jerked, rising in spurts. Seth did not close his eyes. He wanted to watch the sky grow closer as the monks cranked the winch. The net twisted, and he spun inside himself, but he kept his eyes open. He would see. He would ascend.

At the top, the crane swiveled, its wood creaking. Seth landed hard in the light, on a stone floor laced with skeins of sand. Above him, statues of the sun gods—Hyperion, Helios, Eos, and Thea—loomed. Their outstretched, linked hands made arches over him as he climbed free of the net. Dressed in thin robes of sun-bleached linen, the monks approached.

Seth breathed deep. He opened his mouth to speak, but one of the monks lifted her finger to her lips and beckoned for him to keep silent.

"For the first year," she said, "you will be whipped if you speak anything but a whispered prayer. Do you understand?"

Seth looked back to the door, the opening where the crane stood on a protruding rock. He knew Geldar would already have begun his trek back across the sand, to seek the demon priest and stop his heretical ranting. Seth closed his eyes, took a long breath, and nodded.

The moon did not rise that night.

Now Seth was at sea on another moonless night. They'd all been moonless since he'd gone to Teshur.

The ship drifted, bobbing enough that his stomach churned. The Bishop approached, her boots loud on the deck.

"Chew this," she said, passing Seth a bundle of green leaves.

"For my breath?" he asked.

"For your stomach."

"Thank you." He bit it and tasted mint.

She followed his gaze forward, to the east.

"How long?" he asked.

"A while yet still," she said.

The cadre filled the ship's meager barracks. Three of the hounds had come with them, including Argos. Lathan had seemed surprised, but the pup would not be parted from Seth. He'd whined and then howled when the cadre had tried to leave him behind.

"He has chosen," the Bishop had said, and that had been that.

Seth refused to spend the entire voyage on his back, hand clutched to his aching belly, so he'd forced himself to his feet and climbed onto the deck. He ate little, which at least had stopped the vomiting.

There was only the sea around them, endless blue-black water. With the sails furled Seth felt better. The mint in his stomach helped. He was hungry, but feared he'd lose it all again if he ate a true meal.

"How is your control, Seth?" the Bishop asked, reading the doubt in his expression.

"I am afraid to test it," he confessed. "I have not performed my penance."

The ship would burn if he lost control.

"And yet you must."

Her eyes were hard, and he knew she was thinking of the beach, of those he'd burned.

Nothing she said could equal the feel of the hard weight in his chest when he remembered that night.

"You will master the flame, Seth. That is required for you to stay in this cadre."

"You still want me in the cadre?"

"You are part of my cadre," she said, voice firm as stone. "You will master the flame."

"Yes, Bishop." She turned to walk away.

He would try. He had failed so far, but he would try. He would make up his penance when they reached land, when he would not endanger others.

"Father," he prayed. "Let me be yours, or let me burn."

25
MOON

The waves brushed Raef back to consciousness. Countless stars, unobscured by Grief or smog, twinkled above him. He lay in rocky sand, a bit of seashell jabbing into his back, the plank of broken ship he'd used as a raft was nowhere in sight.

Kinos. Cormac. They were gone.

Kinos.

Cormac.

Blood stained his shirt, but the wound in his side had closed.

How long had he been in the sea? Not long enough to starve or die of thirst.

He remembered the cold of the water, remembered the loss washing through him, so much worse than the fog and silence. The waves had pushed him along.

Now he was here. Wherever here was.

Alone or not, his stomach wanted him to move.

Many of the constellations had set. It was late.

Holding in a groan, Raef stretched, sat up, and took in his surroundings.

He'd landed on a small island. He walked and climbed until he could see more of where he'd come.

South of his little rock, which was one among many other little rocks, lay a larger land. It was no great distance. Had there still been tides, he might have even been able to walk to it when the water was low.

Not that he would.

Across the shore, pressed into a thick crowd, were shades. This was no Grief, no mere shade mist. This was an army.

They were the ghosts of peasants, farmers, and fisherfolk. They stood straight, each shape distinct, each face clear, and every dead eye was trained upon him.

"Thiva," he whispered, his voice hoarse.

This was the Isle of the Dead.

Raef blinked and wiped his eyes to clear them.

He'd first thought it was a lighthouse. That made sense with the jagged stones dotting the water, but no, the shape was too familiar, a spire of white marble and black basalt. Seven buttresses ringed it, their heights rising and falling to mark the phases. The final phase was the door.

Beyond the ghosts, above the twisted, thorny trees covering the hillside, stood her tower.

Phoebe's Tower.

Thiva's temple to the moon, a twin for the one in Versinae, stood intact on the larger island. A lightless little town nestled in its shadow.

All that lay between Raef and it was a short stretch of water and an army of hungry, willful shades.

"I can wait," he said, taking them in one more time before he climbed back down to the beach. "I can wait for morning."

The water would protect him. Then he could cross. Still, Thiva's ghosts weren't like the other shades he'd seen. They hadn't dissolved into Grief. They were aware and awake, which meant they must have a regular supply of blood upon which to feed.

Raef passed the night huddled against the rock, his arms wrapped around himself. He wanted to sleep, if only to quell the hunger in his stomach. It nearly matched the hunger in his mind, but when he closed his eyes he saw Kinos sinking beneath the waves, silently calling Raef's name as he drowned.

The sight wouldn't leave him.

Raef shivered inside Cormac's sodden coat and almost missed the dreams of fire. He knew them well, and they were always warm.

Dawn would come. He'd reach the tower. His palms itched with the need to riffle through its books, to uncover its secrets. There had to be answers for the mysteries that had upended his life.

The tower's height might also give Raef enough of a vantage point to see more of the island, to spy other survivors. Maybe, just maybe, he wasn't the only one who'd made it to land alive.

"I can wait," he repeated.

The sun had fully risen when he dove into the waves. He regretted leaving the coat, but there wasn't an easy way to carry it. The cold shocked the lethargy from his limbs.

Hunger forgotten in his push to get there, to prove that the tower wasn't a mirage, he kicked until he reached the harbor of abandoned fishing boats.

Shivering, he climbed ashore.

The town was all low buildings, whitewashed houses of clay and brick.

Everything was sunbaked and brine-stained. It would have been pleasant, peaceful even, except for the silence and the complete abandonment.

The Thivans had painted their doors and shutters a happy

blue, but the lack of life already nibbled at the upkeep. The paint was chipped and faded. Grass grew among the clay tiles of the roofs.

No people came to greet him. No birds roosted in the trees.

Then there were the vines. Gigantic, they overshadowed the houses. Rugged, the bark bore no leaves, just thorns as long as his arms and red blooms that emitted a cloying scent. It reminded Raef of rotting apples mixed with the too-familiar taste of blood.

The vines wormed everywhere, snaking across the island. They'd even crushed some of the houses.

The shades weren't visible, but Raef could feel their dead eyes on him. He checked his wounds, the cut on his arm, and the splinter in his side. Curiously, both were almost healed.

He'd swim back at sunset, spend the night across the water, and explore more by day, every day, until he had answers, until he could form a plan beyond the now.

Perhaps one of the boats at the dock was seaworthy. Perhaps he could handle it by himself, load it with what supplies he could find, pick a direction, and sail away.

The tide of black and blue, the loss of Cormac, of Kinos, rose suddenly, threatening to overwhelm him.

Raef forced it down.

He had to be quick. He had to be careful. With any luck, he'd soon have answers.

Hurrying up the unpaved road, he climbed toward the tower until his stomach reminded him of practical matters.

Each house had a little garden. Those not starved for light by the creeping, weedy vines had grown wild since the shallowing.

He filled his stomach from an orange tree, swallowing even the seeds. The fruit was almost overripe, too soft when he clawed his way inside the skin.

The sticky juice reminded him how thirsty he was. He found

a well in the town square, dredged up a bucket, and drank before taking off his shirt to wash the salt from his face and chest.

Sated, no longer parched, Raef made his way to the top of the town. It rose in a slope to the hill where the tower stood.

The thorn tree wound in a thick ring about its base, but kept its distance. The red flowers made a carpet in the space between, as though the vines besieged the tower but had yet to breach its walls.

He found a gap where he could squeeze between the thorns and took the broad steps in twos. The doors, twice his height, were sheathed in iron. It reminded him of the box, and he took that as a sign. They weren't freezing to the touch, but were locked. In the tower's lee, the shadowknife slid from his wrist without prompting, as anxious as him to get inside.

They opened and Raef came face-to-face with Phoebe.

He'd known her statue would be there, but still he choked, shaking, on the verge of tears.

She stood in her boat, the crescent moon, ready to row the dead to the Underworld. The half of her face not veiled by her basalt cloak hinted at a cryptic smile. He'd spent many hours contemplating her stone visage, meditating on whatever he'd done wrong that day. It had been one of Father Polus's favorite punishments, probably because he knew it bored Raef so much.

"Lady," he said.

Bowing, he kissed her sandaled feet, wiped the dust from his lips, and found a smile for her before returning to his mission.

The rest of the first floor matched Versinae's. Slender columns began in basalt, then rose to fluted white marble. They reached for a ceiling tiled in jet and marked with silver stars. Pilgrims and supplicants would have loitered here. It took a larger donation, a rare text or an oblate, to buy access to the higher floors, to the shrines and the library, her most sacred space.

Raef still did not know who his mother was. She must have received something for him, in exchange. He'd been made in the tower itself, at the Spring Rites, which was strange.

The priesthood cared for orphans, but to keep a baby bred there? His mother must also be noble. She must have been devout.

He made for the stairs hugging the outer wall and found a body slumped on the first landing. Its black robe hung loose and stained around its skeleton. Raef knelt to look closer. He could spy no cause of death, no broken bones. The stiff robe didn't look cut or pierced in any way.

"What killed you?" he asked.

He'd get no answer, at least not by day. The windows brought light enough to keep the Grief at bay. The day was young, but he did not have long. Raef ignored the memories that stirred in the dust around his feet and hurried upward.

The dormitory, with its narrow bunks of beds, could have been his own. He'd best slept to the sound of the other children snoring and dreaming, which had made joining the Lost a comfort.

Corpses filled these bunks.

This was not his tower, these were not his playmates, but he clutched a post to keep upright at the sight of the bones.

"I'm sorry," he said.

He hadn't understood the safety he'd had, not until a few nights on the streets had taught him what he'd lost. Raef squeezed his eyes shut to force down the tears. He had to find the answers.

He bolted for the stairs. So many of his punishments had been for running. He'd get distracted by something then find himself late for prayers or lessons.

The tower is a temple, not a gymnasium, the Hierophant would chide him.

Raef had spent entire days in the old man's office at the top, reading one book or another as Father Polus went about tower business. Raef would ask him endless questions, but Father Polus wouldn't answer. Instead, he'd send Raef to fetch books from the library and bring them back so he could find his own answers. He'd read and read in that little room. At times he'd hated it.

Chest aching, Raef opened the office door, half expecting to see Father Polus's burned shade sitting behind the desk, working his mouth to impart one final secret, but the portrait on the wall depicted a woman. Her auburn hair crossed her shoulder in a braided rope. She wore a kind smile Raef hadn't expected. The plaque named her Arden, the tower's High Priestess. Father Polus had never smiled like that. He hadn't been jovial, not like Father Hanel or some of the other priests.

None of Arden's papers helped. The drawers held moth-eaten vestments, a ledger that tracked deliveries, shipments of books from the other towers or the docks, and a necklace, a disk of black glass hanging from a cord.

Raef looked through it. He knew these. They were lenses for looking at an eclipse, as well as a symbol of darkness.

It may be tied to the Black Sun, but Raef needed to know about the shadowknife, about the box—what it might be and why someone would want Kinos inside it.

He needed to know if he had truly heard her, truly seen her, or if he might be going mad.

Raef left the office and entered the library, the tower's heart. Two open stories of shelves and balconies contained all the scrolls and books the priests had collected and copied. Cult statues, hooded priests, and lesser deities were worked into the pillars. Each held a finger to their lips, pleading for silence in the goddess's most sacred space. Raef longed to linger here, to take one of the ladders to the higher stacks and read the first book that caught his eye. He could have spent his life reading. He'd been meant to spend his life reading.

The place looked untouched, like the priests might return at any moment and demand he dust the desks or fill the inkwells. For all its familiarity, the air lacked the smells of coal and industry. Here was only sea salt, sun-warmed vellum, and a touch of old death, the bodies that had withered below.

These books had been the priests' passion—Phoebe's passion. He'd been an irreverent child, but he recalled the day he'd smudged a page with an inky fingerprint. The priests had punished him, but it hadn't compared to the shame he'd felt, the sense of having marred something precious to the goddess.

Raef scanned the shelves, not knowing what to search for. A heavy volume with the mark of Dodona's tower, an oak leaf inside a waxing crescent moon, perched on the nearest desk. It was a treatise on wheat.

Phoebe was the goddess of the moon, of knowledge both hidden and revealed. Hadn't that been the point of all the Hierophant's lessons, of making him read so much? Knowledge was won and wisdom mined. They weren't freely given.

What Raef needed wouldn't sit where some clumsy visitor might stumble onto it. This tower was the same as Versinae.

Damn it, he cursed silently. Even with all of them dead, with her dead, he wouldn't say it aloud, not here.

Raef had known what to look for all along, a carving that was not a carving, a door that was not a door. He'd let his homesickness overtake his wisdom.

He hurried down the stairs, past the barracks and the statue, through the bronze doors, and into the undercroft.

The shadowsight came as the vaults and cellars opened before him.

He had to be careful. There was no light here, nothing to keep the shades at bay.

Raef almost slumped to the ground at the sight of the black door. The carving was here too, but it stood broken, shattered from the center, like something had clawed out of it.

He called the shadowknife and ran it through the glass. He felt for a catch, like he did with any lock, like he had with the box, but he knew it wouldn't open again. No matter what day or night it was, this was not the door he needed.

He remembered the collapsed vaults in Versinae, the drowned texts he couldn't read.

Traces of an old odor, like rotten meat, tainted the air as he progressed.

Raef drew his knives and stalked on. The first tunnel had been crushed in Versinae, but Thiva's ended in a room full of little beds and child-sized cages.

He knew this place, remembered its twin. A ladle stood in a cauldron, encrusted with fossilized porridge. More bodies, slight and still, child-sized, lay beneath their blankets. Someone had covered them.

Raef did not want to look, but he knew he had to. Somewhere deep in his guts all the things he'd swallowed down, all the things he did not want to remember, rose.

Trembling, he reached for a blanket. There were only bones, but Raef recoiled, and forced himself to look again.

The child had a tail. The child had horns.

Heart rabbiting, he darted from the room. He had to put that skeleton and the horrible truth it represented behind him. He had to—but he couldn't ignore it.

It was true. It was all true.

The priests were heretics. They'd consorted with demons. More than consorted, they'd housed them, fed them. They'd . . .

Raef reached the ledgers and plucked a volume from the shelf. Its spine labeled it as Dodona, a polis far west of Versinae. He opened it to the middle and flipped through the pages. Lines connected unpronounceable words to names. A date marked every connection, sometimes resulting in a vertical line leading to a fresh name.

Cormac had said the priests courted nobles for the rites. He replaced the book and selected another, looking for his tower, for Versinae.

Finding it, he flipped through the pages to find his year. He read, and slumped to the floor. He read it again, trying to force it into his mind.

New Moon
Cormac Deslis -- -- -- -- -- -- -- Sati
21 Coeus 1434
Hraefn

Raef threw back his head, hitting the wall hard enough to hurt his skull. The pain almost made enough room for the truth to fit.

He had a birthday. And he had a name.

"Hair-eh-fin," he whispered, testing the syllables. Hraefn. They'd called him Raef because they couldn't pronounce his name.

His real name. His demon name.

He'd denied the rumors about the priests, that they'd consorted with the gods' enemies. He'd thought it a lie, something the Inquisitors had concocted to justify what they'd done to her. Now he understood. That was the purpose of the black doors. They were gates to the Underworld. They'd summoned demons, bred them with nobles—with Cormac, to make him and children like him.

This was what he was? He could have retched.

Cormac, his father, his mother, the silver-masked woman—Sati, a demoness. Raef couldn't breathe.

He sat, head aching, heart aching, until a wave of cold crept up the corridor.

Raef's breath came out in a puff of fog as the shadowknife pulsed in warning.

The hairs on his arms stood straight as he found his feet, quietly as he could, and peeked around the doorframe.

A shadowy thing came up the passage. It blocked the stairs.

It was a shade, of a sort, but it had many legs, many arms, and faces, all grimacing with pain. Thorny vines ran through it, stitching the ghostly flesh of many shades together. It lumbered awkwardly, its dozens of dead eyes swiveling in all directions.

Raef pressed his back to the wall.

The cold intensified, as though the shade drank the heat from the air.

It had nearly reached him.

He wasn't bleeding, but like the spirits on Thiva's shore, this shade seemed aware as it searched the vault.

The spirit stiffened. All of its eyes swiveled, faster than its body as it turned back toward the entrance. It scrambled that way, quick as its many feet would allow, leaving a trail of mist.

Raef followed. He crept around the corner as golden light lanced like a sunbeam out of the dark from atop the stairs.

The knights had come.

Raef rocked back on his heels. He had to stop them. He couldn't let them destroy the tower.

The spirit flinched, raised its many arms to shield itself, but made no sound as it burned. The smell was like chalk, dust, and sour blood thrown into a fire. Raef gagged on the taste.

The fire flashed again, bright enough to drive away the shadowsight.

He gaped. Seth, the knight from Versinae, stood atop the stairs.

The spirit extended several of its arms. Thorny veins, red and ropey, shot toward Seth. He countered with fire, but the spirit poured on. The vines beat back the flames. Seth faltered. The thing would have him soon.

"Damn it," Raef said.

He reached for the table with its ancient, uneaten meal, and tossed a plate like a discus. It shattered against the spirit's back. The thing turned. Raef tossed another, catching it on one of its larger faces. He wasn't going to hurt it, but he could distract it, give Seth a chance to escape.

The shade raised its hands, ready to strike at Raef with the same tendrils.

Fire flashed as Seth drew his sword. He leaped and landed, cleaving the thing in two. The shade burned away.

Raef and Seth faced each other in the light of the flaming sword.

"What are you doing here?" each demanded.

26
MOON

"Who are you?" Seth demanded.

"There could be more of them." Raef heaved. "We should get out of here."

"I asked you a question."

Seth lifted his sword to better see Raef by its light.

"I was hungry. I thought there might be stores, food."

"There are better places to find food, but I meant on Thiva. There's no one alive here."

"I was shipwrecked."

The sword sizzled, burning away the ghost's old, bitter blood.

Raef needed to get Seth away from here, away from the ledgers and the tower.

"Can I tell you the rest outside?" he asked. "The sun will set soon."

"It is still morning, but you are not wrong."

Seth gestured toward the stairs.

Seth had been gentle and awkward in his flirting at the prince's ball. Now he seemed gruff and focused.

"What are you doing here?" Raef repeated.

"We have a mission," Seth said brusquely. "It's not your business. You're just lucky I was here."

"I could say the same."

So there were other knights. Not good, not for Raef or the tower.

The heat of the sword warmed the back of Raef's neck as he climbed the stairs.

Despite the threat, Raef almost laughed.

Seth didn't recognize him.

He'd worn a mask and a hat to the ball. His scant beard had grown back, his hair longer, and he'd spent day after day in the sun. He looked nothing like the noble he'd posed as when Seth had approached him.

They emerged from the vault.

Seth paused to stare at Phoebe's statue. He didn't strike it. He didn't try to burn it or curse her. He simply looked sad.

"I wish I could forgive you," he muttered.

Like it was Seth's place to judge a goddess, to judge his goddess. He was too young to have taken part in the attack on the towers, but he remained a Knight of Hyperion, and the knights had broken the world.

"We need to get out of here," Raef stressed.

It was not yet noon, but he had to get away, swim back to his rock, any rock, before sunset.

Outside, Seth turned to close the tower doors.

With a long kick, Raef swept his feet out from under him and flew down the steps. Someone had cut a convenient hole in the ring of vines.

A sharp whistle sounded from behind and a golden blur pounced from the trees, tackling Raef, knocking the breath from him.

A Hound of Hyperion, far smaller than the one that had chased him and Kinos in Versinae, pinned Raef to the ground with its body. He stared up into its slobbering mouth as it opened its jaws wide enough to snap his head off. Then the hound licked his face, its broad tongue scratchy across his chin and forehead.

"Eww," Raef said.

"Argos!" Seth chided the beast, though there was no heat in it. "Bad hound! You're not supposed to lick him. He's a bad guy."

The hound nearly crushed Raef as it rolled off him to run to its master.

Seth glared down at Raef.

"That was foolish. Try it again and I'll leave you behind."

"Where are you taking me? We have to get off this island."

Seth took Raef's knives and fished a length of rope out of his pack.

"I'll deliver you to my Bishop. She'll decide your justice."

"I'll have even less of a chance if you tie me up."

"There's nothing to threaten you if we stay in the daylight," Seth said, though he eyed the vines and the shadows with obvious worry. "But you weren't wrong. We must return to the cadre before dark."

"We could swim out to one of the rocks," Raef said. "The shades can't cross water."

"I suspect you would know."

"What do you mean by that?"

"We passed a wreck on the way. She was clearly a pirate. That was your ship?"

"Probably," Raef said. "I don't think anyone else made it."

He hated the obvious grief in his voice, but Seth's expression softened. He didn't say anything as he tied Raef's hands in front of him. Raef considered his options. Shadowknife, a well-placed knee. He could bite, but the matter of the hound remained.

"I'm sorry," Seth said. "But you should know . . . we found bodies when we landed."

The heat left Raef's veins.

He had to know, had to, but could not ask for details, not if Seth was clever enough to connect Raef's description to Kinos.

"Can you show them to me?" he asked, voice hoarse. "I need to see them."

"My cadre is there," Seth said, eyeing the sun's position in the sky. "But if you try to run again, Argos will catch you, and next time, he will be on fire."

Raef should have trembled at the threat, but he was too chilled by the idea that Kinos and Cormac might have drowned. He squeezed his eyes shut, tried to force away the sight of Kinos's secret smile, the one in the dark that only Raef got to see. He tried not to picture Cormac's approving nod when Raef lifted a sword with the right grip.

They'd had so little time together.

To lose both of them now felt cruel, but if the gods had possessed any mercy they'd never have let the towers burn.

Seth marched him east, following the coast.

The vines wound everywhere and often blocked the way. Seth used his sword to burn and hack a path. The wood sizzled beneath the blade. Thick sap the color of drying blood oozed from the cuts as the vines uncoiled from the road. The smell was like the shade Seth had destroyed.

"I don't like the look of that tree," Raef said.

"It's more like a grapevine." Seth prodded the wood with his sword. "But grapes don't have thorns."

"How do you know?"

"I lived somewhere they grew."

Seth smiled, just for a moment. Then it turned sad and vanished, buried in the grim visage of the golden-haired knight.

Raef didn't challenge him further. He only wanted to get to wherever Seth was taking him, to see what he had to see, the bodies on the beach.

"Will we make it by sunset?" he asked.

"Yes."

Seth might manage the Grief with his sword's flame, but if the other shades here were like the one in the undercroft— well Seth couldn't win against more than a few of them. He'd nearly lost to one.

"What is your name?" Seth asked.

"Why?" Raef asked.

"We're traveling together. It seems only polite to ask."

Raef scoffed.

"I'm a prisoner," he said, lifting his bound hands.

Seth cringed.

"Pol," Raef lied. "I'm Pol."

"Pol the Pirate," Seth intoned. "What kind of life is that?"

He sounded disgusted. Who would have thought that Kinos would have anything in common with a Knight of Hyperion?

"If it's any consolation, I've never killed anyone," Raef said. "I never really did much of anything."

"Then why do you carry these?" Seth asked, tapping his free hand on one of Raef's knives where he'd strapped them to his belt.

"It's a dangerous world," Raef said, wiggling his bound hands as proof.

"It is," Seth agreed. "I'm guessing that blood on your shirt isn't yours?"

Raef looked to the stain. Thank the moon the sea had washed so much of it out. He'd healed so fast. Was it proof of demon blood?

"We were attacked," he said. "Tetheans. They killed—well, they killed a lot of us. Most of us, I think."

"I'm sorry."

"You don't think we deserved it? They were pirates. We were pirating."

Kinos had been right. It didn't matter that it had been privateering, legal in the mind of the prince. They'd been pirates.

Raef hadn't known the crew well enough to like them, but to die like that, drowned in a watery grave . . .

"The gods weep for any life unredeemed," Seth said. "They could have come to the light, had they been given a chance."

Raef did not answer. He'd seen what Hyperion's light could do, and he'd burn before he walked that path.

The twisting branches thickened, not quite to a forest, but enough to cast shadows across the rocky hills.

Orchards of pomegranate and apple trees grew inland. There were fields of wheat and thick olive trees. He'd brave the thorns to eat his fill.

"What about you?" Raef asked.

"What about me?"

"You asked my name. What do they call you?"

"Seth."

"Seth the Knight does not have the same ring as Pol the Pirate," Raef said.

Seth laughed. He actually laughed. It was a pleasant sound, reminding Raef of the man he'd met at the ball.

Argos stalked through the trees, occasionally wagging his tail and looking to his master when he discovered an interesting smell. Like Seth, the hound was young. Both were less deadly or serious than what Raef had expected. He wondered if Argos could even conjure the fire that had burned Boat

Town. Seth had threatened Raef with it, but so far he'd seen no proof. Still, more knights, and probably more hounds, lay ahead.

The path dipped into a valley full of leafy trees. Fruit piled around their trunks.

"Are those apples?" Seth asked, breaking into Raef's thoughts.

His stomach grumbled.

"Now will you untie me, please?"

"Come here," Seth said. He obliged, undoing the knots. "Don't forget about Argos."

"I got it," Raef said, making an exploding gesture. "Whoosh."

"It is noon," Seth said. "We'll stop here for a while."

Rising from where he'd bent to lift an apple, Raef blinked at him.

"Shouldn't we keep going?"

"It cannot be helped. I must pray and perform my penance."

Seth turned away from Raef and began to undress, stripping to his smallclothes without a word.

Perching on a boulder, Seth closed his eyes. His sword, loose in its scabbard, lay in reach. Free handed, with a nearly naked captor, Raef was tempted to run.

This might be his only chance, but he knew he wouldn't try to.

The thought of their faces, blue and lifeless—he forced the image aside and reached for an apple.

Dusting it on his shirt, he ate and reached for another.

Seth's murmured prayers sounded like confessions, like pleas for forgiveness. Warmth filled the air.

The muscles did not surprise Raef. He'd seen those thick arms in motion, but he blinked at the pale lines running across Seth's back. The knight had been lashed, often enough to leave many, many stripes against his skin. They reddened from the heat he'd summoned.

Chewing, Raef circled, trying to get a better look.

Seth had a scar on his chest, right over his heart, like a burn mark.

Argos let out a small growl, warning Raef to move no closer. He lifted a hand to assure the hound.

The tone of Seth's prayer did not change, but he began to sweat, to steam as the heat rose.

His skin smoldered.

Raef waited for the taste of roasted flesh, but it didn't come, not even when Seth's breathing grew ragged and pinpricks of blood welled across his skin. Argos gave a little whine.

Raef froze in place. He shouldn't care. Seth was a Knight of Hyperion and his captor. Raef should wish him pain, but could not.

Seth finished his prayer and opened eyes full of sparks.

Raef stared, not even trying to hide that he'd watched.

"What was that about?" he asked.

He'd known the knights were zealous, but this—self-torture—it was so much worse than he could have imagined.

"Penance," Seth said.

He stood, somewhat stiffly, and began to dress.

"Burning yourself?"

Raef hadn't realized the knights could be burned. He'd thought them fireproof, like the hounds.

"The likes of you would not understand."

"What's that supposed to mean?"

"You're a pirate." Seth drew his tunic over his head.

"So?" Raef asked.

"You're a thief. You steal from people. You live a life without remorse."

"What are you going to do, burn me?"

Seth blanched. He looked wounded, like Raef had slapped him.

"Why would I do that? Didn't I save your life?"

"Oh," Raef paused. Seth had, hadn't he?

"Wait, didn't I save yours?"

Seth considered it for a moment then smiled.

"I suppose you did."

He doesn't know who you are, Raef reminded himself. *He doesn't know what you are.*

Then again, Raef wasn't so sure about those things himself. Not anymore.

An oblate, sure, of a sort, but also a demon, a half-demon. Did that explain the shadowknife? He'd assumed it had come from Phoebe. That's what the priests had told him about the shadowsight, that it was a gift from the goddess. Maybe both were from his mother, the mysterious Sati.

Raef had assumed it was Phoebe's voice he'd heard in the crypt, her that he'd seen from time to time. What if it was someone else? What if it was his mother?

He'd met Cormac, liked the man well enough, but didn't expect a reunion with a demoness to go as smoothly.

"Hold out your hands," Seth said.

"Really?"

"Really."

Raef scowled but offered his wrists.

Thiva, so much greener than Versinae's lands, unfolded around them. Everywhere the vines did not grow fields and fruit trees sprouted. Rhea had clearly blessed this land. In another time, with better company, this could have been a pleasant walk along the coast.

Raef wondered if Eastlight were like this, or if it were

all rocky and stale. He wished for Kinos's company, not a knight's.

"Where did Argos go?" he asked, realizing the hound had disappeared.

"I don't command him," Seth said a little defensively. "At least not fully."

"Does he always lick people like that?" Raef remembered the scrape of the hound's tongue along his cheek.

"I do not know. We haven't been paired very long."

"I never had a dog myself." Raef tried to sound sympathetic.

"Me either."

The rush of the waves came and went as they skirted the shore. Raef had lived his entire life beside the sea. The idea that he could go inland where the water and the freedom it represented wasn't in sight left him feeling strangely caged.

Aegea was a continent, but Raef had never thought to explore it. When the knights came for Kinos, he hadn't considered running that way.

In a way, as awful as the tower's fall had been, it had freed him. He hadn't had to stay in Versinae, and yet he'd never wanted to leave, not until the box, not until Kinos.

Kinos or no Kinos, Raef had to go to Eastlight. He had to try that door. It had to be intact. It had to be. If it failed he'd try again, every sunset, until the Day of the Black Sun.

If it didn't open—then he didn't know what he'd do.

He covered the crescent of hope in his chest that finding Kinos had brought, shielding it from the breeze of his doubts. It hung entirely on the door and what he'd find on Kinos's little island. If it died, he wasn't certain what would remain of his heart.

Something clicked in the hollows between the trees, bringing Raef out of his thoughts.

"What is that?" he asked.

"Don't try to trick me again," Seth warned.

"I'm not. It could be the wind, knocking branches together."

"There is no wind."

Seth lifted his sword, called its flame, and took a fighting stance.

The familiar smell of chalk and sour blood rose around them. The clacking sound increased.

"Whatever they are, they're getting closer," Raef warned.

"We've nothing to fear during the day. Hyperion protects us from the dead."

"I don't think these shades share your faith," Raef said.

Several shapes lurched out of the woods.

They looked like people made of wood. Mud oozed between the woven branches. Leaves clothed them in random patterns. Their faces were empty masks. Their limbs were coiled twists of the thorny vines. The red flowers jutted and sprouted everywhere along their bodies.

Raef forced the shadowsight, trying to see deeper, like he had in the fog. *There.* They were spirits, the same kind that Seth had destroyed in the undercroft, wrapped inside the plants to hide from the sun.

"Cut me free." Raef lifted his bound hands toward Seth.

"No."

"I don't want to die here, Sir Knight. I won't run. I swear."

Seth held out the sword's edge. Raef ran the rope over it, holding his hands as far apart as he could to avoid the burning metal.

"Can I have my knives back?"

"What good would they do?" Seth asked.

"You have a point," Raef conceded.

There was nothing alive here, nothing to stab. It wasn't like the shades to approach the living, not if they weren't bleeding.

"That's why there are no animals," Raef said. "No birds."

"What?" Seth asked, turning back and forth, looking for an angle of attack.

"The shades here are awake. They've eaten them all."

Here, the dead hunted the living.

"We need to run," Raef said as one of the makeshift figures creaked and clacked toward them.

Seth cast about, but the ring of figures, more than a dozen, was closing in from all directions.

"I don't think we can."

"They're using the sticks and leaves as shields," Raef said. "Can you burn them?"

The shape nearest to Raef's right lurched forward with unexpected speed. Seth shouldered him aside.

Raef slammed into the ground as Seth spliced the thing in two. The moldy scent of burning leaves and old blood filled the air. Exposed, the spirit dissolved.

"Yes," Seth said with grim satisfaction. "Yes, I can."

There wasn't time to thank him. More of the things came on.

Raef found his feet but had nowhere to run. The ring was closing, a barbed fence they couldn't leap.

Seth stepped toward Raef, turning his sword left to right, trying to shield him. It was a noble, stupid gesture.

The day was too bright for the shadowknife, and Raef wasn't certain it would help.

Seth whispered a prayer. The air warmed. Raef stood trapped between the fire and the closing ring of thorns and spirits. Seth might burn many of them, but not all.

One of the things lashed out, the vines reaching like a whip. Raef caught it between the thorns and twisted, breaking it off. Exposed to the sun, the spirit inside sizzled. The thing remained where it stood, wounded but undeterred.

"That was too close," he said.

Another slash of Seth's sword cut away another whip.

The ring closed.

A wall of fire appeared a toe's length from Raef's boot. He fell back against Seth, interrupting the knight's prayer. Centered on them, the circle of flames burst outward, burning leaves and twigs. The spirits made no sound as their cover dissolved. They burned away, leaving only ashes and the wet stink of singed vegetation. Black marred the ground in a perfect circle around Raef and Seth's position.

"Your faith is strong, Seth," a new voice said as Raef struggled to get his shuddering under control. "But you lack wisdom. These spirits aren't like the others we've encountered."

"No," he agreed. Dousing his sword, he sheathed it and fell to his knees at the sight of the approaching woman. "No, they are not."

She stood a little shorter than Raef, with hard lines on her arms.

She wasn't large, but she carried herself proudly. Her long hair was woven into braids. She'd seen battle. Dimples and smudges scored her brazen armor. Her heavy mace was dented from much use.

Reaching them, she knelt over one of the smoldering piles.

"Rise, Seth," she commanded. "Who have you found here?"

"Pol, a pirate."

"Shipwrecked," Raef interjected. He could speak for himself, but it might be wise to let Seth do the talking. He'd come to think of Seth as almost friendly, but this woman radiated strength, and she clearly showed a mastery of the god's fire his companion didn't possess.

"Come then," she said, slinging the strap of her mace over her shoulder. "We may have found some of your fellows."

"Seth told me."

"Then you know that they were all drowned. We brought the bodies ashore."

"You did not leave them to the sea?"

The Bishop cocked her head.

"The gods wish us buried in Rhea's arms. We will burn them so they do not add to the Grief."

"Show me. Please."

She began to march.

Head bowed, Raef followed.

Seth didn't tie Raef's hands again.

"What else did you find?" the Bishop asked. "Aside from—"

She gestured toward Raef.

"Pol," Raef whispered.

"The town is empty. No people. No animals."

Seth didn't mention the tower. He didn't mention the undercroft or the very flammable, intact library.

"But as you said, the spirits here are not like others. They attacked me, even by daylight. Pol saved me."

The Bishop raised an eyebrow in Raef's direction. He shrugged in response.

She led them to a rise. Below, on the beach, another ten knights had laid out a line of bodies.

A full cadre, and it would take only one of them to see the mark on Raef's wrist to recognize what he was. Then it would all end in fire.

"Pol?" Seth asked, laying a hand to his shoulder. Raef did not miss the look of disgust one of the other knights, an auburn-haired man, threw Seth's way. "Are you all right?"

"Yes. I just . . ."

"Make your peace with the dead," the Bishop said.

"Then what will you do with me?"

He didn't know how to read her grim expression. Did she mean to burn him, to leave him here with the others?

Seth hadn't seemed to think so, and his expression was kind now, concerned even.

"We will keep you with us," the Bishop said. "You would not survive without our protection."

Raef exhaled, letting out all of his breath. He couldn't put it off any longer and looked to where he did not want to.

The knights had laid the bodies faceup. Raef walked the line of familiar, waterlogged corpses, tensed for the inevitable blow, the sight of the face he loved, and for the man he could have called father if given time.

The cabbage-eared drunk.

A tattooed man who'd sung beautifully.

Other faces he knew.

But he'd learned none of their names.

No Cormac.

No Kinos.

They could both still be out there. They could both still be alive.

"Do you know them?" the Bishop asked.

"Yes. Thank you for bringing them ashore."

Their faces were blank, their eyes closed. Sand-brushed and sodden, but not anything like the bodies the Tetheans had left in the sea as bait.

Raef hadn't known these people well or even really liked them, but no one deserved that fate.

"Of course," the Bishop said with a little softness. "If you tell us their names, we will pray for them."

"We were on the same ship. That is about all I can tell you."

She cocked her head at him.

"I wasn't there long," he said. "Hadn't been to sea long."

Maurin would have slapped him for admitting it. He wasn't thinking right.

How could he?

He felt scraped raw, inside and out.

Perhaps he simply no longer wanted to hold his tongue, though he had to. For Phoebe. For Kinos.

He might still be alive.

"You said you hadn't killed anyone?" Seth asked.

"I haven't," Raef said. It was true. He hadn't even killed Zale, the knight in the crypt and counted himself beyond lucky that the grizzled veteran was not among the cadre.

Raef had to focus, to step carefully, and avoid anything that might give him away. He'd let Seth's unassuming nature distract him. The Bishop would not be easy to fool.

"What are you even doing here?" Raef said. "Why stay here?"

"We're searching for someone," she said.

"Who?"

"A black-haired man," Seth said. "At first, I thought you might be him, but his eyes are green. Yours are black."

"Sorry to disappoint you." A scream of something, hope or joy, bubbled in his throat and had to be swallowed down. He couldn't trust it, and he could not reveal it.

"How do you know he's here?" he asked.

"An Oracle," the Bishop said. "She sent us here, to search the eastern side of the island."

"Why are you on the north shore?"

"The cliffs and brambles make it impossible to land to the east," the Bishop said. "We must march overland. Our ship will return for us."

"And you'll be coming with us," Seth said.

He grinned, like it was a jaunt, like it wasn't a hike across a haunted island where the shades were hunting them.

Still, they were here for Kinos. He was on Thiva. If this Oracle of Hyperion could be trusted then there was a chance, and it was everything.

Despite Raef's best efforts, the hope in his chest waxed brighter.

The knights had shown up unexpectedly, impossibly.

He could have laughed. The Bishop was right. He needed their protection.

The Knights of Hyperion were his only chance to find Kinos alive.

27

MOON

"It's afternoon," Raef said. "Can we get there by nightfall?"

"Unlikely," the Bishop said. She turned to the knights. "We'll march east. Form up. We've said the blessing, Seth. See to the bodies."

"I—" he stammered.

"I know you have the fire for it," she said sharply.

Seth set his mouth in a thin line.

"Yes, Bishop."

"Come with me, Pol," she commanded.

Raef followed as she put some distance between them and the dead pirates. He hated this, that they'd use fire, even though he understood that there would be fewer shades this way.

He imagined the flames licking at his skin.

Seth stood trembling near the line of corpses.

Raef narrowed his eyes. The other knights clearly had the fire. They should not expect Seth to do such a duty alone. He was too kindhearted. It was probably part of a knight's training, to grow his strength and faith, or it was cruel, like his self-inflicted penance.

Then the flames fell from the sky in a wall, splashing across the beach.

The Bishop's fire was crimson, but Seth's was golden, liquid, and all too familiar. The taste of everything burning was all too familiar.

Raef stumbled backward as the sand blackened like it had in Versinae. It ran, glossy and sparkling, burned to molten glass.

Seth had the fire. He had more than enough fire.

The flames stopped raining. The bodies were ash. Even the bones were gone.

Raef understood now.

Seth could have saved them from the spirits who'd attacked them, but there'd been too great a chance that he might kill Raef and perhaps himself. Raef had thought him gentler than the other knights, but truly, he was the worst of them.

Seth lacked control.

He'd been holding back in the vaults. He could have brought the tower down. He could have burned Raef to a cinder.

The tremor racking Raef's limbs almost brought him to his knees, and he wasn't alone. Shaking, Seth wiped his eyes before he turned to meet Raef's stare. Then he slumped to his knees. His tears shone in the last of the firelight.

Raef's heart pounded. He needed to run—but the shaking had quelled.

A question rose, overwhelming the tremble.

Why?

Seth could have burned him to a cinder. He could have brought the tower down. Why hadn't he?

He trudged his way toward the column of knights.

They didn't speak as they marched.

For once, Raef had nothing to say. He let the question circle in his mind, a way to keep the fire and the worry for Kinos at bay.

"Bishop," Seth said, nodding to where the sun had begun to set behind them.

"We'll seek shelter now," she announced. "The dead will come in force tonight."

"There's a hilltop," a knight reported, returning from scouting ahead. "Rocky, flat on top. We should be safer there."

"Can we leave him behind?" one of the knights asked another, nodding to where Seth lingered at the rear of their march. The other scoffed.

"We leave no one behind," the Bishop said in a rigid tone.

Still tasting ashes, Raef fell back to walk beside Seth.

"Are they always like this with you?"

Seth nodded.

"I—I am flawed. The fire burns me. I lost control of it and people died. That is why I do penance."

"You mean burn yourself?"

"Yes."

"Who were they, the people who died?"

"They were on a beach. They attacked us."

Raef had already figured that part out, and he had a hard time feeling bad for the Sharks. They'd been fools to attack the knights, unreasonable in their demand for gold when there'd been so much at stake. He'd been forced to call the Grief on them to get past them.

Still, no one deserved a death by fire.

"At least you're sorry for it," Raef said.

"It doesn't matter." Seth's face twisted with sorrow. "I don't want to hurt people."

Raef pursed his lips.

"What?"

"Nothing." Raef shook his head. "Just—you surprise me. You're not what I expected in a Knight of Hyperion."

"We earned the people's fear," Seth said. "I earned it. The most I can do is try to make up for that."

Raef let Seth walk on before he hurried to catch up.

They reached the hilltop.

Camped atop it, they could defend themselves, or make a last stand if it came to that. Raef listened to the brush of the wind across the rocks and trees. He hugged himself for warmth.

There were three hounds, Argos being the smallest. Raef couldn't be certain but one of the larger ones might have been the one who'd chased him and Kinos through Boat Town. He took little breaths and held them before letting them out. Surely it would have attacked him if it had his scent. The legends said the Hounds of Hyperion could track you anywhere if they tasted your blood.

The knights sank to their knees and prayed toward the sunset. Phoebe's priests would have done the same at moonrise. Raef could see the value in their prayers. The knights' faith brought the fire. They'd need it against the shades. Still, something in him tore to think how the full moon would have hung over this island, over the sea, shining and silver, if not for them.

Lady, he prayed silently. *Give me the chance to bring you home.*

Then it was dark, and the only lights were the endless stars and the knights' swords, flaming like torches. The air chilled before the now familiar, terrible odor drifted over the hilltop.

"They're coming," Raef whispered.

"Stay close to me, Pol," the Bishop said.

She cracked her neck and gripped her mace.

The hounds surrounded her, forming an inner ring while the knights held the outer.

"They will not harm you," the Bishop said, catching Raef's expression as Argos came nearer. "They were bred to fight demons."

What if the hounds sensed what he was? What he partly was?

"They can summon fire," Raef said, hoping she'd send them further away. "Shouldn't they go after the spirits?"

"You have no magic," the Bishop said. "I want them protecting you."

"Thank you," he said, meeting eyes with Argos.

Seth stood in the ring with his fellow knights, braced for the fight, but a small tremble rippled over his shoulders.

Raef should not care. He shouldn't, but he didn't want to see Seth harmed.

The cold deepened. Raef resisted the urge to hug himself again. He felt useless. Despite everything, he felt grateful for the warmth of the god's fire.

Raef opened and closed his fists. The shadowknife pulsed in its mark, beneath the leather cuff. It raced with his heart as a shape crested the hill.

It was a child, a peasant girl in a plain dress and rough skirts. Her unbraided hair made a wild nimbus about her head. Her eyes were empty white, but focused on him. She carried a toy, a doll made of mud and sticks. It wore one of the red flowers in its straw hair. Lifting it, she held it to her ear as if to listen to its whispers.

Sparks lit along the hounds' fur.

"Hold," the Bishop ordered.

The hounds stopped pawing the ground but they kept growling, low and menacing.

Raef could feel it too, like a blade whispering over his skin, just on the verge of cutting. The mark burned with cold. The shadowknife wanted to fight this cousin of his, this—

"Demon," he whispered.

Shades gathered behind the girl, a waiting army.

These were the ghosts Raef had seen lining the shore. Most

wore simple clothes. They carried hoes and pitchforks. All had ravenous eyes, but they weren't blank. They were focused on Raef, like he was a prize to be taken.

The girl smiled. Her eyes filled with red, and the spirits charged.

28
SUN

The shades rushed forward to flow around the girl in a tide of gray.

"Wall!" the Bishop ordered.

Seth lifted his shield and held it in line with the knights on either side of him.

Each knight sent fire through their shield. They lit, one by one, to make a blazing wall.

The spirits swirled around them, like their formation was a rock in the current of a cold river. The spirits broke against it, burning to ash. Flecks of their remains clouded the air. One landed, icy like a snowflake, on the bit of exposed neck beneath Seth's helm.

He poured the fire through his shield, straining to keep it blazing but not so hot that it burned him.

He could not see through the flames but felt the tide pour on as the cold advanced. They must be burning hundreds of them away, but still they came.

There had to be an end to them. There had to be.

Next to Seth, the wall of flame faltered.

He pushed his fire further, to cover the gap and shield more of his fellow knights.

Father, grant me the will, he prayed. *Grant me the control.*

The flames closed the breach.

The knight beside him sighed in relief.

"Thank you," he said quietly.

"Praise Hyperion," Seth said.

Any other words, any more distraction, might cost him too much focus. He'd managed, so far, to not let the fire spill back onto himself.

Down the line, one of the knights tired. His fire flickered. Seth pushed himself, straining to cover that gap as well. The heat singed him through his gauntlet, but still he willed the flames onward. He had to push them, push himself, but not lose control. His flames would not hurt his fellow knights, but he could burn Pol to a cinder if he lost focus.

The flames did not make it in time.

Seth hadn't even learned the knight's name. He went down in a haze of red and gray mist as the spirits tore the blood from him. One of the hounds let out a wail. Seth didn't think it was Argos, but he couldn't turn to see.

The ghosts poured through the gap as more of the knights weakened.

Seth knew there were limits to faith, to the power a knight could wield.

"Close!" the Bishop yelled.

The knights stepped together, closing ranks. The Bishop had not summoned her fire yet.

And there was Pol, behind their shield wall. He did not deserve what the shades of Thiva would do to him. No one deserved that.

Guard him, Father, Seth prayed. *Save us all.*

Bolstered, Seth pushed back at the fire, made it flow outward. It wasn't enough. He could smell burning flesh and knew it was his.

Still, he pushed as another knight faltered. A third. Holes opened along the shield wall. Those knights fell back before the spirits could take them.

Seth clenched his teeth until he thought they'd crack. Fire had filled his vision, and still the shades came on, pushing against his shield, against his faith. Their ashes fell like snow. They dusted the ground and chilled him, trying to douse his resolve.

How many were there? Why would they sacrifice themselves like this? He'd never seen ghosts show such will.

A wall of molten scarlet, the Bishop's fire, rose between them and the tide of spirits.

"Contract!" she commanded.

Seth's drills with her and Lathan had him obeying without pause. He felt a flicker of pride as they stepped back, closing ranks again.

Only the dead knight remained behind.

The tide of spirits finally broke, but Seth did not relax.

The girl stood on the path they'd taken to the hilltop. She and the Bishop eyed each other. The scene was silent save for the knights' ragged breathing, and the constant, almost synchronized growls of the hounds.

The Bishop lifted her mace. A beam of pure sun split the night.

The girl moved, faster than possible, almost faster than the light.

The beam struck the side of her face.

The flesh burned and red roots wormed free, wriggling and searching.

The girl screamed, an inhuman shriek that could have shattered glass.

Slight chest heaving, she lifted her doll and twisted, breaking it in two. Red dust, pollen, filled the air.

Several shapes, the patchwork spirits bound in vines, crested the hilltop. Thorny vines trailed them like chains. The crimson flowers clothed their misty skin.

The girl, half her face burned to char, her remaining eye still red and gleaming, grinned.

Seth understood the rush now. That onslaught had weakened the cadre; it had cost them precious fire and one of their number.

The patchwork spirits halted their advance. He could see his breath, but the air behind him had warmed. They'd retreated to the hounds' inner ring. Argos shifted closer, sharing some of his heat with his master. Seth's heart lightened. He dared not look behind him. He'd trust the Bishop to keep Pol safe. Seth lifted his shield. He could, he would, endure.

Then he saw it, the thing. It was like the others, stitched together, like the one in the undercroft, but so much larger, a hulking giant. The girl swung her broken doll through the air like it was flying.

The giant's dozens of faces opened as if to scream in rage. It made no sound, no noise as it lumbered forward, and that was so much worse. The dead sewn into it had no voice.

Some were large, adults. Others were tiny, the ghosts of children. All of their eyes stared forward, past the knights, toward Pol.

Of course they'd want him. He had no fire, no faith, no means of protecting himself.

But how could they be enough against this?

He saw the girl's plan clearly then.

The knights' power was tied to their faith. The giant cast doubt. Their wall of fire buckled even before it strode forward.

The Bishop's prayer poured down, a column of flame. The other stitched spirits rose and swirled, sacrificing themselves to shield the giant.

It lumbered toward them, reached out with a face-lined arm, and struck the center of their wall.

Lathan.

His fire died as he fell backward, knocked to the ground. His shield clattered away.

"Close!" the Bishop shouted. "Close!"

Lathan lay sprawled, clearly too stunned to retreat.

The giant lifted its foot. Vines wriggled loose from its sole as it prepared to crush the fallen knight.

Twisting, Seth stepped to the right. He poured all of his fire into his sword, pointed it at the giant, and pushed everything he had, all of the flame, all of his faith, through the blade.

Light burst across the hilltop like the beacon of a lighthouse.

The giant burned.

Pain raced up Seth's arm. The taste of his own singed flesh mixed with the sour blood and chalky ash.

The others had fallen back, obeyed the Bishop, leaving Seth and Lathan exposed.

Fire. All was fire. It filled his vision. The spirits glittered in it. He burned them away. He burned them all, set them free. It could all burn.

That would be good.

That would be right.

He was barely aware of Lathan scrambling backward.

"Seth!" Pol shouted. "Come on!"

The plea snapped him back to the moment, to the hilltop, and the now.

Seth retreated, covering Lathan as the knights parted for them.

The ashes of the burned spirits and the giant continued drifting down, but the night was warmer, heated by what he'd unleashed.

The battle was over.

The girl had vanished.

The cadre had survived, but they'd lost one of their own.

Seth took heaving breaths. He should have been stronger. He should have been able to save them all. And still there was the fire, that moment when he'd seen everything in gold and sparkling embers, like he'd stared into the sun with open eyes and not been blinded.

"You do not break formation!" the Bishop shouted.

Seth faced her and she struck him, her mailed gauntlet ringing against his helmet.

He blinked, then understood. He'd disobeyed. His training was imperfect. He was imperfect.

With a nod, Seth knelt, removed his helmet, and offered her his other, bared cheek. She slapped him again, the edge of her gauntlet cutting him.

"What are you doing?" Pol demanded, stepping between them.

"You do not break formation," the Bishop repeated, her chest heaving from the night's efforts. "You could have gotten us all killed."

"He saved us!" Pol shouted. "He saved that knight!"

"Pol," Seth snapped before gently adding, "she is right."

Seth turned his face, offered his other cheek again. The Bishop seethed but she did not strike him a third time.

"Search in pairs," she told the knights. "Take the hounds, but do not go far. Cry out if you see anything, any sign of her."

The cadre obeyed. Pol remained at the Bishop's side, shaking. Seth had the urge to put an arm around him, to comfort him. He looked stricken. He had to be terrified.

"What was she?" Seth asked the Bishop, though he thought he knew.

"Bring wood," she said without answering. "We will burn Dion and build him a cairn."

So that had been the dead knight's name.

"Yes, Bishop."

He blinked when Lathan stepped to his side, silently offering help. They moved down the hill, swords held high, watching every shadow. Seth skirted the thorns and black vines. They grew thicker toward the east.

"Father," Seth prayed aloud. "Let us find our quarry. Let us leave this terrible place."

A little voice, one he could not quite silence, wondered if the Hierarch had hoped they'd die here, if he hadn't sent them to Thiva with the intention that they not return. Father Geldar had hinted at that, but no, the Oracle had said to send a cadre, that they would find their quarry on the eastern cliffs. Still, the Hierarch did not have to choose the Bishop's cadre.

She had not answered his question, but Seth had seen it in her eyes.

Demons.

They'd been taught that the gods had killed them centuries ago.

It could not be completely true. If it were, then who had Phoebe's priests consorted with?

The Hierarch could not be wrong, but there must be demons alive somewhere. One was on this island. Her influence might explain the spirits. Like the doll, she'd stitched them together to create abominations.

"How's your arm?" Lathan asked as he bent to break a fallen branch into pieces that he could carry.

Seth looked to his sword arm. His gauntlet had protected

his hand and wrist, but above that, his jerkin was burned. Blistered and red, the flesh beneath it had begun to ache.

"I can fight."

"I saw that." Lathan's features narrowed in confusion. "You saved me."

"Of course I did."

"I wasn't kind to you."

"No, you were not," Seth said, because it was true. He gathered his own logs.

"I was the opposite of kind."

"So you deserve to die?"

"No, but . . . I think I misjudged you, Seth."

Seth narrowed his eyes.

The Bishop had been right. He'd broken formation. He lacked the discipline of a true knight, but at the same time, he wouldn't let anyone die if he could prevent it.

"No, you didn't," Seth said. "I'd do it again, save you, but I am what they say, Lathan. I'm not the knight I should be."

"Maybe not," Lathan said. "And maybe that's not such a bad thing."

Seth followed him back up the hill, his burned arm chafing against the wood he carried. They arranged it into a long pile, placed Dion atop it.

The Bishop said the blessing and lit the pyre.

Pol stepped away, his eyes full of fear.

Seth's armor felt very heavy.

After, when the flames had cooled, when Dion was ash, they set a watch and settled down to sleep.

All were quiet, even Argos, who curled at Seth's side. Pol continued to shiver.

"Here." Seth took the dead knight's bedroll from his pack. He handed over his own blanket as well.

Pol blinked. "Don't you need it?"

"I will do without tonight. It can be part of my penance."

Pol took the blanket, clutched it in his hand, needing it but wary of charity. Seth's heart sank a little. The man clearly wasn't used to kindness.

That was easier to accept than the idea that he was afraid of Seth, though why shouldn't he be?

He'd tamped it down, banked it inside him, but still it burned. It whispered, telling him to light it all, to burn everyone, even Pol, away.

29
MOON

Raef lay curled in the dead man's bedroll, but found himself unable to sleep.

He wrapped a hand around the cuff on his wrist. The shadowknife slept now, but the thrum of it, constant through the battle, echoed in the bones of his arm. It had wanted out, to fight, and did not appreciate being denied.

Knowing only he could see, he risked a look.

The mark had grown. Soon it would be too large for the cuff to cover. The knights would see it then. Seth would see it.

Dawn came too soon.

Raef dragged himself into a sitting position, forcing his stiff body into motion. The knights didn't seem any better off. They packed their gear slowly and spoke their prayers with dim enthusiasm. They'd won. Most of them had survived, thanks to Seth, but the battle had cost them.

The knights tied two sticks together and stood Dion's scorched armor atop the cairn that held his ashes.

"Let his spirit rest in the god's light," the Bishop prayed. "Let his ashes rest in Rhea's arms."

"No shadow shall stand," the cadre responded as one.

Seth wasn't among them.

"What now?" Raef asked the Bishop.

"We push east, and retrieve our quarry as Hyperion wills. You will carry Dion's pack."

He opened his mouth to protest, but she cut him off with a glare.

"You have no gear, and clearly need his bedroll. He'd want you to make use of his supplies."

Raef nodded, and stretched, trying to work out the kinks in his shoulders. He followed the knights down the hill with sluggish steps, trying to grow comfortable with the new weight on his back.

On the ship he'd slept with Kinos, and the nightmares had retreated. Now they came in force.

The giant lingered behind his closed eyes, it and the dead faces along its body. The *Ino* sank and the tower fell. Fire raged in every scene, lurked in every corner.

Seth reappeared a while later with Argos at his side.

The long night had stripped away the knight's eager, upbeat nature.

Raef opened his mouth to say hello, but his stomach grumbled before he could greet the pair.

Seth laughed.

"You are always hungry. Turn around."

Raef obeyed and Seth sifted through the pack.

"Here," he said, passing Raef a bit of dried meat.

It tasted like salt and leather, but it eased the near constant gnawing in Raef's belly as Seth fell into walking beside him.

"How are you feeling, Pol?"

"It's not like I was hurt."

Raef didn't mention the dead knight or the cut on Seth's cheek. It had already faded to a dark pink.

"Still . . . What you saw." Seth ducked his head, his expression sheepish. "It was a lot."

Raef bit down on a smile. Here was the awkward man from the prince's ball.

"Why do you think the spirits here are like this?" Raef asked before biting off another chunk.

"I don't know." Seth glared at the ever-present vines. "Perhaps it has something to do with that."

And the demoness, Raef thought.

That little girl had eyed him with more intelligence than any shade he'd met, even more than Father Polus's ghost. She'd also screamed. The dead were silent.

He remembered a line from an old hymn that spoke of the silent paths of night, how they made no sound when Phoebe rowed them to the Ebon Sea.

Raef had to step carefully. He did not know how much common folk and pirates were supposed to know about the demons.

They were similar to the gods, immortal, but Raef felt he could understand the gods. They ruled over domains: night and day, earth and sea. They had families. The demons were wilder, ruling over emotions or impulses like greed or pride.

He could not help but wonder about Sati, about what she valued.

He couldn't understand what the priests of Phoebe had been thinking to summon them, let alone to breed them with people to make children. He needed to know why.

He hoped they'd limited themselves to the lesser demons. The worst of them, the highest, were associated with humanity's darkest impulses, like murder and rage, and they'd been powerful enough to war with and kill the gods.

The demon who'd attacked them had proven her guile.

She'd commanded an army, been smart enough to wear the knights down before she'd unleashed the giant upon them. Only Seth had saved them.

The vines thickened as they went east. They hadn't seen the last of her.

"Where are we going?" Raef asked Seth.

"We have a mission," Seth said.

"Can you tell me more about it?" Raef asked. "The Bishop said you're hunting someone to the east. Who is he?"

Seth shook his head. "I'm sorry, Pol. It's not my place. Ask the Bishop. She will tell you if she wants you to know."

"All right," Raef groused.

He wouldn't. He knew better than to risk it.

The spark of hope still danced in his chest.

They were going east, hiking toward cliffs, heading toward Kinos.

The knights paused at a fork in the dirt road, waiting for scouts to look ahead. A cracked, wooden statue marked the spot. It showed a pregnant woman, her hands fixed on her round belly. Raef could just make out her kind smile.

"Rhea," Seth said. "The Harvest Mother."

"I know who Rhea is."

"I would think a pirate would pray to Tethis. She's the goddess of the sea."

"I didn't say I prayed to Rhea. I said I knew who she was."

"So who do you pray to?"

He didn't sound judgmental, only curious. He wanted to know, probably so he could try to convince Raef to pray to Hyperion.

"I try not to." There he went, being honest again.

"Why not?"

"Because the answer is usually no."

Seth gave a thoughtful nod, but the warmth from their banter faded as they marched.

The other knights had marked the two as outsiders and kept their distance.

Raef knew he did not belong, but wondered what Seth had done to warrant it.

He'd fought bravely at the hill, saved them. He had more power than any of them. Seth had so much of it that he could burn himself. Perhaps he'd put the fear of the fire into the other knights.

Good, Raef thought. *Let them know how it feels.*

One of the scouts returned to the main column.

"There's a monastery ahead," she called.

"And the road?" the Bishop asked.

"It continues east, toward the coast."

"We go that way then," the Bishop said. She turned to Seth and nodded toward the other fork in the road. "Go find Lathan."

"You're sending him alone?" Raef asked.

"They have their hounds," the Bishop said. "And they have their faith."

"Can I go with him?" Raef asked.

She raised an eyebrow, and Raef did not like how long she considered him.

"Fine," she said.

Seth whistled for Argos. The pup ran toward them with so much energy that Raef thought he'd bowl them over.

"Calm, Argos," Seth gently chided.

The hound obeyed, content to playfully herd them down the road.

The vines grew thicker as they left the knights behind. The cloying scent of the flowers filled the air. Raef began to wonder if he'd ever taste anything else.

"I didn't think the Bishop would let me come with you," he said.

"Why not? You're not our prisoner."

"You tied me up," Raef reminded him, trying to rekindle their earlier camaraderie.

"I am sorry about that. It wasn't kind of me, but you did knock me down."

"I did."

"The Bishop is gentler than she seems. She is hard, but fair."

"She wasn't gentle or fair last night, striking you like that."

"Her anger was warranted. I broke formation. Yes, I saved Lathan, but I could have caused the line to fail. Everyone could have died because of me, including you."

"But they didn't, and she cut you. She put you in danger."

Seth pressed two fingers to his cheek. It had been little more than a scratch. But it had bled.

"A cadre is only as strong as its weakest member, Pol. And that is determined by how well they fall in line."

"Only you're not the weakest member. You saved them. You saved me."

Seth smiled and turned away.

"We should hurry," he said.

They walked faster, ducking beneath the vines, climbing their roots, being careful to avoid their thorns. Seth did not draw his sword or call his fire. Raef did not know if he was conserving it for the next battle or if he did not want to make Raef afraid of him.

Raef listened, scanned for movement—trying to find

anything amiss. Thiva's silence was helpful as he listened for the clack of sticks. He hoped, surprising himself, that they did not find Lathan dead.

The shades could hide in leaves and mud, which was most of Thiva.

Forcing the shadowsight, Raef examined the vines, and found what he expected. The shades lay curled inside, but they did not sleep. Their eyes followed him. The dead waited, biding their time until dark.

He stretched a hand toward the bark. The wood did not curl or snap toward him, but he could feel the hunger. Just a drop, just a scratch, and all would change.

"Pol," Seth called, waving for him to catch up.

Lathan stood ahead, staring at a mound of refuse. His hound prowled nearby, ears straight, but she wasn't aflame.

"What is it?" Seth asked.

Lathan pointed.

Dozens of mounds stretched across the hill.

"Bones," he said. "They're all just . . . bones."

Raef leaned closer.

There were rusted shovels, abandoned carts, some half-dug pits that overflowed with the forgotten dead. It was no way to treat corpses.

"I don't understand," Raef said. "Why aren't they buried? Why weren't they burned?"

"They've been here a long time," Lathan said. "Probably from before the Grief."

"We should get back to the cadre," Seth said. "The Bishop is ready to march."

"Targ," Lathan called his hound.

They walked back in silence, Argos trying to play with his elder, much to her annoyance. He and Seth were well-matched.

Raef could not miss how Seth looked to Lathan from the corner of his eye, seeking approval much like Argos did.

Looking away, Raef pondered the mounds of bones. Kinos would have tried to pray for them.

They rejoined the cadre, and Lathan reported what he'd found.

The Bishop said nothing, but her stern face looked troubled. With a wave she led them toward the monastery the other scout had found.

Little houses of piled stone huddled together like bee skeps. Fields and gardens, as overgrown as the rest of Thiva, ran out from them in rings. The vines did not intrude here, and the sight of other flowers should have eased the weight on Raef's shoulders.

"Rheites," the Bishop said.

It made sense that Thiva would venerate the Harvest Mother. The entire island was a breadbasket, green and full of fields. Her touch clearly lingered, even through whatever had claimed her people. It had to have been terrible. Rheites would not leave their dead in the air. They would follow their tenets and return the dead to her arms, to the soil—unless they'd been unable to.

The knights fanned out to search.

Seth tried a closed door.

"It's nailed shut," he called.

A crude X was painted on it in faded whitewash.

"That's the sign for plague," the Bishop said.

Seth staggered away from the door.

"That explains the bodies," Lathan said. "They were overwhelmed. It killed them too fast to keep up with the burials."

Raef could picture it, the living, drowning in the dead, weeping as they did what they could, sprinkling a handful of dust to appease the Harvest Mother. He imagined she wept too, grieving her children as she grieved any lost too young.

The Bishop cast a final, sad glance over the huts.

"Let's keep moving."

The ground grew rockier as they climbed higher. The sun reached its zenith, and the Bishop commanded they stop for prayers.

Raef closed and opened his fists, frustrated to see them waste this time.

Seth slipped away, but Raef could understand why. He was trying to master the fire, to stop another incident like the beach in Versinae, and it hurt him to do so. Raef had seen the red, angry skin where Seth's sleeve had burned away. He remembered Seth's bare skin smoldering when he performed his penance.

Raef finished sifting through the dead man's pack. He cast aside anything heavy, keeping the blanket, bedroll, the little bit of coin, and the rations. He'd need all of that if he found a way to escape with Kinos.

Seth jogged toward him. Raef tried to ignore the scent of fire.

"How's your arm?" he asked, nodding to the prior night's injuries.

"Better." Seth held it out for inspection.

The flesh was pink, but not raw or scabbed over. Seth may not be immune to the god's flames, but he didn't burn as another would.

"I'm glad." Raef meant it.

He was becoming what, friends, with a Knight of Hyperion?

He had to find Kinos. And he had to figure out how to handle the knights when they found him.

"Let's catch up." Raef hoisted the dead man's pack onto his shoulders. "We have to get there soon."

"Yes." Seth sounded worried.

Raef shot him a questioning glance.

"Our power comes from our faith," Seth whispered. "It is stronger when Hyperion is in the sky. I worry about doubt."

"Me too," Raef confided.

He also worried about the demon and what traps she might lay. The shadows grew as the sun began its downward slide and mist pooled in the valleys to the south.

He wasn't certain the knights could survive another onslaught, and he was ready to find Kinos and escape whatever was happening with him and Seth.

Raef hadn't trusted anyone for years, extending the minimum he could to Maurin and Eleni. Even then, he'd held back so much, had kept his secrets and not talked about his past. Then, Kinos had come along. Now he felt disarmed, naked to emotion and too trusting.

He had to focus on the demon. Unlike the gods, they were tied to emotions. If she was controlling the shades, and she seemed to be, then deciphering what they felt might tell him more about her.

He'd like to talk it through with Seth, but how could he do that without exposing what he was, how he knew things Pol the Pirate would not?

"The girl—what is she?" he asked. "She's not a ghost, at least not like the others I've seen."

"I think she's a demon," Seth whispered, as if naming what she was might call her forth.

"I thought the gods killed them all." Raef tried to sound surprised and hoped he wasn't overselling it.

"Most of them," Seth said. "You probably know why the knights were commanded to destroy Phoebe's Towers?"

"No."

"Her priests consorted with demons, and when the Inquisitors found proof—it left the knights without a choice."

"You sound sad about it."

"I am." Seth looked ahead, but whether to their destination or to where the moon would have arisen, Raef did not know.

"But yes, there are demons in the world still."

"Is that why the girl can control the ghosts?"

"I've never heard of it," Seth said. "But I don't know everything about them. They prey on people's emotions."

Right, Raef thought, feigning patience. *Put it together . . .*

"She must have some hold on them, some feeling to get them to obey her," Seth mused. "She'd have to promise them something. In the stories there's always a bargain, deal."

"Fear," Raef said. "These shades are willful, solid. She's keeping them from falling into Grief. That's the bargain they made when the plague came."

"You are very clever, Pol."

"I—I'm sorry," Raef said.

"Don't be. I like clever men."

Seth flushed, and they walked on.

Raef was soon winded. The weight of the pack did not help.

The vines here grew thicker than houses. They burst from the ground like arching bridges, leaving space enough for the cadre to pass beneath them.

Ahead stood a broken castle, its walls riven with cracks.

The vines flowed from there.

Behind them, in the twilight, the mist had thickened into a lake.

The scent of the flowers was a miasma, but blood and rot rode the air too.

"Our quarry lies within," the Bishop said.

She sounded so certain, but how did she know? An Oracle had sent them here, but why hadn't it warned her about Raef, the night child—the demon—in their midst?

"You will remain here, Pol."

Her bronze eyes were hard.

"What?"

"No."

"It will not be safe for you. You have no faith, no fire."

"I won't be any safer here," he said, gesturing at the mist below.

He could see faces in it. The shades were gathering.

The knights began to shed their packs and gear, keeping only their swords and shields.

"Argos will guard you."

"No!" Raef said. "I won't let you leave me behind!"

"Tie him to a tree, Seth."

"Yes, Bishop."

Seth crouched to take a length of rope from his pack.

The other knights started marching toward the castle, leaving Seth behind despite his power. Raef almost felt as though they deserved what they were about to face.

"Don't do this. Please, Seth."

"I have to. I'm sorry."

He put a hand to Raef's chest and nudged him until his back met bark.

"Why?"

"You'll be safer here." Seth wound the rope around Raef's chest. "I would not see you come to harm."

"You're not like the others." Raef squirmed but found no slack as Seth knelt to pet Argos. "You don't have to be like them."

"But I want to. They're what I strive to be."

"Why risk yourself for them? They treat you like shit."

"The others have a right to be wary of me."

"You keep saying that." Raef heard his own desperation. "But why, because of your flames?"

"No."

Seth stepped closer.

Raef could see the spark of fire in his eyes and feel the heat of what ran beneath his skin, but didn't flinch. Seth would not hurt him. Raef knew that. Even this, tying him up, was a misguided attempt at protecting him.

"Because you're right, Pol. I'm not like them. I grew up somewhere else."

"A monastery," Raef said. "You told me."

"No." Seth shook his head. He looked so sad. He trembled. Afraid. "Before that."

"What could be so bad that they'd treat you like they do?"

"If I tell you, you won't want to be friends with me. You won't want to know me at all."

He sounded so young, and Raef wondered if he'd ever had a friend, had ever been close to anyone in his life.

"That won't happen. I promise."

And he meant it. Lady Moon, he meant it.

Seth chewed his lip, took a breath, and said, "I was raised in the tower, Phoebe's Tower, in Dodona."

"You were a neophyte?" Raef asked. "An orphan?"

He almost couldn't get the questions out.

Seth folded in on himself. Despite his broad shoulders and greater height, he seemed smaller than Raef in that moment.

"No. They made me, and others like me, from the demons. I'm impure. That's why I burn. An Inquisitor found me, took me away. He brought me to the Hierarch as proof of what Phoebe's priests had done."

"They didn't burn you?"

"The Hierarch showed me mercy." Seth looked to the gathering mist and the sprawling vines. "Until now, until he sent me here."

"Do the knights know?"

"Yes. It's why they act as they do toward me. I'll understand if, well, if you do too."

Raef's world tilted as Seth turned and ran away. Raef might have fallen over had the ropes not bound him upright.

Oh, Mother Moon, he thought. *Oh, Phoebe. He's like me.*

30
MOON

Shouts and the sound of battle reached Raef at his tree. Argos whined to hear the howl of a fellow hound. The demon had sprung her trap.

"Idiots," he muttered.

He pushed himself up on his toes, wriggled, but found no give in his bonds. Argos growled as Raef strained against the ropes.

"I'm just trying to help." Raef grimaced as he pushed again. "I don't want him to die."

Seth was like him.

The knights had twisted him, made him hate himself, but that didn't mean he deserved what he'd find in the castle. The Bishop knew. They all knew. A demon waited for them, but they'd marched in anyway.

"Idiots!" Raef repeated.

Kinos was in there. If the knights failed to capture him, if they all died, what chance did Raef have?

"You could help you know," Raef told Argos. "Don't you want your master to survive?"

Argos stopped growling and sat back as if to consider the suggestion.

Seth's knots wouldn't give, so Raef would have to.

He tried to use the force of the ropes to pop his arm from the socket. He jumped, yanked, pushed until he saw red, but he could not bring enough force to bear.

"I'm not strong enough. Please, Argos."

Argos leaped, jaws open. Raef let out a yelp, but sagged forward as the hound sank back. He kept his eyes on the hound as he shrugged off the severed rope. Argos had bitten through it.

"Thank you."

Argos let out a little yip.

"We're friends, right?" Raef asked.

Argos yipped again.

The keep was ancient and crumbling, a round tower with a great crack that split its side. It rose behind a square outer wall marked by a gatehouse.

The smell of burning wood washed over Raef. He took his knives from Seth's discarded pack.

"Let's go find them," he told Argos.

The hound yipped and followed when Raef started walking.

"Never thought I'd be happy to have a Hound of Hyperion at my back," he admitted.

The cadre had made it inside the outer wall, leaving the gatehouse doors open behind them. Raef passed inside, intending to cross into the courtyard, but paused to see the thorny vines carpeting the walls and ceiling of the gatehouse. They writhed, twisting like a veil of serpents. The flowers blinked open and shut like watching eyes.

One of the knights lay strangled in the vines, impaled on the thorns. They curled around her, obscuring her face.

Argos growled as Raef moved closer.

The shadowsight showed him the spirits in the wriggling green. The thorns had pierced her, found the exposed skin and joints in her armor. They'd soon suck her dry.

She coughed, startling him. She wasn't dead.

Raef took a long breath, drew a knife, and started cutting her free.

"Thank . . . you," she sputtered, her breath heaving.

"You're bleeding. Can you call your fire? It will close the wounds."

She choked on whatever answer she'd meant to give but nodded.

Raef found her sword and pressed it into her hands.

"Stay with her, Argos." He didn't expect the hound to obey him any better than it would its master, but the knight was clearly stunned. "Burn anything that gets near her."

The doors to the courtyard stood open, charred and smoldering. At least there were no more bodies, but there was a new smell of meaty rot, like a compost heap mixed with a butcher's leavings.

Thorns and flowers coated the inner walls and much of the ground. The hulking, stitched shades were everywhere, floating in and out of the smoke that filled the space.

A hound howled in pain and fell silent.

The shades had broken the knights' formation. Many of them lay sprawled, unmoving as vines crept to ensnare them.

A flash of fire led Raef to Lathan. He crouched with two others behind some derelict carts and debris. A pair of the stitched-together shades came at them. The fire cut them down and drove them back, but Raef could see that the knights were weakening.

"Where's Seth?" Raef shouted.

"Ahead with the Bishop."

The doors to the cracked keep had rotted off their hinges. Its dark maw looked like the only path. The building was nearly as much branch and thorn as stone.

"You've got to get out of here," Raef shouted as another pair of shades emerged from the keep. "There's too many of them."

"Not without the others," Lathan called, standing to cleave another spirit as it drifted toward the trio.

They wouldn't last long if they didn't run. Raef had to find the Bishop, get Kinos and Seth, then get her to order a retreat. Raef clenched his jaw and ran toward the keep's doors.

He'd almost reached them when one of the giant shades stepped into the doorway, blocking his passage. It raised a fist and tendrils snaked free, aiming for him. Raef drew the shadowknife, ready to test it against the thing, knowing he'd never be quick enough to keep it from catching him.

A ball of fire struck the giant's chest, knocking it back. At first Raef thought Lathan had thrown a spell, but the flames uncurled and growled. Argos snarled as he clawed and bit his way through the shade's heart.

The hound leaped free as the spirit fell, breaking apart as it struck the ground.

"Good boy," Raef said, breath heaving more from panic than exertion. When he looked back, he saw that the knight he'd saved had joined Lathan's group. "Let's go find your master."

The entrance opened into a round space, the keep's base.

Raef walked the bottom of a wide, dry well. The floors above had collapsed, broken by the vines. Blades of sunlight filtered through the opened roof, lighting on piles of debris and ruined furniture.

He tried to stay hidden, though he doubted his success with Argos glowing as he followed. The hound's flames were near enough to almost singe the hair on the back of his neck.

He exited the passage and saw a body, a peasant hanging, impaled on the thorns.

The man took a slow breath, his skin so colorless that Raef nearly mistook him for a shade. Raef stumbled inside and found the rest of them, countless people impaled at every angle, ringing the well from base to splintered roof.

Red petals drifted downward. They carpeted the ground.

The latest victims hung closer to the ground. The knights. The Bishop. Seth. The vines pulsed, drinking deep. Their captives did not stir.

Raef froze when he found Kinos.

He hung on the thorns, pale and still as a marble ship's prow.

One of the thorns had pierced through his shoulder. Another, his side.

The spirit girl stepped out from behind an empty throne. Raef's guts twisted at the sight of her blood-filled eyes. Her face had healed. It seemed they all healed quickly, even half-breeds like Raef and Seth.

"It's the perfect solution, cousin," she said.

"Killing them slowly?"

Keeping their distance, eyes locked, they circled each other.

"They make blood. The shades feed and thrive. The rimmon tree keeps them alive."

"You call that living?" Raef nodded to the shriveled bodies.

"That was the bargain they made with me. The price they paid. You should have seen them weep when they killed their own, offering them to me in sacrifice, but it was the only way to survive when the servants of Hyperion came."

"What are you talking about?" Raef gauged the distance between them. The shadowknife would likely stop her. It certainly wanted to. It thrummed, his second heartbeat. "Thiva's tower still stands."

"Yes, it does. The island's prince would not allow them to raze it. He brought an army against the knights, sent the peasants, but even the Knights of Hyperion wouldn't murder them, and so the Inquisitors came, creeping like spiders among the people. Oh, and the poison they brought . . ."

"You sound impressed."

"I was. They died so fast, too quick to be buried."

"But not you." Raef inched closer.

She was almost in reach. He could leap, tackle her, and drive the shadowknife into her heart.

"You're something else, aren't you? You're the thing that crawled out of the Moon's Door."

The vines curled nearer, the thorns dripping with dark sap. Raef had to keep her talking.

"No, little cousin. I was invited. The fools summoned me. Then the plague took them too. The survivors were happy to accept my offer. Their fear of death is all I need to walk this world."

Kinos twitched. He shook, like he might wake. The vines curled closer, tightening their grip on him.

"They're dreaming," Raef said.

"Their nightmares feed me. Their blood sustains their spirits. Now the servants of Hyperion will feed us too, and here we'll all remain."

Shades crowded through the door. Shuffling forward, trailing vines like chains, they carried the bodies of Lathan and the other knights. Raef heard the squelch as they pressed the knights into the vines. Lathan screamed as the thorns pierced him. Then he fell quickly silent.

"It can't last forever. Someone will come to stop you."

"Who?" She stopped circling and opened her hand. A red flower bloomed on her palm. "Who's left in all this dying world to care about me?"

"Maybe I care," he suggested. "You called me cousin."

"Because you are another child of the Sunken Garden, even if you are a mutt."

"A demon," Raef said.

She hissed. "That is their word for us, their lie."

"What would you call us, then?" Raef could charge her. He was close enough to make it, but he needed to know. He may never get this chance again.

"We were gods before they came, before they killed the greatest of us." She spun, her face lifted to the sky. The blood in her eyes overflowed and ran like tears. Her skin rippled, some other form threatening to surface. "This was our world."

"Why did the priests summon you? What did they want?"

"To make you," she said. "To make those like you."

"But why?" Raef asked.

"You don't know," she teased. Her skin browned, rippling like the rough bark of the vines. She laughed. "You don't know what's coming, do you? You don't know who is coming."

He could stall no longer.

Raef tensed to leap, but the vines exploded from the earth beneath her, pushing her skyward, beyond his reach. Riding a mass of roots like a great skirt of thorny tentacles, she loomed above him.

She wasn't a girl. She was the tree.

Argos whimpered as the vines and thorns caged him. The hound sparked as he tried to call his fire, but he was too young. He'd used up his flames to save Raef. The thorns pierced him, and he fell silent.

The shades pressed in behind Raef, closing off the tower's entrance.

"What shall I do with you, cousin?" she asked, her voice

something else now, a terrible choir of all those she'd ensnared. "Shall I make you a bargain?"

He was surrounded. Even with the shadowknife, he would not be able to fight free, and he'd never leave Kinos and Seth behind.

"What do you want?"

"Serve me. Carry my seeds beyond Thiva's shores, and I will let you have one of your mortals. I'll let him live and you can sate your own hunger with him, whatever it is you crave."

She gestured, pointing a long, thorny finger at Kinos.

"Not that he has much blood left. He came to me half-drowned. He won't last long. But they both dream of you, and oh, the things they dream. Pick one."

"And the other?"

"He stays with me, forever, to ensure your loyalty. It is a generous bargain."

Raef pretended to consider her offer. He pretended to be torn.

"All right," he said. He pointed to Seth. "That one."

"Interesting," she purred.

The thorns withdrew like sheathing blades. Raef rushed, catching Seth as he fell.

"Pol . . ." Seth whispered.

"It's Raef, actually. My name is Raef."

"You—you lied to me."

An ember glowed in Seth's golden eyes.

"You heard?" Raef asked.

"Yes."

"That's right, I lied to you. I'm a demon." Raef struggled to say it aloud. "Just like her."

"Like me."

Raef wanted nothing more than to tighten his grip, to pull

Seth to him, and say he wasn't alone now, that they weren't alone now, but he couldn't. Something inside him cracked to say what he had to, to do what he had to do now.

"So what are you going to do about it?" Raef asked. "You have to burn me, don't you? I lied to you. I betrayed you."

Seth grew warm in Raef's arms.

"I know—" Seth choked. "I know what you're trying to do."

"Then you also know why," Raef said, voice low, cracking. "You have to let it out."

"Oh, sweet nothings," the demoness sang. "Is that what you feed on, cousin?"

"No." He looked up at her. "It's curiosity."

Father Polus had always called him mind-hungry, and he'd never been happier or more content than in the library, reading while others read, copying texts while others copied.

"Boring, but we're all the god of something."

"I'm no god." Raef helped Seth to his feet. "We made a deal. Where are these seeds?"

She grinned and rose higher. Stretching out her spindly arms, she began weaving her palms together.

"The people—" Seth whispered. "It will kill them."

"You can control it. I know you can."

"Please don't make me do this."

"I'm sorry," Raef whispered. "But you have to. It's the only way any of them are getting out of here with us."

"I can't."

"You can. You, we, are so much more than you think. You're good, Seth, a good man. You won't hurt those who don't deserve it."

"Argos?" Seth asked.

"She has him," Raef said, looking to where the hound lay impaled on the thorns.

"It's time, cousin," the demon said. "Are you ready to carry me beyond these shores?"

In her palm she held three pits, like the stones of plums. They were the same color as her eyes.

Seth choked once. It might have been a sob or a gulp of air.

"Get behind me," he said.

31
SUN

The fire came unbidden. Fed by the truth about Pol, by Seth's own pain, it poured from him.

He wasn't alone. He wasn't the only one left, but what that meant . . . just trying to comprehend it cracked his heart open and fire poured out.

The flames filled his vision. The demon screamed. She ranted, but Seth didn't hear it.

The roar filled his ears. Glorious and golden, its light filled his eyes. Seth grappled with it, forced it to his will, to spare the lives of those entrapped and burn only the wood, the tree, and the thorns. It burned him as well.

The flames snarled, crackled, and lashed at him, but he would not give it its freedom.

Only the wood, he willed, pushing and pushing the flames higher, further.

Someone was shouting his name, but it sounded so far away. Seth couldn't really hear it. Not this time.

The burning went on and on. It was like trying to weave a

tapestry at lightning speed. His mind ached, but somehow he kept up. He kept the flames leashed. Like a score of hounds, they pulled, were almost beyond him, outracing his control.

Someone struck him.

The Bishop. His helmet rang like a bell. The fire cleared from his sight. Everything smelled of burning wood and sizzling blood.

Ash fell like snow, hot and cold by turns, as the tree and the spirits inside it burned.

Seth came back to his body, to awareness, full of aches, bloody where the thorns had pierced him.

On the dais, Pol squared off with the demon.

Raef. He said his name was Raef. He'd survived. The Bishop had survived. Seth took a heaving breath. He'd mastered the flames. He needed to get to Raef, to help, but his strength was spent.

Raef held a knife, a sliver of perfect blackness that Seth knew had come from Phoebe, from the darkness they shared in their corrupted blood.

Seth wasn't alone. Raef was like him, had hidden right beneath his nose.

His broken heart sank in his chest. Of course he'd find someone who intrigued him and of course he'd be Phoebe's. Seth could never escape where he'd come from.

He forced himself to straighten, to stand, but the Bishop put a hand to his shoulder.

Raef and the demon circled, taunting each other. He'd lunge. She'd sidestep. Seth inhaled, trying to find a little more fire, but he felt empty, bloodless in a way that even the carnivorous plant had not engendered.

"You could have lived," she snarled, casting about for cover, but all the furniture and the vines were gone. Only ash and the comatose Thivans remained of her kingdom.

She no longer resembled a child. Her true form was a monstrous woman made of the bound vines and red flowers. Blood ran in streams from her eyes.

"They're not yours to feed upon," Raef said.

"They are insects!" she said.

It was her turn to lunge, her arm extended, her fingers spiny thorns meant to pierce Raef's chest.

He was quick. He dodged her strike and drove his black knife into her side as she swept past him.

She hissed and whirled, her other arm lashing out, coiling like a barbed whip around his throat. Raef choked, bloodying his hands as he tried to break her hold. She grinned, red eyes narrowing, her teeth a row of thorns.

Seth put aside his aches.

"Father, guide my hand," he prayed.

Seth lifted his palm and summoned flame. It lanced out, slicing through the vines strangling Raef.

The demon screamed. The blood sap oozed from her severed arm. It rewound, strips of vine reforming into a hand.

It took her long enough that Raef tore himself free. He charged her again.

The black knife emerged from his hand. It was part of him.

He drove it into the demon's heart.

She screamed as blackness spread from her center. Chest heaving, Raef watched her fall, his dark eyes narrowed, as veins of shadow spread from the wound.

Raef stepped to her as she struck the ground. He crouched to meet her darkening eyes.

"I'm sorry, cousin, but I can't let you hurt anyone else."

"They'll turn on you," she rasped, gaze dropping to Seth, to where their quarry lay weak and coughing. "They know what you are now."

"I don't care," Raef said.

Seth knew now that Raef was a liar. He was a good one, but not when it came to this. He did care, at the deepest level.

The demon saw it too.

She laughed, a rasping, creaking sound.

Raef lifted his fist, called the knife again, and plunged it into her heart a second time.

She burned away, as if the darkness were a different kind of fire.

Seth felt cold. The flames lay spent and sated within him, and the only arms he could imagine warming him belonged to another of his ilk. He didn't even have the strength to shudder.

Raef's neck was collared in blood. His hands, too, were painted with it, but he was in no danger. Seth had burned away the shades. Only ash-like snow remained.

"You've got it all wrong, you know," Raef said, looking to him. "We're not evil. You're not evil, just because we're born from them. We have a choice."

He nodded back to the black-and-red stain that had been the demoness.

"You don't know me," Seth said.

Raef laughed, perhaps a little madly.

"Sure I do. Who else could?"

"You don't know what I've done. That beach—those people."

"I was there, Seth, and at the ball too. That was me in the mask. It was me you asked for a dance."

Seth swayed, ready to fall to the ground again.

"I went to get him." Raef nodded to their quarry. He did not look well. "I stole him. I'm the one who opened the box."

"Why are you telling me this?"

"You know what I am now. What's the point of hiding? I

can't leave him. If you take him, I'll follow. If you kill me, I'll haunt you."

It hurt, the intensity he showed for their quarry, the feeling in his eyes and words. Hyperion, damn it—it hurt when it shouldn't have.

"We're made from demons," Seth whispered.

Raef held up his arm, tore off the leather cuff he wore, and showed Seth the mark there. At first Seth thought it was a tattoo or a bruise, but he could see it was a series of black moons, their crescents woven together in interlocking rings.

"Maybe," Raef said. "I don't know why they made us, but we decide who we are and what we become."

Seth shook his head.

"I don't think that's true. I don't think it can be."

A shuffle and clink of metal brought Seth around. The cadre had gathered, limping together, trying to assess their wounds.

Raef knelt by their quarry, his face full of concern.

"Kinos—Keen?"

The man opened his eyes.

"Raef?" he asked.

"Yeah," he said, smiling. "Found you."

Kinos looked around them. His eyes settled on the knights.

"No," he said. "It wasn't supposed to go like this."

"It's all right." Raef gathered the slighter man into his arms. He turned to the Bishop with a fierce, protective expression that twisted Seth's insides.

"What happens now?" Raef asked her.

"We do as we were ordered," she said. "We take you, both of you, to the Hierarch."

"Will you resist?" Seth asked.

Raef scoffed. "Like I could. But no, I won't fight you, not if you make sure he's all right."

More shapes shuffled into view. The Thivans, those who'd survived the vines. Seth wiped his eyes.

He'd done it. He'd mastered the flames, and yet in the moment he could find no joy or solace.

Nine of the cadre remained. Two more had fallen here.

"We should not let him live," Lathan said, nodding toward Raef. "He's like her."

"He saved me," one of the scouts, Sera, said. "Whatever he is. He saved my life."

"We will take them to the Hierarch," the Bishop commanded. "Alive."

Seth crouched to check Argos's injuries. The holes in his flesh had already knit.

"Thank you, Father," Seth prayed tiredly.

The other knights moved tenderly. The sap remained in their veins, slowing their movements as they shuffled outside. Across the island, the vines had gone, burned away with the demon. The red flowers remained. They melted all around them, rotting to a sticky liquid.

"We'll march back to the ship," the Bishop said, looking over the survivors.

"What about them?" Seth asked, nodding to the Thivans.

They cowered together, so thin they looked like skeletons.

"May Hyperion forgive their choices," the Bishop said.

Choices.

We decide what we become, Raef had said.

Yes, they'd trusted a demon, but so had he. Seth had listened to Raef in those moments, and Raef had believed in him, believed he could control the flames. And he had. Seth had mastered them.

"This is their island. We will leave it to them," the Bishop declared. She turned to the knights. "Prepare to depart."

"Kinos is too weak," Raef called from where he half-carried their quarry from the keep.

The Bishop narrowed her eyes and knelt to make certain he was not lying.

"Carry him, Seth," she said. "We'll make a stretcher when we reach the packs."

"Yes, Bishop."

Seth opened his arms.

Raef swallowed.

"I will not harm him, I swear."

Raef nodded.

Seth lifted Kinos gently. He was not heavy. The vines had fed deeply from his veins, leaving him thin, though he looked far less sickly than the surviving Thivans.

"I hope you return to health," Seth told them. "I will pray for you. Beg the gods' forgiveness, and perhaps you may have it."

Some of them nodded, but none of them spoke. He did not know if it was weakness or shame that drove their silence.

Raef followed closely as Seth stumbled under the addition of Kinos's weight.

Seth wanted to ask what they were to each other, but it was obvious how Raef's feelings ran. The fire stirred at the thought.

"Do not try anything," Seth said to Raef.

"I won't," he answered. "Just be careful with him. Please."

"You used us to find him."

"Yes," Raef said. "It was the only way to safely reach him."

"Why were you really in the tower?" Seth whispered, low enough that no one else would hear.

"I wanted answers about myself, about him. Why was he in that box?"

"I don't know. We are not to question our orders."

"It was the Hierarch who sent you here?"

"His Oracle. He sent me to guard the box."

"I am sorry for lying to you."

"What did you find?" he asked, unable to hold the question in. "In the tower?"

Raef's eyes darted from side to side, ensuring they were not overheard.

"I found out who my parents are. There are ledgers in the undercroft."

Seth stiffened and nearly dropped his sleeping cargo.

"You found your parents?" he asked.

"My father is human, but my mother . . . well, all I know is that she was like her."

Raef nodded back toward the clifftop and the broken castle.

"I don't know who my parents are," Seth said. "I don't know if they're even still alive."

"I'm sorry," Raef said. "I truly understand."

Seth let out a breath.

Raef seemed sincere, but how could Seth ever know? He had no guile and so he could not see it in others. Raef could have been an Inquisitor. He was that good of a liar, but suspicion was too heavy for Seth's heart to carry. He decided to believe that he'd gotten a glimpse of the real Pol, the real Raef.

"Thank you," he said.

Raef was, well, a lot of things, but he felt something like a friend. Yes, he was angry and ashamed that he'd been lied to and fallen for it, but Hyperion forgive him, he wasn't alone anymore. He had a friend.

PART FOUR

A LIGHT IN THE EAST

❧

*This world was old
when the gods arrived.*

—GRAFFITI CARVED INTO A
MARBLE SLAB ON EASTLIGHT

32

MOON

The ship, smaller than the *Ino*, rocked back and forth, riding the waves rather than slicing them. A window, far too small to escape through, freshened the little cabin's air. A prism set in the ceiling cast a gleam of emerald light.

Raef sat, his back to the wall, with Kinos sprawled across his lap.

Kinos hadn't awoken again, but his breathing remained steady.

They had sea bread, a pitcher of fresh water, and a pallet of hay with enough blankets to keep them warm.

Despite the knights' kindness, Raef held no expectations about the hospitality they'd find when they reached the Hierarch.

"I don't know how we're going to get out of this one, Keen," Raef whispered.

He laid his hand atop Kinos's, afraid to do more, afraid to cause any more pain.

The thorns had pierced him all over, leaving holes and

bruises. Raef didn't have to ask if Kinos was like him or Seth. He wasn't healing quickly.

The knights were groggy, but the demon had held Kinos longer. He'd remained unconscious through it all, boarding the ship, a priest's ministrations, and sailing away from Thiva.

"At least they're taking you toward home," Raef said, bending to lay a gentle kiss atop his head. "We're sailing east, not back toward Aegea."

Kinos groaned, stirred, and opened his eyes to a crack, like even that bit of light might hurt them.

"You're awake?"

"Wish I wasn't," Kinos croaked. "Everything hurts."

Raef rushed to pour him a bowl of water and hold it to his lips.

"What happened to you?"

"The ship was sinking." Kinos sipped, then gulped. He fixed worried eyes on Raef's. "I couldn't find you."

"It's all right." Raef carefully combed his fingers through Kinos's hair. "I found you."

"How?"

"Drink some more and I'll tell you."

Raef spilled out everything he should have from the start and everything he'd learned since, that Cormac was his father, that his mother was a demon. He left no secret unexposed.

"That's—a lot," Kinos said when Raef was done.

He looked better, a little color had returned to his face.

"Why tell me now?"

"There's no point in hiding anymore. And you deserve to know."

Kinos shifted until he sat beside Raef, their backs pressed against the wall. He set the bowl aside and took Raef's hand in his.

"It will be all right," he said, leaning to prop himself against Raef.

"How do you know?"

"It has to be," Kinos said.

Raef felt the rocking of the boat, so much slower than the racing of his heart.

"They're taking us to the Hierarch."

"You could have run, back on Thiva," Kinos said.

"No, I couldn't have."

Kinos reached, turned Raef's face to his, and kissed him.

"You taste terrible," Raef said.

"Jerk."

Raef laughed and kissed him back.

"Whatever happens," Kinos said as he pressed close, his green eyes intense, "we're together, right?"

"Together," Raef agreed. "You really don't care—about what I am?"

"I meant what I said. You're not what I expected, but I'm not sad it's you I feel this way about."

They sat huddled together, until the ship shuddered, rippling as her anchor dropped.

"We're here," Raef said.

Unnecessary, he knew, but he hadn't known what else to say.

It was about to end, that they'd come here, where they'd meant to go, only for Raef to die, only for Kinos to return to the box, or worse.

The door to their little cell opened. Lathan and a knight Raef did not know stood on the other side.

"Out," Lathan barked.

Raef and Kinos did not argue. They marched ahead as the knights followed them onto the deck.

An island, rocky and desolate, stretched out before them.

Raef could see the olive trees that Kinos had mentioned. The ruins outnumbered them by far. Tumbled columns of marble and half-collapsed walls of sandy stone filled his view. A murmuration of birds, like a cone, danced above a hill, winding and unwinding in a slow, beautiful dance.

The ship had anchored in a bay. The island's arms curled around it like a crescent, much like Versinae hugged the water.

"This is Eastlight?" Raef asked.

Lathan tied their hands in front of them. He gave the ropes a little tug but did not make Raef's knots painful.

"Yes," Kinos said.

"Which one is yours?" Raef asked, nodding to the whitewashed houses of the little town.

"None of these. I grew up on the other side of the island. Look, Raef, I need to—"

"March," Lathan said, nudging them toward the gangplank.

They obeyed. Raef wanted to look behind them, to see if Seth was among their escort, but he couldn't bring himself to face the knight.

Whatever connection they'd made wouldn't be enough to save them now. Seth had said the Hierarch had spared him. Raef wouldn't tie Seth's destruction to his own.

Several armored figures in red capes waited on the dock. The Knights Elite. The Hierarch had arrived before them.

Raef seethed. It was broad daylight. He couldn't call the shadowknife. His hands were bound, and even if he could engineer an escape, Kinos could barely walk, his strength too sapped from his ordeal.

This was the end. Raef had thought he'd shake or cry, but all he felt was a strange emptiness—like this was how it was always going to be. At least he'd saved Kinos from the box, even if it was just for a while.

The Knights Elite formed a circle around the two of them. They left Lathan and his companion behind.

There had to be a way out.

There was always a way out.

The townsfolk watched from behind the glassless windows of their little houses.

Raef itched to go and see the massive, fallen statues half-buried in the sandy soil. He doubted the Knights Elite would appreciate it, so he marched along the road of cracked and ancient cobbles, taking in everything he could.

Birds called between the scraggly trees. He choked when he inhaled a swarm of gnats. A lynx stalked among the stones and weeds.

Raef kept quiet through it all. This place demanded it. Even if it hadn't, he wouldn't know what to say.

The shadowknife lay still, sleeping in the bright light. Perhaps it was certain of his fate.

Perhaps there would be mercy for Kinos.

Lady. If you hear me, save him, please.

The moon did not answer him, but Raef felt certain something lingered here, some touch of the gods. Whatever Eastlight was, it was important, holy.

In another time he could have spent his life here, trying to discern the island's secrets.

The ruins ahead stood a little taller, a little more intact. They'd reached Eastlight's heart.

"The Columns?" Raef asked Kinos.

"No talking," one of the Knights Elite barked.

Kinos gave a little nod. He looked pale, stricken. Raef couldn't take his hand, but he nudged Kinos with his shoulder.

"Together," he whispered. "No matter what."

"Together," Kinos whispered.

"No talking!" the knight barked again.

The temple was built from a dark stone Raef did not know the name of. It must have been massive, though only one building remained among the piles of rubble.

Any friezes or depictions of the gods honored here had been worn away, but Raef could feel it. She'd walked here. This place was hers, as much as Versinae was hers. He had no doubt that were he to pray, he'd hear the whispers of the gods. He knew he'd never get the chance.

A massive, robed statue stood at the center of the columns. She had no face, no features. The shape was not the same as the ones in the towers, but Raef knew her. Despite everything, the terror, the march toward whatever the Hierarch would do to them, despite the temple's missing roof and the sunlight reaching where it should never touch, Raef knew her.

Behind the statue stood the thing he'd meant to find, a black mirror, the door, like the ones in Versinae and Thiva, but undamaged. It could open. If he could just reach it, drive the shadowknife into it, maybe she'd return.

It was too soon, he knew. The Day of the Black Sun remained far away. He realized he'd been counting down to it, night by night. The old rhythms and calendars remained engraved on his memory. They'd outlived the priests who'd taught them to him.

They turned the corner, passing the temple into what must have been the courtyard at the center of the buildings.

The Hierarch waited for them.

The head of Hyperion's faithful sat on a padded chair, surrounded by more Knights Elite. He wasn't that old. Older than Cormac, surely, but he showed no sign of frailty. He wore his golden armor like he'd come here to do battle, which was laughable. Raef was bound, unarmed, and utterly defeated. He wouldn't try to escape as long as they had Kinos, and Kinos was in no shape to fight.

The Hierarch had won, and he knew it. They all knew

it, but if Raef had to guess, something else floated in his eyes. Relief, or perhaps fear.

Their escort filed in around them, filling the space among the ruins.

Seth stood beside the Bishop, slumped inside his armor.

One of the Knights Elite put a mailed hand to Raef's shoulder, forced him to his knees, and held him there.

Still standing, Kinos shook.

Raef tried to give him an assuring look, even as several of the Knights Elite carried a familiar box into the courtyard.

All was not lost. Not yet. There was always a way out.

"Nephew," the Hierarch said, his face full of victory. "Did you find the key?"

Raef blinked. He was talking to—

"Kinos?" he asked.

Kinos paled.

"Yes, Your Holiness. I found it."

"Kinos?"

Kinos took a step forward. He put himself between Raef and the Hierarch.

"It is in a mark on his wrist, but I beg you, do not hurt him. He is not what you think." Kinos looked over the faithful, the knights, and the Bishop. "What we think."

He didn't look at Raef, but tears shone in his eyes.

The Hierarch rose, stepped forward, and lifted Kinos's chin with a hand. He stared him in the eye, seeking something.

"Did you play your game too well?" he asked. "Actually fall for this creature?"

"Raef isn't evil. He can come to the light."

The Hierarch burned through the ropes binding Kinos's hands with a touch.

Something red and raging bubbled in Raef's gut. The little

spark of hope, the flame, went out as something inside his chest shattered.

"Why?" he asked.

"Because Phoebe must not return," the Hierarch said. "If she does, she will bring the worst of the demons with her."

"You're lying," Raef said. "She wouldn't do that."

"Oracles do not lie," the Hierarch spat. "Hyperion does not lie!"

He stomped past Kinos to strike Raef across the face.

Raef fell to the dirt, tasting blood. His tooth had cut the inside of his cheek. At least it was daytime. Not that the Grief mattered now, not that any of it would ever matter again. He'd had a hope, a tiny sliver, and now he had none.

The horror on Seth's face was obvious. The Bishop was not so easy to read, but Raef thought he saw disgust in the lines around her eyes.

Raef shook his head and wished he hadn't. It still rang from the backhand.

"Smash that," the Hierarch said, gesturing to the obsidian door. "Make sure he sees."

"No!" Raef screamed.

"Don't worry, boy," the Hierarch said. "It won't hurt for long. I think you're almost ready."

Raef thrashed in the knights' grip as they lifted him and forced him to watch as two of the Knights Elite destroyed the Moon's Door.

He couldn't sob. He couldn't weep. Everything within him had just stopped, like it had died.

"This is the end of Night," the Hierarch said, leaning over him. "The final end. No vestige, no echo, shall remain."

Raef stopped fighting. He could not look at Kinos, at Seth. He could not look anywhere.

He'd been a fool. He wanted to retch, to sob, but could only stare at the ground and feel the tears stream down his face. There was no way out. There was no one for him. If some trace of Phoebe had remained, surely they'd removed it now.

The Hierarch gestured to the box. "We brought it for you, for the bearer of the key."

"I thought you'd burn me."

"I would, but the Oracle was quite specific. You had to be lured. You had to be broken. The box will only take the willing. This way you can sleep, safe forever, and the door will never open."

"Uncle—" Kinos stepped forward, but the Hierarch warned him back into place with a glare.

He looked like he'd been the one to be slapped, to have his heart ripped from him.

Raef might have spat a curse in his direction, but he couldn't even summon hatred. He ran his eyes over the box. Maybe that was for the best. He could just lie down, go into the dark, and forget all the treachery and disappointment. If he was very lucky, he wouldn't even dream.

His gaze locked on the worn, faceless statue. Maybe, just maybe, he'd be with her.

In that moment, it became apparent. He'd lost her. He'd lost Kinos. He'd never had Kinos. He'd just . . . lost.

"That's it then? I'll sleep?"

"Yes," the Hierarch said, almost gently. "We will take you to Drowned Gate and you'll sleep forever in its depths. It's a kinder fate than what we've given most of your kind."

Most, but not all. They'd spared Seth, let him become a knight, even if he hated himself for what he was.

"Why?" Raef asked. It was the only question left.

"She has touched you, and if I burn you she might find another before that cursed day."

He'd been right. The Day of the Black Sun was part of it. The Moon's Door and the shadowknife were part of it, but they did not matter now. Nothing mattered now.

Raef could see it, looking back over the months since he'd opened the box. Kinos had been a trap meant just for him. Curiosity had led him to open the box, to steal Kinos. When his trust was earned, and the last of his secrets out, Kinos had slipped the knife into his heart.

"Bring him."

The knights dragged Raef to his feet and marched him toward the box.

The Hierarch raised a hand.

"The matter of the key remains," he said.

"The key?" Raef asked.

"You opened the box before," the Hierarch said. "We must cure that."

"No!" Kinos shouted.

"Nephew," the Hierarch barked. "You are my blood, but this is what will be."

"You don't have to do this," Kinos sputtered, but he froze in place.

The Hierarch did not answer, but Raef saw it in his eyes. He didn't have to do it. He wanted to. It was cruelty that drove him, cruelty and zealotry born of fear. That twisted sort of faith could not be reasoned with.

A knight seized Raef and forced him forward, pushing his left arm across the box's lid. A second man grabbed his hand, pulled his arm straight. His mailed grip crushed Raef's fingers to the point of breaking. The shadowknife pulsed with his panic, hurting him nearly as much. The knight behind him leaned in, pinning Raef to the cold metal.

"Seth," the Hierarch commanded. "Prove yourself to me. Make the cut."

Raef screamed with all his breath, tearing his throat until the knight behind him clamped a hand over his mouth. Raef kicked, bruising his shins on the knight's metal greaves.

Seth stepped forward. He drew his sword a few inches from its scabbard and met Raef's eyes. Sparks danced there.

"No," he said. He let the blade slide back into its scabbard. The fire left his eyes.

"You deny me?" the Hierarch demanded.

"I cannot do this. I will not do this."

The Hierarch opened his mouth, perhaps to order Seth's demise, when the Bishop spoke.

"Hyperion will not grant him the fire if he does not believe in the rightness of the act," she said.

His strength depleted, Raef took heaving breaths.

"Give me your sword," the Hierarch said.

Seth did not move.

"Do you deny me?" the Hierarch repeated, his voice booming over the old stone. "Do you deny Hyperion?"

Seth drew the blade and tossed it to the ground.

"I cannot do this," he repeated. "I will not do this."

Eyes fixed on Seth, the Hierarch lifted the sword. Fire lit the metal. It sizzled and whitened. Raef screamed again, too loud for even the knight's mailed hand to smother.

The Hierarch swung.

33
SUN

The Hierarch dropped the sword. Seth could no longer think of it as his. It clattered against the ground. The box ceased its whirring, clicked once, and fell silent.

"It is done," the Hierarch said with a heaving breath.

Seth did not move. He could not look up. As much as he wanted to turn from the blood, from the lifeless hand with its curled fingers, he could not.

He walks the silent paths of night, he thought, remembering the old hymn he'd once loved to sing. *Lady grant him light. Lady guide his way.*

"Pol," he whispered.

Raef. His name was Raef.

Seth would not cry in front of the Hierarch, in front of the Knights Elite, but how he wanted to. He nearly retched, but swallowed it down, tasting the acid in his throat. It rolled in his stomach like sharp stones.

His mind raced, trying to understand. Their quarry was not their quarry. Raef had gone into the box and Kinos stood watching, his face as fixed as stone.

"Nephew," the Hierarch said. "You have done well. You have earned your rope."

Kinos, who Raef had loved, was the Hierarch's nephew.

"Thank you, Uncle," Kinos said, head bowed low.

All of this had been a trap for Raef, to find and imprison him forever.

"Take that to the ship," the Hierarch commanded with a dismissive wave at the box.

The Knights Elite obeyed, bearing their burden to the docks, leaving the dead, severed hand, the blood, and the feeling that all the world was wrong.

"Bishop," the Hierarch said, turning to her. "I think it is time your young charge take his pilgrimage."

"Your Holiness?" she asked.

"If Seth would be a Knight of Hyperion, a full knight, then he must complete his pilgrimage, yes?"

"That is the order's tenet."

"Then send him. Get him gone, somewhere far away where I shall not soon find him."

"Yes, Your Holiness," the Bishop said, her eyes narrowed. "Walk with me, Seth."

He did not look to Lathan or the other members of the cadre as they left the ancient temple behind.

The pilgrimage was the order's final rite of passage, but it was not the Hierarch's place to declare it. The Bishop would give Seth his mission when the time came. She would say when he was ready.

Only then would Seth set out alone, to retrieve some artifact of the demon wars or aid those in need. It was something he dreamed of, his final step to becoming a true knight. This was an overstep of the Hierarch's authority. To hear him declare

that Seth go now, like it was another errand simply to be rid of
him, felt like tarnish on something that should be incorruptible.

Seth kept quiet as they marched. He felt empty and strange.
His steps were too light without his sword.

"Is Argos able to travel?" the Bishop asked.

"I don't understand," he said, meaning everything. He
needed to catch his breath. He needed to pray.

"Is he fit, Seth? Are you?"

"Yes," he said with a nod. "We will go wherever you send us."

She should know that. He'd come here after all. He'd
witnessed what he'd seen, and not stopped it. He should have—

"Then you must leave," she said, breaking the course of
his thoughts. "There is another town on the other side of the
island. There are ships there."

Stopping, she pressed a heavy purse into his hands.

"Hire one. Now. Get off this island as quickly as you can."

"Where will I go?" he asked. "Is this truly a pilgrimage?"

"You have lost your sword," she said, hands still cupped
around his. "You must have a weapon, so I charge you to seek
another. Find the Forge of Helios. Draw from the arms there.
One will choose you."

It felt pointless. The Hierarch wanted him gone again, just
like when he'd been banished to Teshur—when he'd been sent to
guard a box the Hierarch wanted opened. He'd been expected to
fail all along. The Hierarch's plan required it. Was this any better?

"But why?" he asked, voice quiet. "I can use any sword,
can't I?"

"I am not so certain that you can," the Bishop said, laying
a hand on his shoulder. "Hyperion will guide you, and I will
pray that he protects you. Take Argos and go now."

"Bishop?" He met her eyes. Strong as she was, as imperi-
ous and blazing, she seemed small then, at least too small for

what she might face. He had to ask, though he did not want to. "Will he harm you?"

"I do not think so, but we will go where he commands. He remains the Hierarch until Hyperion chooses another."

"Am I—" Seth paused. Uncertainty filled him and stole his summoned confidence. "After—I mean, am I?"

"You are one of my cadre," she said. "You are not of Teshur. You are not of Phoebe. Wherever you came from, you are of Hyperion. I've been certain of that for a long time. Whatever else you might become, Seth, you will always be one of my knights."

She'd known. She'd known all along and hadn't turned him away.

"Thank you."

Unable to say anything else, he made the god's sign.

She returned it.

"Go with his light, Seth, but go quickly and with care."

The Forge of Helios was a legend. If it was even real, Seth had no idea where it lay. It was a secret, and secrets were the realm of Inquisitors. He did not know its location, but Father Geldar might.

He almost smiled.

The Bishop was wise. She'd likely guessed that seeing his old mentor would be what he most needed. Perhaps some knights had guile after all.

What had happened to Raef was not his fault. It wasn't. Seth had held no part in the Hierarch's plot, but he could see now why he'd been chosen to guard the box. The Hierarch had known he would fail, had needed him to fail.

Kinos had escaped because Raef held the key, and now Raef would sleep forever, trapped inside, without anyone to save him.

It wasn't his fault, but they couldn't have succeeded without him, without Seth being who and what he was. Had the Oracle known? Had she told the Hierarch to send a cadre to

Thiva because she knew he'd choose theirs? He would likely never know, was uncertain if he wanted to.

It was not his fault, but if he hadn't been there, had not found Raef in Thiva's tower, where he'd gone, drawn by his own curiosity—it felt like a broken bottle punched into his chest.

He tried to push the pain aside. It was unseemly to pity himself, after what Raef had suffered . . .

"I must pray."

The sun had begun to set. He hated autumn, the shortening days. They reminded him of Dodona, where Rhea held sway, and of the harvest dances. He'd watched them from the tower windows, let them distract him from his prayers. He did not think upon those days, had tried to erase them, and realized now that he mostly had.

Argos looked behind them and sniffed the air.

Seth scanned the low, dry hills and the scattered ruins, but saw no one.

"It's likely best we do not travel by night," he conceded.

Seth had craved a cadre for so long, but now he only wanted solitude.

He found a little temple atop a hill. Its roof had partly collapsed, but it would serve for a night. He could watch the sunset through its portico. He could pray for peace. He could pray for Raef.

He removed his armor slowly, set it aside with care.

"Father," he prayed, staring at Hyperion's disk.

It touched the Shallow Sea and made a road of glittering fire on the water.

He wanted to say more. He longed to offer penance, but felt his body had paid enough. He was done with that.

"I offer you a sacrifice," he whispered. "Take my heartache. Please."

Surely he'd grown it large enough.

On Thiva, when he'd hung on the thorns, teetering between conscious and unconscious, he'd dreamed of burning, of driving a knife into his own heart to set the fire free, to burn away the demons and the things that crawled toward him. He'd dreamed of killing them all, the Thivans, the knights. He'd dreamed he'd brought the broken castle down and crushed them all.

Then Raef had chosen him, just for a moment, and it had felt right, until he'd seen the reason.

It had been the easiest thing for Raef to goad him into calling the flames, but Raef had been right. Seth hadn't hurt anyone.

He'd mastered the fire, but now it felt dim, doused. For once it truly slept within him.

"Father, let him sleep in peace. Spare him from nightmares."

But dreams had been of Phoebe. Then again, so was prophecy, and he'd seen the Hierarch's Oracle, a being of sun and light.

Argos settled against him as he stretched out atop his bedroll. The warmth was welcome. With the hound there, Seth's cloak would make an adequate blanket for one night.

"You did not think he was evil, did you, boy?" Seth asked, stroking Argos's fur.

"Raef," Seth whispered, testing the name, trying to make it stick.

But Argos was already snoring. Seth chuckled. The pup had so much energy—until he did not. At least he healed quickly too. His wounds from the thorns were already gone.

"He saved us," Seth whispered.

Raef had saved them all, revealed himself despite the cost. Seth didn't have to hold back the tears now.

He let them fall.

What he'd learned, what he'd seen the Hierarch do—he

remained the Hierarch, as the Bishop had said, but it was clear she had opinions about that.

It was not Seth's place to judge, but how he wanted to.

He kept seeing the lifeless hand, the mark on its wrist burned away by the cut.

How he wished Hyperion had chosen another for his voice in the world.

His sword. The Hierarch had used Seth's sword.

It was strange how much he still wanted to retch. He wasn't certain he'd ever eat again.

The old pain, his loneliness, had been replaced with something rotten, a stain. He had Argos. He wasn't alone. He still had his faith.

"Thank you, Father," he prayed. "For shelter. For Argos. For the Bishop and Father Geldar."

Seth paused. He inhaled the scent of the darkness. Dust and a hint of dry, sunbaked wood.

"Thank you for Raef."

))) ❭ ● ❬ (((

Argos let out a little growl sometime before dawn. Seth reached for his sword only to remember that it was not there.

A hooded figure too solid to be a spirit blocked the starlight shining through the temple door. Seth had no time to spring to his feet.

The man had nearly reached him when he straightened, lurched, and fell to the side. A gurgling sound filled his throat. His armor clanked as he hit the ground.

Behind him, a slighter figure moved into view.

"Who are you?" Seth demanded. Lifting a hand, he lit the darkness with a whorl of sparks.

"Careful, Seth," Kinos said, brushing an ember from his shoulder. "This old place would easily burn."

"Are you here to kill me?" Seth clenched his hand. The flames flickered between his fingers.

"That was the order," Kinos kicked the dead Knight Elite at his feet to roll him over and extracted a throwing knife from the man's neck.

The aim was perfect, right between the helm and the shoulder.

All of Kinos's weakness and softness were gone. He wore a brown robe with a white rope.

"So why aren't you?" Seth asked. His eyes flicked to the corpse as Kinos took a seat on a bit of broken roof, like it meant nothing that he'd just killed a man.

"Because I think the Oracle that guides my uncle is not what she seems, and more importantly, because the voice of Hyperion in this world cannot be without mercy."

Kinos's green eyes looked hard in the starlight, like unpolished emeralds.

"Who are you?" Seth asked. "Really?"

"I never lied to Raef, not much. My name is Kinos, and I did grow up here, but my family are the faithful. Now I am the youngest Inquisitor to earn my rope. It's all I ever wanted, to follow in my uncle's footsteps. It's all I can remember ever wanting . . ."

He trailed off.

"Before Raef," Seth said.

"Yes."

"But you were in the box. You and he—"

"Don't try to think, Seth. Knights aren't meant for it. My uncle's Oracle asked for me, specifically, to go into the box and catch the last son of the Night. We had to make sure it was him, that he was the one with the key that could open any door, because he could open the Underworld with it. He could bring back Phoebe, but the prophecy said she wouldn't come alone. She'd bring the worst of the demons with her."

"But why you?"

"Because I could trick him, because he would love me, and that would blind him to what I was. But the Oracle lied, at least by omission. She didn't say that I would love him back, that doing what I had to do to him would cut out my heart."

I didn't think you had one, Seth thought.

He should be kind, but did not know how to be kind to this man.

"You let the Hierarch cut off his hand," Seth said. "You could have tried to stop him."

"We both could have tried harder," Kinos snapped. He dropped his eyes to the ground. "I didn't know Uncle was going to do that."

His eyes shone with tears that wouldn't quite fall.

Kinos was beautiful, and Seth could see the trap, how Raef would want to protect him. A quick glance at the dead knight revealed the truth.

"I lost him forever in that moment," Kinos said. "How could he ever forgive me? I'll never forgive myself. But you can get him back."

"He's gone. They're taking him to Drowned Gate."

"He's not dead," Kinos said. "There's still time."

"I don't know where it is," Seth said. "Do you?"

"I do not," Kinos said. "I'm too new for such a secret."

"Everything you did, that you did to him, was for that rope." Seth nodded to the belt at Kinos's waist. The fire rose in his belly, stoked by anger and grief. The sparks swirled faster in his fist. Some leaked to drift in the air between them.

"Yes," Kinos said. "As I said. Try to keep up. We don't have much time."

He knelt to search the dead man's pockets.

"We won't be the last assassins my uncle sends after you. And it won't take him long to realize that I let you go. You must be quick, and you need to stand out less. The giant hound isn't going to help."

"You killed a Knight Elite," Seth said.

"Yes. Easily. I just told him you were in here, that the demon was sleeping."

"You were watching me."

Kinos nodded. "You lot aren't very subtle."

"But the Hierarch—"

"Will send others, Inquisitors, and you won't see them coming."

"I . . ." Seth stammered.

"Keep up, Seth," Kinos growled. "I can't come with you. You have to find Raef. You have to get him out of the box. And you'll need a weapon."

"I'm on my way to find one," Seth said.

"You could take his," Kinos said, nodding to the corpse.

It was a weapon, a sword sworn to Hyperion.

The knight wielding it had come skulking, an assassin determined to end Seth's life while he slept. How was that honor? How did that serve the god?

The knight had forgone his vow. His weapon was forfeit.

Seth swallowed.

"It will serve for now. But we still have no idea where Drowned Gate is."

"Yeah," Kinos said. He reached into his robe to withdraw a bundle of bloodstained cloth. "That part is up to Argos."

34

MOON

Everything burned. Everything. He'd swallowed fire and it dug at his heart like a sharpened spoon.

"Poor broken blackbird."

The voice, musical and feminine, called to him.

Raef could not feel his hand, only the fire—the cut—the place where it had been.

"Not a bird," he said, his voice dry and creaking, hoarse from disuse. "No wings."

"Look again," she said.

He opened his eyes. He lay naked on a metal floor, arms straight at his sides. Metal shavings scraped his back.

Raef tried to rise, but his body felt like stone.

"Who are you?" he asked.

She stepped into view.

She wore a cloak of swirling shadow. It floated around her, a nimbus of darkness that reminded him of the moonless sea. Her eyes were black.

"Hush," she cooed. "I'll make it better. I will help you fly."

She leaned closer, an inkwell and pen cradled in her hands. "What are you doing?" he asked. "What is that?"

He tried to squirm, to thrash, but could not move.

"This is water from the Ebon Sea."

She dipped her pen into the ink and reached for his severed arm. "You had a little before. It's time for more, every drop for every feather."

Raef looked where he did not want to, to the swollen, misshapen place where his hand had been.

"Don't touch it," he said. Tears spilled off his face, dripped into his ears. He couldn't shirk or roll away. "Please."

The pen pricked his flesh. The ink oozed and flickered like a thing alive, like the mark. Its touch stole the unbridled heat that had rolled through him. It chilled worse than any ice, any winter.

Raef could only sob as she used his skin for parchment. It went on forever. She drew along his arm and over his heart. Then she went lower, circling his belly in thick, spiraling lines.

"Why are you doing this?" he ground out when she paused.

"To make it better," she said, lifting Raef's leg to encircle his ankle in the freezing ink. She left no part of him unmarked. Done with his body, she knelt to scratch across the floor, drawing him a set of wide, feathered wings.

"I don't understand," Raef said through chattering teeth.

"No one placed the mark upon you. Phoebe didn't give it to you. It has always been a part of you. The Ebon Sea has always been part of you."

"You're not real. You can't be. I'm imagining you."

"Oh, I'm real enough. I'm here."

Raef tried to focus on her, but her features flowed like water. He did not know her.

Down in his gut, in the break in his heart, he knew her name but could not say it.

Sati. This was his mother, the demoness who'd birthed him.
"Where am I?" he asked.

He could not see much. The place was all metal, welded
together. A flickering darkness gathered around them, fingers
of black flame the shadowsight could not penetrate.

A cold sweat broke across his naked skin.

"This is Helios's Forge, where he crafted the weapons of the
Gods' War. I brought you here to mend you, Hraefn. Then you
can open the Moon's Door for me."

"They smashed it," he said. "They took the key. They
took—"

He looked to the end of his arm. She'd ringed it in black
whorls. The cold of the ink had dulled the fire.

"The key was never the mark, never just your wrist," she said.
Reaching, she cradled his arm in her hands. "You have always had
everything you need. You've always been everything you need."

"Why?" he asked, failing to hold back the tears. "Why show
yourself to me now?"

"Because time grows short. The day approaches, the one
day when Hyperion doesn't guard the way."

"The Day of the Black Sun."

She nodded and gently added, "And who else am I to haunt?
Who is here for me?"

"I met another," he said. "On Thiva. I killed her."

"Haerwen," she said, shaking her head. "There was always
too much madness in that one. Do you feel better now?"

"I feel cold," he said. "I still can't move."

"You will, when you awake."

"This doesn't feel like a dream."

"It is and it is not." She shrugged her slight shoulders. "This
is twilight."

"Why?" he asked. "Why did you have me?"

"I've already told you." She paused and cocked her head as if listening to someone he couldn't hear. "But I can tell you a little more, since it's just the two of us. I serve he who would return."

"Who is he?" Raef asked.

"Only the Moon's Door matters, child. Open it. Let your goddess back into the sky. The Grief will recede, the tides will return, and you will save the world."

"And your master will return."

Her mouth bent, but her head dipped with a demure nod he felt certain she did not mean.

"Yes."

"The Hierarch was right, wasn't he?" Raef asked.

Even with all of the terrible things Logrum had done, murdering Phoebe's priests, sending Kinos to trap Raef. Despite all of it, he'd been right: the demons would come back too.

"Who is he?" Raef asked. "Who do you serve?"

"It doesn't matter. Awaken, find the Moon's Door, and live."

The paralysis ended without warning. Cold metal remained beneath him, but he was no longer naked.

He was inside the box.

Raef squeezed his eyes shut, forced himself to calm and see if the cold would take him back into sleep. It did not. He tried banging on the lid with his remaining hand, but with so little room to maneuver, he could only knock. It wasn't going to open this way.

"No," he moaned.

His other arm ended in a cauterized stump. They'd taken the mark. Sati's drawings were gone.

His chest tightened. He gulped but found far less air than he needed. It was the crypt again, the knight—Zale—choking him. Blackness crept in at the edge of his vision.

She'd said he had everything he needed. With nothing else

to trust in, Raef forced his body to lie still. He searched inside himself, down through the wide, wide break in his heart.

The fire of the Hierarch's cut burned, seared him inside and out, but he reached past it.

The shattered glass feeling was worse, so much worse. Just touching the place where he'd come to care for Kinos, all he'd done—the betrayal—it felt like dropping into a cauldron of molten glass. He wanted to flee from it, to not feel it, but it had happened. It had.

He had to reach past it or he would not survive.

The pain cooled when Raef found the place inside him where the shadowknife lived. It slept, pulsing, black and blue, like a dark star.

The blade emerged from Raef's truncated wrist. With it came a ghostly hand. It did not feel like flesh, but he could grip the knife.

Tears welled, but he had too little time.

The blackness was closing in. His lungs ached as if he'd dove to the bottom of the sea.

With another labored breath, Raef twisted, trying to make enough room to push the knife into the center of the lid. That's where he'd hit the lock before.

He willed the knife to solidify, turned the hand. Nothing happened. He coughed, rasping. He sucked in breaths, but found no air. Eyes wide, teeth clenched, he fished around inside the metal until the knife caught on something.

The box hummed and rattled. It took too long. He'd pass out. He'd die.

The lid unlatched.

Raef pushed it open and gulped down air. Feeling trickled back into his limbs. Climbing out, he stumbled free and landed on his back.

Though he could flex the fingers, his new hand had no feeling, no sensation. Raef could sense the shadowknife inside him, waiting to be called. Knowing he had not lost it filled him with such relief that he collapsed. He leaned against the box, racked by sobs born of pain and relief.

35
MOON

The fire had cooled, and he could almost think clearly. His hunger, always a constant, took second place to his thirst. He needed water.

He didn't know if Sati had really been there. Yes, he was awake, free of the box, but there were no markings on his skin. No black whorls. He had no wings.

At least the shadowsight remained.

There was no Grief here, only a natural dampness that laced the air with salt and the smell of old stone. The taste of rotten eggs came and went in drafts.

Drowned Gate. This was the Inquisitors' prison from which none had escaped. They used to tease each other about it in the tower yard.

"Watch out or they'll take you to Drowned Gate," Father Hanel had said after one of Raef's more outrageous pranks had gone awry. He couldn't remember if it had been when he'd put live eels in the cistern or when he'd switched the bakers' salt and sugar barrels.

It didn't matter now. The prison was a wide, stone well, a water-slicked shaft cut into the world's bones. The box had landed on a ledge, atop a pile of rocks and rubble. A corner was crumpled from the impact. Somehow Raef had slept through even that.

His mother had woken him. His mother wanted him to bring back Phoebe.

A low, constant rumble came from everywhere and nowhere. He saw only misty water when he peered down to the well's bottom.

He was alone.

There was no light.

Another, thinner ledge stood above him. A passage opened onto it. Raef could climb to it, if the shadowhand came when he willed it, and if he could control it enough.

"Come on," Raef said, shaking his arm. The pain returned, blinding him with a wave of red and black.

He slumped against the box with a groan.

Teeth gritted, he squeezed his eyes shut and saw the glowing sword, felt the agony anew. He had to push it down, but it felt like swallowing knives.

Raef knew he'd have to digest it. He'd have to feel it in pieces, bit by bit, before it ate him from the inside out. He breathed, in and out, trying to stop the swirl of pain. He sobbed, tears and snot running free. He wiped it all on his right sleeve. The knights had torn the left from his shirt.

Eventually, thirstier than ever, the damp air soothing his scalding flesh, he calmed.

Raef threw his head back and found pairs of lights, golden eyes, blinking open at the top of the well. A dozen shapes, lithe and silent, descended toward him. He blinked, but they didn't vanish. Whatever they were, they were real. They could see him, and they were coming for him.

Raef jerked himself to his feet.

He could run, but this ledge went nowhere. He'd have to climb to the next.

"Please," he begged.

Concentrating, Raef felt inside himself. There. The knife. The hand.

They were a part of him.

The hand emerged. It felt much like the knife, cold, but a lifeless extension of his flesh.

He had no time to wonder.

The things above him were getting nearer. They began to yip, making a sound between dogs and men. There were almost words in their yips, and that made them so much more terrible than howls.

With clumsy, uncertain movements, Raef climbed the wall.

He'd gotten a few feet off the ground when the pain returned, a blaze of fire sparking through his veins.

The black hand vanished. Raef fell. The landing sent a fresh shock of agony through him. He lay there, shifting to feel if anything had broken.

"Get up." The pain would wait. It had to wait. "You can cry when you're safe."

The hand came more easily the second time.

The creatures were closer. He could hear the scrape and scrabble of their claws now. He climbed again, reached the higher ledge, and collapsed onto it.

"Not there yet," he said, forcing himself to stumble into the tunnel and move as quickly as his depleted strength would allow.

The walls were smooth, waterworn, not hewn. They glistened. The way opened into a cavern full of stalagmites that littered the path like so many melted candles. Raef slipped between them to put as much space between himself and the well as he could. He took every turn he found, squeezed through every narrow crack to lose his pursuers.

The yips fell away. The sound of running water grew louder.

Perhaps he'd lost them. Perhaps they feared this place and he'd trapped himself with something worse.

Ahead, mist flowed from a milky stream. Raef reached to drop his head into the water.

A hand seized him by the shirt collar, holding him back like a puppy by the scruff. Jagged fingernails scraped his neck.

Raef struggled, fought his way loose, and flipped over. His strength fled before he could kick or strike whoever stood over him.

"That's not water," a ragged voice said. "It's acid."

The man looked deflated, like a bladder with the air let out. His skin hung pink and waxy on an aged face. Sallow-gray hair, like dirty snowmelt, crowned his bald scalp. One hand remained extended toward Raef. The other clutched a dead, upraised lantern. Scarred pits lay where his eyes should be.

The man nodded toward the stream.

"One sip of that and your throat will melt."

The scrape and yips echoed up the passage.

"They're coming," Raef rasped. "The things. Whatever they are."

"They're demons, of a sort," the man said. "Can you read?"

Raef froze.

"Can you read?" the old man demanded.

"Yes. I can read. What does that have to do with anything? We have to get out of here."

The man smiled. His few teeth were stained a mossy green.

"If you can read, then I can help you."

"All right." Raef found his feet. "Let's go."

The blind man shuffled into the cavern. He didn't seem to be in any rush despite the approaching pack.

Raef took in what details he could as the space opened. Metal walkways, many of them rusted, connected more of the waterworn passages.

The place was full of little abandoned chambers. Many were barred, but empty. Several held the bones of things or people long dead and molded. Some of the doors had been broken open, their bars had rusted away. The sound of claws came and went as the blind man led Raef onward.

"You said they were demons?"

"Yes. Bred and left here." The old man giggled at something he didn't share and waddled on, taking Raef through the tunnels, his dead lamp lifted like it shone for them both.

The man muttered, sometimes cursing, sometimes laughing, until he slipped inside a crack so quickly that Raef almost missed it.

The old man was faster than he looked. Raef would have to watch out for that.

He followed the smell, like old cheese and urine, into the narrow passage. Setting his lantern aside, the blind man tugged at the rock. The stone pivoted, tilting on a hidden counterweight to hide the way out. On the other side, another stone ground, moving until the way opened, leading deeper into the rock.

Outside, the demons passed by, yipping and growling. Raef could almost understand them, these cousins of his. They were in pain. They'd been abandoned. They called for blood in their doggerel tongue.

Mad. He was going mad.

"Through there," the old man said, pointing for Raef to head inside.

Raef froze.

"It's a library," he gasped.

Niches riddled the cavern's smooth stone. Books and scrolls, parchment and tablets, all lay shoved together at jumbled angles. The air here was drier, free of the sulfuric tang.

"When I heard you out there—I thought they'd dropped in something useful. They do that. Sometimes."

Raef hugged his maimed arm to his chest as his strength deserted him again. He slumped to the floor.

"Do the Inquisitors ever come here?" he asked, hearing how broken he sounded.

"Not anymore." The man fixed the pits of his eyes on Raef. Lifting his lantern, he turned the little wheel as if to adjust the missing wick. "Why are you here?"

"What?"

"There are only two types here, heretics and demons. Which are you?"

Both, Raef thought, but he was too weak to fight if the madman took offense at his faith or bloodline.

"Neither," he lied.

"Then why are you here?" the man asked. He cradled the lantern like Raef might try to steal it, like it was precious, a babe or pet, and not a bit of garbage.

"I don't know exactly," Raef said. He remembered black hair and green eyes like spring leaves. Everything threatened to rise, to overcome him. He took a long steadying breath and said, "There was this Inquisitor—"

"Which one?" the man snapped.

"Logrum." Raef could not call him the Hierarch anymore, much like he couldn't say Kinos's name.

The madman growled. Then he wailed, once, loudly, before collapsing into sobs.

"Is he the one who put you here? Is Logrum the one who blinded you?"

The madman had covered his face with his hands, but he nodded.

"Did you know that Inquisitors are allowed to lie?" he asked.

"Yes," Raef said.

He did not want to remember the dark, the rocking of the ship, or the brush of lips. The thoughts, even pushed away, ripped open all his wounds.

"Heretic," the old man said, jabbing a thumb at his chest. "They feed us to the demons, unless you're smart."

"You must be smart then," Raef said. "To figure out that door."

"I could read once," the man said. "Can you? Are you something useful? I'll let you stay if you are something useful."

"I could read to you."

The old man straightened, grew animated.

"Then you can sort the books," he said, his voice shrill. "They'll make sense again."

Raef wondered how long it had been since this man had talked to anyone else, how long he'd been down here with the terror and loneliness chipping away at his sanity.

Raef's heart ached for him, and he was surprised that he could still feel anything for another person. He wondered how long it would take for him to become just as insane as his new companion. Probably not long.

"If I could read again, I could see the way out," the wretch muttered.

"There's a way out?" Raef asked.

"The gate—" the man paused to giggle. "The gate is drowned in acid."

Raef thought back to the bottom of the prison's well, to the misty water like the stream he'd almost drank.

A scraping sound, claws on stone, came from outside. Raef hugged himself.

"Can they get in?" he asked.

"No. They're all too mad for doors."

Raef lacked the strength to run any further. He had to get it back and his thirst still pained him.

"Is there anything to drink?" he asked. "To eat?"

The madman gestured to a fountain filled by a drip from the wall.

Its basin was coated in green, the stuff that had stained the madman's teeth.

"Algae?" Raef asked.

"It is a safe one," the man said. He turned and slumped into an old chair, cradling his lantern.

I've had worse, Raef reminded himself.

The stuff went down, slimy in his throat. He did his best not to taste it.

The old man snored. Sweat beaded his bald pate. Raef stepped away from him, wiping his mouth on his sleeve.

"I'm just going to look at your books," Raef whispered.

The texts were ancient, disorganized, and in every form. There were bound volumes of leather and stacks of loose paper, vellum scrolls, and even tablets of bark or stone.

Father Polus would have traded the orphans for these, Raef thought.

He lifted a shard of red clay and found the sort of writing he'd seen in Thiva, the same sort that spelled out his true name.

"This language," he said. "It's what the demons used."

"Demotic," the old man said, giving Raef a start. "It's called Demotic. That was not their name for it, of course."

"But these are heresies. Why weren't they destroyed?"

"Drowned Gate wasn't always a prison. The Inquisitors used to study here, not just destroy. The word means to question. They used to question everything."

Raef had known that but had forgotten. He'd associated the Inquisitors with so much worse for so long that he'd let their history fade in his memory. They probably had too.

Reading and thinking, he pondered the hoard of knowledge beneath his fingertips. It calmed the black and red still roiling within him.

"Do they know these are here?" he asked.

"They know," the man said. "They do not forget. But they cannot reach them. They do not come here. Between us and them is a legion of insane demons. There are other things, I think, higher up, but they've gone mad since their maker disappeared."

"There's a way in," Raef said. "So there must be a way out."

"It's a joke on us, on the punished. You'd never swim past the point where the acid floats atop the water. You'd never have enough air. You'd burn away before you reached the bottom."

"Has anyone tried?" Raef asked.

The man's breath became ragged, as though this bout of lucidity was an uphill climb.

"Many," he said. "Especially the new ones. Sometimes they surface, scream a little, then sink."

"So we're trapped here."

The man rocked in affirmation. "Most of us are already mad. I'm a little mad. I used to be . . . well, I used to not be. I could read. They took my eyes because I read too much. I read the thing they did not want to know."

"They maimed me too," Raef said.

His hand. His heart.

The Hierarch had taunted that he'd been ready, as though the box required a sacrifice. Perhaps it did. Perhaps his heart, his love, had been the price.

He remembered lying on the *Ino*'s deck with Kinos at night, hands clasped, eyes fixed on the sky free of Grief and the city's haze. The stars had been beyond counting, a belt of them like a road for the gods to walk, or a river for Phoebe to sail, back when she had done so.

He'd felt completely full in that moment. His belly, his heart. All he carried now was fire and ache.

Maybe that had been the cost the box required, the price to sleep within it, a fatal wound within his chest, even if he didn't bleed. If so, perhaps he'd woken because he could heal.

His mind seemed mostly intact, but how would he know? Could he? Would he feel the break, the cracks in his sanity? Would it come on gradually or all at once?

The old man knew that the Hierarch had broken him, which had to be a terrible thing.

Something about him seemed familiar, something Raef's mind wouldn't yield to him. Perhaps that was the first sign. He pushed it away to pick at later, like a half-finished meal he'd return to when he could stomach more.

Raef opened his mouth to ask the man what he'd found, what he'd been punished for, but the fire returned, flaring from nowhere, stealing his vision.

He dropped to the ground, racked and burning. He screamed, long, throat-scorching screams.

"You burn," the madman said when Raef could scream no more. "They put the fire in you too."

"Will—" Raef clenched his teeth, afraid he'd bite his tongue if he didn't. When the fire ebbed, he gasped, "Will it pass?"

"Never completely," the man said. "But it will lessen."

Raef groaned as convulsions overtook him.

The wretch took him by the ankles, dragged and dropped him near the pool, atop a pile of fetid rags that must have been his own bed.

Raef did not know how long he lay there. Days? A fortnight? Sweat drenched his hair and ruined clothes. The
madman scooped algae from the fountain and trickled it into
his mouth. Starving, feeling like he hadn't eaten in a year, Raef
swallowed handful after handful and collapsed back into the
nightmares.

Cave mouths tempted him, teasing him with freedom, but
when he ran for them, eyes the color of poison opened above
him. The cave snapped shut when he reached the exit, taking
his hand, always his hand.

It was there. Then it was not. His arm itched. It *burned* as
though a thousand needles jabbed it.

Something almost shapeless slithered in a darkness the shadowsight could not penetrate. Hundreds of hands moved with
a singular purpose. Each palm bore a blood-filled, jaundiced
eye. The world of his nightmares was perfectly dark, and for a
moment it comforted him. Then it burst into flames, burning
him from within.

Always aflame, Raef died and died again.

He lost count of how many times he woke screaming. He
lost all sense of day or night. He lost the count he'd kept since
the moon had died, if the box had not already taken it.

The madman came and went, muttering a song Raef should
have known, drumming on his lantern as erratic and mad as
Raef's heartbeat.

Then he awoke, shivering and soaked, to find the madman
standing over him, rasping out rough breaths, the empty sock-
ets of his burned eyes focused and sad. Raef knew him then,
at last, the memories drifting up from the depths of his mind.

"Father Hanel?"

Hanel didn't answer. Insanity glazed his greasy face. He
clenched and opened his fists in time with his breathing. The

sound tightened and slackened. He wheezed like an old bellows. Raef straightened, unsure whether to back away or embrace him.

This man, this wretch, was so far from the jolly teacher Raef remembered. He had thought he'd have no pity left after what Kinos had done to him, but his heart found a little more room to ache for the old priest.

"Father? It's me, it's Raef."

"Raef?"

"I thought you died with the others."

"I . . . I didn't mean to kill you. They told me they would spare the children. That was the deal we made."

He settled his bulk into his chair, lifted the lantern and cradled it. He hummed a lullaby, one Raef now recognized from the tower.

"Raef, my boy?" Hanel asked, looking up with burned-out eyes. "Did you know that Inquisitors get to lie?"

"Yes, Father," Raef said. "I knew that."

Hanel's jaw worked as he sang to the lantern. He cooed to it, calling it by the names of the children he'd tried to save through treachery. It had never occurred to Raef that someone had betrayed her, told the Hierarch her mysteries and exactly when to strike the towers down. It had never occurred to him that Father Hanel could betray them.

But Raef was too tired for anger, too weary for hate or vengeance. The fire in his blood had cooled.

He did not want to sleep anymore. He did not want to have more nightmares, but the blackness would not release him. He sank into it. He saw no more green eyes, no more closing cave mouths, only the shadows that he could not peer through. When there was light, it came from a distant sliver, a tiny moon he reached for but could not grasp.

36
MOON

Raef woke reeking, hungry for real food, but no longer exhausted. His mind had cleared.

Hanel didn't answer when Raef called for him. The air of the cave tasted stale, but Raef didn't want to risk whatever lived in the passages. He called for the black hand and nearly wept when it answered. He could control it, could summon it, at least in darkness. If the hand worked like the knife, then he would lose it again in daylight.

He swallowed all the algae his stomach would take, and found the hole Hanel used for a latrine, holding his breath until he was clear of it.

After, he returned to the books.

He scanned tablets and pages, setting things in order as he went. He worked until his eyes hurt, rested, and rose to read some more.

He lost all sense of time, but a history of the gods, of their war with the demons, told from the side of the vanquished and translated by the Inquisitors, emerged. Raef's head spun with the implications and revelations.

"Where are you?" Hanel asked, surprising Raef from the foot of the ladder.

Book in hand, Raef froze. He relied on Hanel's blindness to protect him if the old priest turned violent.

"Where. Are. You?" Hanel punctuated each word as if stabbing the air with spittle.

"Here," Raef said, setting the book back into its niche. "I was reading."

"What?" Hanel lifted his lantern.

"Reading, Father Hanel. I told you I could."

"Did you find it?" he asked, his rage forgotten. "Did you find the thing I had to unsee?"

"I think so." Raef joined him on the ground. "These texts, the people who wrote them, they didn't consider the demons evil or even monstrous. They thought them gods."

"So they were. The higher demons at least." Hanel fluttered a hand, showing a hint of the jovial scholar Raef remembered. "The lower ones are less, somewhere between the gods and men."

"So it's true?" Raef asked.

"Yes." Hanel deflated, became suddenly small and tired. "Banished by their children, our gods invaded this world. They warred with the gods here, and branded them demons to win the people's faith."

"I can guess who came up with that strategy," Raef said, remembering how thoroughly the Inquisitors had whispered lies and truth to turn the people against Phoebe.

"How did you find this?"

"Logrum. We were paired on pilgrimage. We went to Teshur, to study the fire temples beneath the desert. They believed we'd be good for each other, that my mirth would temper his seriousness. The steles there—the carvings we found told us the story."

"And you told Father Polus."

"Yes. The Inquisitors already knew of course. They don't forget. Then Polus started making the children. I told Logrum what Polus did, how to stop him so he'd spare them. They were innocent. You were innocent."

"But he betrayed you," Raef whispered. "He blinded you and threw you down here."

"Yes. I dedicated my life to teaching, to ensuring the gods' truth. What I found, that the gods are no better, no worse than the demons. I could not bear it. I could not. It is a mortal wound when your faith breaks, my boy."

Hanel sobbed, though no tears filled his dead eyes.

"What do you mean, that the gods are no worse than the demons?"

"The Knights of Hyperion made the hounds, bred them to fight the demons, bred them from the demons here." Hanel caught himself on a shelf, as if speaking it wounded him. "Their excuse for killing her was for doing what the knights and Inquisitors had done in Hyperion's name."

Raef's vision narrowed to a tunnel. The rank hypocrisy of it lit a cold fire inside him. The ink, the marks, thrummed beneath his skin. There was some rage left in him after all.

"Why then?" Raef growled. "Why did they really kill her?"

"Because the Hierarch told them to. He said it was necessary, that he heard a prophecy from an Oracle. They killed us, their brothers and sisters. They killed our Lady and all of her children. I told them how, and it was hypocrisy. All of it."

Hanel's face went slack as if he'd spent his lucidity. It drained away, leaving the defeated old man who'd saved Raef from the acid.

Raef struggled to tamp down the cold fire, the rage, even though he didn't want to. It eased the blacker maw in his heart.

He took in the jumbled library, the shelves and stacks that held everything he'd ever want to know.

"You have to go," Hanel said. "I thought it would be different, but I'm not sane. You have to get out before I hurt you. You have to tell someone the secret."

"I will, Father. I'll tell everyone. I promise."

"Good," Hanel said, sounding small. "That's good."

"Can you tell me anything that would help me reach the surface?" Raef asked. "Anything about the way out?"

"You can't reach the surface," Hanel said. "The only gate is drowned in acid."

"So you said," Raef reminded him gently.

"I wish you could stay and read for me. Maybe you could find it, the thing I need to know. Maybe I could understand again."

His words dampened the fire inside him. Hanel had already forgotten. Perhaps that was a mercy.

"Me too, Father."

"I can't take you. I don't know the way out."

"It's all right." Raef bent to take in the old man's face, to remember it. "You stay with the books. Keep them safe for me."

"Maybe you could come back. Maybe I'll be better. Maybe then you could read to me."

"I'd like that."

"Take my lamp." Hanel offered it like a delicate, precious thing.

"It's all right, Father. I have my mother's eyes. I can see in the dark."

37

SUN

They left the docks behind. Seth wore his armor with a cloak over it to fend away the looming winter. He didn't think it would conceal him. Kinos had been right about Argos being a clear giveaway.

"We are not meant for skulking in the dark," he told the hound as he bent to scratch the top of his head.

He'd talked a lot to Argos on the journey. He knew it was a habit born of loneliness, and that many would consider it a weakness. He let the habit form anyway.

Seth had no experience with money, but he'd found a ship to take them back toward Aegea. He hoped the price was fair.

There'd been room for him and Argos in the hold, and the captain believed that having them aboard would bring fortune from Hyperion. Seth did not feel like a good luck charm. He felt cursed.

At least he wasn't alone. Argos's ears twitched as he listened. Intent upon his master's voice, he'd yip in agreement or cock his head in question. Seth would have sworn that the hound understood his words. Then Argos would lick some rude part of himself and Seth would doubt his own sanity.

There was no more music in the walled-off gardens, no more arguments or fights in the alleys. Versinae lay still beneath the Grief, and it had thickened in their absence.

It had been troubling, sailing into port. They'd moored in the fog, the ghost mist so thick that Seth couldn't see more than a wagon's length past the prow.

He almost wished he was back on the ship. Something had cured his stomach, and the rocking waves no longer troubled him. He'd been safer there, but he had to do this. Even if the Bishop hadn't tasked him with the pilgrimage, he had to find Raef.

Seth remained a knight. He would always be a knight, and everything inside him said he had to right this wrong. Even if Raef could not forgive him for his part in things, Seth would do his best to wipe the stain from the order's honor.

"Got anything yet?" he asked Argos.

He'd fed the hound his grisly meal before they'd left East-light.

Not knowing how much of Raef's blood it would take, Seth had given Argos the entire hand. The hound had crunched it down, bones and all, working it between his teeth to the point where Seth had been forced to turn away.

Seth had no proof that what they said about the hounds was true, that once they'd tasted someone's blood they could always track them, but he prayed it was. Anytime they'd gone on deck, Argos had walked to the prow to stare westward, but he'd only pawed at the ground since they'd landed.

Seth wished Lathan were there, or the Bishop—anyone who might make this all feel less impossible. He would've even welcomed Kinos's help, distasteful as he found the man, but Seth had no idea where the young Inquisitor had gone. Hopefully he'd hinder some of his uncle's efforts against Seth's life.

"It's just us now, boy," Seth told Argos.

The Grief obscured the city's spires. So few lights remained. Versinae had been filthy last time. Now the refuse was gone, no doubt burned to make what light and protection the people could.

Seth padded along. He'd be a fool to sleep at the temple or even tell the priests that he'd returned to the city. Most of the Bishop's purse had paid for his passage. He didn't want to risk the cost and exposure of an inn, but he might have no choice. He could not sleep in an alley, not with the Grief so heavy.

"Father, guide me," Seth prayed quietly. "Keep us safe."

Argos stopped with a long, low growl in his throat.

The Grief swirled over the dark streets, obscuring whatever came for them.

"I didn't miss this place," Seth declared.

He let the fire come, brought it near to the surface. It had lain quiet after Thiva, sated, but the urge to unleash it was rising now.

"Then you shouldn't have come back," a woman said.

Flanked by two others, far enough apart that Seth could not strike them all, she stepped out of the shadows. They wore gray cloaks, a means of blending into the Grief.

These weren't knights. They weren't Inquisitors. Rough-looking, they were closer to the gang he'd faced in Versinae's slums, but carried themselves with confidence.

"We should thank you for making it so easy," she said. "You're worth a tidy sum, boy."

He could take at least one, Argos, another, but they'd be pressed against these odds.

Seth did not want to use the fire that way, to hurt people.

"I can guess who sent you," he said. "But there is no need for this. I'd prefer to let you live."

He drew his sword and called the fire. It no longer burned him, though it still tested his control.

"I doubt you can pay us what we're worth, let alone what he will."

Seth shook his head.

"I don't want to hurt you," he said, trying one last time. "Please walk away."

The men drew long knives from beneath their robes. The woman lifted a crossbow, all were banned weapons by Versinae's prince.

"Forgive me, Father," Seth whispered. "Forgive them."

The flame brightened. Something whispered through the dark, a sound like a darting bird. It moved too fast for Seth to see.

One of the assassins lifted his hand, brushed his cheek. His fingers came away red.

His eyes went wide with panic. He opened his mouth, but shades swarmed out of the mist, gray hands and teeth clasping and ripping. His scream was short.

The remaining man charged.

Seth swept out with his sword and a wave of fire arced toward the woman as she pulled the trigger. Argos leaped. Terror filled Seth but the hound landed, a bolt caught between his teeth.

The woman burned, then the Grief took her too.

Argos had already dropped the bolt and charged to meet the final assassin. The man lifted his hand, ready to catch Argos in the throat with his knife.

Another whisper in the dark and the man's raised wrist stood lined in blood. The knife clattered against the cobbles as the shades took him in a swirl of red.

Breathing ragged, Seth panted as a new figure stepped forward. He tucked the dart gun back inside his cloak and reached to pet Argos's eager head.

"It's not safe for you here, my boy," Geldar said by way of greeting.

Seth wanted to smile. He wanted to rush forward and embrace the old man.

"I had to come," Seth said. "I have something I need to know."

"He'll kill you if he catches you." The Inquisitor eyed the bloodless bodies. "And he won't stop trying."

Seth's hands were trembling. He'd taken another life, but did not feel bad about it, at least not as bad as he had before. The woman had intended to kill him. He would pray for forgiveness, to not lose the regret that should come with killing anything, even if he'd done it to survive.

For now there was Geldar and the looming question. They were both sworn to obey the Hierarch, the voice of Hyperion in this world, and Seth was at the old man's mercy.

"What will you do?" Seth asked, knowing he would not resist if Geldar chose to bring him to the Hierarch.

"I will choose my faith over my church."

Stepping closer, Geldar wrapped Seth in his arms.

Seth sagged against his mentor, this old man who'd saved him again and again.

"Come," he said, letting Seth go. "I can give you a place to rest. Then you can tell me what it is you need to know."

"This way, Argos."

The hound barked, sounding anxious, his nose pointed toward the temple. Perhaps he wished to rejoin his pack. Perhaps his family was there.

"This way," Seth repeated.

Argos followed.

Geldar led them back down into the shallowed bay, into the slums.

The Grief had never been so thick. Faces and vague shapes flickered as it swirled around them. The ghosts brushed, cold and mostly shapeless, across Seth's skin.

He lifted a hand to call a warding light, but Geldar took him by the wrist and shook his head.

"You've exposed yourself too much already."

They walked on, the priest leading him by memory. None of the cookfires burned now.

"It's getting worse."

"Yes," Geldar said. "The cycle of life is slowing. There are fewer and fewer babies, more and more ghosts."

He brought them to a ship painted in garish colors. It was tagged with graffiti, most of it inscrutable, some of it foul, but the inside wasn't ransacked. The old man lit a candle, light enough to keep the Grief at bay. He pulled a thick curtain over the sagging door cut into the ship's hull.

Argos perked up. He circled, sniffing.

"The woman who lived here had a reputation," Geldar said, settling into a chair. "It helps keep the locals away."

Argos gave a little yip.

"Raef lived here, didn't he?" Seth asked.

"Yes," Geldar said. "When this business started. I tried to scare him off it, but he did not listen. Your sort always were stubborn and doggedly curious. Two traits of the breed it seems."

"Why?" Seth asked. Argos gave up and nuzzled Seth's knee until Seth scratched his head.

"Something in the way Phoebe hoarded books I think. She encouraged questions, learning, and her priests had a dangerous habit of forming their own opinions." He looked sad. "I tried to warn them too, to talk Polus out of his plan."

"Why did you want to scare Raef off?"

"For the same reason I'm protecting you," Geldar said. "The Hierarch is misled in this business."

"He's the voice of Hyperion in this world," Seth said automatically, though without any of his old conviction. The man had maimed Raef. He'd sent assassins. These were not acts Hyperion would condone.

"It doesn't mean he's infallible, and it doesn't mean I will let him take you from me. You should run, Seth, get far away from here."

"I need to find Raef. I have to find him."

"Like draws like." Geldar's smile saddened. "Is that how it is then, between you?"

"No. He is—was—in love with Kinos. That was how they trapped him."

"I know." Geldar closed his eyes, pressed his back against the chair, and let out a long sigh. "That boy is too ambitious."

"Who is he?"

Kinos had saved his life, but Seth could hardly think kindly toward him. He knew that he'd have to let it go someday, offer it to Hyperion and hope the light burned the resentment away, but today was not that day.

"The Hierarch's nephew. He's always been ruthless, but this business . . . when the Oracle named him to the task, he accepted with vigor, practically leaped at the chance. To lie, sure, we do that. But to seduce someone, to feign love? That is not Hyperion's way."

"I don't think it worked out so well for him. I think he came to love Raef back. He sent me to find him. He wasn't faking that."

"It hardly matters now. We cannot have a Hierarch who would do what Logrum did or what he plans to do."

"What do you mean?"

"Logrum has always looked to the future. He plans for Kinos to succeed him."

"But that's not how it works. Hyperion chooses the Hierarch. It is not a dynasty!"

Geldar smiled. "Your faith runs deep, my boy, but Logrum has always had more interest in temporal matters. He wishes to be more king than priest."

It was too large, too much for Seth to know where to start fixing it, or what part he could play. This issue was far larger than him or Raef. It was corruption in the temple itself. Politics were a game he could not understand or win. He already had two impossible tasks before him.

"I have to find Raef. Then I have to find Helios's Forge. The Bishop set that as my pilgrimage. Can you help me with either, Father?"

Geldar laughed, bringing Seth's head up. He blinked.

"Your Bishop is wise, my boy. Both are closer than you think."

"But Raef is in Drowned Gate."

"So is the Forge. I suspect she knew this," Geldar said. "There were some among the knights who did not approve of the Hierarch's actions, especially the murder of Phoebe, though they cannot say so openly."

"But I don't know where Drowned Gate is."

Geldar's smile turned sharp as he leaned forward.

"That's all right. I do."

38
MOON

Raef crept along the tunnel, every sense tuned for the sound of claws on stone or steel.

Drowned Gate was a labyrinth, but there was something familiar in its rumble. Water ran everywhere, in rivulets and showers from above. Raef could not tell the acid from the pure, so he kept as dry as he could and made his way upward, working round and round in the climbing passages.

Again and again, his path brought him back to the central well. Each tunnel opened onto a ledge, but none had a way to reach the opening at the top of the prison.

Retreating again, he climbed, choosing only upward paths, and found a room with walls covered in ancient parchment. It looked something like the tower's Scriptorium, where the priests had copied books, but these were drawings of flayed flesh, organs, and bones. Detailed notes filled the margins and loose pages were piled on the rusty tables stained by all sorts of humors.

Raef wished he could retch, but everything he'd seen had

hardened his stomach too far for that. His heart still ached at least.

"Thank you, Lady," he whispered.

He was still alive, still human enough to feel, even if it hurt him so.

A stairwell led him higher than ever before, giving him a cautious hope. He entered a familiar room.

He knew these metal floors and walls. He'd seen these forges, vast enough that entire families could have made homes inside them.

Helios's Forge—that's what Sati had called this place. A stack of familiar shapes stood propped against a wall. Some were complete, others in pieces, but all were boxes with the same moon symbol worked into the lid.

Raef lifted a bit of brass, shifting it awkwardly with the shadowhand. It moved stiffly.

The fire in him stirred, threatening to rack him once more, to send him out of his mind again. He breathed in and out, willing the flames to douse, to fade back into embers. He thought of Seth. This must be how it was for the knight, always fighting the fire within him, always pushing it down. No wonder he'd been so broken.

Raef passed tools and half-finished weapons, many whose make he did not understand.

A bronze frieze wrapped the ceiling. In it the gods fought the demons. Raef knew the faces of Phoebe and the other twelve, but the demons were strange, inhuman. One figure was a ring of hands, an eye in each palm. Another was a storm cloud, a third, a swarm of locusts. The lesser demons mixed the shapes of man, beasts, and plants, like the jackal men here in Drowned Gate, like the woman of vines on Thiva. Haerwen, his mother had called her.

The two other walls showed the battle, the gods and demons at war, their followers clashing. They led great armies. The final wall showed a sad procession, Phoebe and Hyperion walking hand in hand. Between their palms they carried a half-moon, half-sun, their light mixing, reflecting one another as they stood mourning with Rhea. A young man rested inside the open coffin, his arms crossed over his chest.

Helios, Raef presumed.

The figures were in the ancient style, like those on Eastlight, rougher but recognizable. Whatever this place was, wherever the box had come from, it was ancient, older than the temples and shrines Raef knew from Versinae.

He took it in.

The gods were a family. They might quarrel as families did, but they were not enemies, not the opposites the knights made them to be.

Yet they'd taken this world. It could not be simple. The demons could not all be evil. If they were, then that made him evil. It made Seth evil, and he refused to accept that possibility.

It followed that the gods could not all be good. No good god would allow the Hierarch or Kinos to do what they'd done.

None of it helped. He had more answers than before, but the Moon's Door was gone. Even if it had survived, the Day of the Black Sun had likely passed.

Raef knew now why Kinos had gone into the box, but not why Phoebe's priests had made him.

He climbed higher, through the Forge's metal chambers. More machinery, more metal, scraps and pieces.

A scraping, jagged claws on steel, sounded behind him.

These creatures were like him, or at least like Argos. The hounds had been bred from them, but Raef did not think they'd be as tame as Seth's pup. He should run, but still, he wanted a look at them, to see if he could spy any part of himself in these distant cousins.

The howling began.

He retreated to the well. From this higher ledge he could see the many openings and passages below. He kept the shadowknife ready. The plan was simple.

Yipping and snarling, the demons raced up the passage, coming toward the ledge. They crowded together, leaving no room for him to slip past them, even if he'd been foolish enough to try.

They looked something like people, with sickly green eyes and matted, yellow fur covering their naked bodies. Their teeth were long and yellow beneath their snouts. Their smell, like oily meat, preceded them. They ran on all fours, claws scraping and clicking, ready to leap for him.

So much for a family reunion.

He'd seen enough to satisfy his curiosity.

The dome of stone, the well's roof, was not much higher. Another passage lay between him and it.

Raef's control over the shadowhand was not perfect, but he knew how to use the knife.

Calling it, gripping it, he drove it into the wall and willed it to harden. He found a purchase for his right hand and toes.

He pulled the knife free, reached, and drove it into the stone again.

With the shadowknife as an anchor, Raef climbed.

The demonkin reached the ledge. They leaped and yipped, trying to catch him.

He'd made it about halfway before one of them started climbing after him. It lost its grip and crashed back into the pack to leap and scramble on the ledge.

Another demon found better purchase. It nipped, its jaw latching onto Raef's boot. He hung by the knife, but lost his other grips. He tried to kick, to lose the demon's hold. No one would be dropping an oar this time.

He straightened his foot and let the demon drag the boot free.

It fell, wailing to land in the acid far below. It surfaced once, screaming, and did not reappear.

That cowed the rest of them. They retreated from the ledge, seeking another upward path. Hopefully they couldn't find what he hadn't.

Weak, he climbed on. He'd lost strength in the box and here, feeding on only algae. He had to leave this place while his body and mind allowed it.

He was almost to the next ledge when someone caught his hand and pulled him up.

"Easy," a familiar voice said.

Raef blinked at the pair of boots before his eyes.

"Is it you?" he asked. "You're really here?"

Seth pulled him up, over the ledge and into safety. Raef collapsed against it. He rolled to his back, trying to look upward. A furry face filled his vision, and a long tongue scraped across Raef's cheek.

"Yes," Seth said, laughing. "It's us."

"How?" Raef asked through brimming tears. "How are you here?"

"How are you out of the box?" Seth asked.

"That's a story."

"We can trade them," Seth replied with sadness.

Raef frowned to see the shadows in the knight's eyes.

"What?" Seth asked.

"I'm just glad you're here," Raef lied.

He remembered what Hanel had said, that it was a mortal wound when your faith was broken. Had it come to that?

He hoped not. He had no love for Hyperion, but he did not want that for Seth.

Seth offered Raef a hand.

Taking it, Raef let Seth help him to his feet.

Seth lifted his right hand. It glowed with fire, a little ball of sun to light their way. Raef's shadowknife and shadowhand glinted silver before they faded.

Seth blinked at the sight. He stood close.

"I have to smell pretty rank," Raef said, mostly because he did not know what else to say.

"It's fine," Seth said, nodding toward a passage. "We'll get you out of here. This way."

"How are you here? How did you find me?"

"The Bishop sent me to find the Forge." Seth lifted his hand so the light danced across the space. Argos padded along behind them.

"And it's in Drowned Gate," Raef said.

Seth's eyes shone when he smiled.

"And both are beneath Versinae."

Raef blinked.

Seth chuckled.

"What's the date?" Raef asked. "Has it happened yet?"

He'd lost count. After all this time, after ten years—he'd lost count.

"It's the twentieth day of Rhea's moon."

Two days. Two days remained.

"It would be waxing, almost full . . . before."

"You kept the count," Raef said, tears brimming again.

"I never forgot her, though I tried." Seth sized up the portal to another chamber. He looked abashed. "The Bishop sent me to find a weapon."

"Your sword . . ."

The one on his belt was not the one Raef knew. It was shorter and the leather of the grip was red. Another story lay there, but Raef would ask about it later.

"I'll never use that blade again," Seth said coldly.

Raef nodded. He understood, and he was honored, had no other word for it.

They took in the Forge and the weapons in various states of completion. "How did you even find this place?"

"I'll show you when we leave," Seth said. He eyed the blades and hammers. "But Argos helped."

"How?"

Seth grimaced.

Raef made a disgusted sound, but he knelt to scratch the hound's head.

"I'm glad you're all right, boy."

Argos wagged his tail in thanks as Seth faced the heavy door ahead of them.

Burnished bronze, they stood as tall as the doors to Hyperion's temple.

"What's in there?" Raef asked. "It looks like a vault."

A trace of the old greed rose with his curiosity. The contents, an ancient mystery, had to be valuable.

"I do not know. I cannot open it, but I think it's why I'm here."

"There's no keyhole." Raef stepped closer. He ran his right hand over the metal. "Did you try knocking?"

"It's Helios's Forge. I tried fire."

"Perhaps your knife?" Seth asked.

"I don't think so."

The ceiling held a frieze like the one below, all the gods gathered in a ring, holding hands. Phoebe stood beside Hyperion above the vault door. They carried their half-moon, half-sun.

"Let's try both," Raef suggested. He nodded to Seth's lit hand. "Put that out for a moment."

"I don't understand," he said but did as Raef asked.

"Put your palm to the door." Raef called the shadowhand and laid it on the metal. "Then call your fire."

Seth stepped forward. Raef used his good hand to guide Seth's to the metal. Seth flushed a little at the touch.

"And . . . now," Raef said.

Shadow and flame.

The metal doors swung open without a creak. Argos let out a happy bark at the trick they'd performed.

"The gods aren't enemies," Raef said.

"They're family," Seth added.

A little light glowed inside.

The interior was pristine, free of dust and damp. Several crystals, set into the ceiling, glowed like captured candleflames.

Raef stood back as Seth wandered among the racks, eyeing the swords and axes. He paused before a long war hammer, considering it.

"This one," he said. Sparks danced in his eyes. "This is the one."

"Will you be able to use a shield with that?"

"No. And I won't fit into the cadre's formation when I wield it, but it does not matter. This is the one."

Even Raef could admit that the craftmanship was beautiful. Forged of some brassy metal, it was worked with woven designs from head to pommel.

Part of him liked the way Seth's arms flexed when he lifted the weapon, but the feeling quickly faded.

"Now we just have to get out of here," Raef said.

"We'll show you," Seth said. "Won't we, Argos?"

The hound perked up from where he'd guarded the vault.

Back in the Forge, Raef watched the door close behind them.

Lighting the way, Seth led Raef and Argos into a small room, a metal box. Raef tensed.

"How is this the way out?" he asked, feeling short of breath.

"You'll see."

Seth laid a hand to the wall, called the fire, and the floor shifted.

The room shook and rose, leaving the broader Forge behind. Raef could hear the clank of chains above. The doorway passed stone both dry and glistening.

Raef beamed at Seth.

"Wondrous," he said.

The room swayed a little, and his weakness threatened to return. Seth lifted a hand, ready to catch him, but Raef kept his footing.

The chamber finally stopped. The open door faced bronze, not stone.

"We'll need to be quiet for this part," Seth said, stepping nearer. "I have a lot to tell you, but the Hierarch is not happy with me. He's tried to kill me twice. He will try again."

Seth let the light fade and pressed a part of the metal wall. It shifted, swinging open silently.

Raef recognized the smell of dead flowers and candlewax.

They stepped into the crypt beneath the temple of Hyperion.

The door to Drowned Gate was the shrine to Helios. The bronze relief slid back into place, fitting so tightly that Raef would never know it was there.

Raef scanned the crypt for flaming swords and let out his breath.

Fewer candles lit the space now.

The three of them crept up the stairs. Raef went first, using the shadowsight to watch for danger.

The sun had set, leaving the dome's interior in darkness.

Offerings were piled about the altar, scribbled prayers and supplications.

"The Hierarch is here," Seth whispered.

"He's in Versinae?"

"Yes. He brought you, in the box. He probably knows I'm here now too, but not that you're free."

"Then we have a chance," Raef replied as they crept toward the doors.

"At what?"

"To fix this," Raef said. "To fix everything."

"How?" Seth's eyes were wide.

"I'm not quite sure yet," Raef lied.

It was easier than telling him what he'd realized in the Forge. He couldn't say it out loud, not yet. The truth of it, the acceptance, had to grow, to settle in what remained of his heart.

Argos padded along, much quieter than his master. Raef tried not to scowl at the rap of the knight's boots on the marble.

"You are really bad at this," Raef hissed.

"I know," Seth whispered back. "Sorry."

The doors were unguarded. Raef could not open them. He was weaker now than when he'd come to steal Kinos, but Seth lifted the beam barring the way and leaned, using his weight to open them to a crack.

He pushed them closed when they'd squeezed outside.

"Now where?" Seth asked, taking in the darkling city.

"I have an idea," Raef said.

"Boat Town?"

"I think we can do better than that."

39

SUN

Seth let Raef lead him by the hand. Argos kept close. Even he did not seem to want to wander with the Grief so thick. It obscured the way ahead and the path behind them, leaving the three of them to float in a little island of light when the rare brazier pushed back the shades.

Raef released him when they reached their destination.

He showed no shame or fear as he stepped to the ornate door, raised the bronze knocker, and spoke calmly to the guard.

"Now we wait," he said.

Shivering, as though the small exchange had further exhausted him, he retreated to Seth's side.

"I wasn't expecting to come back here," Seth confessed.

"What were you expecting?"

"Another wrecked ship, a hole. Maybe a sewer, but not the prince's palace."

Raef had played the part of a wealthy noble when last he'd come here. Now he wore one boot and a stained shirt so torn that he may as well have gone without it. Despite what Seth had said, the smell was pretty bad. Then there was the hand, or rather, the lack of it, the place it should be but wasn't.

"Stop staring at it," Raef said. He shivered. "Please."

"I'm sorry."

He slung the hammer off his back, unbuckled his cloak, and settled it on Raef's shoulders. Raef looked up at him, his eyes full of something as he hugged the wool to his body.

"Thank you," he whispered.

"I should have thought of it sooner."

Raef smiled, and for a moment he was Pol again, the pirate who'd never seen kindness. That hadn't been a lie, Seth decided. Raef had not had it easy since his tower had fallen. Someday, maybe, he'd hear the story and maybe Seth would tell his own, how Geldar had stolen him from Dodona's tower as proof of heresy, but could not bring himself to slit Seth's throat. He doubted Raef would find much love for an Inquisitor, especially after the events on Eastlight, but Geldar had contended with the Hierarch, begging for the life of a demon boy, and he had won.

Argos sat between them, head darting back and forth at every sound. Seth narrowed his eyes, but his sight could not pierce the Grief.

The door opened and the guard waved for them to hurry inside.

A thin, straight-backed porter waited for them. He wore a crisp emerald coat and polished boots despite the late hour. A badge like a coin, showing the hawk-nosed prince flanked by two crows, was pinned to his chest.

He was old, though not as old as Geldar, with gray hair cropped close to his head.

Seth recognized him. He'd come with the prince to the temple when the Hierarch had first arrived in Versinae.

"This way, Master Raef," the porter said, waving for them to follow him into the palace's sweeping hall.

"You know me?" Raef asked, blinking.

"Of course. Lord Cormac is not presently here, but we will send a message."

"He's alive?" Raef choked out the question.

"Yes," the man said gently. "He has not stopped looking for you. He's at the docks now, preparing another search."

"Can you tell him that I'm here?"

Raef's eyes glistened. He swayed on his feet, and Seth braced again to catch him.

"We have already sent runners with torches. This way, please."

The house was lit, not as brightly as it had been during the party, but enough that Seth could see how harshly Raef contrasted to the pristine interior.

He did not feel so clean himself, not with his boots and the stink of the journey still upon him.

"I have beds prepared," the porter said. "Unless you prefer one."

Seth blinked.

"Uh . . ." he stammered.

"Two please," Raef said.

"I'll have baths brought and call for his lordship's physician."

Raef looked like he might protest, but bit off whatever argument he'd been forming.

"Thank you."

With a nod, the porter left them at the doors of two rooms and marched away.

Raef let out a weary chuckle.

"What?" Seth asked.

"All that business with the mask and shaving." Raef reached to scratch at the faint beard lining his jaw. "I could have just walked up to the gate and announced myself."

"Do you want to tell me what's going on?" It came out harsher than Seth intended. He did not like being confused and suspected Raef of teasing him.

"Do you remember how I told you that I found my parents? Adrian Deslis is my uncle, by way of my father, his brother Cormac."

Seth sank a little. He'd believed he and Raef similar, the same, but this put them back on a different footing. Raef was noble, and his uncle was hardly anyone Seth admired.

Seeing his expression, Raef's face turned gentle.

"You said you don't know who your parents are?" he asked.

"No. I thought I was an oblate until Father Geldar told me the truth, that I'd been bred in the tower."

Raef reached for him with his shorter arm, caught himself, and wrapped his right hand over Seth's.

"The ledgers on Thiva have the lists for Dodona. You could find them."

It had not occurred to him what the future held. He'd rescued Raef. He'd found his weapon. He would return to the Bishop, but it was not as though the Hierarch would stop hunting him. The future, for the first time since he'd set out for Teshur, felt obscured.

He could say with certainty that he finally understood what Geldar had meant, about being more complete, about dreaming bigger. He wanted more than knighthood, even if he didn't dare yet voice his hope.

"Would you—I mean, would you go with me?" he asked, saying as much as he dared.

"If I can. If I survive what's coming."

They'd circled each other for so long. The gods had to have a hand in it, that the two of them, probably the last of their breed, should meet over and over. They'd danced like the moon and sun, like their gods, like night and day.

The porter returned, leading servants with steaming jars. They moved in and out of the rooms, up and down the stairs like lines of ants.

"We need to make certain no one else knows we're here," Raef said, voice faint. He looked wan, like the last of his strength had fled.

The porter nodded.

Seth had a thousand more questions, but they would keep. They were safe enough for Raef to rest.

The servants led him inside his room. Seth opened his own door.

As promised, there was a wooden tub, full of steaming water. Stripping, he eased into it, and realized how much he needed it. He scrubbed himself clean, shedding the dead skin, salt, and the grime of travel.

Argos yipped happily.

"Did you want to join me?" Seth asked the hound. "You could probably use one too."

Argos's response was to curl into a ball by the hearth.

)))) ● ((((

There were clothes when he awoke, simple but far nicer than anything he'd ever worn. They fit him, which was unexpected. His armor and the hammer lay untouched where he'd left them but everything else was gone.

He rose, opened the window, and found a sunbeam to pray in. It was weaker than he liked. The palace was above the city's tall towers, but a heavy fog lay over Versinae. At least it wasn't Grief, not entirely.

"Thank you, Father," Seth prayed. He wasn't certain what else to say, how to capture everything he felt.

He'd found Raef. Argos had survived. They had a moment of safety.

Seth felt he needed little else, though his stomach disagreed, growling so loudly that it woke the sleeping hound.

"Thank you," Seth repeated.

He'd prayed to Hyperion for so long, seeing him as the Father, as the light, but in some ways it had blinded him. He'd always thought it was his blood, the flaw of his birth, but he'd never heard Hyperion's voice, never felt the god's hand directly on him.

Finding the hammer, feeling it had chosen him, had changed that. It felt like a gift from the god himself. Maybe it had something to do with the way he had finally mastered the fire, maybe it had been Raef's influence, the feeling of rightness when he'd stopped trying to burn away the parts of himself that had come from Phoebe or the demons.

Perhaps the hammer meant Seth did not belong in a cadre. Perhaps he would be a different kind of knight. He felt strangely at peace with the idea. He felt at peace with Hyperion, and with himself, for the first time in so long.

Rising, Seth opened the door to see a man standing outside Raef's room, his hand raised to knock but frozen in place, like he could not quite bring himself to it.

"He's probably still sleeping," Seth whispered. "He needs it."

"Oh," the man said. He was slender, around Raef's height, with hair just as dark but tied into a tidy rope at the back of his head. "How bad is it?"

He looked like he could use some sleep himself.

Seth almost wished he could lie, say he did not know, but that was not Hyperion's way.

"The Hierarch took his hand. Beyond that, he's very tired and maybe heartbroken."

The man squeezed his eyes shut, took in a long breath and let it out.

"You're Cormac? The one he wanted to get a message to?"

"Yes."

"You're his father."

"Yes."

Something red and jagged slipped into Seth's heart. They weren't so alike, Raef and him. This was new, this jealousy. It was very different from what he felt when he thought of Kinos. Anger tempered that feeling. This was something else. He understood why people called it green with envy. It swam in his guts like too many unripe apples.

Even with the ill feelings, he could admit there was something healing, something that made him feel more alive and complete than before, like another piece of him had fallen into place.

"Tell me everything you can," Cormac said, his stricken expression reminding Seth that he wasn't the only one hurting on Raef's behalf.

"I don't know everything, just the parts I was there for and what Kinos told me."

"Tell me those then."

"All right."

He followed Cormac to the palace kitchens. Servants brought food: thin, fresh bread, olives, and a soft cheese that Seth had never had before. They ate while Seth told all he could.

Sating his hunger was only part of it. Telling the story had soothed the ache, like a lengthy confession.

For Cormac's part, he looked pained, weighed down by what Seth had unburdened onto him.

"It is nearly noon," Seth said when he had finished. "I should pray. You are welcome to join me."

Cormac shook his head.

"I don't think Hyperion and I are going to be right for a long while."

Raef might be half-demon, but his father might be the source of his temper.

"Hyperion did not wrong him."

"Tell that to the Hierarch. After all, isn't he the god's voice in this world?"

Seth had no answer for that, because it was true. He found his way back to his room.

Argos wasn't there.

Seth shouldn't have left the hound alone. The servants would not know what to do with him.

Noticing that Raef's door was open to a crack, Seth peeked inside to find Argos curled at the foot of Raef's bed.

Argos lifted his head slightly, acknowledging his master, then settled back in place. Raef did not stir, though Seth could see the steady rise and fall of his pale, too-thin chest. He had a little dark hair there, and no scars, not like Seth's. The only clear injury was the arm that ended shorter than the other.

"I'm so sorry," Seth whispered.

He'd promised not to stare. He pulled the door closed and returned to his own room.

He preferred the open sky for prayers, but the window would do. At least the sky had cleared. The light was brighter, and he could see the temple's dome, rising over the city, just a little higher than the palace. Seth stripped and sat. Eyes closed, he focused on the light, on its warmth.

"Father," he prayed.

But he did not know what else to say.

He'd found Raef. He'd been chosen by Argos.

But he'd also killed to save his own life, and could not regret it, could not ask for forgiveness.

He'd completed his pilgrimage, become a full knight, and yet he felt incomplete.

Seth conjured the flames, let them roll through him. But he did not smolder. He did not steam.

He had changed.

He felt it more than heard it, but the message was clear.

His penance was complete.

Seth lifted his face, closed his eyes, and felt the light. The fire did not roil inside him. It did not fight for escape. It filled him, warmed him. It was part of him. The darkness was there too, a contrast, a complement.

He did not call it, but the flame gathered in his palm and took shape.

A long blade glimmered in his hand, so bright that the glow shone through his closed eyelids. It whirled and twisted, flattening, spinning into a shield.

Seth opened his eyes. The light vanished.

A sword and shield of fire. No knight he knew could conjure that.

"Father," Seth prayed in wonder. "What am I?"

No answer. He was alone.

"No," he said, smiling, feeling the warmth within him. It did not burn. It did not singe his skin. He was not alone. Never truly.

Seth had lost his faith in the Hierarch but not in Hyperion. He had not lost his god's love.

He had Geldar and the Bishop. He had Argos.

He had—

"Seth?" a voice asked from behind him.

Raef leaned against the doorway. Still pale, he was at least clean. He wore a pair of soft sleeping pants and a loose shirt of gray linen with a pattern of leaves woven at the hems. He was barefoot, and there was something about that, about its vulnerability, that pained him.

"You're awake."

Raef nodded, and even that seemed to take some of his strength.

"Thank you," he said. "For coming for me."

"You got yourself out of the box."

"Thank you anyway. I never would have found my way out."

"You need to lie down." Seth nodded to the bed.

"Yeah," Raef agreed. He moved that way, felt at the bed like he didn't trust it, then climbed into the bedding that Seth had left bunched in hills and valleys.

Seth put a blanket over him, but Raef did not notice. He was already asleep again.

From there it was visitors. Cormac had chairs brought. They sat together, watching over him. The physician arrived, a large woman with curling red hair in a purple gown. She shooed them out. Even Argos obeyed. The harried-looking man carrying her bag shot them an apologetic look as he closed the door behind them.

When she opened it again, she left a confused looking Raef behind.

"Barbarous," she spat, eyeing Seth and Cormac like they'd made the cut. "But it's clean. He needs food and sleep. That is all."

Cormac nodded as she shuffled away, her assistant scurrying after her.

Raef lay propped against the headboard.

Cormac's eyes remained focused on Raef's left arm.

"It's all right, you two," Raef said, turning between them,

holding it up and laying it to rest on his chest. "This is who I am now."

Seth did not quite believe him. He was a good liar, but his eyes darted that way now and again.

"Sit," Raef said. "Both of you."

Cormac took a chair. Seth dared the edge of the bed.

"I know what I have to do," Raef said, looking between them, meeting their eyes. "And neither of you will like it."

40

MOON

The occasional bob of a watchman's lantern came and went in the distance. No one living walked the streets. Even the best thieves had surrendered to the Grief and stayed indoors.

No one guarded the Garden wall. Raef called the shadow-hand and scaled it quickly. Reaching the top, he turned his gaze beyond the city.

The press of the shades extended into the hills, making a second, misty sea. Beneath him, Versinae lay too still, too quiet, an island besieged in gray. He might save the world, but it might be too late for his home. His limbs felt heavy despite his new-found strength in darkness. He'd felt it when night had fallen, when he'd finally woke from the last of his stupor to eat his fill in the palace kitchen. He was stronger when Hyperion had set, stronger than he'd been before Eastlight and the box.

He took a breath, ready to test his limits, and to see if Sati had told him the truth.

Concentrating, Raef pulled forth the shadowmarks that she'd drawn into his skin. He pushed them further, let them unfurl around him into a pair of diaphanous wings. He could flex them. He could barely feel them. Like the shadowhand, they felt *other*, more like a boot or clothing than a part of him.

Raef stepped forward and let himself fall.

He could not fly, but he could glide, awkwardly. He needed practice.

His heart sank that he wouldn't get the time.

Raef landed with a thud in the garden. Neither it nor the ruins had changed since he'd sheltered here with Kinos.

Thinking of him still brought the broken shard feeling to his chest. He inhaled the chill garden air. Perhaps there would be a moment when thinking of Kinos wouldn't feel this way, but he knew he wouldn't have time for that either.

He returned to the undercroft, to the domed ceiling and dusty floor. The splintered carving, the black door, showed his reflection as he approached it.

He rubbed the black hand over it, gingerly brushing away any soot and dust.

Sati slipped into his reflection. His mother, the demon, wore a sad smile.

Raef had thought he'd feel something stronger in this moment, having put it all together, but the resolution, knowing what he had to do, weighed him down.

"You solved the puzzle," she said.

"Can you read my mind?"

"I do not have that power, but your expression is grim enough to tell me what you are thinking."

She stepped forward and he could see her better, looking as she had when she'd marked him. She met his stare. "And it's not hard to guess your thoughts."

Raef examined her reflection. Translucent, as if painted onto a dingy window, she was thin, even in the shadowsight.

"You're a spirit, aren't you, a ghost?"

"Yes. Flesh is weak. I am an echo." She examined her hand. Her nails were black, like her eyes, like his eyes. "As all our kind are."

"The priests brought you here, where you could be with Cormac."

"Yes." Her smile seemed genuine. "Your father was a delight that evening."

"Then what, I was born and they killed you?"

"No, little blackbird. They were trying to stop our extinction. They honored me as befitted a daughter of the Sunken Garden."

"Why?" he asked. "Why did they do it?"

"Phoebe realized the sins of her kind. She wished to make peace in our ancient war, but I died for you, to bear you."

"I'm so sorry," he said.

"It is I who owe you an apology. I sloughed my skin, got to linger and watch you grow, but without flesh I was forced to trade my fealty for survival."

"To the higher demon. He who would return."

"My clever son . . . Yes again. He knew the secret, how to remain, but I had to trade to gain it. All I've done to you, all of it." She hung her head and he lost sight of her eyes in the veil of black hair. "I wormed my way into Logrum's dreams, whispering that he had to become the Hierarch by any means, that he had to kill the moon. So earnest that one, so eager for murder when I gave voice to his ambition."

It did not surprise Raef. Logrum seemed more than capable of assassinating his predecessor.

"You were his Oracle?"

"Yes."

"But why kill Phoebe if she was trying to make peace with you?"

"Only she can descend and return through her door, but she guarded it too closely for my master to slip past her. Now Hyperion guards it, but tomorrow he will sleep. When you open it, she will return, and so will Rerek."

"And Kinos?" Raef asked.

"Oh, Logrum's darling, doting heir." She met Raef's stare again and smiled. It was not kind. "Even though he acted as my puppet, he had to pay for hurting you. I knew he would love you, and that Logrum would lose him forever when he realized what he'd done."

"You almost sound like you care about me."

"I do, in my own mad way, but to survive I needed you to break, to force you to see what you are, crack open your heart and grow your sacrifice. You will open the Moon's Door and Phoebe will return. My debt to my master will be paid, and I will be free to walk the Sunken Garden again."

"What does that mean?"

"That's not what you really want to know, is it?" she asked. "You want to know what will happen to you."

"I'll die," Raef said with a shrug. "That's the sacrifice."

"Yes, and if you do not offer it, the world will drown in Grief."

"I have to die." He'd known it, but saying it aloud, it still did not quite feel real, inevitable as it was. "You've made certain of that."

"So I have." She did look sad as she reached to press her hand to the glass. "It's almost dawn, Hraefn. It's time for you to go."

He returned the gesture, pressed the shadowhand to the cracked obsidian. He could not feel her, did not know how to feel about her. She'd done this to him, known the price he would pay for her survival. All his life he'd wondered where he'd come from, imagined a parent somewhere, loving him, missing him. What parent could claim love for a child they'd willingly sacrifice?

"No, Mother," he said. "It's time for me to burn."

That was the answer of course. Phoebe's light was simply Hyperion's reflected back. There could be no moon without the sun.

Raef had realized it in the Forge, where the gods made their weapons of war, where they'd sealed the vault by means of both light and darkness.

Opening the Moon's Door would take Hyperion's fire.

Retreating to the flooded room, he fetched one ledger. It was molded over, illegible, but it would serve for his plan.

He took his time climbing the wall, reveling in his strength and speed before Hyperion rose.

Telling himself he wanted to see the city a final time, he walked the streets, meandering between the towers, but he could admit that he did not know how to say goodbye to those he had to.

Then he could delay no longer. The sun had risen high when he went to the temple plaza.

Cormac and Seth waited for him, at the sprawling fountain with its marble tritons and fantastic sea dragon.

Around them, the city woke. The people gathered outside the doors, crowding together as noon approached.

His broken heart filled at the sight.

"Thank you, Lady," he prayed.

He'd thought them fled or dead, but the people of Versinae proved themselves as resilient as always.

Cormac looked side to side, wary and worried.

"There has to be another way," he said.

"There isn't." Raef surprised him with an embrace, knowing it would silence further arguments. He'd lose the will to do this if either of them protested too hard.

"You're not anything like what I imagined," Raef said. "But I am glad, Father, that we had the time."

"Me too." Cormac let Raef go and wiped his eyes.

Raef turned to Seth.

"I wish I had more time to make it all up to you."

Then it was Raef's turn to be surprised as Seth kissed him, quick, hard, and fiercely. Raef didn't pull away. He never wanted to pull away from this earnest, golden-haired man who could understand him like no one else could, who looked at him like no one else ever had.

"Just come back to me," Seth said. "That's all the making up you need to do."

"We both know that's not going to happen."

"Then I'll find you on the other side."

Raef found a smile.

"If anyone could, it's you."

They flanked him as he pushed his way through the crowd in the plaza and through the tall bronze doors of Hyperion's temple.

"Why are there so many people here?"

"I might have sent runners to spread the rumor that people should come today," Cormac said. "And Adrian might have put a little silver into it."

"You know, I might decide to like Uncle Adrian," Raef said before diving into the tide of bodies.

They jostled him, stepped on his toes, and Raef grinned through it.

The tide sheered Cormac and Seth away from him. That was better. Raef did not want them too close. If the gods showed mercy, they wouldn't see what was about to happen.

He broke through the crowd and came to a halt, eyes wide. The Hierarch had changed since their encounter on Eastlight.

Deep circles ringed his eyes. His crimson robe and golden coat no longer hung tight on his hunched frame.

Voice trembling, no longer booming, he spoke the Rite of Transgression.

Raef knew the ritual. The priest spoke it to take the fates of the people onto himself, to appease the gods through self-sacrifice and privation. Logrum's hand trembled as he lifted the wreath of bay and laurel from his head to lay it upon the altar.

Raef pushed forward, clearing the crowd and stepping into the light beneath the oculus.

"Logrum!" he shouted. "You lying fraud! Hyperion does not hear you!"

His blasphemy brought a collective gasp from the crowd. They shuffled back, distancing themselves from the heretic.

The Hierarch met Raef's eyes. He opened his mouth to speak, but could only gape.

"You profane his temple with your false prayers," Raef continued.

"I am the voice of Hyperion in this world," the Hierarch said, sounding labored.

"You are a hypocrite."

Raef lifted the ruined book he'd fetched from the undercroft.

He had the crowd's attention. Near silent, they listened. He found the Bishop's stern, bronze eyes. She turned to the knights winding their way toward him and halted their advance with a nod.

Raef wondered if Seth had anything to do with that.

"Should I tell them the truths I dredged up from Drowned Gate? Where you threw me after you took my hand?"

The Hierarch pointed a trembling finger at the volume.

"That book is heresy."

"It's from the Inquisitors' own library," Raef called. "Proof that the Hounds of Hyperion were bred from demon stock, that you killed Phoebe for doing what Hyperion himself once commanded."

"Is this true, your Holiness?" the prince asked.

Raef hadn't seen Adrian among the nobility. The crowd began to murmur. Restless, they tried to pick a side.

The prince's expression narrowed, like a predator scenting blood. He'd come to twist the knife, but it remained on Raef to drive it home.

"You killed the moon for a lie," Raef accused. "You stole your crown and brought the Grief!"

"I killed Phoebe to protect us, to protect you all from the demons. Demons like him!" Shouting, the Hierarch pointed to Raef. The room warmed. "And it worked. This would be the Day of the Black Sun, but it did not come. She is dead. It can never come."

"Do I look like a demon?" Raef stepped closer to the altar, leaving the crowd safely behind. He lifted his severed arm. "Were I a demon, I could have kept you from cutting off my hand."

"Give me that book!" The Hierarch reached out. Despite his commanding tone, the grasping gesture was almost pleading.

"No," Raef said. "I'm giving it to the people. I'm giving them the truth."

"Knights!" the Hierarch bellowed.

"Hyperion is the light, Your Holiness," the Bishop said, her voice carrying. "The light is truth, and the truth must be known."

"Lest we all be lost in darkness," the knights finished together.

At this, the crowd divided. Some called Raef mad. Some looked ready to rush him. All hesitated, watching to see what would unfold.

Guilt and anger warred in the Hierarch's eyes. Sati had done her job well. The same mad terror Raef had spotted on Eastlight ran openly across the Hierarch's face.

He only needed one more push.

"I know what you did," he said, quiet enough that only Logrum would hear. "I know how you earned your robe and ring. I'm going to tell them. I'm going to tell everyone."

The Hierarch snapped, faster than Raef had expected, just as Raef needed him to. Fire and light poured through the oculus. Raef caught a glance at its swirling column. Then the searing heat took him.

The crowd screamed and ran for the doors.

Agony washed through him. He drank it in, let the flames fill the cracks in his heart, the break Kinos had made for it.

The Moon's Door was never a carving. The carving had been a mirror, showing only himself. He'd never held the key. The moon reflected the sun. Hyperion's fire was the key.

Still, it hurt beyond anything Raef had imagined. His greatest fear, the death he'd always known would come for him, arrived.

The tears sizzled off his face.

The crack broke open. The place where he'd loved Kinos, where he might love Seth someday, where he loved Cormac and Phoebe exploded into a thousand suns.

The light and fire carried him away.

41

MOON

Waves, the Ebon Sea, stretched to the horizon. Nothing, not the inside of the box, not his worst winter on the streets, could be as cold as this place, and yet he did not freeze. Instead he burned like incense, embers slowly eating away what remained of him.

He'd died, yet he could feel his heart pounding in his chest. The water whispered to him, a song, a chorus of voices. Raef could almost make out the words.

The rough stone of the shore scratched his bare feet. He felt a pang of loss for his boots. He'd finally had a new pair, one all his own, thanks to Cormac. Raef tried to laugh that he would care about such a thing here, in this most final of places, but no sound came.

The inky water brushed the silent shore. Hyperion could never come here. Every mortal had to. The fire washed through him again, bringing a ripple of agony. He wouldn't last long. He couldn't. More of him flaked away.

Am I dead? he wondered. *It shouldn't hurt so much to be dead. You're on the other side of the Door.*

She stood next to him, wrapped in her cloak of starry night. Raef hadn't seen her approach. She hadn't been there. Then she had.

Half her face peeked through the hood. Black throughout, without a gleam, a statue carved from jet. Lightless, as she must be, in the forever night of her exile from the sky.

Lady. Raef fell to his knees.

It was her, really her—and her voice. It had been the one he'd heard in the crypt, not Sati, not a trick. She had been with him.

Raef, she said softly. *My raven. Rise, child.*

But the pain would not let him. His heart, broken so many times, had finally given out. It surely would have killed him, were he not already dead.

Did it work? he asked, looking up at her. *Did I get it right?*

Yes. Her smile wiped away so much of his agony. *You brought the light to me, the fire. You have opened the way. Now I can return. You only have to give it to me and your pain will end.*

Raef wanted to sigh, but he had no breath.

Good, he said. *An end, once and for all.*

Don't you want to know more, to ask why I made you?

Raef gestured at the void around them, at the fire roiling inside the cage of shadow written on his skin. He pressed his hand to his heart.

I thought it was for this.

No, my gentle boy. You've done a terrible thing, opening yourself this way, necessary though it was. You are the door and the bridge between us, between our worlds.

What about the demons? Won't they come back too?

Yes. Some will be good. Some will be evil and they will need to be stopped. Mortals bred with gods have always been our greatest weapons. We cannot breed with mortals as our children can, and we swore we'd have no more of our own when they banished us. Only Helios came with us, and we lost him in the war. I used what gods this world had, to make you, son of my heart. You are the child I could not bear.

I guess it no longer matters. Seth, or some other half-breed, will have to be your weapon. I am sorry to have failed you.

You, my clever boy who is not always so clever, could never, have never, failed me. Rise and I shall open the way.

Raef found the strength to obey, and she touched his heart with an obsidian finger.

All the fire in him, everything he'd carried here, the flames and anguish, left him in a rush. Now he froze, just as badly as he'd burned before.

Then he was in her arms. Phoebe lifted him as if he were tiny, a child. Sati may have given birth to him, but this was his mother, his only mother. She was so much bigger than he, growing as the fire filled her. Waxing, brightening, she carried him to a little boat shaped like the crescent moon and laid him down. He realized this was how she carried the souls, ferrying them gently to this place so they might sink into the sea and find their peace.

She took up a long pole and looked just like her statue. Raef smiled.

He'd have kissed her feet, if he'd had the strength to move.

Stars winked into being high above them. They kept lighting until more than he'd imagined possible shone above them. They began to fall, to gather, a blizzard of silver light, and in it, a stream, the road beyond. The boat began to glow, shining as she did, full of silver light.

Are you ready? Phoebe asked, a smile peeking out from her cloak of stars. *Are you ready to go home?*

Don't I have to stay here? he asked, the tears leaking from his eyes as he forced them to stay open, even if it blinded him. He did not want to miss anything. He did not want to forget, even as he knew that this moment was more akin to a dream than waking. It had already begun to fade.

Have you not yet guessed? she teased. *The fire cannot burn you. I made you as they made the hounds, to hold and withstand Hyperion's flame.*

That was why. That was how. He'd opened the door when the tower burned. He'd burned. That was what he hadn't remembered. He'd come here, just long enough to escape. Then he'd slipped back into the world, into Versinae. He'd forgotten in the shock of it all.

I don't know if I can bear it, Lady, Raef confessed. *Bear living, after all that's happened.*

You can. You must, for I am not yet done with you.

Moonlight filled everything and Raef felt hot metal beneath him. He opened his eyes and found himself lying naked on the sun. It took a moment to realize that the light was merely the reflection of Hyperion on the temple's golden dome. He lay naked atop it.

Through the oculus, he heard the crowd's shouts and shock at the Hierarch's actions. They were still bolting into the plaza. The sun hung overhead. Raef had only been gone a moment. He'd survived.

"Lady . . ." he prayed, his voice shaking.

The sky above him darkened. The din inside the dome and in the plaza turned to startled cries. The reflected light on the golden dome dimmed as the moon slid over Hyperion's disk.

Raef's skin tingled to see her hanging there, blocking the sun's light. Out past the city walls, the Grief rose like a tide of gray. It twisted, spiraling into thick strands full of faces and shapes. The threads rose, flowing upward, weaving skeins of mist, rivers that poured through the open door.

In the sudden night, Raef felt strong.

He called his wings, stepped off the dome, and landed near the temple's laundry yard. He tugged on a pair of breeches with little consideration for size, grabbed a shirt too small, and selected another. Dressing remained difficult. The shadowhand, especially the thumb, was not as agile as flesh.

Raef blinked. He could not be certain, but he thought he saw dozens of hands, each with an eye in the palm, grasping and reaching in the ring of sunlight that haloed Phoebe's disk.

The last of the ghosts passed through her, and she moved, letting Hyperion back into the sky they shared.

42
MOON

Raef flicked his wrist and sent the two coins, a pair of coppers, chasing one another around the bowl. It had taken a bit of practice to master this simple trick with his one daylight hand. Most times, when eating with the shadowhand, the fork still hit his cheek instead of his mouth. His lip curled to know that he still couldn't write his name any better than a first moon neophyte. It was especially unfair as he'd always been good with a knife in either hand.

The year turned toward winter. Raef pulled his black robe around himself and thanked Phoebe for the heavy cloth, though really he should thank his father since Cormac had gifted it to him. Raef leaned back against the wall, at his post beside the hole Seth and the knights had hammered open for him so he did not have to climb it on sunny days.

The mark, the shadow, slept, waiting for night. Then he'd have two hands again. Then he could run the roofs, do whatever she asked of him.

A golden shape loomed over him. Something heavy dropped into his bowl, dipping it toward the cobbles.

"A golden Hierarch?" Raef asked, looking up from the coin.

Seth smiled down at him. Back in his armor, his hair shorn, he practically glowed. He wore his hammer on his back. The brass inlay caught the light.

He looked good. He always looked good. Raef returned the smile.

"I thought you could use it."

"I can."

"Cormac sent me. He'd like to see you at the palace."

Raef bit the coin and picked himself up. He waved to the priests of Hyperion across the plaza. Some waved back. Others nodded awkwardly, still uncertain how to take the return of a Night Brother. Some looked away.

"How much have you made today?" Seth asked, leading Raef across the plaza toward the palace.

"Including this?" Raef asked, nodding to the coin as he tucked it into a pocket.

"Yes."

"One golden Hierarch and two coppers."

"And you're really doing this the hard way?"

"I'm doing it the right way, thank you," Raef said. "That's what Phoebe wants. At least I think it is. She's less talkative on this side of the Door."

"She really spoke to you?" Seth asked again, as he had so many times before. His eyes always filled with wonder at the answer.

"Yes, though it's like a dream now. I can't remember most of it and what is left is fading."

Seth slipped his hand into Raef's.

"For whatever it's worth, I think it's the right way too."

"Too bad we're not immortal." Raef squeezed Seth's hand. "At this rate I'll have enough to hire masons to clear the rubble in ten years. It should take about two hundred more to rebuild the tower. You'd think people would be more grateful."

"The city is still recovering, and there are still a lot of ghosts."

"She can't take all of them, the ones without any spirit left, any mind. There might always be a little Grief."

"But the fish have returned with the tides. People can eat."

"Yes," Raef agreed.

A few merchants had appeared with goods to sell. Peddlers trickled in, both overland and with the ships. Versinae was ebbing back to life.

Raef spied an urchin working the plaza and flashed an L for "Lost." The girl rolled her eyes but she flashed it back.

The roads grew safer, so long as you didn't bleed too much. Tethis remained especially haunted, but after the trouble they'd given Cormac, Raef couldn't say he sympathized.

He lowered his hood as they passed through the palace gates. A guard tapped the butt of his halberd against the ground in salute.

"I'll never get used to that," he said. "I never expected my uncle to acknowledge me. Even if I wanted to go back to stealing, I'd never get away with it. All the guards know me now."

"At least you'd probably get a nicer cell," Seth said.

"Not likely. Uncle has acknowledged me, but he's not fond of me."

The feeling was mutual. Raef knew too well the difference between how the prince and the people lived. Cormac often reminded him that having Adrian's ear would allow Raef to negotiate for those in need, so he did his best.

"Your father has acknowledged you too. That should keep you safe enough—if you can stay out of trouble."

Raef gave Seth a look of mock affront as they approached the granite crenels and green copper spires. They passed into the great hall. A long series of frescoed figures, ancestors he knew nothing about, looked down upon him.

Court wasn't in session. The servants either ignored Raef and Seth or gave a slight nod in greeting. They weren't friendly, not exactly, but they accorded him respect and notice. It made the back of his neck itch.

"I wonder if they'd let me stay for dinner."

"I wonder if they'd let you bathe."

"I've got to say, Sir Knight, I never expected you to have a sense of humor. Or to play errand boy for the palace."

"It gave me a chance to see you." Seth let Raef's hand go and pecked him on the cheek. "Head to your uncle's solar and I'll see if I can find some bread and cheese for my beggar priest."

"Do that, and maybe I'll take that bath with you."

Seth blushed and ducked his head. Raef smiled, headed upstairs, and braced himself.

In the solar, Cormac sat beside the prince at a round table laden with letters and maps.

Prince Adrian Deslis, Cormac's elder by five years, wore a perpetual scowl. Like Cormac, he dressed elegantly, in a doublet of black velvet and a pair of fine rings set with emeralds. A tendency toward the material appeared to be a family trait. Raef may be a raven, but his uncle and father were magpies.

Raef bowed. "Uncle."

"Bastard," the prince greeted.

"He has a name," Cormac snapped.

"And you have a new ship," the prince said. "You can get back to it at any time."

"Uncle just wishes me to remember my place," Raef said. He closed his eyes to tamp down his temper.

It seemed shorter lately. He wondered if his demon blood were to blame or if it was just a side effect of having gained a family.

After a short breath and a quickly whispered prayer, Raef opened his eyes and asked, "You wanted me, Father?"

His uncle opened his mouth, but Cormac cut him off. "We wanted to tell you that the Hierarch has quit the city. He's returned to Ilium and left Versinae's temple to the Bishop."

"So I can watch my back a little less."

Seth could have told him that, though he probably hadn't out of his desire that Raef get along with his newly acquired relations. Raef's knight could be meddlesome when he thought he was up to good.

"What else is there?" Raef asked.

The prince gestured for Raef to sit. He took the chair across from them.

"There is to be a council of the princes." Adrian waved a hand to the letters scattered around him. "We will meet to discuss the Hierarch's influence in our affairs, measure it, and consider if it is proper for the representative of Hyperion to exert so much influence over temporal matters."

Raef sat back in his seat. It was unheard of, but the Hierarch had overstepped. If they were ever going to weaken his influence over Aegea, now was the time.

"You're finally putting him in his place," Raef said. "Good."

"It will not end well for him," Cormac said. "He tried to incinerate you in front of the entire city. That cost him greatly."

"It's worse than that," the prince added. "With the truth out, the Sun House's power is broken here. Diminishing the Hierarch has acted as a beacon to every cutpurse in Aegea. It's not just petty crime. Murders and robberies are surging. This city belongs to the shadows now."

It might not be that. Raef had brought back Phoebe, but she hadn't come alone. There were demons in the world again.

If one were responsible, he'd find it, this cousin of his.

He'd do his duty to her, and above all keep the balance.

"It's not the shadows, not the night or the day," Raef said. "We can't survive without Hyperion any more than we can without Phoebe. We need them both."

"It will take time for the people to find their faith again," Cormac said.

"I understand how they feel." If anyone could convince him to forgive Hyperion, it was Seth, but even then, it would take time. "What do you want me to do?"

"Your father tells me you have contacts," Adrian said. "Friends on the streets. I want you to find out what you can. See who is in charge. Perhaps we can strike a deal with them. If there are interlopers, perhaps our native gangs would assist us in defending their territory."

Adrian was shrewd, Raef had to give him that.

"I know someone, but she'll want payment, pardons, and aid for the children she cares for."

"If she helps, she'll have all three. You can go."

Cormac looked offended at the blunt dismissal, but Raef smiled to assure him. He was glad to have a father, but he could fight his own battles.

And they were a family, new as it was, rough as Adrian could be. They would find a balance too.

Seth found him again that night, once the sunset prayers had ended. Raef had answered Hyperion's priests with one of his own, though he doubted anyone could hear his solitary voice. He imagined doing a solstice procession. It would be rather sad. All the priests of Hyperion would come halfway to the tower ruins, and he'd meet them alone.

Argos dug in the garden below as Raef and Seth sat together atop the wall. Tucked between two of its crenels, they waited. Raef stared toward the east, past the temple dome and the city walls. He needed acolytes, but hopefully not too soon. He had nothing to feed them, no way to clothe them, and no idea what to teach them. The collection of knowledge was her first tenet, but the library was gone. The wisdom of the elder priesthood was gone.

He could try to retrieve Hanel from Drowned Gate, but was not certain how the old man would fare out of the darkness, or how he would care for someone so mad. Nor did he have food or space for Hanel. At least Seth had kept his word and brought Raef bread and cheese for their supper.

Tomorrow Raef would seek out Maurin to bring her Adrian's terms. He'd find out what she could tell him about the city's new troublemakers.

"Did you mean it?" Seth asked, pulling Raef from his thoughts.

"Mean what, the sunset prayer? Of course."

"No, what you told your uncle and father, that we need Hyperion and Phoebe."

"Eavesdropping, Seth?" Raef spared him a glance though he kept his focus on the horizon. "That's not very Sun House of you."

Seth smiled.

"You might be rubbing off on me a little."

"I meant it," Raef assured him. "Though I don't know if I can ever forgive the knights. I know I can never forgive Logrum."

Seth's gaze flicked to Raef's arm. His smile faltered.

"I don't think I could ask you to."

Raef had to admit, there was some appeal to a world without a sun. He'd dreamed of it once or twice, an endless night where he never lost his second hand, where he could run and fly without limit.

The world would freeze without Hyperion. A sunless Aegea

would be worse than one without a moon. Raef shuddered, shaking off the dream before it could turn into a nightmare.

They stared at the horizon for a while, waiting together.

"What are you thinking about?" Raef asked, because he was curious, because he loved the sound of Seth's voice, especially when he sang at dawn, his earnest hymns spiraling up the wall.

"Thiva," Seth said. "You promised we'd go."

"I meant that too."

"I was thinking about the tower there, not just the ledgers, but the books. Maybe there's gold or silver in the vaults. It's not like that would be stealing. It's already Phoebe's coin."

It was not a bad idea. Raef smiled.

"Do you think the Bishop would give you the time, another pilgrimage?"

"I don't think she knows exactly what to do with me. I don't fit into the cadre's tactics anymore. She'd likely be glad to have a respite from me."

"I doubt that's true."

She was a hard woman, but Raef suspected the Bishop cared for Seth as she seemed to care for all of her knights.

He did not pry too deeply into the politics of Hyperion's faith, but it seemed Seth would survive the Hierarch's disgrace. The Inquisitors, likely at pressure from Geldar, mostly pretended that Seth did not exist, that he was just another knight. Another pilgrimage might be just the thing if he were drawing too much attention.

Much remained uncertain, but Raef would not allow anyone to hurt Seth.

"Of course. We'll go together, whenever you want. And if we have the time, after, I'd like a closer look at Eastlight."

Seth gave him a worried glance.

"Not for the reason you think," Raef said. He had no interest in finding Kinos. No one had heard from him since the night Raef had lost his hand, and he'd be happy if that were the end of the youngest Inquisitor.

"That place is special to the gods. I felt it. I'd like to know more."

"That's all?" Seth asked.

He reached out, closed his hand over Raef's wrist.

"That's all."

Seth's thumb felt strange against his severed flesh, but Raef did not pull away. He did not call the shadowhand to cover it. This was who he was. He wouldn't hide it.

"I'm so sorry I lied to you," Raef said.

"When?"

"Before, on Thiva."

"Why are you apologizing now?"

"Confession is good for the soul," Raef said with a shrug. "Isn't that what you're always telling me?"

"I forgave you, remember?" Seth shifted and pulled Raef into his arms until Raef's back rested against his chest. "You came back to me. That's all the making up I asked for."

"I don't think it's enough. It doesn't feel like enough."

"Then promise me no more secrets." Seth tightened his embrace. "No more lies. Just tell me everything."

"There are parts you might not want to hear."

Seth's lips brushed Raef's ear.

"Tell me anyway."

"All right." Raef thought carefully, trying to put the truth, the entire truth, in order. He wouldn't lie, not even by omission, if he could help it.

A silver glow glinted on the horizon.

"The first time I saw you," he began, "I almost killed you."

ACKNOWLEDGMENTS

First, thank you, reader. I hope this book brings you dreams.

Thanks to Rick Bleiweiss, Deirdre Curley-Waldern, Isabella Bedoya, Isabella Nugent, Sarah Bonamino, Josie Woodbridge, and everyone at Blackstone for making this lifetime dream come true.

Lesley Sabga for being the most amazing agent.

Nicole Resciniti, for telling me to dream bigger and convincing me to listen.

Sarah Riedlinger, who brought everything to life in a cover and interior art that made me feel exactly the way I'd always hoped to when I saw it.

Jake Shandy, who made the perfect map for this dark and twisty world.

Kendra Merritt, who helped intensely with a sensitivity read.

Veronica R. Calisto, who always helps me get some details right.

Brian McNees, Jo Dunn, and Neva Murphy for being the family I chose and for choosing me back.

Thank you to the ones who never said I couldn't: Brian Staley, Liz Freed, David Myer, Erin Kennemer, Anitra Van

Prooyen, Kyle Freeman, Aaron Wood, Nikki Cimino, Kim Lajevardi, and Nikki VanRy.

To Barbara Ann Wright, Helen Corcoran, Sara J. Henry, Alex Jay Lore, and Cecy Robson.

Thank you to some of the authors who showed me the road and left a trail I could follow: Shaun David Hutchinson, Cale Dietrich, Trip Galey, David Mack, K. D. Edwards, Jennifer Estep, Jonathan Maberry, Gregory Ashe, Lynn Flewelling, C. S. Poe, Darynda Jones, James Persichetti, Lisa Brown Roberts, Shiri W. Sondheimer, Gail Carriger, and Jenna Lincoln.

A special thank you to all the readers, artists, booksellers, and librarians who've read my work and supported me.